Praise for the first novel in the
Ancestry Detective Mystery series

MURDER ONCE REMOVED

"For mystery lovers of any generation, S.C. Perkins has penned
a captivating new series that is equal parts dangerous and delightful, witty and well-plotted. *Murder Once Removed* has
it all: a plucky heroine, effortless prose, and a healthy dose of
Southern Charm, along with fascinating genealogical details,
wonderful characters, and a multi-generational crime to solve.
This is cozy crime fiction at its finest."

—*New York Times* bestselling author Kate Carlisle

"Terrific . . . *Murder Once Removed* kicks off this series with a
bang. Here's to many more to come." —*BookPage*

"A quirky-meets-cute whodunit!" —*Woman's World*

"[A] fun debut. Lucy's officemates and other quirky friends add
spice to this delightful cozy. Readers will look forward to Lucy's
further adventures." —*Publishers Weekly*

"Take an original cold case, a savvy 'ancestry' detective, and a
compelling new voice in cozy mysteries, and you have a home
run from the talented pen of S.C. Perkins. From the first heart-
stopping line to the final conclusion, *Murder Once Removed*
is a clever page-turner. Tracing family lines can certainly be
deadly—and oh, so much fun!"

—Carolyn Haines, *USA Today* bestselling
author of the Sarah Booth Delaney mystery series

LINEAGE
MOST LETHAL

S. C. PERKINS

St. Martin's Paperbacks

Published in the United States by St. Martin's Paperbacks, an imprint of St. Martin's Publishing Group.

LINEAGE MOST LETHAL

Copyright © 2020 by Stephanie C. Perkins.
Excerpt from *Fatal Family Ties* copyright © 2021 by Stephanie C. Perkins.

All rights reserved.

For information, address St. Martin's Publishing Group, 120 Broadway, New York, NY 10271.

www.stmartins.com

ISBN: 978-1-250-75031-0

Our books may be purchased in bulk for promotional, educational, or business use. Please contact your local bookseller or the Macmillan Corporate and Premium Sales Department at 1-800-221-7945, ext. 5442, or by email at MacmillanSpecial Markets@macmillan.com.

Printed in the United States of America

St. Martin's Paperbacks edition published 2021

10 9 8 7 6 5 4 3 2 1

For Claire and Paul, with all my love

ANCESTRAL CHART

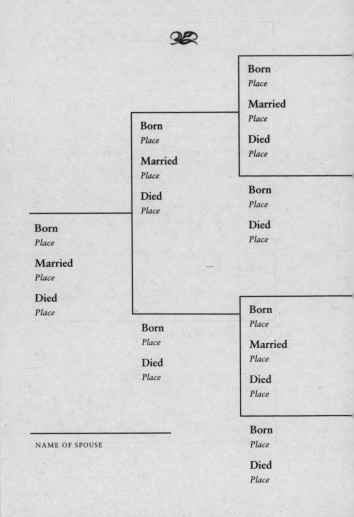

Born
Place

Married
Place

Died
Place

Born
Place

Married
Place

Died
Place

Born
Place

Died
Place

Born
Place

Married
Place

Died
Place

Born
Place

Married
Place

Died
Place

Born
Place

Died
Place

NAME OF SPOUSE

Born
Place

Died
Place

CONTINED ON CHART _____

CONTINED ON CHART _____

CONTINED ON CHART _____

CONTINED ON CHART _____

CONTINED ON CHART _____

CONTINED ON CHART _____

CONTINED ON CHART _____

CONTINED ON CHART _____

LINEAGE
MOST LETHAL

ONE

❧

Stop," I begged. "Please."

Her trancelike gaze swiveled my way, curly tendrils of graying brown hair sticking to her damp forehead. My eyes darted from her round, blotchy face to the mound of white powder she held in her gloved hand.

"No," she said. Despite the cool day, sweat trickled down her temple, mingling with a smudge of mascara and blue eyeliner. "It's what I have to do."

She drew her arm up, her thick wrist flexing backward. She was going to use the entire handful. Oh, the damage it could cause.

I reached out, latching on to her wrist. With a yelp, her fingers opened and the powder fell in a fluffy white shower onto the grass.

She whirled on me. "Hey! What was that for?"

Palms outstretched, I said, "I'm so sorry, but I couldn't let you do that."

She looked down at her glove, which was coated in powder.

It also dusted most of her purple stretchy knit pants and the hem of her multihued striped cardigan.

"For heaven's sake, why not? It's just all-purpose flour."

Pulling off her gloves, she began brushing the flour from her knit pants with angry strokes. "All I'm trying to do is get a clear look at that unreadable gravestone"—she jutted her chin in the direction of what would have been the target of her flour bomb—"which I'm pretty sure shows the resting place of my great-great-grandma."

The name and date were indeed hard to read, as the stone had been worn with time, dirt, and lichen. "I saw online that if you rub flour onto it and then brush some of it off, the words will show up nice and clear."

"Well, technically that's right," I told her, holding out a clean washcloth I'd pulled from the tote bag that had somehow stayed on my shoulder. She snatched it from me. Her eyes were a clear gray, and they were shooting me icy daggers of annoyance.

"See? Then why did you grab me and knock the flour out of my hand?"

"Because of what happens when flour gets wet," I said.

She went silent, giving her pants two more rough strokes with the washcloth, then finally grunted, "It gets gummy." Her voice went defiant again. "I was going to brush it all off, you know."

"I don't doubt it for a second." Nodding toward her still floury legs, I said, "But as you're reminded, it's hard to get all the flour off, and any residue that's left behind can trap moisture and speed up the deterioration of the gravestones."

She gestured toward her intended target. "Then how am I supposed to read it? My mama's not well enough to come out here and see the grave herself, and it's taken me almost a year to find where my great-great-grandma was in the first place. I'd planned to do one of those rubbings you hear about." She pulled a thick crayon from her pocket and indicated her own tote bag. Inside, along with an open bag of flour, I glimpsed a piece of rolled-up butcher paper.

I tilted my head toward the entrance of Comal Cemetery. Located forty-five minutes outside of Austin in the town of New Braunfels, it was the final resting place of a good two dozen ancestors of my latest client, hotel heiress Pippa Sutton. "Some cemeteries allow rubbings and some don't. This one doesn't. Usually you have to call ahead or check the website, but this one also has a 'no gravestone rubbings' sign on the gate you entered through."

Her shoulders drooped. "So what am I supposed to do?"

"I'll show you." Rummaging in my bag, I pulled out a soft-bristled brush and a plastic bottle filled with liquid. "This is a biological solution for cleaning gravestones. You can buy it off the internet or at certain stores. First, we need to wet the stone with water. Then we'll spray on the solution and suds it up, and the white lather will settle into the etchings and make them readable, just like the flour would have. From there, you can take lots of photographs with your phone."

Dousing the stone with water from a nearby spigot, I then sprayed on the biological solution. "Afterward, we'll rinse it off again, but the agents in this stuff won't harm the stone or the surrounding grass." I grinned. "It'll give it a nice cleaning to boot."

The would-be flour attacker looked dubious, but didn't stop me as I went to work. Once the stone was all lathered up, I smoothed off the excess and the words became clear. I turned around to find her grinning ear to ear, a mist of tears filling her eyes as she saw the name on the stone.

"I found her," she whispered. "We were thinking she'd been lost forever." She leaned over, touching the stone with reverence and giving me a clear view of the cemetery entrance, where an old man stood, leaning heavily on a cane, as a car approached.

A breeze lifted what patchy wisps of hair were left on the top of his head. His gray suit hung limply from his frame, and it took him two tries to open the car door before he began lowering himself into the back seat with effort. I wondered whose grave he'd been visiting. That of a loved one? A friend? A newfound ancestor like my flour-happy companion?

As if he felt my gaze, he paused and looked straight at me. I had a fleeting impression of something I couldn't place before interference in the form of a colorful striped cardigan broke our connection.

"Now what do we do?"

My new friend looked hopefully at me, shifting just enough so I could see the car carrying the old man disappearing down the side road. I smiled and focused. "Now we take some photos for you and your mother before we rinse off the solution." I showed her how to work the filters and extra editing features on her phone's camera to make the words even clearer.

"My goodness," she said, her cheeks now pink with happy surprise.

I said, "For gravestones that aren't as badly worn as your ancestor's, sometimes you can just take a photo and use filters to make the words stand out."

The woman gave a hefty sniffle, wiping her nose with the washcloth I'd given her. "How do you know all of this?"

I held out my hand to her. "It's part of my job. My name is Lucy Lancaster, and I'm a genealogist."

TWO

I admit it, Luce, I'm a little jealous you get to be in the lap of luxury at the Hotel Sutton for the next five days and Josephine and I have to wait until New Year's to join you," Serena said. "All my travel in the past two months has been bloody exhausting, and I'm ready for a staycation."

"Seriously, who makes your schedule? You should sack her this instant," I teased.

This was met with an amused snort from both Serena and Josephine, my two best friends and office mates. All three of us were self-employed and shared an office space in a small historic building in downtown Austin, just a block south of the Texas Capitol. On the third floor of the Old Printing Office, as our building was known, I operated my genealogy business, Ancestry Investigations, while Josephine Haroldson was a sought-after translator and Serena Vogel was a successful style blogger and influencer. While all of us had been busy over the holiday season, Serena had been more in demand than usual. In fact, Josephine and I had barely seen our friend since early November.

"Note to self," Serena drawled, "fire self for overscheduling self like a total prat."

"I love how you two have picked up on my native British lingo," Josephine said. "It makes me long for London—and feel as if I've been *une très bonne influence*."

"Considering we've mostly picked up on your native British swear words, I'm thinking you've been a very good *bad* influence," Serena said.

"Oh, you've definitely influenced us, Jo," I said with a grin that neither of my friends could see, since they were at the office and I was in my car, driving back to town from New Braunfels. "Only it comes two years after we had you saying 'y'all' and addicted to queso and guacamole, so I'm thinking Serena and I were the better bad influencers."

"More like the unfair advantage of two against one," Josephine retorted, before adding, to Serena, "Though now I want some guacamole. Care to make our Lucy jealous by having happy hour at Big Flaco's Tacos?"

"High five," I heard Serena say, and there was the sound of slapping palms.

"Oh, now that's just a low blow," I said. My scandalized tone only made them snigger.

"Anyhoo," Serena said. "We actually called to check how your schedule with the Sutton project was going. Would you fancy a facial with us at the hotel spa on New Year's Eve morning? I called and they still have one spot open at ten a.m."

Turning off West Cesar Chavez Street, I hung a left onto Delta Drive. The semiprivate road angled sharply toward Lady Bird Lake for two-tenths of a mile, past a line of tall juniper trees marking the boundary of the Sutton estate, before depositing me onto the crushed-granite parking lot of the Hotel Sutton, where I was about to start my own luxurious staycation.

Well, mostly. I was still officially on contract, with a few days' work left to do for Pippa Sutton, my twenty-four-year-old client who was the last descendant of the famed nineteenth-century Texas land baron Reginald Sutton and his stylish English wife, Sarah Bess, to bear the Sutton surname. Though Pippa was an only child, she had a whole bevy of cousins she was close to, most of whom I'd interviewed over the preceding six weeks.

Part of the reason I was staying at the Hotel Sutton was that I had more interviews scheduled with two of Pippa's out-of-town cousins so I could add their oral histories to the documentary-style video I'd created. Afterward, I would edit the videos and put together the final presentation that would be shown on New Year's Day to Pippa, her mother, Roselyn, and nearly a hundred other descendants of Sarah Bess and Reginald.

I'd show it twice, in fact. Tomorrow, at Pippa's request, I'd be unveiling a draft version to a small group of her closest family members, all of whom were first cousins once removed or second cousins, and one great-aunt known to everyone as Aunt Tilly. They were the relatives who'd banded around Pippa and her mother after the death of Pippa's father eighteen years earlier.

With her paternal grandfather's passing last year, Pippa had become the sole heiress of a nearly hundred-year-old dynasty of small but high-end hotels in Texas and other parts of the South. Knowing she was the last official Sutton in the family line was the impetus behind Pippa's decision to hire me. My job was to help her preserve the Sutton name and its history. Not just for Pippa herself, but also for her other family members, including future generations.

"So, what do you think?" Serena's voice said through my car speakers.

Inwardly, I sighed. My best friends would be snogging their

boyfriends on New Year's Eve, but when the clock struck midnight, I would be singing "*Alone* Lang Syne." Still, maudlin wasn't normally my thing, so I made sure my tone was bright.

"Sure, ten o'clock will work."

My response was met with the silence of friends who know you better than you think.

"Yeah, we heard that fake cheeriness, Luce," Serena said in dry tones. In the background I heard Josephine's "Mmm-hmm," but she added kindly, "You don't have to come with us if you don't want to, love."

"No, no," I said, "of course I want to. Book me the appointment, Serena. If I only get to look dewy and glowing for myself and you two, that's enough for me. It'll be fun."

"You'll be even more beautiful than usual," Josephine said. "Walter and Ahmad will notice, too, no doubt."

Serena added, "But they always think you look great."

"Okay, okay," I said with a laugh. "I know it's the end of December and there's a chance it may snow on New Year's, but there's no need to tack your own snow job on top of it. I'm fine. Really. And the facial sounds great."

Catching sight of my determined face in my rearview mirror as I put my car in park, I said, "In fact, while you're at it, see if you can also book me a massage. I deserve it."

"Too bloody right," Josephine said.

"Heck yeah, you do," Serena agreed. "I'll call the spa back now." And I only just heard Jo sing out, "See you on New Year's, love!" before my friends hung up on me.

Just beyond the Hotel Sutton's parking lot, the afternoon sun was casting its last glints of the day onto the surface of Lady Bird Lake, the Colorado River reservoir named after former First Lady and Texas native Claudia "Lady Bird" Johnson. I hefted my suitcase from the trunk as a double-decker riverboat chugged slowly westward over the water, groups of tourists lining its railings and enjoying the pleasantly cold December air. A near constant stream of walkers, joggers, and cyclists made use of the ten miles of trail skirting the lake.

One woman, running by with a shaggy mixed-breed dog, faltered in her pace for a moment, staring up the terraced lawn at the Hotel Sutton for the seconds it took her to pass. I was familiar with the sensation. The hotel, once a grand private house, suddenly and gloriously appeared out of the trees as you came along the path, its elegant beauty proud in the clearing, and vanished just as quickly behind the veil of oaks, cypresses, and sugarberry trees as the trail curved away.

Slinging my tote bag over my shoulder, I rolled my suitcase over the crushed-granite pathway and around a stand of topiaries and leafless crepe myrtles to the front of the hotel, carried it up the wide steps to the deep front porch, and pulled open one of the heavy wooden double doors.

A lovely smell of furniture polish and fresh flowers met me in the foyer, as did a large Aubusson rug in shades of gold and cream on a field of aqua. A runner in complementary tones ran up the grand staircase, while the adjacent front room held prim emerald-green velvet sofas and rugged-looking distressed-leather armchairs.

Dominating the left wall over a large fireplace was a gilt-framed 1901 portrait of Sarah Bess Sutton, Pippa's three-times-great-grandmother. On the opposite wall, underneath the fluted balusters of the grand staircase hung a Warhol-esque painting of a long-haired dachshund, his ears and tail up as if he'd spied a rat to flush out of a hole. Sarah Bess's dark green eyes seemed to be perpetually regarding the little dog with the hint of an amused smile.

The mix of feminine and masculine, stately and cheekily modern—it was all Pippa's doing, and it all worked perfectly.

"Lucy, welcome back, my dear. You're just in time for cocktails."

If I hadn't recognized the voice, I would have thought Sarah Bess herself had spoken to me. Instead, at the back of the room, pink-cheeked Mrs. Pollingham was beaming at me from her post, a huge curved desk fronted by tufted saddle-toned leather.

"Miss Pippa went to her cottage, but she'll be back in a flash," she continued. "She asked that you leave your suitcase for the bellboy and meet her in the bar for your progress update."

"Happy to," I said. The bar was mere feet from where I was standing and a fire was already crackling merrily in the fireplace behind the marble high-top tables and brass-accented barstools.

"Excellent," Mrs. Pollingham said. "She wants to try something called a Napoli old fashioned on you to see if it's worthy of the happy hour menu. It has a shot of Chef Rocky's homemade blood orange liqueur in it, as if all the bourbon weren't enough. I've already told him to be sure and send you two out something to eat before you start drinking that lethal-sounding concoction."

I grinned. "Old fashioneds . . . a warm bar . . . anything made by Chef Rocky . . . I like the way you and Pippa think, Mrs. P."

Parking my suitcase beside a Queen Anne chair upholstered in bold striped satin, I started to pivot in the direction of the bar, then stopped in my tracks as the look on Mrs. P.'s face went from its usual sweet expression to a frown. Eyes in a crystalline blue were locked onto my legs as she made her way around the front desk and crossed over the Aubusson to stand in front of me, hands on her hips.

Somewhere in her fifties and a longtime employee of the Sutton chain of hotels, Mrs. P. was all softness, from her curves to her hair, which was gingery with a bit of gray and worn in a chin-length pageboy that was often tucked behind her ears. She was barely taller than my five foot two but her capable, no-nonsense presence made her a giant at the Hotel Sutton. She was called the Force of the Front Desk, and everyone loved her, including me.

"What's this? What happened to you?" she asked.

I looked down at my dark jeans. Or what had been dark jeans when I drove to New Braunfels at lunchtime. Now they were dusted with so much flour, they'd lightened by two full shades.

"Holy cow," I said. "Hyacinth's bag of flour must have spilled on me when I carried it for her. We were talking so much I didn't even notice."

To Mrs. P.'s curious look, I explained, "Hyacinth's a woman I met at Comal Cemetery when I was there taking photos of the Sutton family gravestones. She was trying to use flour on her ancestor's stone to get the name to show up better. I explained why she shouldn't, of course. She was very nice once we got to talking, though, and very interested in learning more about genealogy."

Mrs. P.'s eyebrows rose slowly at the earnestness in my voice. "My dear, other people go to New Braunfels to have a good time floating down the Comal River in inner tubes. It does make me wonder that your idea of a good time is to go to Comal Cemetery."

"Hey, it's never a good time until you go hunting for dead people, Mrs. P.," I quipped. "Everyone knows that."

Her eyes lit with mirth. "How did you fare, then? Did you find all the dearly departed Suttons you wanted?"

She gently turned me back toward the door as she spoke. I took the hint. I was to rid my legs of flour before reentering her carefully guarded front room.

"I did," I said as she opened the front door for me and we stepped out onto the porch, with its classic Haint blue ceiling. I pulled my phone from my bag, showing her a handful of photos, including the gravestones for Sarah Bess and Reginald. The last photo was of the gravestones of James and Nell Sutton, Pippa's paternal great-grandparents.

"I need to ask why James and Nell aren't in the same row as James's parents, or his siblings and their spouses. I'm wondering if James didn't initially expect to be buried in New Braunfels, being that he went back to England for so many years and fought in World War Two as a British citizen."

"You're spot on as usual, Lucy, as my great-granddad would say," came a voice from behind me.

THREE

❧

Pippa Sutton, wearing a white blouse under a sedate black blazer, a pencil skirt, and low heels, was rounding the far corner of the wraparound porch. Her hair was pulled back at the crown and fell past her shoulders in chardonnay-hued waves. A simple strand of pearls was at her neck, and gold studs adorned her ears. The leather-covered iPad she was holding to her chest halfway covered a brass name badge.

I'd seen her wearing this uniform of sorts a few times. I also sensed the now familiar frustration underneath her professional smile. Pippa, the owner and chief operating officer of multimillion-dollar Sutton Inc., was filling in for the events manager again.

Since Pippa prided herself on saying all Sutton employees, herself included, had working knowledge of every job within the hotel, I wouldn't have thought twice about her being the de facto events manager—if the chronically absent employee hadn't been Roselyn Fischer Sutton, Pippa's beautiful, intelligent, talented, and, based on what I could tell from all my dealings with her, completely self-absorbed mother.

Mrs. P.'s quick glance reminded me to be careful showing my annoyance with Roselyn in front of her daughter.

"Pippa thinks so highly of you, dear," she'd said to me only last week, "and the fact that Roselyn hasn't been as . . . well, as reliable as usual, is embarrassing and upsetting to her." Mrs. P.'s face had briefly clouded, and I could tell it was upsetting to her as well.

I couldn't lie—I wasn't the biggest fan of Pippa's mother, especially when she dumped more responsibility on her daughter's already busy shoulders. Yet I had to give Roselyn a good deal of credit. She'd never stopped working in her thirty-year career, despite marrying her wealthy hotelier boss, Bracewell Sutton, when she herself was a newbie event planner. Nine years into their marriage, after Bracewell had died tragically in a skiing accident, Roselyn hadn't needed to continue working. Her husband's will had seen to her every need, though the Sutton hotel business had all gone to Pippa, Bracewell's only child and heir. And yet Roselyn had kept working, proving herself an accomplished and in-demand event designer year after year as she helped her young daughter learn the business and prepare to eventually take over Sutton Inc.

It was strange; women like Roselyn Sutton usually made me want to throw them a ticker-tape parade and hold them up as a poster child for fabulous, hardworking, impressive women, yet there was something about Roselyn I couldn't quite warm to, no matter how hard I tried.

Oh, and the fact that she was adamant about not wanting her side of the family included in Pippa's genealogy project? Yeah, that didn't really help my opinion of her, either.

I'd had clients whose family members weren't interested in my work many times before, of course. However, they usually changed their tune once they understood the wonders of how their family came into being, struggled, persevered, and grew over the centuries. In Roselyn's case, however, no matter how excited Pippa became at each interesting Sutton-family tidbit I uncovered, she remained dispassionate, even occasionally becoming snappish whenever Pippa suggested I could do the same for her family tree.

Thankfully, I felt my irritation with Roselyn abate when the creases between Pippa's eyes began to dissolve, humor washing them away as she took in my floured jeans.

"What did you do? Insult Chef Rocky when he was making his fresh pasta?"

I explained about Hyacinth, the flour, and the cemetery. Then I showed her the photos of her own family's gravestones, stopping as before at the ones honoring her great-grandparents.

Pippa smiled at me. "You know, even though I can barely picture my great-granddad in my mind anymore, I have two strong memories of him. One was him smoking his pipe while reading the newspaper in the back parlor"—she tilted her head toward the Sutton's interior for emphasis—"and the other is him telling me how he had never intended to come back to the States until he met my great-grandmother."

She smiled wistfully and pulled her iPad closer to her chest. "To be honest, Lucy, most of what I know about him is actually from the letter you found a couple of weeks ago."

"Hey, I'd never have come across it if you hadn't insisted I see the dovetail joints on that seventeenth-century writing desk," I said, holding my hands up in mock outrage. "You're the one who told me the joints were best viewed up close. Heck, you practically *made* me pull the drawer out fully."

Pippa's laugh was surprisingly throaty, hinting at the warm and open personality hidden beneath her reserved exterior.

"Well, *you* made the mistake of telling me you share my

obsession for antiques, so that's on you, my friend," she said. "Still, I've probably pulled those drawers out a good dozen times over the years and never noticed anything. It was you and your lucky genealogist's touch that made the letter reveal itself."

The letter, which was unfinished, had been written by Pippa's great-grandfather to one of his friends in 1967. It had somehow fallen behind the drawer, never to be completed or sent. When I'd extracted a folded sheet of stationery from inside the slightly crumpled, yellowed envelope, we saw *James Bracewell Sutton* embossed at the top, and James's precise penmanship filling the front of the page and half of the back.

Mrs. P. looked at us with fondness. "I happen to think you two girls were meant to find that letter together," she said. "And what a romantic tale it told of how Mr. James and Miss Nell met back in 1943."

I put my hand to my heart. "It was super romantic. Both of them on leave in London. He in the RAF, she one of Eisenhower's secretaries. Literally colliding with each other in the lobby of the Dorchester Hotel, so hard his flight cap fell off, and she caught it."

Pippa and I exchanged dreamy sighs. "The scene keeps running around in my mind, too," she said.

Mrs. P. laid her hand on my arm and said, "You do really have a gift for opening up the past, my dear," and I felt my cheeks glowing with pleasure.

"On that note," I said, "Pippa, I was going to wait until tomorrow to tell you about something else I discovered, but I don't think I can now."

Pippa and Mrs. P. both looked at me expectantly.

"I was able to locate some of your great-grandfather's war records," I told her. "He wasn't just in the RAF during World War Two—he was also in the SOE."

Pippa's brows knitted. "What's the SOE?"

"The Special Operations Executive," I said, noting that Mrs. P., a fellow history lover, was nodding at my side. "Your great-granddad worked in intelligence."

"He was a spy?" Pippa said.

I nodded, then changed that to tilting my head side to side. "Maybe," I conceded. "SOE agents did a bunch of jobs within intelligence, but it's highly possible he was a spy. I'm still waiting on the records I requested, which include his time in the Royal Air Force as well."

Pippa's eyes, which reminded me of the color of fresh jalapeños, went a half shade brighter. "I wish my dad could have heard all of this. My granddad, too."

"Me too," Mrs. P. said, patting Pippa on the arm.

"And I wish I'd been able to meet your great-granddad," I told Pippa. I put my hand to my heart in history-geek ecstasy. "I would've asked him *so* many questions about the SOE."

Pippa nodded vehemently in agreement, and the chuckle that always seemed to live in the back of Mrs. P.'s throat erupted as she put her arm around my shoulder for a squeeze.

"If he hadn't already passed, no doubt you would have talked him to death, dear Lucy," Mrs. P. said. "Now, stay out here and get yourself rid of that flour so the two of you can try some Napoli old fashioneds. I'm going to go see where our young bellboy has got to. We have a newly married couple scheduled for check-in at any moment."

She gestured for Pippa to go inside like an impatient mama duck herding her wayward duckling. My floury jeans and I were left outside under the rapidly darkening sky, enjoying the warm glow I always felt after giving clients news that made their faces light up like Pippa's had.

FOUR

M y glow didn't warm me for very long, though, since the sun was setting at a breakneck pace. I began to shiver as I brushed at the flour on my jeans, puffs of white erupting with each stroke.

We'd had a mild winter thus far, and with the weather giving me a sunny, cloudless sixty degrees as I jaunted out to the cemetery in New Braunfels, I hadn't needed more than a down vest over my cashmere sweater. Now, as my jeans began to lighten to a slightly faded dark blue, I gazed up at the hotel, looking forward to warming up properly in such beautiful surroundings.

I loved the huge wraparound porch on the first floor and the deep veranda on the second, both of which gave stunning views of the water from the south side of the house. The rooms on the north side afforded an equally pretty view, allowing guests to look out over the expansive and colorful English-style knot garden created by Sarah Bess, who'd been an avid gardener.

Built in 1895 by Reginald Sutton, the house had remained in Sutton hands for a hundred twenty-five years and counting. Yet like most big, old houses, the upkeep had become harder over time. With Pippa's vision, it had been carefully and thoughtfully overhauled into twenty beautifully appointed rooms, with a state-of-the-art day spa and a restaurant featuring Chef Rocky, one of the hottest new chefs in the country.

It wasn't long after Pippa opened the hotel, which had easily racked up the four stars they'd been awarded for luxury, that she'd decided to hire me.

While I couldn't say I was overjoyed that she'd found me through the publicity surrounding me back in November, when I used my genealogy skills to help save Senator Daniel Applewhite from being killed by his fourth cousin, twice removed, I was thrilled I was getting the younger generation interested in knowing about their ancestry. At twenty-four, Pippa was only six years my junior, but even so, finding a whip-smart young professional who wanted to research her family tree made me all kinds of giddy.

Almost the moment the last ray of sun streaked across the sky, the hotel's white fairy lights popped on. Strings of them encircled the trunks and crawled up the limbs of nearby crepe myrtles, bigleaf maples, and pawpaw trees, dramatically accentuating their leafless states. Softer landscape lighting then made the evergreen magnolias and fringy Montezuma bald cypress trees positively glow from the inside, sending droplets of warm light bouncing off the water of Lady Bird Lake. Carriage lights and more landscape lighting came on around the hotel itself, transforming the Hotel Sutton from charmingly welcoming to utterly romantic.

Despite myself, I felt an annoying prick of tears behind my eyes. New Year's Eve was rapidly approaching, and with it the charity gala the Suttons would be hosting at the hotel. Of course, I'd be with Serena and Josephine, two people who always made my life better and brighter, but they would also be cozying up by the stone fireplace with their boyfriends. Essentially, I would be hanging with the four of them, sipping champagne and trying to ignore the couples' lovey-dovey gestures while I played the fifth wheel.

My best friends didn't know it yet, but I was planning on disappearing to my room within seconds of shouting "Happy New Year!" along with the crowd of well-dressed revelers. Oh, sure, I could get a pity kiss from Walter, Serena's longtime love, or Ahmad, Josephine's latest besotted boyfriend, but that wasn't what I wanted, and I didn't have a special someone of my own to kiss me as the clock struck midnight. Not anymore, anyway.

A few weeks ago, for two hours and three long, amazing kisses, I thought I'd had a special someone in the form of slightly insufferable, history-loving FBI agent Ben Turner—though when I first met him, I couldn't have imagined enjoying those kisses for even one second. Ben and I had locked horns spectacularly during our first couple of—okay, several—meetings, but I admit, by the time I'd helped him discover who was threatening Senator Applewhite's life, I'd fallen for him.

Afterward, as a thank-you for all the times Ben helped me and didn't throw me in jail for interfering in a police investigation, I'd insisted on finding his mother's Daughters of the American Revolution patriot so she could gain admittance to the historic service organization. I'd successfully traced Mrs. Turner's line, proving she and Ben had not just one, but four Revolutionary War soldiers in their family tree who'd fought for America's independence.

With a scowl, I slapped at another streak of flour, remembering how excited I'd been to send Ben the documents proving his genealogical connections, plus an extra attachment containing the filled-out paperwork for his mother to submit so she could finally become a member of the DAR. He hadn't written me back instantly like I'd thought he would, though, and the hours of radio silence had quickly begun to crawl into the double digits.

When the total no-response time neared a full week, I realized I'd been ghosted. I didn't even get so much as a curt thank-you text for my work, or for the photograph I'd emailed him of one of his Revolutionary War ancestors, fabulously named Ebrington Chaucer FitzHugh, who looked so much like an eighteenth-century version of Ben that it still made my breath catch to think about it. The two men even sported the same expression, making me wonder if Ben's stern Fed Face had been passed down through genetics rather than learned working for the FBI.

Huffing out a breath, I attacked another large flour streak, as Ben's blue eyes touched with green around the pupils flashed in my mind. The way they'd looked into mine when he'd leaned down to kiss me on the Congress Avenue Bridge, while Austin's Mexican free-tailed bats were flying out from seemingly under our feet in a wave of flittering black wings. That kiss had been . . . wow. So were the two that had followed, with a promise of more to come, though I knew it wouldn't be immediate since he had to fly out to DC the next day for some follow-up on the case I'd helped him solve. I hadn't counted on him deciding the wait should be permanent.

Serena and Josephine, always having my back, had initially attempted to be positive.

"Maybe he's on another assignment," Serena had suggested at the time.

"Yes, love," Jo had said. "It's possible he's deep undercover somewhere and can't contact you."

My reply was to remind them how Ben himself had told me he was a white-collar agent who never did any undercover work. To that, my friends had no other recourse but to march me down to Big Flaco's Tacos for what Serena called "Break-Up Queso and Margaritas."

"You can't actually break up when you were never going out," I'd said, scooping up a tortilla chip full of Flaco's special spicy queso all the same.

Josephine ignored this and told Julio "Big Flaco" Medrano we would be following up our queso with "Break-Up Churros with Break-Up Mexican Dipping Chocolate."

With that, Flaco, who made no frijoles about the fact that he considered me his fourth child, had pulled his aviator sunglasses down on his nose and eyed me with a penetrating look that would have had most people wondering if they should run for the hills, but which I knew was actually silent worry.

He'd liked Ben, too, which had made it worse.

"Suck it up, Lancaster," I whispered to myself with heat, as the sound of a car's wheels in the hotel's parking lot jerked me out of my reverie. "If Ben isn't interested, then he isn't interested, and there's nothing you can do about it. Get over it."

Footsteps crunched on the pathway. They sounded labored, like someone was struggling with heavy luggage. Dollars to doughnuts, it was the expected newlyweds, and one or both of them had brought half their wardrobe.

Brushing the last remaining white streaks from my jeans, I jogged up the stairs. Seeing through the leaded-paned windows of the front doors that neither Mrs. P. nor the bellboy were in the foyer, I stopped, figuring I'd do the newlyweds a solid by holding the heavy door open for them. Grasping the brass pull, I waited, listening to the erratic scuffing noises coming from beyond the wall of shrubs that blocked the view of the parking lot.

"Holy cow, they must really have a ton of stuff," I said under my breath. Looking out toward the parking lot, however, I saw nothing more than the shadows cast by fairy lights, shrubbery, and trees. Then one shadow began moving, slowly becoming larger and longer.

"Finally," I muttered. Yet what staggered into view wasn't a couple, but one man—balding, tall, and thin, sweating profusely, his face more ashen than the color of his suit. He stopped under a pool of carriage-lamp light and stared up at me, his gasping lips twisting into an odd expression.

For a moment, I merely watched in surprise, then I flew down the stairs, grabbing his arm just as he stumbled. I focused in on his face, catching his glassy, bracken-colored gaze for a brief moment. I registered relief in his eyes, mixed with something else. Recognition, maybe?

Then his hand came over mine and I felt a piece of smooth metal being pressed against the back of my hand.

"Keep them safe," he said, his voice ragged, barely more than a whisper.

His lips pulled back into a semblance of a smile, and I caught a glimpse of a badly broken front tooth. Without another word, his arm slid from my grasp and he collapsed, the pen he'd been pressing to my hand dropping to the ground like a cylindrical metal stone.

FIVE

oly mother of—" I whirled toward the front door. "Help!"
I called, pulling my cell phone from my vest pocket to call
emergency services. "Someone help!"

The emergency operator answered just as the bellboy, tall,
gangly, and pimply, flung open the door. His dark eyes widened
for a second at seeing the man on the ground. Then he jumped
into action. "I'll get Mrs. P. and the defibrillator!"

I knelt next to the man and said to the operator, "A man has
collapsed at the Hotel Sutton." Steeling myself, I reached out
and felt his wrist. There was a creepy nothingness where a pulse
should be. "There's no pulse. He's not moving. Please send an
ambulance."

Somehow I already knew an ambulance wouldn't do this
poor man any good.

"Do you know CPR?" the operator asked me.

"Yes," I said, though I barely knew I'd spoken the words.
After my ordeal a couple of months back, I'd decided I needed
to do something to make myself feel whole again. Instead, I did

three things: I took a CPR class, a self-defense class, and went to see a counselor. All three were good decisions, and I was back to being "me" once more, but I'd hoped I'd never have to make use of the CPR or anything I'd learned in self-defense class.

No such luck.

"Was that a yes?" the operator said in my ear.

"Yes," I repeated with more strength. "I just learned last month. I'm supposed to sing 'Stayin' Alive.'"

"That's right," the operator said. "You can do this."

Putting my phone on speaker, I brushed a stray lock of hair from my face, closed my eyes, and started whisper-singing the Bee Gees' 1977 classic. The operator hummed the tune along with me. It was the beat I needed, not the words. It was how fast I was supposed to push on the man's chest.

A breeze kicked up and the pen he'd dropped—a nicer black writing instrument with gold trim that glowed in the lamplight—skittered sideways for a moment. I wanted to reach for it, but I didn't stop CPR, not even when I heard the sounds of movement from all angles. Some of them were coming from inside the hotel, others from across the vast side lawn, where Pippa and her mother had separate cottages on the edge of the property. The first runner made it to me well before the others due to having four legs instead of two.

"Boomer, no!" I said to Pippa's stocky yellow Labrador retriever as he happily sniffed and snuffled at the inert man, wagging his thick tail at a speed that made it dangerous to stand behind him unless you liked bruises on your legs. I managed to keep up the CPR beat, knowing it wasn't doing any good.

"Get on," I wheezed to the dog, using the command I'd heard Pippa say a thousand times.

It's been said that if you really want to feel humbled, try

ordering around another person's dog, and it was true. Boomer ignored me as he nosed and snorted around the mysterious man.

"Boomer, no! Get on!"

It was Pippa's voice this time, and she called out with authority. I glanced over my shoulder to the porch to see her skidding out the front door from behind the bellboy.

The dog, hearing his human, finally obeyed, darting off with happy abandon toward the cottages as two small headlights of a golf cart appeared. Roselyn had arrived in her personal cart. Whether she knew of the problem or had just finally decided to make an appearance at the hotel, I didn't know. In the distance, I heard the faintest wail of a siren as the hotel's front doors opened once more and Mrs. P. rushed out carrying a portable defibrillator.

Her eyes were bright when she reached me, already ripping off the paper that would allow the contact strips to stick to the man's chest and electricity to pulse through his skin. I was light-headed with exertion and relief.

"I'll take over from here, dear," she said with soothing authority. I sat back on my heels, puffing hard. Mrs. P. announced herself to the 9-1-1 operator and began checking the man's vitals.

"I was a nurse for ten years. I most certainly do know how to work the defibrillator," she told the operator. With confident hands, she ripped open the man's button-down shirt and applied the strips to his chest.

Pippa extended a hand and grasped mine, pulling me to my feet with a steady grip. When I was upright, though, I heard the shakiness in her voice.

"Lucy, what happened? Are you all right? Who is this man?"

"I don't know," I said, wiping my brow, grateful now for the cold breeze. "He came from the pathway. He was staggering and sweating and seemed confused. He stumbled and I tried to help him . . . but he just collapsed."

Pippa turned to her mother, with whom she shared the same long legs, blond hair, naturally arching eyebrows, and full lips. Due to Roselyn's regular trips to a wizardlike dermatologist and the fact she was wearing nearly the same outfit as Pippa, she and her daughter looked like sisters.

"Do you recognize him, Mom?" Pippa asked. "I don't at all."

Roselyn merely stared at the body, horrified. "He's not moving," I heard her say finally. She wrapped her arms around herself, and Pippa dutifully moved to put an arm around her mother's shoulders.

Down on the ground, Mrs. P. had removed the strips and conscripted the stalwart bellboy to keep up the CPR beat as she pulled on a latex glove. She opened the man's mouth, giving me another peek at his broken tooth, then used her thumbs to raise his eyelids. She pursed her lips, then took my phone off speaker and spoke to the operator. Even over another rush of cold wind, I distinctly heard the words, "No signs of life."

"Oh my God," Roselyn said, literally clutching her pearls, her voice brittle with stress as Mrs. P. fished for a wallet from the man's coat pocket. "Is he dead?" Her eyebrows made a motion like they were lifting, but no lines appeared in her forehead.

"He sure is," Mrs. P. replied. From his wallet, she extracted two dollar bills, a grocery store receipt, a driver's license, and a ticket stub to a local live theater, the last two of which she held away from her, squinting to better read the information on them.

"What do you mean?" Roselyn's voice went up an octave, rivaling the pitch of the sirens that were drawing nearer. "You need to keep working on him, Mrs. P. We can't have a"—she lowered her voice to a hiss—"*dead person* on the premises."

Mrs. P. held out her hand to Pippa, who helped her to her

feet. Brushing crushed granite from the knees of her black trousers, Mrs. P. said, "Not much we can do about it now, I'm afraid. I suspect he's been dying for days or weeks, and we just saw the tail end of it, when delusion finally hit."

She held out the contents of his wallet to Pippa. "Hold these, would you, dear?"

I glanced around; everyone looked stunned, including three hotel guests I hadn't formally met, but I knew from photos were Pippa's Aunt Tilly and her first cousins once removed, Catherine and Ginny.

"Are you sure?" Pippa and I said at the same time. When she didn't take the items Mrs. P. was offering, I did, looking down at the ID on autopilot.

"Positive," Mrs. P. said as she packed up the defibrillator. She gestured to the man's ashen face, the sheen of sweat still on it. "He's displaying all the signs of someone who's been going downhill. This wasn't a sudden thing. He may have had a terminal disease, or been mixing medications, or even been a drug addict. But he was a dead man walking, without a doubt." Looking at me, she asked, "What's his name again?"

"Edmund Hugo Markman," I said, reading off his driver's license.

Mrs. P. took off her latex gloves, each one rolling off with a squelching *snap*. "What did he buy, out of curiosity? Medications of some kind?"

Scanning the receipt, I said, "Nope. A couple of frozen dinners and a six-pack of bottled water."

"And the theater ticket?" Pippa asked.

I held it out to her. It was for the musical *Oklahoma!*, which had been in town for the past few weeks. It was one of my favorites, actually. I'd taken Josephine to see it and we'd sung the catchy songs for days afterward.

Pippa glanced at the ticket. "Did he have anything else on him?"

I remembered the gold-trimmed black pen and spun around, my eyes scanning the ground, searching for it in the darkening night even as the wind whipped my long hair into my face.

Then a gurgling sound made my head jerk up. Roselyn Sutton was holding her fingers to her mouth and turning pale. Pippa and I both started toward her, but Mrs. P. merely tut-tutted and took Roselyn gently by the arm. "Don't worry, my dears, I've got her." Her voice softened, as if she were speaking to a scared child. "Come on, now. Let's go inside and get you some peppermint tea." When she looked up to see more people were coming out the hotel's double doors, identifiable as guests of the hotel's restaurant by the starched napkins some had in their hands, she turned Roselyn away, saying, "We'll just go round back, shall we?"

With Roselyn in good hands, Pippa was already up the steps, reassuring the guests that the situation was under control even as flashing lights in the parking lot heralded the arrival of the ambulance.

As the EMTs rushed toward us with their gear, I gave the man one last look, watching the thin hairs on the top of his head lifting upward in the breeze. I had the feeling I'd seen him before, but where, I couldn't say. Mentally shaking off the thought, I stepped aside as the EMTs went to work to confirm what Mrs. P. had already determined.

The poor man was dead.

SIX

❧

A nd he said, 'Keep them safe'?"

"That's correct, Officer . . . Carr," I said, peering across at the name badge of the policeman with a strong jaw and wheat-hued crew cut.

Shifting in a club chair in the hotel's pretty sitting room, I fought the urge to clench my teeth. I had great respect for law enforcement—despite my dubious history of sassing a certain FBI agent—but I hadn't had anything to eat since long before watching Mr. Markman collapse. Since lunchtime, in fact, and now my brain was feeling fuzzier by the second, even as my patience was dropping like a lead balloon. Didn't cops know it was never a good thing to interview a witness who was hangry?

"What do you think he meant by 'keep them safe'?" Officer Carr asked.

"I've no clue," I said. "From what I understand, this man may have been ill for some time. It's possible he was having delusions when I came across him. Has someone confirmed whether or not he is, in fact, Edmund Hugo Markman?"

Officer Carr's face smoothed into a familiar professional mask, and I held up a hand with a sigh to stop the words on his lips.

"It was silly of me to ask. I know y'all are looking into the situation and you can't tell me. All I know is that I've never seen him before and I don't know what he could possibly have been talking about."

Officer Carr's response was to change the subject. "Please give me a timeline of your day."

I told him that I'd spent the morning cleaning my one-bedroom condo from top to bottom. "Then I packed for my week here at the Sutton and drove out to Comal Cemetery in New Braunfels. I was there for nearly two hours—"

I stopped when Officer Carr's cell phone buzzed. He took the call, easing out of his armchair and walking over to the far end of the room, where a Hepplewhite sideboard stood with a tray of Burleigh stoneware mugs in their most famous patterns. Flanking the tray were two silver urns, one kept continuously full of coffee and the other filled with hot water for tea.

I finally took a sip of my own tea. It was Earl Grey, sweetened liberally with sugar. I normally took my tea straight, with maybe a dash of milk from time to time, but Mrs. P. told me a good cup of sweet, hot tea was what I needed after witnessing that poor man's death.

I began to feel the dragon that was my low blood sugar settle down a bit. Sipping again, I looked around the room, taking in all the nods to the Suttons' English and Scottish ancestry in the furniture and décor. Even without my help, the descendants of Sarah Bess and Reginald had already known they were mostly British.

"My mom, though?" Pippa had said. "She tells people she's 'just Texan.' Both sides of her family didn't come to America until after World War One, and she knows next to nothing about them. I honestly think she doesn't know what else to say because she doesn't know who she is, so to speak."

Remembering Roselyn's near swoon, I decided I didn't have space in my head for her dramatics at the moment and twisted in my seat to look out the window at the knot garden.

Sarah Bess's creation was beautiful even at night. Crepe myrtles lit with more fairy lights stood guard at each corner, and strategic landscape lighting made it easy to stroll the paths between the carefully shaped boxwood hedges filled with winter-blooming flowers and vegetables.

Boomer the Labrador seemed to appreciate it, too. He trotted into the garden and stood, ears perked, as he assessed something in the distance for the appropriate canine response. His lips were curled up, and at first I thought he was sensing some danger. My skin prickled for a moment, but eased when I looked harder. Boomer was merely holding something in his mouth. Whatever it was, he was carrying it around carefully.

"Ms. Lancaster?" Officer Carr said. I blinked. He'd once again settled into the armchair across from me. "I asked, what time were you at the cemetery in New Braunfels?"

Massaging the back of my neck, I forced myself to focus again on Officer Carr.

"From around two thirty p.m. to about four. I wouldn't have stayed there that long if it hadn't been for Hyacinth and her attempt to flour-bomb her great-great-grandma's gravestone."

When Officer Carr's eyebrows went up, I explained about Hyacinth. "That's why I was outside when Mr. Markman showed up and collapsed." Indicating my jeans, which still bore a few white streaks, I added, "Mrs. Pollingham, the front-desk manager, made it clear that flour-covered guests were not allowed in her lobby, so I was outside, dusting myself off."

I sipped my tea. Officer Carr asked me to take him through

the moments from when I first saw our victim to the time the paramedics arrived.

Starting with the reminder, "Well, I heard him first, I didn't see him," I answered his questions, feigning patience. When I'd given him every detail I could remember, I put down my tea mug, hopefully signaling that I was done. Officer Carr either didn't get the picture or didn't give a rat's tuchus.

"And there's nothing else you remember that might be of interest? Besides the"—he checked his notes—"sweating, confusion, and broken left front tooth? Oh, and that he was holding a pen. A 'nicer writing instrument with gold trim,' you said, not just an everyday writing pen. Any idea where it might be now?"

I explained that the wind had picked up, so I was guessing the pen had ended up blown into the bushes or found by the groundskeeping team, who'd swarmed the front entrance with rakes and applied a fresh layer of golden-toned crushed granite after the ambulance had departed. Within ten minutes, the outline left by Mr. Markman's body had been erased. It was as if he'd never existed.

Officer Carr nodded. "It's December twenty-seventh," he said. "You'll be here at the hotel for five nights, until New Year's Day, I understand?"

"That's correct," I said, then explained my role as Pippa's genealogist. "I've created a video for the Sutton family that I'm showing to my client and about twenty of her closest relatives tomorrow. Then I'll conduct a couple more interviews this week and edit them into the final version of the video, which I'm showing to my client's extended family on New Year's Day. After that, I plan to do nothing but relax here at the hotel with my best friends before heading home."

"Which is here, in Austin." Flipping to a page in his notes, he rattled off both my home address and my work address.

I confirmed both and he finally put his notepad away and got up. I stood, too, holding out my hand to him. "Thank you, Officer Carr, and happy New Year."

"Likewise, Ms. Lancaster," he said, straight-faced, before turning and striding out of the room. I blanched at his retreating back. In that second, he'd sounded just like Ben, all formal and stuffy and by-the-book. I put down my mug with a frustrated sigh.

From the front room, I heard Mrs. P.'s voice saying, "Good night, officer, and thank you," just as movement in the garden caught my eye. Boomer was trotting by once more, his lips still curled around whatever he held in his mouth. This time, the landscape lighting hit it just right, and I saw that it was a long, thin cylinder. A black cylinder with gold trim, to be exact.

"Well, I'll be darned . . . ," I said, chuckling despite myself, and hurried out of the sitting room.

Mrs. P. was manning her station at the front desk, her eagle eyes watching a passing guest, no doubt for signs one of her temporary charges was experiencing symptoms like Mr. Markman had earlier. She was so engrossed, she about jumped a mile when I appeared in front of her.

"Och, Lucy," she said, putting her hand to her ample bosom. "You nearly had to use the defibrillator on me, too. Scared the life out of me."

I grinned. "A thousand apologies, Mrs. P., but I'm on a mission. Do you have any dog treats? Boomer picked up the pen that poor man dropped and has been carrying it around. I need to get it from him before he tries to chew it up and hurts himself."

"A pen?" Mrs. P. echoed. "I didn't see a pen."

"That's because Boomer stole it off the ground before you got there, when I was doing CPR on our guy." I jerked my thumb over my shoulder, out toward the front of the hotel.

Mrs. P. stared at me for a moment, as if her mind were replaying the scene outside, then rolled her eyes heavenward. "Oh, that silly dog. Pippa took him to training when he was a puppy, but little of it seems to have stuck." Then she abruptly disappeared behind the desk. When she straightened, she was unscrewing the lid of a glass jar filled with dog snacks. She fished out two, her button nose wrinkling at the strong liver smell.

"Here," she said, placing them in my hand. "He goes crazy for these things, for reasons only he knows. He'll do anything you want once he gets a whiff of them." Mrs. P. shook her head like Boomer was more trouble than the most finicky guest at the hotel, but with an indulgent smile. Even the Force of the Front Desk couldn't pretend she was immune to the charms of the goofy Lab.

"Do you think this pen may be evidence?" she asked me, her blue eyes lighting up with sudden curiosity.

"I seriously doubt it," I said with a shrug. Worried Boomer would wander off again before I could get to him, I started toward the back porch, tossing over my shoulder, "but I'll be giving it to the police anyway, just in case."

"Good," I heard Mrs. P. say with satisfaction. She wouldn't have had me do anything less.

SEVEN

I got lucky. Boomer was still hanging out in the knot garden when I walked out the French doors onto the back porch. He wagged his tail furiously at the sight of me, but didn't approach. The pen was still firmly in his mouth, unchewed.

"What's up, buddy?" I said, sitting down on the porch's topmost step. Boomer, his excitement overtaking him, took two steps toward me, then stopped. He knew the rules of dog and human: if he came too close, I could nab him and probably get him to drop his new toy. No way was he having that.

All casual like, I put one liver treat in my hand. Boomer's soft golden ears perked up and his black nose twitched. He took two steps closer, unable to resist the smell, which seemed to have been modeled after stinky feet.

"Want a treat?" I asked him, holding it out on my palm.

It was the magic phrase. He raced up the stairs, eyes bright with anticipation. I didn't even have to say "Drop" to get him to spit out his prize. The pen landed at my feet with a deep *thunk* and Boomer stood staring at the treat with the look of a drug addict in need of a fix.

Showing he did have some manners, he waited for me to hold my hand closer before he inhaled the treat and chomped it in rapid, slobbery bites. I bent forward, grabbing up the pen. With one last lick of his lips, Boomer went the still of a hunting dog, his sweet brown eyes fixed on the pen once more, which was laced with slobber and gravel grit.

"Oh no, sweetie. You can't have this back," I told him before giving him the second treat. Rubbing his ears, I examined the pen.

It looked like your everyday black affair with a gold clip, the only other ornamentation being four gold bands encircling the pen cap. Three of the bands were delicately thin, but the fourth was close to an eighth of an inch wide. I could tell it wasn't new, both from the weight, thickness, and indications of use over the years in the form of fine scratches on the barrel, cap, and clip.

Turning it endways, I saw that it was a Montblanc, the distinctive "snow cap" emblem on the tip mimicking the snowy top of Mont Blanc mountain, for which the brand was named. Without thinking, I wiped it on my leg to get off the excess dog slobber and granite dust, then froze.

Rats. Could I have just wiped off evidence?

Boomer and I looked at each other. "You slobbered on it first," I whispered to him. "Okay if I just blame you?"

His tail thumped the steps in response as I held the pen up to the brightest part of the porch lights. There it was, the faint red hue beneath the black resin, signaling to me it was a real Montblanc, not a fake. My paternal grandfather had taught me that trick.

I smiled, thinking of my grandpa. He had a thing for Montblanc pens, and still used one for anything he wrote to this day.

He'd given my sister, Maeve, and me each a lovely one from his collection for our respective college graduations, and we both used them for signing important documents. As I examined the pen, I thought about Grandpa, and smiled.

Boomer whined, watching me turn the pen over in my hand, using every ounce of his manners training to not snatch it out of my hand. Sliding off the cap, my eyebrows went up. Though I knew it was older, I'd somehow been expecting a regular ballpoint. Instead, it was a fountain pen, with a beautifully engraved gold nib. A very sharp, pointy nib.

"Sorry, darlin'," I said, using my knuckles to rub Boomer between his eyes. "I had to confiscate this before you chewed it up or swallowed it. Pens aren't good for puppy dogs, you know." I smiled when he gave in, sat down and leaned into my rubbing, accepting my affection in place of his toy.

I turned the Montblanc over once more, admiring its clean lines, wondering if it were from the 1950s or earlier, which Grandpa preferred. I was sure it was a Meisterstück, which meant "masterpiece," the Montblanc company's most classic pen line, because the nib was engraved with the numbers 4-8-1-0, the height of Mont Blanc in meters.

I looked again at the gold nib and saw it was more elaborately engraved than most, including a scroll-like motif and—I squinted—what looked like two feathers crossed at the bottom. *Grandpa would love to see this pen*, I thought. He adored ones with intricate engravings. I could show it to him over FaceTime, which he'd just learned to use a few months ago and had taken to, as Josephine had said, like a pigeon on a french fry.

All at once, Ben's voice was in my head. "We don't know if the man's death was natural or not, Ms. Lancaster. You should call the police now and turn the pen in. There could be prints on it or other evidence connected with it."

I scowled, feeling a swoop of irritation that I could still remember Ben's voice so clearly. Even when he'd so thoroughly left me behind, he was somehow still trying to boss me.

I mean, really, the police already had Mr. Markman's ID, right? They didn't need this pen to confirm that. So would it really make that much of a difference if I turned it in after I showed it to Grandpa?

I checked my watch. Grandpa would be in bed by now, and calling him at night would only make him worry, even if it were only for the amount of time it took him to put on his glasses and answer his phone. It would definitely have to be tomorrow, even if I grudgingly knew the Ben voice in my head might be right.

I looked at Boomer with a rueful smile. "I think my brain is feeling the need to taunt me with thoughts of annoying FBI agents who sucker nice genealogists into falling for them." But Boomer just sighed and nuzzled my hand, maneuvering it until I was scratching his neck. Smart dog.

I slid the cap back into place and made my decision. I'd give it to the police tomorrow, after showing it to Grandpa over FaceTime. Flicking off one last tiny nugget of granite clinging to the barrel, I put the pen in the pocket of my down vest.

From the far side of the hotel, I heard Pippa's voice call, "Boom-er! Here, boy!"

Boomer jumped to his feet and dashed toward his human's voice without a glance back at yours truly. I had to laugh as I walked back inside.

"Another love 'em and leave 'em type," I said. "Apparently, I'm a magnet for them."

But I was barely five steps down the hall when I stopped in my tracks, an odd feeling creeping up my spine. Like I had eyes on me.

I looked around. To my right was the sitting room. On my

left, the back parlor. Was someone in one of those rooms, watching me?

Slowly, I stepped into the sitting room, which was still brightly lit by several lamps. Empty. I eyed the back parlor across the hall, and goose bumps popped up on my arms. On my first visit, Pippa had told me it was reputed to be haunted. At the time, I'd laughed it off. Now, with the room mostly in shadows, it was an easy tale to believe.

Making myself be brave, I peeked in. The furniture, all dark woods, leather, and suede, had been arranged into five separate seating areas with several large, cushy armchairs, two leather Chesterfield sofas the color of tobacco, and several paintings of bird dogs, horses, and hunting scenes on the wall, one of which I was positive was a Stubbs. Besides two dimmed lamps, the only other light was from the large fireplace along the south wall, which was emitting a low, flickering glow.

My eyes darted around the room, which was quiet other than the soft ticking of the grandfather clock. I recalled Pippa's tale and how her light Texas accent had affected a thick drawl.

"The menfolk used to sit here after dinner, smokin', drinkin', and gamblin'. Two of 'em died in here in 1908, in fact, after pullin' their pistols on one another when they both accused the other of cheatin' at cards." Her drawl eased, to be replaced by a note of ghoulish amusement. "Their spirits are said to live on in here, brandishing their pistols at one another. Several family members and guests throughout the years have seen them."

"Have you?" I asked, fascinated.

She grinned. "Nope, but occasionally you'll hear a noise that sounds like someone having the wind knocked out of him."

"Oooh, creepy," I said with a shudder. "Were you related to either of these dueling men?"

She shook her head. "But both were rumored to be lovers of

Sarah Bess's." Her green eyes lit up again, this time with mischief. "She was a beautiful and wealthy widow by that time, after all."

I'd grinned along with her, hardly shocked. The notion of puritanical Americans in Sarah Bess's era, before, and since, was as much of a myth as it was a fact. It was refreshing to have a client who already knew their third great-grandmother hadn't been some pristine angel, and wasn't judging her for it, either.

I took in the large portrait of Reginald Sutton hanging in pride of place between two of the parlor's windows, lit from above with a brass picture light. If his portrait were a true likeness, then his pronounced widow's peak, turn-of-the-century garb, and dark eyes gave him an uncomfortable resemblance to a vampire.

Another rush of a chill stole over me, like I've always heard happens when ghosts are nearby. I readied myself to see two apparitional gamblers raising pistols in my direction.

There was nothing, though. The room was silent, except for the continued ticking of the grandfather clock. I nearly jumped out of my skin when it began softly gonging the hour.

"Holy frijoles," I said under my breath, my hand over my racing heart.

"Lucy? Whatever are you doing?"

I whirled around with a gasp. Mrs. P. was standing in the hallway, holding a clipboard, looking at me with a mixture of concern and amusement. I nearly wilted against the parlor's door frame, then began laughing like a fool at the relief of seeing a real human and not a pistol-wielding ghost.

"Oh, not much, Mrs. P. Just going a little nuts here from a long day, low blood sugar, and Pippa's ghost stories, that's all." A couple of snort-laughs escaped, and I held my hand over my mouth to try and compose myself, making Mrs. P. chuckle.

Then, much like she'd done earlier with Pippa, she made shoo-ing gestures with her clipboard.

"Go on, then, you silly goose, get out of here. I've got my evening check to do before I go home and Pippa's waiting for you in the bar with those cocktails and some of Chef Rocky's pasta carbonara. Go have yourself a stiff drink and some food. You've had a long day."

"Right you are, Mrs. P.," I said with a grin. I turned and began walking off, then whirled around again, pulling the fountain pen out of my pocket. "Oh, and thanks for—"

At that moment, Roselyn Sutton had come in the back porch doors, looking polished and calm once more. Her eyes coldly assessed me as I waved the Montblanc with my loopy grin, then they slid to Mrs. P. without so much as a hello. I opened my mouth to ask Roselyn how she was feeling, but caught Mrs. P.'s look that told me it would be a bad idea.

"You're welcome, dear," Mrs. P. said pointedly to me with a reassuring smile and a nod.

I took it as my cue to skedaddle for the bar. If I didn't need a potent drink before, I sure as heck did now.

EIGHT

Lucy! Good morning, my darlin'." After a blurry moment, my grandfather's beaming face came into focus on my iPad.

I blew him a kiss, which he pretended to catch and put on his cheek. "Good morning, Grandpa," I said. "You finally got over that cold. I'm so glad to hear it." I had to turn the speaker volume down a couple of notches, his voice was coming over so clear, but it made me happy to do so. He was in his early nineties now, so colds weren't the trifling things they once were.

He chuckled. "Not much can keep me down for long, you know." As I knew he would, he changed the subject, never one to want to talk about his health. "Now, to what do I owe this lovely pleasure? Did your mom and dad get off on their cruise all right?"

I nodded. "They just boarded. Mom said she'll be sending you, Maeve, and me a group text once they set sail for Turks and Caicos."

"And Maeve? She and Kyle are still with his parents in Vermont?"

"Yep. Skiing to their hearts' content," I said.

"Good," he said, before eyeing me sideways. "Then you're not calling to tell me you have other plans for brunch next week, are you?"

I laughed, tucking my feet under me on the black-and-white zebra-striped armchair. Each of the hotel's rooms was named after one of Sarah Bess's favorite flowers and decorated in the same elegant but eclectic style as the rest of the hotel. My room, with its wainscoted walls painted a high-sheen dusky blue, was the Plumbago Room.

There was a silky duvet in a dark lavender color on my bed, which had a tufted leather settee acting as a footboard. On one wall, a large painting of the English countryside hung over an art deco bar cart, where a crystal ice bucket and highball glasses stood alongside a matte-black coffee machine. On the wall by the bathroom, three black-and-white photos of 1960s classic cars were positioned in a step pattern, giving the impression that the Corvette Stingray was winning. Dark-wood side tables, French doors opening to the veranda, and heavy blackout drapes in a bottle-green color finished off the room.

I'd already opened all the drapes, looking out over the veranda to find a gray sky with the trees shrouded in mist. On Lady Bird Lake, two kayakers braving the cold were paddling by with smooth strokes, their bright watercrafts, helmets, and life vests lending pops of color to the monochrome morning.

"No way am I canceling on our brunch date next week," I told Grandpa. "I'm craving the diner's chicken and waffles something fierce."

"Then chicken and waffles you shall have," he replied gallantly as he moved into the better light of the kitchen and settled himself onto one of the barstools. His image on the screen became clear again as he rested his elbows on the butcher-block countertop.

Grandpa was probably my favorite person in the whole world. The oak desk I used in my office in Austin, with its gloriously scuffed top and large crosshatch carved into the right corner, had been his. And it was Grandpa whom I wanted to call whenever I had had a rough day and just needed to hear the voice of someone who thought everything I did was wonderful. My late grandmother said Grandpa and I were two peas in a pod, and my mother was forever saying the blueprint for my soul had been taken straight from my grandfather's, he and I were so alike. We both considered it the best compliment.

Luckily for me, Grandpa lived only forty-five minutes southwest of Austin, in the pretty little town of Wimberley, where he tended to his garden, built birdhouses that he gave away to anyone who wanted one, and walked to his favorite diner for lunch, like he had every day for the past ten years, ever since my beloved Gran passed away. He was my hero, and the only other man who could hold a candle to him was my own father.

"Grandpa, you have to hear what happened to me yesterday," I began.

"I'm all ears—almost literally, these days," he said with a chuckle as he plucked his glasses off the neck of his gray sweater and put them on.

"You're still the handsomest man I know," I said, and it was the truth, even if his ears, which had always been a smidge on the big side, weren't getting any smaller, and his dark, wavy hair had long since turned white and thinned. Photos of him from his younger years showed him to be matinee-idol handsome, even with the ears. Serena and Jo had almost swooned over photos of him in his army uniform during the war, and I knew from many stories my grandmother had told me that she'd practically had to beat other girls off with a stick when she and Grandpa were courting.

Grandpa gave a bark of laughter and waved my compliment away. "Enough of that tosh. What's this interesting story you have for me?"

"Well," I began, "yesterday a man died at the hotel where I'm staying."

I saw his brow furrowing at my words. *Rats. Shouldn't have made him worry by saying that.*

"Anyway, when he—"

"A man died, you say, Lucy?" Grandpa cut in.

"Oh, it had nothing to do with me," I hastened to reassure him. "He wasn't a guest at the hotel or anything, and the police don't think there's a connection at all. Mr. Markman—that's the guy's name—was likely very ill, and was probably delusional, bless his heart."

I wasn't going to tell my grandfather the man had died right in front of me, right after uttering those final cryptic words. No way, no how.

Seeing the look of relief on my grandfather's features made me recall the look in Mr. Markman's eyes before he'd collapsed. It had been odd, the way he'd seemed almost comforted to see me. I pushed it out of my thoughts. Surely it was just an effect of the poor man's deluded mind.

"Anyway, this man had a Montblanc pen on him," I continued. "My client's dog, Boomer, picked it up, and I didn't get it back from him until after the police had left. It's a fountain pen, a Meisterstück, I'm pretty sure, and looks old, like some you have in your collection. I wanted to show it to you before I handed it over to the police. I'm curious to know how old it is, and since you're practically an expert, I figured you'd be able to tell me."

A grin split my grandfather's face. "I'll do my best to impress you, then. You've kept it somewhere safe where it wouldn't get scratched further?"

I gave a teasing roll of my eyes. "Of course, Grandpa. Who do you take me for, some heathen's granddaughter?"

"Well, you do have your grandmother's blood, too, and you know what she was like," he said with a wink.

I grinned. My grandmother was notoriously unsentimental about any inanimate object and was famous for keeping her gemstones mixed with her costume jewelry and storing both in a cardboard shoebox.

"Gran would have chucked it in her purse, dog slobber, dirt, and all, that's true," I said with a laugh.

"And then she would have given it to me a month later, when she finally cleaned out that purse of hers, and it would have had peppermint wrappers and ten different receipts stuck to it," Grandpa said.

"I think you'll approve of where I stored it, then," I said, showing him my hinged sunglasses case, a tangerine-colored hard shell. I popped it open, revealing not my sunglasses, but the Montblanc, on the soft chamois interior.

"You're right, it is a Meisterstück," Grandpa mused as I held the pen up, moving it slowly so he could see it from all angles.

"It's fairly basic," I said, "except for these gold bands." I suppressed a giggle when I saw his hitherto mild interest turn into a sharp squint as I pointed out the cap's three thin gold bands and the fourth thicker one. "And the engraving on the nib is interesting, too."

It looked like Grandpa's nose was about to touch his phone screen when I pulled off the cap to display the pen's gold writing nib.

"It's hard to see, but there's a scroll motif and some engraving under the forty-eight ten." I pointed to the spot. "It's very pretty. Looks like two crossed feathers amidst all the scrollwork."

My words were met with silence. For a moment, I thought the connection had frozen, but then I saw whiskers and the calico face of Bertie, Grandpa's cat. She'd jumped up onto the table and butted her head against his hand, making the phone move. As she purred, her tail made like a fluffy windshield wiper across the screen.

"Grandpa?" I said.

He gently nudged Bertie out of the way. "Can you take a close-up photo of the nib, Lucy, and send it to me? And one of the cap, too."

I nodded. "Sure thing. Will that help you determine the age?"

Grandpa's blue eyes were fixed on the pen. "What?" he finally said. "Oh, yes, I think that will help in this instance."

I capped the pen once more and smiled. "This one must be rare, huh?"

My grandfather was rubbing a veined hand over the white stubble on his chin. It was a gesture I recognized that told me he was deep in thought. "Why do you say that?"

I turned the pen over in my fingers. "Because up until now, you've been able to tell me the general age of a fountain pen within seconds of seeing it."

For another moment, Grandpa was silent, but as soon as I opened my mouth, he straightened up, looking pointedly at his watch, his lips twisting into a resigned smile.

"Oh, my goodness. Lucy, my darlin', I'm afraid I promised John McMahon I'd have breakfast with him this morning and I nearly forgot. You know that old so-and-so, he'll call me every five minutes if I'm not on time." He shook his head in mock exasperation. "I've already steeled myself to listen to him drone on about LSU's chances of beating A and M in the Sugar Bowl on New Year's Day, I don't need to have him—what did Serena tell me to say? She's such a pistol, that one . . . oh, yes, I don't need him 'blowing up my phone,' too."

"Oh, okay. No problem, Grandpa," I said after a moment's hesitation. "Have fun with John. And tell him for me he's plumb crazy if he thinks the Tigers will beat the Aggies."

He chuckled, giving me a thumbs-up that clearly displayed his own Aggie ring, worn down so much now that it was almost a featureless lump of gold. "With pleasure. And you'll send me those photos?"

"You'll have them before you get to the diner," I promised.

"Good," he said with a nod. "Until later, then, my darlin'." Then he blew me a kiss, which I caught and put on my cheek just as the screen went dark, leaving me feeling like something not right had happened.

"Huh," I said to myself as realization dawned. "I can't believe it, but I think Grandpa just blew me off."

A moment later, my phone buzzed with a text from Pippa and I switched gears.

> Everyone's here and excited to hear your
> presentation! See you in 30!

Hopping off my armchair, I gave myself a mental high-five for being smart enough to do my makeup before calling Grandpa. I dressed in a pair of black pants paired with a silky blue V-neck blouse, black wedges, and simple gold jewelry. Then I took some close-up photos of the Montblanc's nib and cap and sent them off to Grandpa, before putting the pen back in my sunglasses case and stashing it in my tote among all the other things in there, including three folders, a few peppermints, and more than a few receipts.

Slinging my tote over my shoulder, I grasped the handle of my wheeled rolling cart, which held a box containing all the Sutton family memory books, a box of restored photographs, and a four-foot-long cardboard tube that held a painting I'd commissioned of the Sutton family tree. Wheeling everything out the door, I headed for the ballroom to set up.

NINE

❧

The screen faded to black after a few poignant heartbeats of Pippa Sutton looking out over her great-great-great-grandmother's garden, pride and emotion glowing in her eyes.

The assembled twenty-two descendants of Reginald and Sarah Bess Sutton broke into applause. I blushed with pleasure at how well my video had turned out, and how well they'd reacted to it. Nearly every last one of them had screen time in one way or another, even if it was simply a photo and a quote that recalled a particular family memory. I'd worked hard on this project for the past six weeks, and I was proud of what I'd done to preserve the history of this family.

They'd also loved it when I'd pulled out the rendering of their family tree. Painted as a huge, wide magnolia, its leaves showed the names, birth dates, and any applicable death dates of the family members, from Reginald and Sarah Bess on down to Pippa and her eight younger cousins, the newest generation of the clan. The painter I'd hired had done an amazing job, and the family all clamored to sign up to receive a poster-size print.

"I can't believe we're related to Princess Diana and the Spencer family," one fortysomething second cousin gushed.

"Well, only *way, way* back," said another cousin, but with a look on her face that told me she'd be crowing about that connection for the rest of her life.

"How about the fact we have so many dukes, knights, and barons in our line?" said Matthew, Pippa's second cousin once removed, who, at sixteen, was Pippa's closest younger cousin in age. "What did you call them, Lucy?"

"Peers of the realm," I said.

"Yeah, that," Matthew said. "It's really cool!"

"I didn't know we were related to one of the signers of the Declaration of Independence," boomed one of the other older cousins, a big man with a shock of red hair inherited from the other side of his family.

"And that we have so many entrepreneurs and social influencers in the family," breathed another woman with an earnest expression. She was one of Pippa's older first cousins once removed, but was so much like an aunt that Pippa called her Aunt Melinda.

Pippa turned to me. "Personally, I can't believe how much Sarah Bess went through to get from England to America," she said. "I mean, first her chaperone died on the ship, leaving her all alone at barely eighteen years old. Then the ship got caught in bad weather and they were adrift at sea for days. Then she and half the passengers were sick when they came into Ellis Island."

"It was Castle Garden, actually," I said. "Ellis Island didn't open until 1892, and Sarah Bess arrived in New York in 1887."

Pippa grinned. "That's right. Everybody always thinks of Ellis Island. I'd never heard of Castle Garden until today."

"It's definitely overshadowed in history as an immigration port," I agreed. "Sarah Bess had barely recovered from her journey and illness after arriving when the Great Blizzard of 1888 hit in March."

"I'm amazed you found that newspaper story of how she helped other families survive the blizzard by bringing them food and blankets and taking some of the children into her home." Pippa's look of awe at my newspaper sleuthing made me grin.

"I'd already found evidence of Sarah Bess's philanthropy from her life in England, so I wasn't surprised at all to find she jumped back into it as soon as she was on her feet in America," I said.

"And she continued helping others for the rest of her life," Pippa said. "She's truly my hero, and makes me want to be a more active giver than I already am."

I saw her glance across the room at her mother, who I knew was one of Pippa's heroes as well. Until recently, at least. Roselyn, looking fully recovered from yesterday's trauma, now appeared bored out of her mind as she made small talk with one of the family. She'd barely watched the oral-history video, choosing to spend most of the time looking at her phone instead. Those sitting around her had been too engrossed to even notice, though I'd seen Pippa briefly frown at her mother before giving the video her full attention.

Only when Roselyn heard her own voice did her head snap up. I saw her straighten with pride at how good she looked on film, and she'd looked around for someone to confirm it. When no one did, she'd gone back to her phone, her thumb moving up and down on the screen, no doubt scrolling through photos on social media.

Her look of boredom shifted only one other time, when something she saw on her phone made her stiffen, her thumb hovering over the screen. From where I stood, just behind her and at an angle, I couldn't see what it was, but I'd caught her glancing at

Pippa with a strange expression before going back to scrolling, her daughter none the wiser.

Another cousin joined us, a handsome man with wide-set blue eyes, chestnut-brown hair, and a build like a former soccer player starting to thicken around the middle. As even family members sometimes did, I had to blink. He looked remarkably like Pippa's late father, but was, in fact, Bracewell Sutton's first cousin.

Automatically, his stats popped into my brain in short bursts, like bullet points. He was David S. Eason—the "S." standing for Sutton. Aged fifty-two, one of the three Eason siblings, who included Melinda and Laurie. Divorced from his wife of fifteen years, David had one teenaged son who lived with his ex-wife in Colorado. He'd been a respected antiques dealer in Houston for most of his career, but was currently on what Pippa referred to as a "sabbatical." On Pippa's charts, he was her first cousin once removed. To Pippa, however, he was one of the cousins who'd really stepped up after her father's accident, earning him the title Uncle Dave. It was how I now referred to him as well.

"Hi, Uncle Dave," I said. "What did you find most interesting about your family tree?"

Smiling, Uncle Dave handed Pippa and me each a Burleigh mug holding steaming coffee, then took a third mug for himself. We moved as one to the sugar and cream and began doctoring our java.

"Without a doubt, it was my grandfather James and his service in the war. I mean, I knew he fought as a British soldier and was one of those who helped to liberate Paris, but I had no idea he worked in intelligence. While my mother was alive, I asked her many times what Gramps did in the war, and she always said she never knew, that he never spoke of it." He cocked his head slightly in a way that reminded me of Boomer. "How did you even find all this out?"

"It's there in his service records," I replied. "You just have to follow the right protocol to request it from the National Archives. You'd be able to find out the same information if you had the time. I can just do it a lot faster and pull in a favor or two, if needed."

Uncle Dave shook his head in reverence. "Well, to quote my young nephew, it's really cool."

Pippa nodded with enthusiasm. "I'd love to know more about him. You told me yesterday you'd requested other records, Lucy. Do you think we'll be able to find more on what he did in intelligence?"

"There's no guarantee, but I think the odds might be good," I said. To their excited faces, I held up a calming hand. "You have to understand, there might not be any documents. Or, if there are, we might not be able to gain access to them. All I can do is request them and see what we can come up with." I lowered my voice to a whisper. "I also have an ace in the hole at the National Archives in DC, though. If I have to, I can play that card."

Uncle Dave turned to his younger cousin. "You know, Pippa, I thought it was a trip when you told us you'd hired Lucy here to do our genealogy, but I didn't think it would be this much fun, or this interesting." He gave her a one-armed hug.

"High-five," I said to her.

She laughed and slapped her palm to mine. "High-five, totally."

Uncle Dave put his palm up as well, and Pippa and I both obliged. Then Mrs. P. bustled in with a fresh tray of cookies and scones. The younger cousins made a dive for the pastries, and I smiled when a dark-haired little girl named Claire brought Pippa and me each a chocolate chip cookie with a shy smile.

"Oh, thank you, sweetie," I said, taking the cookie and biting into it.

"What? No cookie for me?" Uncle Dave said. Claire disappeared, but was back in moments with a cookie for her older cousin. Uncle Dave gave her a courtly bow, and Claire ran off, giggling, to join her other cousins.

Nibbling on our cookies, Pippa and I looked out the windows to see another couple of young cousins playing tug with Boomer.

"He just loves having so many kids to play with," she said with affection. "He's such a good boy."

Behind us, Mrs. P. snorted. "He's a menace, that's what he is. Especially when he jumps in the river and then goes running like a terror through the knot garden." She looked at me. "Last week he came straight from the river and rolled in the compost the head gardener had just put out. I thought the poor man was going to have an apoplexy!"

Pippa and I laughed, though I noticed Uncle Dave merely regarded Mrs. P. coolly. For her part, Mrs. P. acted like he wasn't even there.

"Speaking of Boomer, I'm so glad those treats worked and you got that fountain pen away from him," Mrs. P. said.

"Fountain pen?" Pippa echoed, even as we stepped back to accommodate two waiters bringing fresh drinks. Mrs. P. moved off to direct them, and I explained about Boomer being a pen thief and how Mrs. P. had shown me the stinky-treat way to his heart, effectively saving the Montblanc from becoming the dog's latest chew toy.

"So that's why he scampered off after that man collapsed instead of coming to me like he normally would," she said.

Uncle Dave's eyes narrowed with interest. "A Montblanc, did you say? My, that's a nice pen. A new one can be over a thousand dollars. A vintage one could go for several times more, depending on certain factors."

"I hadn't thought about that," I said. Another thought swirled around in my brain. Could the pen be the thing our dead man wanted to keep safe?

No, his voice had been raspy, but the words had been clear. He'd said, "Keep *them* safe." *Them*, plural.

"I did show it to my grandfather over FaceTime, though," I continued. "He collects Montblancs. He didn't say what it was worth, but he did seem very interested in it, especially when I showed him the intricate scrollwork and feathers engraved on the nib."

"Now my curiosity is definitely piqued," Uncle Dave said. "Where is this pen now?"

"It's in my tote," I said, gesturing with the last half of my cookie across the ballroom to the far corner. Mrs. P., who was taking out some extra Burleigh mugs from the nearby glass-fronted cabinet, had evidently just noticed my hiding place as well, and was craning her neck toward the corner as she pulled mugs by their handles.

"Could we see it?" Uncle Dave asked.

I glanced at Pippa, who seemed to be examining her cookie, crumbling one edge in her fingers. She'd been looking uncomfortable since Uncle Dave had mentioned the Montblanc's value. Recognizing the heartbeat of silence directed her way, though, her head jerked up.

"Oh, yes, we'd love to see it."

I hesitated. It was the same level of forced cheeriness Serena's and Josephine's voices gave off when I offered to demonstrate my latest genealogy software. But Pippa followed up with a smile and a nod of encouragement, so I stuffed the last of the cookie in my mouth and went to get the pen—making it just in time to help Mrs. P. as she juggled one mug too many.

"Got it," I said, lunging the last step and scooping a pink

calico mug that was slipping from Mrs. P.'s pinky finger. For good measure, I lifted off another.

"Oh, you are an angel, Lucy," she said breathlessly. "We need more mugs in the sitting room. Seems like all our other guests came down for coffee at the same time." She moved sideways to reveal my leather tote bag, sitting open as I'd left it. "These must be your presentation materials and such, then?"

"They are, and I came to get the fountain pen I rescued from Boomer," I replied, digging in my tote, pushing aside a folder full of genealogy relationship charts, feeling under another folder of blank ancestor charts, and finally finding my sunglasses case at the bottom. "Pippa and Uncle Dave wanted to see it."

Seeing her interested expression, I said, "Want to see it, too?"

Mrs. P.'s lips twitched. "You kept that man's pen in your sunglasses case?"

I gave a sheepish grin. "I know myself, and I'd lose it otherwise."

I popped open the case and, at that moment, two streaks of child-size lightning rushed out from behind the window's heavy curtains, just holding in their squeals. It was Claire and her cousin Marilyn, playing some game of their own making. Surprise and fear of accidentally bonking them on the head made me jerk the case away, sending the pen flying over my left shoulder.

"Oh!" I cried as Mrs. P. stumbled backward, nearly losing her balance. I reached out and steadied her.

"I think you dropped this," came a deep voice from behind me.

It was one I knew well, and it made my heart soar, even before I spun around and looked into the handsome face and blue eyes.

"Grandpa!"

TEN

I threw my arms around my grandfather's neck and hugged him tight, breathing in the mixture of cold air, leather jacket, soap, and equal hints of aftershave and pipe tobacco. "What are you doing here?" I asked.

"I was in the area and stopped by to see you, my darlin'," he said, pressing his cheek against the top of my head before pulling back, catching my hands, and looking me square in the face. "Oh, how time flies," he said. "I'd swear you're prettier every time I see you."

I blinked in surprise, though my smile stayed in place. Grandpa was invoking his favorite code phrase from my childhood. One I hadn't heard in years. One he relied on to get out of trouble with Gran, often after taking my sister and me to get ice cream before dinner.

"Oh, how time flies," he'd say to Maeve and me when we walked into Gran's kitchen to find him with his hands in his pockets, rocking back on his heels with a guilty smile. *"You two get prettier every time I see you."*

It meant we were to play along with him. It meant we had permission to deny everything.

Then when Gran would ask Maeve and me directly if we'd just had ice cream, we'd solemnly shake our heads, as if our sticky hands and the telltale drips down our T-shirts weren't in plain view. We figured out quickly that Gran didn't believe any of us, but she was too much of a pushover for her granddaughters— and despite the look of infuriated exasperation she'd throw at Grandpa, she was still a pushover for him, too. Grandpa's code phrase had stayed in regular, cheeky action until my grand-mother's passing, and I hadn't realized how much I'd missed hearing him saying it.

Suddenly, I was glad Maeve wasn't here. We'd probably have burst into tears thinking about how much we missed Gran, spoiling Grandpa's subterfuge in the process.

But why was Grandpa giving me the "play-along" signal now? There was nothing weird going on that I could see. Nevertheless, I gave his fingers two quick squeezes to show that I understood.

"Well, now, who is this handsome man with the silver tongue?" Mrs. P. said, clearly recovered and looking my grandfather up and down with a hint of flirtation.

"Mrs. P., this is my grandfather, George Lancaster," I said. "Grandpa, this is Mrs. Pollingham, the Hotel Sutton's amazing front desk manager."

Mrs. P. offered her hand slowly, as if surprised. Grandpa took her hand and shook it firmly, not just clasping her fingers in the way many men, especially those of his generation, often did.

Mrs. P. looked from me to Grandpa and back again in clear confusion. "Your *grandfather*, Lucy? Not your great-grandfather? But you're barely thirty—" She heard her own gaffe and stopped, looking mortified.

Grandpa put his hand to his heart in mock injury. "And just when I thought I could still pass for a spry eighty-five."

Mrs. P., blushing furiously, started to say, "Oh, no, Mr. Lancaster. I didn't mean—"

I put my hand reassuringly on her arm. "It's okay, Mrs. P. We get this all the time, and Grandpa's just messing with you." I playfully swatted my grandfather's hand, then linked my arm through his. "See, my grandparents married right after World War Two, in 1945, but didn't have my father until nineteen years later."

Grandpa chimed in, "He was a happy surprise after we'd been told over and over we couldn't have children."

"Then my parents married relatively young—right out of college—and had my sister and me by the time they turned twenty-five," I said. "So, I'm one of few people my age whose grandfather is a World War Two veteran."

"And still kicking and going swing dancing once a week," Grandpa added, taking my hand and giving me a deft, tight spin.

"But you must have been very young during the war," Mrs. P. said, looking at him as if she still didn't quite believe the math.

Grandpa nodded. "You're correct, and very astute, Mrs. Pollingham. I was one of those wild young boys who lied about his age so he could sign up and fight for his country. I was tall and had muscles from working on my uncle's cattle ranch, so they believed me when I said I was eighteen."

"And how old were you really?" Mrs. P. asked, her expression finally showing some measure of acceptance.

He leaned forward and said, sotto voce, "Sixteen and three quarters, but don't tell the feds."

"Oh, go on," she said, eyeing him with much humor. "You're pulling my leg."

"Would you like to know how I did it?" Grandpa asked, clearly enjoying his harmless flirtation with Mrs. P., who was nodding eagerly. "They didn't cotton on to me because there was another George Lancaster and I passed myself off as him—at least initially."

Mrs. P. looked well and truly shocked. "No," she breathed.

"I tell you the truth," Grandpa said with a solemn air. "We were both from Houston, though we went to rival high schools. He was two years older and a star football player, so I knew of him, but he didn't know of me. We had the same eye color, and were about the same height"—Grandpa grinned roguishly—"only I was much better-looking. All in all, the army just assumed someone had done the paperwork incorrectly, which was hardly a shock to anyone, and both of us ended up working for Uncle Sam."

Mrs. P.'s eyes had grown round, her lips parted in surprise. "But . . . you didn't really let the army believe you were he, did you?"

Grandpa was unabashed. "I did, and I don't regret it one jot. My commanding officer eventually found out my age, though, and that's how I ended up a war correspondent, traveling with various outfits until I turned eighteen, ending up in the Fourth Infantry."

"Did you ever meet the other George Lancaster?" Mrs. P. asked, enthralled.

My grandfather's eyes were practically glowing. "I did, in fact. One night, George and I both turned up at the same USO dance and I introduced myself, telling him what I'd done. George got a kick out of me using him to con my way into the army."

If possible, Mrs. P.'s eyes went even rounder, then she burst out laughing. "Och, Lucy, your grandfather's a live one, isn't he? I can see where you get your sass now, oh yes."

"I don't have a clue what she's talking about, love, do you?" Grandpa asked me with exaggerated innocence, making Mrs. P.'s cheeks brighten by giving her a wink.

"I just can't believe the coincidence," she said, still chuckling. "Does the other George Lancaster have a granddaughter named Lucy, too? Wouldn't it be a hoot if that happened?"

Grandpa grinned. "Now, that I don't know, but when he died some years back, a few friends thought it was I who had passed and sent my wife condolence cards. My wife joked that she should get to take a boyfriend, since I'd left her a desirable widow."

"I can see Gran saying that," I said.

Grandpa put his arm around my shoulder. "If you think I have cheek, Mrs. Pollingham, you should have met my wife." Before she could reply, though, he turned to me.

"Now, my beautiful Lucy. I think this is yours." He held out his palm, presenting me the Montblanc.

My hand nearly jerked back as I reached for it, but I managed to cover it up with a theatrical flourish as I picked up the black fountain pen with gold bands on the cap. Only instead of four gold bands—three thin ones and one thicker—there were only three bands total. The snowcap on the end was different as well.

This was why Grandpa had said the code phrase. He'd switched the Montblanc I'd found with a different pen and he wanted me to pretend not to notice. But why?

My thoughts raced. It had already been strange when Grandpa had practically hung up on me this morning. Then to appear at the Hotel Sutton out of the blue? That was even stranger. And how did he even get here? Grandpa still had his driver's license, but preferred not to drive long distances. So why was he here? It had to be about the pen—the real one, which was presumably somewhere on Grandpa's person. But could it be that special?

If I had to guess, it was worth a pretty penny, and Grandpa knew it. He would never ask me to keep it from the police, but I figured he'd want to do what he could to establish provenance for it after it was released from evidence—and maybe be the first in line for it, if no other next of kin could be found for our dead man.

Regardless, the best thing I could do was keep my mouth shut and follow Grandpa's lead until he explained everything.

Opening my sunglasses case again, I tipped the stunt-double Montblanc into it, and then turned the case around so Mrs. P. could see. "It's pretty much an ordinary fountain pen," I said with a casual shrug.

She bent over the pen, looking at it from all angles. "It does look rather ordinary, but lovely in its own way."

Grandpa had pulled his glasses from the inner pocket of his jacket, and I held the case where both he and Mrs. P. could see.

"It's definitely a Montblanc," Grandpa said, even though we'd already established this earlier. "A Meisterstück, from the looks of it. From the mid-1940s, I'd wager."

Mrs. P. gave Grandpa a curious look, and I explained, "My grandfather collects Montblancs. The Meisterstück is his favorite type. He has probably thirty of them."

"My, that's quite a collection," she said to my grandfather, before asking me, "You did say it was 'pretty much' an ordinary pen. What makes it different?"

I was about to start stuttering and make something up, but Grandpa did it for me. "I think I know. You see the snowcap emblem?" he said, pointing to the stylized white snow-covered mountain peak on the cap. "There were a small number made after the war where the snowcap is slightly bigger than normal. They were trying it out, but the buyers didn't care for it, so they went back to the smaller version."

Mrs. P. studied it. "How interesting. And this makes it more expensive?"

Grandpa cocked his head. "Well, not for your average person, no. But for an avid collector, yes, being as they're so rare."

Nodding, Mrs. P. looked at me. "Is the writing part," she fluttered her hands, searching for the word, "you know, the pointy part—?"

"The nib," offered Grandpa.

"Yes, the nib. Is it engraved like I've seen on some pens?"

Grandpa looked at me, raising his eyebrows like he'd never seen it and would be just as surprised as Mrs. P.

This was getting weirder, but I picked up the pen and took off the cap. Briefly, I wondered how we were going to swing this with Pippa and Uncle Dave, who were waiting for their very own look at the pen and who knew it supposedly had feathers on it. A few moments ago, I'd seen them watching us curiously from across the ballroom, but they'd made no move to come over—yet.

Desperately trying to think up some excuse for why the nib wouldn't have feathers, I looked down and stood flabbergasted. It indeed had a feather engraved on it. One single feather instead of two crossed ones, but it was there.

"I thought you said it had feathers, plural," said Mrs. P., who'd come up with some reading glasses, looking closely at the nib.

"Did I?" I said, feeling like my voice went up to a pitch only Boomer could hear.

"Did you have your glasses on when you looked at it last night?" Grandpa asked, giving me another significant look while Mrs. P. continued to peer at the nib. "Because maybe you thought the scrollwork around the feather made it look like more than one."

"Come to think of it, I didn't have my glasses on," I said, catching on just in time. "And it was dark, too, so I guess I didn't see it well at all."

Grandpa sent me a wink over Mrs. P.'s head, who was still studying the nib intently. "If you look really closely, Lucy, it's actually a quill," she said. "You know, as in the early writing instrument made from a feather?"

"Is it, now?" Grandpa said in feigned wonder. He took a closer look at the nib. "Well, I'll be dashed. You're right."

"Holy moley," I said, wondering if anyone could see the sweat beads on my forehead yet. "I got it all kinds of wrong, didn't I?"

"Still, it is quite beautiful," Mrs. P. said, looking over her readers at Grandpa. "No doubt this is a valuable pen."

He grinned. "You, my dear Mrs. Pollingham, have the eye of a collector." When she blushed prettily, he said, "And I think you might be right."

"Maybe Mr. Eason will know," I said, as I saw Uncle Dave craning his neck over the shoulder of another family member to see where I'd got to. "He's my client's first cousin once removed, and an antiques dealer," I explained to Grandpa.

"Yes, he is," Mrs. P. said, but added in an undertone, "Though I would be careful inquiring about the value of this pen, Mr. Lancaster."

"Please, call me George," Grandpa said. "And why do you say that?"

Another flush of pink came to her cheeks. "I apologize, George. I shouldn't have said anything. It's just that—" She glanced at me, then at my grandfather, looking agonized as to whether she should continue. Finally, with a furtive look toward Uncle Dave, she said, "It's not a secret Mr. Eason is on sabbatical from his job as an antiques dealer." She rested her hand on my arm. "I assume Pippa told you this, Lucy dear, or otherwise I wouldn't say it to your grandfather." Without waiting for my reply, she squared her shoulders. "Mr. Eason lost his job over a year ago at the company where he worked for many years. He was accused of stealing a valuable item. What few know is that he believes I had something to do with his firing merely because I was in the shop the day the theft happened. And when I was interviewed, I told the truth—that I'd seen him wearing the item in question."

I stood there, nonplussed. Actually, I hadn't known that part, and now I felt embarrassed that she'd told us such private information.

"What was the item?" Grandpa asked, looking only politely interested.

"An Omega CK2129 watch," Mrs. P. said.

I looked blank. I knew Omega watches were a very nice brand, but the model number meant nothing to me. Grandpa, though, let out a low whistle.

"That was a damn fine watch made for RAF pilots who took part in the first wave of the Battle of Britain," he told me. "They called it the Weems model. Only around two thousand were ever made. There's likely very few in existence today, especially ones that are working and in good condition."

"Which this one was, from what I was told," Mrs. P. said.

"If you don't mind me asking, Mrs. P.," I said, "how did you know Mr. Eason was wearing that particular watch?"

"Simple," she replied. "He showed it to me as he was putting it on. Then I saw him leave and he was still wearing it."

I didn't know how to respond to this, so I was glad Grandpa took charge.

"The heads-up is appreciated, Mrs. Pollingham," he said, inclining his head.

"You're most welcome," Mrs. P. said, picking up the Burleigh mugs again. She gave us a dazzling smile, then disappeared through a crowd of Sutton family members.

ELEVEN

W   "ell, that was a mite uncomfortable," Grandpa said once
    Mrs. P. was out of earshot.

Uncomfortable? The past few minutes had been downright bizarre, and I had a slew of questions for my beloved, upstanding grandfather.

As he and I fell into step, maneuvering around another group of Sutton cousins toward Pippa and Uncle Dave, I began firing off questions.

"Want to tell me what that was all about? What did you do with the real pen? How did you even get here? And why are you here? Not that I'm not thrilled to see you, of course."

"I took the shuttle from our senior center, naturally. I'll need to be dropped off downtown by three thirty to make it back. I'll tell you everything else later." He said this cheerfully, looking cooler than a cucumber in an ice bath.

Pippa and Uncle Dave, however, seemed a little strained in each other's presence, though Pippa quickly brightened when I introduced her to Grandpa. If she thought it strange that my grandfather would show up unannounced at the tail end of her family's event, her manners and years of being in the service industry precluded her from saying so.

"Lucy's told me a lot about you over the weeks we've worked together on my family history," Pippa said to Grandpa. "Including one very cute story about how you got Lucy's grandmother to notice you by always being the guy who was reading a book whenever she walked into your local soda shop."

Grandpa beamed. "My Elinor had about ten suitors at the time, all who kept trying to impress her with their muscles. I knew she had a thing for brainy men, so I tried to look the part."

I said, "But she saw through Grandpa, even then."

My grandfather's smile grew. "It's true. It wasn't until the day I was truly engrossed in the adventures of Allan Quatermain in *King Solomon's Mines* and didn't even notice her come in that Elinor finally talked to me. She walked up and asked me, 'Do you like to read now?' and she could tell I was being truthful when I said yes." He sent Pippa a genial wink. "That day, I got the girl *and* a love of books—couldn't have been luckier on both counts."

"What a great story!" Uncle Dave crowed, his bonhomie at an unnatural level. When all our eyes swiveled his way, he cleared his throat self-consciously and mumbled an apology before turning to me with an anxious expression.

"Lucy, Mrs. Pollingham didn't try to buy that Montblanc off you, did she?"

"No, not at all," I replied, startled. "Why would you think that?"

"She's a collector," he said, with what looked to be a light-hearted shrug, though it ended with a slight curling of his upper lip.

"Uncle Dave . . . ," Pippa began, casting me an embarrassed glance before looking up at her cousin. "Mrs. P. collects pocket watches, you know that, and only very selectively. I don't even think she's bought one in years."

"Yes," he agreed, "but collectors collect. She's shown interest in other items before, and what she does collect, she gets the best." Frustration grew in his voice. "I've seen her grandfather's pocket watches. She could get a pretty penny for some of them, let me tell you, and she had her eye on the Weems that day."

I tried to look like the word "Weems" didn't mean anything to me as Pippa tucked her arm through Uncle Dave's, a gesture that was meant to show solidarity as well as shut him up. It worked, though he still looked tense. Pippa then smiled at Grandpa and me as if nothing odd had been said. "Lucy, we'd love to see this pen that's been of such interest, both to that poor man who died and also to all the collectors in our midst. Would you show it to us?"

"Of course," I said. Grandpa, who was holding my sunglasses case, opened it, and I obligingly picked up the Meisterstück and held it where they could see every inch. The gold bands glinted, and I removed the cap to reveal the delicately engraved nib. If either of them recalled that I'd said there was more than one feather on the nib, they didn't say so, thank goodness.

For Grandpa's part, he merely kept his eyes on the pen, nodding in agreement with the little descriptions Uncle Dave was murmuring, verbally cataloging the pen's attributes and dating it to between 1942 and 1945.

"You're taking this to the police?" Uncle Dave asked when I put the pen away and shut my sunglasses case once more.

I nodded.

"Is there any need to?" he said. "I mean, I never saw the dead guy, but I heard Mrs. P. say he'd clearly been ill, so it's not like he was murdered or anything. Does the pen really need to be turned in?"

I didn't need to look at my grandfather for a reminder of right and wrong. I was already hearing Special Agent Ben Turner's infuriating voice in my head again.

I said, "It's highly unlikely they'll need it, yes, but if they happen to find some kind of foul play in the man's death, it'll be considered evidence because he had it on him at the time. It's the right thing to do."

"But surely Boomer carrying it around in his mouth wiped anything of use away," Uncle Dave protested, his tone halfway between belligerent and petulant.

"Uncle Dave . . . ," Pippa said again, albeit more gently. "I agree with Lucy—it's the right thing to do. Even if it's worth a couple thousand dollars, it's not enough to—" She stopped, almost stepping back at the furious look that came over her cousin's face.

"Excuse me," Uncle Dave said curtly, and walked off, his shoulders rigid.

"Are you all right?" I asked Pippa, seeing her stricken face.

She put her fingers to her mouth, then nodded. "Yes, I can't believe I just said that." Watching her cousin stride from the room, not even acknowledging his sister Melinda when she called to him, Pippa said, "Should I go after him?"

"He'll be all right," Grandpa said. "Give him some time to cool off and then make your apologies."

Scraping her fingers through her blond waves, Pippa sighed. "Since I've already let the cat half out of the bag, let me explain before your imaginations run wild."

"You really don't need to," I said. *Mostly because Mrs. P. already unceremoniously dumped the cat right on top of us.*

But Pippa held up a hand. "No, it's okay. I know I can trust you, Lucy." She smiled at Grandpa. "And you by extension, Mr. Lancaster."

I couldn't look at Grandpa for fear I'd start coughing. The man I trusted most in this world had pulled off a sleight of hand right in front of witnesses, for pity's sake!

"Uncle Dave was accused of stealing a valuable watch—the Weems he mentioned earlier, which, as you might be aware, Mr. Lancaster, is a highly sought-after World War Two pilot's watch," Pippa said. "This happened about sixteen months ago, and as a result, he was fired from the antiques company where he'd worked his whole life. He swears he didn't do it and the company agreed not to press charges because the only evidence they had was that of"—she hesitated for the merest of seconds—"one witness. However, the company stipulated he couldn't work in the antiques business for a period of two years, so we've all been saying he's taking a sabbatical."

She looked around for her cousin, but he was nowhere to be found. "It's been hard for Uncle Dave, because he really loves what he does. I actually hired him as a creative consultant at our downtown hotel, the Sutton Grand, this past June, but, well, the hotel business is a particular one, and you either work well in it or you don't."

"And Uncle Dave didn't," I said.

Pippa nodded. "Let's just say I allowed him to quit after six months, so he'll be scraping by on savings until his forced hiatus is over. He's already looking for items he can start selling, though."

"He's hankering for something rare to put him back on the map, I take it?" Grandpa said.

"If not on the map, at least on the right road again," Pippa said, her lips twisting. "I feel terrible for him, but he's almost acting like a shady used car salesman these days. He's trying to get me to sell some of the Sutton antiques to get him going again, and, while he took my 'no' with good grace, he keeps hinting that one good piece could really help him out."

Grandpa gave Pippa a kindly smile. "If you wouldn't mind an old man giving you some of the wisdom he's picked up in nine decades, you were right to say no. I only walked through your lobby once and I saw more fine-looking pieces than you could shake a stick at. If you sell him one, he'll want more. It will be like an addiction, and you don't want to make an addict of anyone if you can. Trust me, I saw much of it in the war, and afterward." He shook his head sadly, adding, "Addiction is an ugly thing that shouldn't happen to anyone."

Over Grandpa's shoulder, Roselyn had approached, her head turned slightly as if she wasn't sure she was hearing correctly, and what she was hearing, she didn't like. The fretful look on Pippa's face was no doubt making her even more suspicious.

"Pippa? Lucy? What's going on here? Who is this man?"

"Oh, hi, Mom," Pippa said, her face easing into a smile. She made the introductions, but Roselyn continued to look wary until Pippa explained that we were discussing Uncle Dave and his desire for a rapid reentry into a successful career. At that point, I thought I saw Roselyn's stomach muscles unclench beneath the fawn-colored cashmere dress that hugged her lithe frame. Now the smile she directed at my grandfather was Madonna-like in its mixture of warmth, understanding, and pity for others' plights. The subtle hint of Chanel No. 5 only heightened the effect.

"You're so right, Mr. Lancaster—"

"George, please," Grandpa interjected.

Sugary tones came into her voice, and she placed a hand on his arm. "George, then. And you must call me Roselyn. You are absolutely right that addiction is something that should never happen to anyone, no matter what form it takes." Roselyn shook back her hair, which had been blown out to a sleek, golden sheet, and gave Grandpa and me her full-wattage smile.

"George, Lucy, would you like some coffee? Or maybe one of Chef Rocky's scones? He's famous for them, you know."

Glancing around the room with pursed lips, she added, "I was looking for him, actually, and wondered if he'd come in here." Pippa looked around, but Roselyn had already turned back to Grandpa.

"I wouldn't say no to a scone to go," Grandpa said. "I was just in the area and came by to see my beautiful granddaughter. I knew she had her presentation this morning, and it seems I gate-crashed the tail end of it." He gave me a hopeful look. "But if you might be done now, I'd love to take you to lunch."

"I'd love that, too," I replied, then turned to Pippa. "Unless you'd like me to stay longer? If anyone has any questions for me?"

Pippa shook her head. "Absolutely not. Your video was incredible, Lucy, and if anyone has any other questions, they can ask them at the final presentation on New Year's Day." She made a shooing motion with a grin. "Go enjoy a nice lunch with your grandfather."

Roselyn had moved off, but now reappeared, holding out two triangles wrapped in blue-and-white toile paper napkins. "And here's your to-go scones, one for each of you."

"Will you still come to dinner tonight with some of my family and me?" Pippa asked me. "Chef Rocky is doing a tasting menu for us, which should be incredible."

"Are you kidding?" I replied. "I wouldn't miss it."

"Good." Pippa turned to Roselyn. "Mom, you really should come with us tonight. Lucy has agreed to let us grill her about our genealogy. I've no doubt she could help you investigate your side of the family as well. I really wish you'd let her try."

Roselyn's smile was still brilliant, but it had taken on the stiff quality I'd seen every time her daughter or I mentioned tracing her ancestral line. Not for the first time, I almost felt like I sensed fear in her, but I couldn't imagine why.

"Oh, no, darling," she said, gracing both of us with her beatific look again. "I've got so much to do tonight with last-minute details for the New Year's Eve gala. But I know y'all will have a fabulous time."

She told my grandfather how lovely it was to meet him before breezing away, leaving us with only a whiff of Chanel No. 5 and the memory of cashmere. When Pippa was hailed by her aunt Melinda, I laced my arm through Grandpa's and we moved back toward the corner so I could get my tote and rolling cart.

"Was it just me, or did Roselyn find the idea of having her family tree done the equivalent of a root canal?" Grandpa said.

"You're not wrong," I said, "but I have no idea why, and neither does Pippa."

All thoughts of Roselyn disappeared when we neared where my tote bag stood. Two little girls were whispering and looking inside it, pointing.

"That one?" Claire said to her cousin, who was nodding emphatically.

Having older female cousins on my mom's side, I knew the temptation of a purse belonging to a grown-up woman who wasn't your mother. There was a glamour about her and all her belongings, and the contents of her purse seemed like magic.

Catching Grandpa's eye, I put a finger to my lips, then crept over to see Claire's outstretched finger pointing at my makeup bag, the clear vinyl pouch showing off the myriad products inside.

"Which lipstick color do y'all like better?" I asked. "The pink or the red?"

They both started, guilt flooding their little faces as they looked up at me. When they saw me smiling, though, they both relaxed, and Claire called out, "Red!" while her cousin, a little more shyly, said, "Pink!"

The two girls skipped off, and Grandpa tapped his chin with his finger. "Now, who do those two scamps remind me of . . . ? I wonder who they could be . . ."

Dropping my sunglasses case into my tote, I grasped the handle to my rolling cart and said loftily, "I'm sure Maeve and I would have no idea who you mean."

TWELVE

It took every inch of patience inside me not to sit my grandfather down under the nearest bright light and interrogate him about the wild charade we'd just played out. As it was, I barely managed to hold in my questions until the moment Grandpa shut my car's passenger-side door. Then they came bursting out of me.

"Okay, what just happened back there? Where's the Montblanc? Why did you switch them? And how on Earth did you do that without me seeing it?"

Grandpa didn't smile this time. He was looking everywhere but at me, and his expression had lost all its usual affability. In fact, it was eerily similar to Ben's Fed Face, which was so not cool.

"Start the car, if you would, Lucy," he said. "Let's go to your office and we'll talk."

I glanced at the time—11:08. "Oh, good, Serena and Josephine probably won't be at lunch yet. They'll be so happy to see you." Then I got a look at Grandpa's expression. "Unless it matters if they're there?"

"It matters for explanations," he said, still looking around as

I pulled out and drove slowly over the crushed granite. "Let's go to your condo first."

"I don't have anything to eat at my place," I said. "I did an end-of-year fridge-and-pantry cleanout before I came here for my staycation. Besides the scones Roselyn gave us, all I've got is instant oatmeal, a box of wheat crackers, and various condiments. Oh, and a jar apiece of homemade pickled okra and garlic dill pickles from Gus Halloran's wife, both of which are really good."

Normally, my babbling would amuse Grandpa. Instead, he just kept glancing at my side mirrors as if distracted. "That's all right, love. We won't be there long and then we can go somewhere good to eat."

Turning out of the parking lot onto Delta Drive, I was picking up speed when I noticed glinting out of the corner of my eye. Out of seemingly nowhere, the Montblanc had appeared in his hand. The real one, with its three thin gold bands and fourth slightly wider band, the one that had been pressed upon me by a now-dead man less than twenty-four hours ago. Grandpa was unscrewing the inkwell from the barrel.

"What are you doing?"

He didn't answer. Instead, he held up the barrel and tipped it over. A small black cylinder fell into his palm.

I was glad we were the only people on the road, because I gasped and swerved into the oncoming lane before straightening out. "What is that?" I asked.

"It's what he wanted you to have," Grandpa said. "Wanted *us* to have."

"Who?" I said.

"Edmund Hugo Markman," Grandpa replied. "Or Hugo, as we knew him."

"Wait, you *knew* him?" I asked, braking to a stop, my voice flooded with disbelief.

My grandfather looked back at me with a grim expression. "Drive us to your condo, Lucy. I'll explain then."

With the University of Texas college students off for winter break, there was far less traffic than usual as I navigated over to Congress Avenue and headed south toward the Travis Heights neighborhood and my little condo complex. I wanted to ask Grandpa a million more questions, but he was radiating a desire to keep a zipped lip, so I drove in silence. The whole time, Grandpa's eyes never stopped glancing at the side mirror, watching every car that drew up behind us. I'd formed an extra two dozen questions by the time I parked in my assigned space and we began walking up the path to my section of the complex.

At the steps that would take us up to the second floor and my little one-bedroom condo, a large flash of orange floof streaked up the stairs, nimbly hopping the last step to stand in an elegant pose that exposed a white chest and paws. Fluffy tail held high and twitching, as if beckoning us to hurry up, the big-boned cat waited for us, finally eliciting a grin from my grandfather.

"He must remember you," I said to Grandpa. "NPH isn't the biggest fan of strangers. He'd never come out to greet me otherwise."

"And NPH stands for again?"

"Neil Patrick—"

"Housecat," Grandpa finished. "Now I remember. I take it he still spends as much time with you as he does with Jackson?"

I laughed. "He does." NPH actually belonged to Jackson Brickell, my condo manager, but you'd never know it by how much time the big tabby cat spent with me. NPH and I were attached to one another big time, so much so that he'd tried to protect me from a bad guy last fall—and when that bad guy had tried to hurt him in return, I lost all sense of self-preservation in order to protect NPH.

We made it to the top of the stairs, NPH mixing happy little noises with his loud, welcoming purr. I knew he really remembered Grandpa when he rubbed against Grandpa's legs for a moment before giving my ankles a light swat and accepting an ear scratch. He led us to my door, making more kitty talk, which was getting louder and more insistent after his initial happy greeting.

"Bertie sounds like this when I spend the afternoon at the senior center playing bridge," Grandpa said. "I think he's chastising you for being gone."

To that, NPH let out a long, guttural meow that I took for, *You're darn right I'm miffed, human. How could you?*

"I'm sorry, I'm sorry," I said to him when, once inside, he jumped up on one of my bar chairs to continue his fussing at eye level. "Please forgive me, your highness."

I followed this with a kiss to his striped forehead, which he seemed to deem an acceptable apology. The two cat treats I gave him didn't hurt, either.

"Now, Lucy," Grandpa said, stroking NPH's back, "if I may have your cell phone and iPad?"

Wordlessly, I gave both to him. He pulled out his own cell and took them all back to my bedroom. He turned on the television in my room and closed the door.

"It's unfortunate to know our devices may be listening, but there you go," was his only comment. I poured us both a glass of water, astonished at my own calm, and Grandpa gestured to the two remaining bar chairs, drawing in a deep breath as he sat down.

"I have some things to tell you, my darlin'. Things your dad certainly doesn't know, and most of which I never even told your Gran." His lips quirked up. "Though I'm pretty sure your grandmother knew more than I ever told her."

"That you're a spy," I said.

I was surprised that it came out so naturally. All throughout our drive to my condo, the notion had been coming to me, and it had seemingly settled into my understanding just in time to hear Grandpa begin his confession.

He inclined his head. "That I *was* an intelligence officer in the war, and remained active as a case officer—a handler—until the year after your father was born."

"If that's the case, you were part of the Office of Strategic Services—the OSS," I said, "which then became the CIA after the war."

"That's correct," he said. "After the war, I was also a part-time reporter for the Associated Press as part of my cover. I was good at it and liked it, so I remained in journalism full-time afterward until I turned sixty-five, just like you've always known."

"Did you tell Gran you'd been with the OSS?" I asked.

"Yes," he said without hesitation, "though I never divulged any classified information or told her of the missions we did, and she knew never to ask." He smiled. "During the war, your grandmother was too young to officially sign up with any of the women's auxiliary outfits, but she worked at the airbase at Ellington Field in Houston. She learned to work on airplanes with the one and only group of Women Airforce Service Pilots trainees in 1942 and '43, before they moved the WASP program to Sweetwater, Texas. She knew how to keep a secret, your grandmother, so when I could, I always told her the truth. And I'll do the same with you."

I nodded. "That's all I can ask for."

I got up and went to my freezer and pulled out something I'd just remembered I had. I scooped generous dishes of chocolate–peanut butter ice cream into bowls and handed him one.

"But Gran would say we should eat something first, then talk," I said, and held my spoon out at an angle with a smile. "Cheers."

A look of relief washed over his face, and I realized then that my grandfather had been worried about my reaction, worried that he'd lost my trust. He clinked his spoon against mine like we always did. "Cheers."

NPH sat up, sniffing the air in case my bowl might be something worthy of his discerning tastes. I gave him another kitty treat, then Grandpa and I dug in. Two bites in, Grandpa started talking again.

"If you're wondering, the story I told Mrs. Pollingham—the story you and Maeve have always known—that my C.O. found out my age and made me a war correspondent—that was true. I actually trained for a couple of weeks under Ernie Pyle. Do you know who he is?"

I smiled. "Only the most famous World War Two war reporter. Won a Pulitzer and had a movie made about him—*The Story of G.I. Joe*, which you've made me watch at least five times over the years."

"Just checking," he said with a grin, before saying soberly, "Ernie was a nice man as well. Killed at the tail end of the war. Anyway, it was Ernie who noticed certain abilities I had."

"Like what?" I asked.

"Oh, like the fact that I picked up languages quickly. That I had mechanical know-how—I could jerry-rig just about anything, too. And . . ." He picked up the pen once more, and it disappeared before my eyes. "I knew a few magic tricks."

My jaw dropped like it had wanted to in the Hotel Sutton ballroom when he'd switched the pens the first time. "Since when do you do magic tricks?" I'd never so much as seen him make a quarter fake-appear from behind my ear, for Pete's sake.

"It was better that I wasn't known for knowing magic, so I tended to only use them in a professional situation." One corner of his mouth quirked up. "I'll tell you what, though, sleight of hand kept me from getting shot several times—and kept me from having to shoot someone in turn. I wish it could have been that way in combat, too."

A wash of feelings came over me. Knowing my grandfather had indeed participated in combat in the war, I always guessed that he, like most soldiers, had shot one or more of the enemy. For whatever reason, I understood this from an early age and never asked him about it, nor had I ever requested his service records as a genealogist. But knowing that the circumstances of war had forced him to take another's life, and that he'd lived with the pain of it for decades, made me see my grandfather a little differently.

"What did you do in the OSS?" I asked. "And how does this pen fit in?" I looked around for it. "Where exactly is the pen, anyway? And what *is* that cylinder thing you found inside it?"

With a smile, Grandpa made the pen reappear; I never saw where it had been hidden. "I have many stories I could tell you about my work with the OSS, but I'll leave them for another day," he said. "Today, my love, you need to hear just one story—but first we need to go to the police. We need an item from Hugo's wallet."

"Okay, but can you at least start with why?"

Grandpa had removed the little cylinder, which I now realized was slimmer in the middle and looked more like a tiny dumbbell. He held it up.

"Because Hugo Markman sent you and me a message, and this will help us read it."

THIRTEEN

Once again, the questions came out before I could stop them.

"He left us a message? How can you tell? And how do you even know Hugo Markman?"

Grandpa ran his thumb over the pen's cap. "When you were telling me your story this morning and you mentioned a Mr. Markman, I didn't think much about it. But then you showed me this pen, and I knew right away that you must have meant Hugo, and that he had sent me a message through you. After that, I knew whom to contact to confirm it was indeed Hugo who had ended up on a pull-out shelf in the county refrigerator."

I made a face at his choice of words, but he didn't notice.

"So, are you going to tell me who Hugo Markman was?"

Grandpa shifted in his seat to look straight at me. He seemed to have made a decision.

"Yes, you deserve some information before we go to the police. Lucy, Hugo was a very nice man who was a full-time forensic accountant and a nearly full-time conspiracy theorist and wannabe spy."

His smile held a sadness for the man who'd died at my feet. "Everybody in the intelligence community in Texas has heard of Hugo. He'd be, oh, in his late fifties now, and has been a consistent hanger-on in the intelligence world since he graduated from college and didn't get accepted into the CIA. Apparently someone encouraged him to go into forensic accounting, telling him he might get to work for the Company that way." Grandpa shrugged. "In the end, though, his tendency to think everything was a government plot continued to hurt him."

"Poor Hugo," I said.

Grandpa nodded. "Still, there was no denying he was a nice guy with a good brain, so he was considered harmless. I'm told he occasionally gave a good tip, too."

"Did you ever meet him?" I asked.

"You could say I knew Hugo a little. Met him in the mid-eighties, well after I'd retired," he said. "I was in Langley one weekend at an OSS reunion and Hugo was there representing his grandfather. Hugo was just out of college and trying to work his way into the Company, but without success. Believe it or not, by this time, he'd already gotten the reputation for being a bit of a harmless nutter. We talked quite a bit that day, and I've heard his name several times since then through friends still in the business, but I haven't seen him."

I had a sudden thought, and clamped my hand over Grandpa's. "Mrs. P. said she thought he might have been slowly dying." I lowered my voice to a whisper, glancing around me as if we were in a public place and not in the safety of my condo. "Do you think the . . . you know . . . the company you worked for . . . may have poisoned him?"

Grandpa was silent for a second, then sat back with a belly laugh.

"No, my love. Hugo wasn't the kind of nutter who needs

silencing. In fact, I was told that in the last decade or so, he'd come around less and less frequently. He apparently worked for a consulting firm out of Houston doing forensic accounting, and they kept him busy. He'd go all over the US for weeks at a time, scaring the life out of corporate bigwigs when he took his eagle eye to their books. The CIA felt he was focusing his mind in a good direction, in catching white-collar criminals, and had become happy." He shook his head again. "No, the CIA had no knowledge of anything against Hugo, and I trust my contact to at least have hinted to me if there had been."

"Okay, but how would Hugo even know me?" I asked. "How did he even find me? And why not you?"

Grandpa gave me a lopsided grin. "Well, your Gran and I moved three times to different cities in the decades since I last saw Hugo. If he were desperate to find one of us quickly, you were the easier to find. You advertise your genealogy services, don't you? Hugo probably found you in a snap," Grandpa said, snapping his fingers for emphasis. "Knowing Hugo's desire to be an operative, he may have even followed you a bit, just to make sure he had the right person, that you weren't involved in whatever this is." He held the little cylinder on his palm, then closed it with a wave of his hand, and it disappeared. A second later, it was back on his palm. "Then when he'd cleared you—at least, cleared you in his own mind—he either knew or hoped like hell you'd show me the Montblanc."

I was nodding, but it turned into a gasp.

"He did follow me," I said. I stared at my grandfather's face, but my mind was seeing the weak-looking old man at the cemetery in New Braunfels. How the breeze had ruffled the wispy patches of hair on his head and how he'd turned to look at me just before he'd been driven off. I told Grandpa about seeing him.

"He was far away, but he looked right at me as if he knew me. Then at the Hotel Sutton, he came staggering up the path. When he saw me, he looked . . . I don't know, relieved . . . like he'd been looking specifically for me."

"What happened then?" Grandpa asked. "Because it's clear you had more interaction with Hugo than just seeing him drop a pen."

I flushed. "I didn't want to worry you," I said.

He reached out and squeezed my hand. "I understand, my love. Now, go on. What happened?"

"I was trying to hold him upright," I said. "So when he gave me the fountain pen, he could only press it against the back of my hand. He said, 'Keep them safe,' and that was it. He collapsed and died. The pen had dropped to the ground and Boomer picked it up before I even truly realized what it was."

Grandpa was quiet for several moments.

"You know, I suppose there could've been a slight chance I was wrong about this," he said, holding up the little cylinder once more. "But that seals the deal. Even though Hugo could be an oddball, he was smart and wanted to do right. His last act was to find you so you could give me this. It was very brave of him."

"I agree," I said, then pointed to the cylinder. It was about a half inch in length, and one end was threaded so that it could screw into something. "What exactly is that, by the way?"

Grandpa gave it to me. "It's a microdot viewer."

"Microdots?" I said, feeling a zing of excitement. "Like real spy intel on something the size of a small dot?"

His eyes twinkled. "Generally the size of a printed period, actually. Go ahead, look through it."

I held it up to my eye, but all I could see was blurriness. Lowering the viewer, I said, "Nothing's there."

"No, unfortunately," Grandpa said. "I was hoping he might have stuck it on the end of the viewer. That's why I gate-crashed your event at the Hotel Sutton and did the old switcheroo instead of arranging to meet you at a more appropriate time."

"So where's the microdot?" I asked.

"It could be anywhere," Grandpa said. "But I think that if Hugo were still lucid enough to get all of this to you before he died, then he would have put it somewhere that was easy enough for us to find."

"Like where?"

Grandpa rubbed his chin. "What else did he have on him?"

"Two dollars, a grocery-store receipt, and a theater ticket to the play *Oklahoma!*"

While he mulled this over, another question came to me. "Grandpa? You don't think Hugo was trying to alert you to an impending national terrorism event or something, do you?"

"No, my love," Grandpa said. "As much as Hugo wanted to be James Bond, my contact assured me he wasn't unbalanced. That tells me Hugo wouldn't have left something of national importance to chance. He'd have alerted the proper channels." Now he scooped up the Montblanc, which was in three pieces, and opened his palm so I could see them. "No, Lucy, this particular fountain pen tells me he's referencing something I worked on in the war."

He'd tacked on that bit of information so casually, it was a good two seconds before I could respond. "Are you serious?" I asked. "Something from World War Two? How can you be so sure?"

Grandpa's smile was grim as he indicated the Montblanc.

"Because only eight of these pens, with this particular engraving and with this cap, were created, for an operation that took place in early 1944. They hold the reader, which can be used on its own if needed, but also screws into another device about the size of a quarter that more easily holds the microdot for viewing."

I held up a hand, confused. "But, Grandpa, Montblanc was a German company. How did these get made for American spies?"

"Well, I can't say I know for sure, but I do know Montblancs were being manufactured in Denmark at the time, not Germany, and could be easily purchased. Also, when I said 'created,' I maybe should have said 'retrofitted.' The eight pens were originally basic black, with no engraving on the nib other than the forty-eight ten—and they certainly didn't come ready to hold a microdot viewer."

"So, what, there was some fountain-pen artisan working for the OSS and he made all the changes?"

My grandfather's blue eyes twinkled. "Very likely. You know as well as anyone that the war drafted people from all walks of life, including artists, jewelers, and craftsmen. Amazing things were done during the war by low-ranking soldiers with high-level skills, believe you me."

"That's very true," I said. "Come to think of it, one of my client's grandfathers had been an artist and set-builder for one of the big Hollywood studios. He was recruited to work with the so-called Ghost Army, creating fake tanks and radio signals and such to fool the Germans."

"Those guys did some cool stuff," Grandpa said.

I nodded toward the pen. "Clearly so did these spies. Go on, tell me more."

He smiled, holding up the pen's cap again. "Lucy, these fountain pens were made so the eight operatives who were issued them could recognize each other. First by the cap, and if the cap were lost, by the nib inside."

"The spies didn't all know each other?" I asked.

"We didn't at the beginning," Grandpa said.

My mouth dropped open. "Wait, you were one of them? Not the handler, like you were later? Or a desk clerk or someone behind the scenes?" I pointed to the pen. "You had one of these and were out in the field, risking your life?"

His grin was amused. "How do you think I recognized it?"

I flung up my arms, making NPH sit up on his bar chair and swat at the gold bangle on my wrist. "I don't know. Maybe you took dictation for whatever general ordered the mission? Grandpa, you were just a kid. What were you in forty-four? Eighteen?"

Now he really did laugh. "I'd just turned nineteen when this mission happened, yes. But, my love, I'd had months of intensive training—and, oh"—he looked up at the ceiling, mentally counting—"at least six successful missions under my belt."

"Get outta town!" I exclaimed. "Really?"

He put his hand on my cheek, smiling. "I'll tell you about some of them, too, but not today."

"Of course," I said, forcing myself to get back to the here and now. "You said there were eight spies connected with this mission. Were you all OSS?"

He shook his head. "It was a joint mission with OSS and SOE."

"Wow. Did you know any of the other spies?"

"I only knew the one I recruited for the mission," Grandpa said. "The other six, I only knew their code names. In fact, to this day, I still don't know any of their real names."

"Seriously?" I said.

"You have to understand how these things worked, my love," he said patiently. "A couple of the operatives I only ever saw for a few minutes, when we passed information. Others, I worked with very closely. We were all part of the same mission, but we all had different jobs to do." He tapped lightly on the Montblanc. "That was another reason for having the pen on us. It allowed us to recognize each other without any code words or looks. One of the guys who passed intel to me? He walked up to me at the designated time and place, in a café in France. I was writing a letter with my pen. We never spoke a word to each other, nor did I ever even see more than the side of his face. He slipped me a coded message and was gone."

"Wow," I said again, with reverence.

"I suppose there's a way to find out who they were, now that a lot of wartime activities have been declassified," Grandpa said, "though I don't know if this one has."

I was fascinated, and dying to ask a million questions, all of them jumbled up in my mind, jockeying for position. One leapt out.

"How would Hugo know about this pen? How would he know that *you* know about this pen?"

Grandpa shook his head. "I'm afraid I don't know, darlin'. Like I said, I know Hugo's grandfather had been OSS, but I didn't know anyone named Markman."

"Then maybe he's the grandson through the OSS agent's daughter," I said thoughtfully. "Did he look like anyone who was part of your mission?"

He considered for a moment. "His demeanor reminded me of one guy. Anxious, jumpy sort of fellow. Always so earnest about everything. He was SOE, however, not OSS." I could see Grandpa going back in time in his memories. "He was dashed smart, though—utterly brilliant, in fact—and when the time came to be brave, he was. His code name was Rupert, but that's all I know." Grandpa sighed, running his thumb over the fountain pen's gold bands. "Rupert's bravery lost him his life, but ensured our successful mission, which helped us win the war." He looked into my eyes. "You and I sit here today because of him."

I blew out a breath and felt goose bumps pop up all over.

"Do you remember the name of Hugo's grandfather—the one you said he was representing at the OSS reunion? Could he have been Rupert? I know some Americans worked for SOE, especially early on, before America came into the war." Smiling, I threw in another factoid. "Virginia Hall was one of them. The Germans dubbed her the most dangerous Allied spy, and she had a wooden leg she named Cuthbert. She also later worked with the OSS."

Grandpa beamed at my spy facts. "Ah, yes, you are correct. The Germans called her the Limping Lady. I never worked with her, but she was a damn fine operative." Then he shook his head. "I never asked Hugo about his granddad. It's unlikely he would've known his code name, though."

"What was your code name?" I asked quietly, almost afraid he wouldn't tell me.

Grandpa held out his hand for me to shake. "Nice to meet you, I'm Robert," he said. "Robert Runyon, but everybody calls me Bobby."

I grinned, shaking his hand and marveling at how naturally the alias rolled off his tongue. "That's a good name," I said.

"I liked it," he said. "Let's just say Bobby and I had some adventures."

"I have a lot of questions for Bobby once this is done," I teased.

Grandpa merely chuckled, so I moved on.

I picked up the fountain pen's cap. "So, these bands. The three thin bands and one larger one. Do they mean anything, or were they merely a specific, but random, decoration?"

Grandpa took the cap and held it out and away from me, then turned it sideways.

"You tell me. If you look at the bands this way, and straight on, what do you see?"

I stared. It took me a long minute and my grandfather waited patiently. If I hadn't known to think about the war and espionage, it might have taken me longer. With those hints, however, I finally saw it when I focused on the width of the bands and what that might signify.

"Three dots and a dash," I said excitedly, reaching out and taking the cap to look closer. "It's Morse code, isn't it?"

Grandpa beamed. "For the letter 'V.'"

The history geek in me came out and I crowed, "For 'Victory!'"

Now he laughed and, taking my face in his hands, gave my cheek a loud kiss. "You make me prouder every minute, my darlin'. V for Victory, yes indeed."

At my exultation, NPH leapt lightly onto the island to check out the pen cap. He seemed to approve of its coded message with a quick rub of his cheek.

"The V also stood for something else, but that's another part of the story," Grandpa said, stroking NPH's back and getting a loud purr in response.

"What about the two crossed feathers and the scrollwork on the nib?" I asked, eager for more spy stuff.

This time, Grandpa pulled out a small, flat object from his wallet and handed it to me. It was a magnifying glass, and I used it to peer at the nib.

"They aren't feathers, love," he said. "They're palm fronds." He smiled again. "But the scrollwork is just that. There to catch the eye so the fronds are less obvious."

"Palm fronds," I repeated with a groan. "I should have recognized them. I see palm fronds on gravestones quite a bit.

They symbolize victory as well. Victory over death, to be specific."

Grandpa looked proud again as he started to put the pen back together, minus the little microdot reader. I realized he hadn't completed his story, that he hadn't told me what was so important about the joint OSS–SOE mission that could have a connection to Hugo Markman's death. Yet at the same time, I felt like he wanted to be sure of his facts before he told me the tale.

If it had been anyone else, from any other time period, I might have thought them a bit ridiculous for not being willing to explain a situation that had happened nearly eighty years ago. But the Greatest Generation were different. They held the war and what happened in it close to their hearts.

And for those who worked in intelligence and swore their oath of secrecy? Well, there were wartime intelligence veterans today who still wouldn't speak of their experiences, no matter how many times they'd been told it was all right to do so. Their honor wouldn't let them break their word. My grandfather was clearly one of those types of veterans, and it was tougher than I'd given him credit for to even tell me what he'd said thus far. I could see it in the crags of his still handsome face.

I got up, scratching NPH behind the ears. "Come on, Grandpa. Let's go."

He looked at me inquiringly.

"To the police station," I said. "You said the microdot is likely in Hugo's possessions, and I trust you and your need to verify before you speak further. So let's go get it and see what Hugo left us."

My grandfather looked at me with emotion in his blue eyes for a long second before pulling back his shoulders.

"After you, my darlin'," he said with a sweeping gesture toward the door.

I first went and retrieved all our devices from my bedroom. My hand was on the front door handle when there was a loud knock.

"Open up!" shouted a deep, gruff voice.

FOURTEEN

Grandpa and I both froze.

"I know you have Lucy in there. Let her go!"

This time, the voice sounded less deep. Less gruff, and with less maturity in tone, too. In the distance, I heard another noise and recognized it. Someone—a second person—was running up the stairs on the side of my condo building. Someone bigger and heavier.

"Yes, open up!" called the second person, his voice tinged with a Mississippi drawl.

NPH, who'd been my attack cat just a couple of months earlier, was at my side. But his tail was up. He knew that voice. He knew both of them, it seemed.

And so did I.

Smiling at Grandpa, I threw open the door.

"Lucy!" they both exclaimed in unison at the sight of me in one piece. The bigger one sighed heavily with relief, his hand on his heaving chest. The smaller one, headphones around his neck, glared over my shoulder at Grandpa, until he glanced at me, then at his big friend, and his expression went uncertain.

"Hi, Diego," I said, grinning at the boy, who was all dark hair, big eyes, gangly limbs, and brand-new braces. "Hi, Jackson," I added to my out-of-breath condo manager, whose mane of auburn hair and butter-yellow cashmere sweater stretched over his belly gave him the look of a stylishly mature lion about town. NPH had dashed out and was curling himself first around Diego's legs, then around those of his actual owner.

Jackson's relief turned to a smile when he recognized my grandfather.

"Mr. Lancaster!" He clasped Grandpa's outstretched hand and pumped it. "It's wonderful to see you again, sir." Looking slightly wild-eyed at me, he added, "Heavens, Lucy, you scared Diego and me half out of our wits."

Grandpa held his hand out to Diego. "Young man, I take it you saw me walking upstairs with my granddaughter, and when you didn't recognize me, you raised the alarm with Jackson here."

Diego, his brown eyes wide, just nodded and shook Grandpa's hand.

"I thank you for doing that, sir," my grandfather said, his tone serious. "I thank both of you for looking out for my Lucy, even though all of us know she's strong and smart and can look after herself."

Diego nodded again, then blurted out, "Lucy told me you were in World War Two."

"I was," Grandpa answered. "Sergeant George Lancaster, Fourth Infantry Division, pleased to meet you." He gave Diego a salute.

"Mr. Lancaster was in D-day," Jackson told Diego.

Jackson didn't know the half of it, I thought.

Diego was agog. "I have to write an essay about the war," he said, before becoming shy, intermittently looking down at his boots, then glancing up at Grandpa. "Can I—" A glance at Jackson, and he said, "I mean, may I ask you what it was like?"

"*Sir*," whisper-reminded Jackson, who had become an excellent de facto father figure to Diego, since the boy's biological father was not in his life.

"May I ask you what it was like, sir?" Diego repeated.

Grandpa smiled. "I would be honored to tell you, Diego. However, my granddaughter and I have some errands to run and things to do, which may keep me busy for a few days. When is your paper due?"

"In two weeks, sir." Diego was currently being homeschooled, but would be going to the local public school at the start of the next school year. As such, his mother was making sure to give him strict deadlines for his projects. If she said it was due in two weeks, it was.

"I expect that should give us more than enough time. When Lucy and I are done with our project, I'll either come back here and you can interview me, or Lucy can bring you and your mother out to my house in Wimberley. How does that sound?"

Diego beamed. "That would be great! I mean, that would be great, sir. Thanks!" And all at once, he was nothing but a kid again, waving to us as he streaked off and clattered down the stairs, NPH in hot pursuit.

Jackson shook his head, watching NPH tear after Diego. "Sometimes, I swear my cat loves you and that boy more than me."

"Ah, but he always comes home to you," I reminded him.

Jackson's response was all tongue-in-cheek drama. "Between NPH and Jud, it's my lot in life to share those I love with others, and wait for them to come home to me at night."

"If you didn't share Jud with others, I'd hog-tie you faster than you could say 'mint chocolate chip,'" I shot back with mock severity before smiling at my grandfather. "You know that ice cream you enjoyed so much, Grandpa? Jackson's boyfriend makes it. He does small-batch only and sells out by lunchtime every day."

"Can he be bribed to set a pint of that chocolate–peanut butter aside for me?" Grandpa asked as I locked my door. "Or three?"

"Jud can't, but I sure as heck can," Jackson replied, and, thankfully, nothing more interesting than ice cream was discussed as the three of us made our way downstairs.

The whole drive to the Austin police department, Grandpa would only tell me that I was giving the decoy Montblanc pen as evidence in place of the real one and that he would be claiming Hugo had something that belonged to him. For the rest, he told me, we would be winging it.

"Winging it?" I repeated. "Don't you think we should have *some* kind of plan?"

"Nah," Grandpa replied. "The only thing you need to do is follow my lead. Just stay as close to the truth as possible and you'll be fine."

At a stoplight, I turned to him, my eyes narrowing. "And what exactly does that mean? What are you planning?"

He just pointed to the light. "It's green, darlin'."

"Grandpa," I said, "you're really enjoying being cryptic, aren't you?"

He merely grinned. "I don't know what you're talking about, love."

The rest of the short drive, I could only think of how much Ben and my grandfather would like each other. I'd come to the shocking realization the latter could be just as infuriating as the former, and both clearly loved infuriating me when they wanted to.

Inside the Austin PD headquarters, the lighting was unnaturally bright, and it was colder than it was outside—which wasn't saying much, since the day was still hovering around sixty-eight degrees.

"May I help you?" asked the young officer with close-cropped dark hair working the front desk.

I looked at Grandpa, just stopping myself from doing a double-take. Gone was his straight-backed posture and watchful but open expression. Now he stood hunched, his head jutting forward like a turtle. He looked like a truly old man instead of my much-younger-acting grandfather, and I didn't know that I liked it. He didn't speak up, though.

Okay, I thought. *We're winging it, and I guess I'm taking the lead.*

"Yes," I replied. "I'm here to drop off a piece of potential evidence relating to the death of a man yesterday at the Hotel Sutton." When Grandpa didn't chime in, I added, "And my grandfather here believes the man who died had something that belonged to him."

The officer showed zero interest in either piece of information, but asked, "Do you know the name of the case officer you dealt with?"

"Officer Carr," I replied.

He asked us to present our driver's licenses and sign in. Grandpa took longer than normal to sign. In fact, he hesitated with the pen for a good second or two before finally, slowly, writing his name as the officer watched. I felt my eyebrows knit, but the officer was already on the phone, speaking in low tones to someone, presumably Officer Carr.

We sat. Grandpa looked around, but didn't speak. Officer Carr strode out after a few minutes.

"Ms. Lancaster," he said, shaking my hand. I introduced him to my grandfather, whose posture had gone even more turtlelike and feeble, while his expression had gone grumpy.

Unbidden, a streak of worry shot through me. Was Grandpa acting or not? I honestly couldn't tell.

Officer Carr was speaking. "I understand you found some evidence? Is this the pen you said had been dropped?"

I nodded, pulling out my sunglasses case and opening it to show the Montblanc. "It got picked up by Ms. Sutton's dog, as it turns out. I'm afraid the dog slobbered all over it."

Officer Carr looked at the pen, which Grandpa had systematically wiped clean before having me hold it to put my prints back on it. "Did you wipe it down?"

I blushed. "I'm afraid I forgot myself when I finally got it away from Boomer—that's the dog. It was *really* slobbery, so I automatically wiped it off." Officer Carr looked like he wanted to roll his eyes, and I said, "Maybe there's some prints on the inside?" Though I knew there wouldn't be.

"You don't need any prints," Grandpa said suddenly, looking at Officer Carr like he was an insolent child. "I *told* you, I know him and he has my ticket."

Then Grandpa turned to me, his blue eyes suddenly huge and childlike. He'd naturally shrunk a bit with age, of course, but now that he was hunched over, his face was very nearly level with mine.

"They're going to give me my ticket, aren't they, Elinor? I need my ticket back."

FIFTEEN

❧

I suddenly couldn't breathe, feeling like I'd just been doused with ice water. Grandpa's eyes looked unfocused, and he'd just referred to me by my grandmother's name.

I glanced at Officer Carr, knowing I must have looked unnerved, and his expression softened with understanding.

Grandpa was reaching out a shaking hand to me. "Hugo had my ticket to the play, Elinor. The one we're going to see together. It's *Oklahoma!*, your favorite, and I can't get in without my ticket." When I grasped his hand, though, feeling like I was about to burst into tears, I felt something. Two quick squeezes. Tears sprang to my eyes, but this time in relief.

Gently, I said to Grandpa, "I'm Lucy, remember? Your granddaughter?"

My grandfather blinked several times, then shook his head as if to clear it. "Yes . . . so sorry, love," he said, with a helpless note in his voice.

I turned back to Officer Carr with a sniffle I didn't have to fake and whispered, "My apologies. Elinor is—was—my grandmother's name."

I swallowed hard. "My grandfather . . . well, he tends to fo-cus on certain things these days and doesn't always remember things in order." With a flash of inspiration, I added, "See, my grandmother loved going to plays, and he still likes to go be-cause it reminds him of better days. I took him to *Oklahoma!* last week, but he's not remembering correctly that we've already gone. Would it be possible for the ticket we found in Mr. Mark-man's wallet to be returned to my grandfather?"

Officer Carr was clearly pitying my grandfather's plight, but he wasn't stupid. "I'm very sorry, Ms. Lancaster, but I can't give your grandfather the ticket. It's evidence until we know what happened to the victim." When Grandpa looked around the room as if easily distracted, Officer Carr leaned in and said, "How did he know it was in the wallet anyway?"

Grandpa's eyes flashed and he jabbed a shaking finger at the officer's chest. "Young man, I'm not deaf. I heard what you just said. I knew about the ticket because it's mine!"

Officer Carr played along. "And how did you know this Mr.—"

"Markman," Grandpa replied imperiously. "Hugo Mark-man. I knew him because we were in the war together." He made a show of standing taller, which, with his head still jutted forward, made him look like a suddenly defiant turtle.

"Grandpa," I said gently. "You were in the war with Hugo's grandfather, not Hugo himself." Looking up at Officer Carr, I said, "Mr. Markman was kind enough to look after my grand-father from time to time and, well, Grandpa can sometimes get Hugo mixed up with Hugo's grandfather."

Officer Carr's eyes had narrowed. "I thought you said you had never seen this man before, Ms. Lancaster. How do you suddenly know so much about him?"

Rats. One step too far, Luce. I went for injured dignity, just to see where it got me.

"I most certainly did not know him, Officer Carr," I replied, lifting my chin while grasping Grandpa's hand. "My grandfather here lives in Wimberley, and when I went to see him today, he was upset, having read about Mr. Markman in the paper. But it wasn't until I'd asked his neighbor that I learned that Hugo—Mr. Markman, that is—would occasionally visit Grandpa, because his grandfather and mine were war buddies."

I felt a quick pressure on my fingers, like you might pump a bike's handbrake. I'd gotten too far from the truth, and Grandpa was telling me to rein it in.

Officer Carr's eyes were still narrowed. "That doesn't explain how this man would have your grandfather's ticket to the play."

I thought fast. "Grandpa . . . well, sometimes he'll give you something he thinks needs to be kept safe," I said. "He knew it was important to not lose his ticket to the play, so I think he gave it to Hugo." To this, Grandpa responded with a vehement nod.

"I did," Grandpa said. "Hugo said he would keep it safe for me until Elinor and I could go. Hugo has my ticket, young man, and I need it." He stared up at Officer Carr with a mulish expression.

"Be that as it may, sir," Officer Carr said, not without respect, "we cannot release the ticket until our investigation into the death of Mr. Markman is complete."

Grandpa suddenly pounded his fist against the plastic-covered corkboard on the wall, making a loud, reverberating noise that had the front desk officer standing up. "I was in the war, damn it!" Grandpa shouted. "I was in Normandy! I fought on that beach, my friends dropping like flies around me, to save our freedom—your freedom, young man—and you're not going to give me my damned ticket to *Oklahoma!*?"

At the ruckus, two other officers had come rushing out, their hands hovering over their service weapons. Officer Carr gave them a quick signal that all was okay.

Grandpa turned back to me, his eyes like blue saucers once more. "Elinor, why won't they give me my ticket? I can't take you without it."

Putting my arm around Grandpa's shoulders, I said, "Officer Carr, would it be possible for us to take a photo of the ticket? Just so that my grandfather has a copy of it as proof? You know, so he can show it at the ticket window and they'll know he isn't trying to gate-crash." I gave the officer an exaggerated wink. "And then, after this mess is over, I can come and get the real one so that Grandpa will have it. Would that work?" I looked at my grandfather, who was giving an Oscar-worthy performance as an old codger in and out of senility. "Would that be okay for the time being, Grandpa?"

"What?" he asked, the gruff back in his voice. "Yes, that would be fine."

Officer Carr studied us for a moment. "All right. Let me escort you to a room and I'll bring the evidence bag for you to photograph."

I didn't expect my grandfather to break his cover as we sat in the interview room, and I wasn't disappointed. He called me by my grandmother's name twice more as we sat at the table, each time asking about the ticket, and I put on my own show by fussing over him, straightening the collar of his jacket, and asking if he was warm enough. He replied crankily that he was, and demanded to be the one who took the photos so he could get a nice, clear shot. I wanted to ask how he was going to get the ticket out of the evidence bag, but I also didn't want to know. No doubt the camera in the corner was recording us, so I wanted plausible deniability.

"All right," I said to him in soothing tones. "You can take the photo."

Grandpa's back was to the camera, and while his "Good" was cantankerous, his eyes were twinkling. I didn't know whether to have a good feeling about this or a bad one. All I knew was that my dearest, sweetest grandfather was a wily old fox.

Officer Carr was back in under ten minutes. He put a plastic evidence bag on the table. Inside I could see the ticket stub to *Oklahoma!*

I handed Grandpa my phone with the camera on. He took it, put it on the table, and spent time smoothing out the ticket in the evidence bag, straightening it, smoothing it some more, and straightening it again until its bent edges flattened and it was a perfect rectangle. When Officer Carr said, "I think it's straight now, Mr. Lancaster," Grandpa gave him a haughty stare and said, "Young man, it will be straight when I say it's straight. In the army, we had to be able to bounce a quarter off our beds, so I know straight and smooth when I see it!"

This time, Officer Carr's lips twitched. I motioned him aside with a grin, whispering, "Let's just give him a minute."

Officer Carr responded with a smile that was really quite nice.

"Thank you for doing this," I said to him. Out of the corner of my eye, I could see Grandpa picking up the bag and shaking it before rearranging the theater ticket again. What could he be doing?

Plausible deniability, Luce. Whatever he's doing, they won't throw him in jail for it, will they?

Wait, I thought. *Would they?*

"You're welcome," Officer Carr replied. I was glad he was looking at me, because now Grandpa was holding the bag to his stomach to smooth it down. "My grandmother is the same way. She obsesses over coupons, though. Can't get enough of them. We've learned it's just easier to humor her and let her have all the coupons she wants than try to change her mind."

"Too right," I said, and laughed, feeling just slightly hysterical now. Grandpa had held the bag to himself again and was almost doing a jig. "Does she ever use them?"

Officer Carr glanced at my grandfather, but when I touched his arm and smiled my brightest smile, he blinked and said, "Ever use what?" He looked dazed—though the good kind of dazed that said his mind was focused entirely on me.

"All the coupons she collects," I said.

But I never got the answer as, suddenly, we heard a sound like plastic crinkling way too fast. Then Grandpa was cursing. More plastic crinkling noise followed as my grandfather turned around.

"Elinor!" he shouted. "Elinor, this blasted bag got stuck in my coat zipper."

My mouth almost dropped as I saw he was trying valiantly to get the bag unstuck from the heavy zipper on his coat, but was only making it worse.

"Grandpa!" I said, jumping forward. "What happened?" Officer Carr had also sprung forward, his expression furious, and grabbed my grandfather's arm, though he quickly pulled his hands away when I snarled, "Don't you dare put your hands on him."

It was utter chaos for the next minute as I tried to unzip Grandpa's jacket and he made attempts to help me, making it worse. Finally, Officer Carr said, "Stop. Both of you."

I glanced quickly up at Grandpa, whose eyes met mine for the briefest second before sliding down to the heap of plastic evidence bag billowing out from his stomach like the Portuguese man-of-wars that popped up on the beaches of the Gulf Coast, ready to sting you if you touched one of their tentacles.

"My apologies, officer," he said, his voice shaky. "I was just trying to smooth it out and it got caught."

Officer Carr sighed heavily. "It's all right, sir. We're going to cut it off you."

He told us to stand still, then stuck his head out of the interrogation room's door and called to someone. Seconds later, a petite female officer with her wavy dark hair pulled back into a low chignon walked in with a pair of scissors and a new evidence bag. She introduced herself as Officer Alaniz, asked Grandpa to sit down with a kind smile, and gently cut the bag away from his coat zipper, with Grandpa helping by holding the bag taught.

With her last cut, Grandpa cried out, "Oops!" and the *Oklahoma!* ticket fluttered down onto the table. He reached out and grabbed it just as Officer Alaniz lunged for it, saying, "Now, Mr. Lancaster, we can't have you touching evidence."

Grandpa pulled his hands back immediately. "A thousand apologies, ma'am," he said. Then he poked his head around to look at me with hopeful eyes. "Think they'll still let me take a photo?"

Officer Carr's world-weary sigh ended with, "Fine. But you do it, Ms. Lancaster. And please make it quick."

I snapped a photo of the ticket, thanked the officers, then took Grandpa's hand and got us the hell out of Dodge.

SIXTEEN

At a stoplight two blocks away from the police station, I finally let myself breathe and wiped my sweaty palms on my pants leg. Grandpa, after looking around—for signs we'd been followed, or for traffic cameras, I couldn't tell—sat up straight, his back cracking as he did, and dropped the feeble, semi-senile old man act.

"Lucy, my darlin', you were wonderful!" His blue eyes were focused and aware once more.

Now I did give a hysterical laugh, partly because I was frightened he hadn't been acting the whole time in the police station. "Grandpa, what are you talking about? We failed. We didn't get you the *Oklahoma!* ticket and the microdot."

"Oh, but we didn't fail. Hold out your hand."

I did as he asked and he touched his index finger to my palm. I looked down, and there was a little black dot, hardly bigger than a period.

"But," I stammered. "How did you get this off the ticket? You barely touched it."

He tapped my palm again and the little black dot disappeared. From the cup holder in my console, he pulled out one of my own business cards, looked at it, and deposited the microdot in the middle. Carefully, he began to fold up my card so it made a protective package for the microdot.

"All it took was one little scrape of my fingernail over the dot on the exclamation point," he said, beaming. "Of course, I had to be sure there weren't other microdots—"

"Hence all your heavy petting of the evidence bag—and only a senile-acting old man could have pulled off the brilliant move of faking getting a plastic bag caught in his coat zipper."

I smiled at him, but he could see that I was searching his face. My right hand was on the center console and Grandpa reached out and squeezed my fingers.

"All an act, love. My bones may be old and creaky and I may make far too many trips to the bathroom at night, but these places"—he touched his temple, then his heart—"I'm lucky enough to say are still working as they should."

Fearing my eyes might mist up if we continued along these lines, I said, "Okay, then. Where to next?"

"We need to go somewhere private to read this baby," he said, tapping his shirt pocket, where he'd slipped the microdot he'd encased in my business card.

"My office?" I suggested. Almost on cue, a text message from Serena came in. I had the car's voice system read it out loud to me without thinking.

> Checking on you after yesterday's weirdness with the
> dead guy. We hope you're right as rain.

"Glad you didn't keep that to yourself," Grandpa said, nodding with approval as the robotic female voice continued to read Serena's message.

Also, a package came for you at the office. Those
fabulous heels you ordered for New Year's Eve. Want
me to bring to hotel? Ben still might show up to snog
the living daylights out of you, and maybe you'll even
get some quality time with HIS pack—.

"O-kay, then!" I sang out, my cheeks heating up as I punched
the button on my steering wheel to cut the playback. Somehow it was even more mortifying in that robotic voice. I started
rambling. "Um, yeah, clearly Serena is at the office, so that's a
no-go. Where to now? Back to my condo? Somewhere else?"

Somewhere I could crawl into a hole to hide and text Serena
that I was going to have her head on a silver platter, naturally.

My grandfather, however, merely hiked an eyebrow my way.
"That Special Agent Turner still hasn't called you?"

"Grandpa . . ." I groaned. My cheeks were surely flaming now.

"Want me to have him taken out?"

My jaw dropped again, but I had to laugh. "Grandpa! I can't
believe you just said that!"

His laugh was both infectious and cheekily unrepentant.

Finally, he said, "I just realized we haven't eaten a proper
lunch yet, and I'm starved. How about we go eat? Afterward,
we can read what Hugo left for us."

"I feel so sorry for Hugo," I said, turning onto Colorado
Street. "I hope the medical examiner finds out what made him
so ill. That broken tooth looked horribly painful."

"Hold on," Grandpa said, his eyes narrowing. "He had a
broken tooth?"

"Yes. I thought I told you."

"You said he looked like he'd been ill, but you didn't tell me
about the tooth. What were his other symptoms?"

"He was staggering, and sweaty," I said.

"Did his hair look like it had been falling out?"

I thought back as I pulled into a parking lot and found a spot. "Well, he was balding," I said. "But he had some hair left on top of his head. Come to think of it, though, it was more like uneven patches of hair."

Grandpa frowned.

"What?" I asked him, turning my car off. "What is it?"

"I'd rather let my contact confirm it before I say anything," he said. "But, regardless, Hugo must have felt there was significant danger to have handled this situation the way he did—following you, making it his last act to get this to you."

He patted his pocket again. "That means someone may already be watching us and know we have this. Or they might not have realized we've found anything of interest yet. The point is, we need to be careful until we know what we're dealing with."

Oh, I didn't like the sound of that at all. I felt frozen in my seat, wondering if we were being watched as we spoke. It was a creepy feeling for sure.

But not for Grandpa, it seemed. He threw off his seatbelt and looked up at the sign in the parking lot with a whoop.

"Big Flaco's Tacos—hot damn, I should have known. I haven't seen Flaco in a coon's age, and I could really use a beer and some of his queso. Let's go."

SEVENTEEN

※

You would have thought it had literally been a coon's age since my grandfather and Flaco had seen each other by the way they embraced just outside of Flaco's kitchen area, exclaiming, *"¡Amigo!"* and rattling on in Spanish for the next few minutes about how they couldn't complain about their lives while simultaneously discussing how the cold made their achy knees act up.

Then Grandpa asked Flaco about his wife and children, listening intently to every proud update, and telling Flaco that his three children were as smart and talented as their parents.

In contrast, Flaco, his handlebar mustache twitching with mischief, replied by telling Grandpa how I was now his most demanding and high-maintenance customer, having become somewhat of a local celebrity after all the nonsense that had happened two months earlier.

"Lucia has so many admirers now, people fight to get a seat next to her at the bar." He waggled his dark eyebrows at my grandfather. "Most of them men."

"¡Mentiras! All of that is such tosh," I said. "I cannot believe

you're feeding my grandfather such lies," I added, hands on my hips, making Grandpa and Flaco roar with laughter.

Then Flaco turned to my grandfather and said, "*¿Pero, que es* 'tosh'?"

When they were done roasting me, Flaco gestured to the dining area, telling us to sit where we liked and that he would bring us something special to eat.

Nearly every table was taken since it was still peak lunch hours. "I guess we're eating here," Grandpa said, not looking remotely put out by it. "But I do wish there were somewhere private where we could get a look at the microdot."

I looked around the restaurant, with its red-vinyl barstools, checkerboard floor, and pockmarked tables. It had the look of a 1950s-style diner that had been beaten with a baseball bat, which was exactly what had happened during the time between when the former owners had abandoned it and Flaco had purchased it to house his taqueria.

"Actually," I said, "I do know of somewhere private." We found Flaco again and I said, "Mind if I show Grandpa your newest addition?"

Flaco's mustache twitched as he pulled a key from his pocket. "The button to open it is working now," he told me. "I have queso and drinks for you when you come back."

I led Grandpa down the short corridor by the kitchen and through a door to the taqueria's storeroom. Passing open shelves full of spices, bags of dried beans, cooking oils, and more *masa harina* than I'd seen in my life, I walked us through a second door, then a third.

The third door opened into a room with black-lacquered walls. A large, half-moon table was at the near side of the room, under a set of black shutters. A handful of clear votive holders shaped like fat pears waited atop the table for their candles to be lit. As of yet, there were no paintings or framed photos or anything else.

I flipped on the lights and pressed a button on the wall. The shutters split apart in the center and drew back silently, with sounds of a hissing, spitting grill and rapid chopping suddenly coming from the other side. We were looking directly into Flaco's kitchen, where Ana, Flaco's best waitress, waved to us while expertly flipping several chicken breasts and repositioning a handful of light green tomatillos that were charring on the grill for one of Flaco's specialty salsas.

The new part-time sous chef, a young man named Juan, was busy chopping onions and was so into his work, he didn't even turn around. Flaco's two other waitresses bustled in and out without giving us so much as a second glance. From the way the shutters opened, no one in the main restaurant could see us, making us almost hidden within the busy restaurant.

Grandpa looked around with delight. "He's built a private chef's table."

"This area used to be two storage closets that Flaco rarely used," I explained. "Since he's had customers begging him for a chef's table for ages, he decided to build one."

I hit the button again, closing the shutters smoothly, blocking out any noise from the kitchen. "He's only booking for Thursday, Friday, and Saturday nights, but it's already reserved for the next three months."

"We'll have to book it for one night, then," Grandpa said. "Get your parents in and whatever other family can come."

"Already done," I said. "I've booked it for your birthday. Maeve and Kyle are even flying in from DC."

A smile split Grandpa's face.

"Okay, let's do this," he said, pulling the microdot viewer

and the little packet from his shirt pocket. Carefully, he removed the microdot from my business card and laid it on the end of the viewer. He offered the viewer to me, but I shook my head.

"Hugo left this message for you, Grandpa. You read it first."

He held the viewer to his eye, turning it until the microdot was level. He didn't study its contents long, then handed me the viewer in silence.

With a thrill of apprehension and excitement—and, I confess, the theme song from the James Bond movies going around in my head—I had my first look at the little black dot.

What I saw almost made me dizzy. My eye was filled with a jumble of numbers. Sets of three numbers separated by dashes, actually.

Then I noticed the letters written underneath each of the first five groupings of numbers. They formed names. I noticed the penmanship of the first two names was neat. The third was much less so. The fourth looked like it was written by a drunk person, and the fifth I could barely make out. The three groups of numbers at the bottom had not yet been decoded. And at the very bottom, so light they were hard to see, were what looked like a series of doodles.

30-5-9 89-6-23 15-9-17 45-2-39 106-5-30 35-2-40
52-4-11 22-2-31 23-1-39 84-3-6 33-9-5 75-8-19 27-3-
22 68-2-20 51-5-21 82-4-27

PENELOPE OHLINGER

60-3-33 27-2-48 6-5-24 33-4-7 84-8-19 10-5-13 32-
6-47 72-3-7 17-3-11 47-7-15 87-5-1 3-5-19

FIONA KEELAND

51-2-16 67-1-23 14-3-14 43-5-36 90-6-19 1-3-100 46-
3-26 23-3-3 96-4-10 23-9-2 113-7-7 35-4-32 56-5-9
20-3-13 81-7-3

ROCCO ZEPPETELLI

34-1-16 67-5-27 84-5-3 24-10-2 43-2-25 4-8-3 59-9-
15 30-8-5 87-15-17 28-3-23 13-6-34 46-4-3

NAOMI VAN DORN

48-2-14 82-2-6 105-4-1 15-6-9 90-9-13 32-6-18 71-
3-10 25-2-9 68-2-19 89-5-25 23-4-42 32-3-5 7-1-17
98-12-6

ALASTAIR NEWELL

76-7-11 15-2-5 47-5-13 20-2-17 38-5-31 3-8-19 70-
2-11 6-4-5 34-6-43 14-3-7 66-5-32 18-1-10 46-3-36
91-7-57 16-7-2 27-2-24 9-2-28
10-2-23 31-4-47 60-2-15 41-6-29 9-4-13 36-7-25
77-2-2 3-6-17 34-2-8 8-3-5 61-8-17 52-4-44 82-9-9
22-1-12
84-4-29 14-3-3 44-9-22 90-5-10 27-3-55 3-8-19 54-
4-20 31-3-26 63-9-15 12-3-30 7-3-14 42-5-6 84-4-10
24-5-18 38-2-9 49-9-27

⊔<⊏∩⅃⊙∨ ⊔⊡∨⅄
⅄ ∧⌐⌐⌐

I lowered the viewer, blinking at Grandpa to clear my vision.
"So?" he said. "What do you think?"

"Well, first off, the main part is code, yes?" I said. "Partially broken by Hugo."

Grandpa nodded. "Yes, it's a book cipher. The first number in the set is the page number to find in the designated key text—meaning a book, of course. The second is the paragraph number on that specific page."

"And the third number?"

Grandpa didn't immediately answer, but looked through the viewer again at the microdot for a long moment. When he straightened, he was rubbing his chin. "I could be wrong, love, but I'm betting the creator of this list used a slightly different method of encoding the cipher."

"How do you mean?" I said.

Grandpa replied, "Normally, in this kind of book cipher, the third number in each set refers to a whole word in the book, not just a letter, and the decoded words are put together to form a message."

He asked if I had something to write with, and I gave him a pen and a sticky note. On it he wrote the numbers *76-7-11*, the first set of numbers from the microdot. "For instance, this should mean you go to page seventy-six of the book, the seventh paragraph, and find the eleventh word within the seventh paragraph."

He gestured to the microdot viewer still in my hand. "But it's clear from what was already decoded that the third number represents only *a letter* from the designated word, not the whole word itself."

I nodded thoughtfully, saying, "It would be hard for any book to contain all those names—especially the surnames, so I'm not surprised."

"I agree, but once we find the key, we can cross-reference it with these decrypts to be sure," Grandpa said. Then he looked at me, his eyes narrowed. "Though why do you think it was Hugo who broke the codes and not someone else?"

I said, "Because the first two names are written fairly neatly, and the others look like they're written by a man who's rapidly getting sicker and sicker."

"Excellent observation, my love," Grandpa said.

My mind was whirring with the sudden thrill of all this. I had a very limited knowledge of ciphers—mostly from movies I'd seen or books I'd read, naturally—but I knew that it was near impossible to break a code without its key.

My excitement was fizzling now. I'd been expecting a clear message. Not just names, but words, in English or some other easily translatable language, that told us why Hugo Markman had sought us out. Instead, he'd left us with precious little to go on, including any clue as to where he found this book cipher he'd partially decoded in the first place.

Maybe Hugo really had been delusional with his illness, I thought. Maybe his mind had been making up alternate realities and had given him a sense of urgency about something that simply wasn't real.

"But we don't have the key to cracking the last three, do we?"

Grandpa's expression was grim. "We are indeed missing the key."

"Do you think they're names, too? Or maybe instructions, or some sort of message?"

"It really could be any of those," Grandpa said. "Or a combination of all. We won't know until we find the right book."

"What about the names we do have?" I asked. "Do you recognize any of them, either as the real names of your fellow spies or their code names?"

Grandpa took a moment to look at the microdot again, answering as he lowered the viewer once more. "None of them are their code names, I can tell you that. I know the name Zeppetelli, but it was Angelo Zeppetelli I knew, not Rocco," he said. "What about you?"

I shook my head, then said, "Well, the name Zeppetelli sounds a little familiar, too, but I can't think of where I've heard it." I held up my palms in frustration. "I hear so many names, you know, and sometimes they all jumble up together like a big pot of alphabet soup."

"Then think of something else for a while and let your mind relax," Grandpa said. "It'll come to you."

What came to me just then was Ben, sitting next to me here at Big Flaco's Tacos last fall, smiling his charming smile. I recalled him telling me to give my mind a break and let my subconscious do the heavy lifting when I knew two ideas were trying to connect in my brain but the bridge between them was being elusive. It'd been good advice, and I took Grandpa's version of it now.

"What about the key text, then?" I asked. "Do you think it's at Hugo's house? I remember seeing on his driver's license that he lives in Houston, but I don't remember the street. Any chance you or your contact knows where he lives?"

Grandpa shook his head. "My contact wouldn't have told me even if I asked. I only know Hugo traveled a lot for his work and often lived in hotels."

"Okay, then," I said. "So, short of you still having another useful contact in the spy world who could use a supercomputer to help us decode this jumble of numbers, we're out of luck."

But my grandfather was looking thoughtful now. "You said 'the main part' earlier. What did you mean by that?"

I said, "Well, there were those doodles at the bottom. Looked like unfinished boxes and triangles, mostly. Some with dots in them. They were faint, but they were there."

Grandpa held his hand out for the viewer and another look at the microdot.

EIGHTEEN

❧

Well, I'll be dashed," he said. "It's a pigpen."

"Really?" I asked. "I mean, those symbols do look a bit crude, yes, but I'd hardly say they're as messy as a pigpen."

He grinned. "No, love, a type of cipher called a pigpen. Also called a Freemason's cipher, amongst other things. The masons were known to be fond of using it, especially during the American Revolution."

"Oh, right," I said, nodding. "I read about a Freemason's cipher once in one of my favorite mystery series. Do you think it will tell us the name of the key text?"

"I'd bet on it," he replied, then rubbed his chin once more. "Though I do wonder why Hugo didn't use something more sophisticated. Pigpens are dead easy to crack. The symbols' meanings are on the internet, plain as day."

"Maybe it was due to his, ah, time constraints," I said. "Maybe he knew his time was short and he used the simplest code possible so you wouldn't be floundering for too long."

Grandpa gave me his proud look again. "I'd bet you're right.

Hugo would know I'd be familiar with it and could crack it quickly."

I was intrigued. "Can you tell what it says just by looking at it?" I asked.

"Nah, not anymore," he replied. "Forty years ago, maybe. Possibly even thirty, but I haven't had the symbols memorized completely since the war." He rolled his shoulders back as if gearing up. "Now, do you have some more paper? We'll need to write all the codes down."

But my brain had been doing some heavy lifting. Not about the familiarity of any of the names on Hugo's list, but about other matters.

"I have a better idea," I said. "Let's go eat some lunch, and then I'll take us to a place where we can better view the list *and* make copies of it."

After a basket of Flaco's handmade *chicharrónes,* followed by two tacos for each of us, including Flaco's newest creation, the Mucho Guapo Taco—strips of beef tenderloin combined with tangy, melty Asadero cheese and topped with slices of avocado—and some *sopaipillas* for dessert, we were back in the car, heading north toward the Texas State Library and Archives Commission. Just as we turned on Trinity Street, Josephine called. I put her on speakerphone.

"Hi, Jo," I said. Reminded of Serena's bawdy text earlier, I hurried to add, "I'm with Grandpa and we're about to hit up the archives. What's up?"

Josephine ignored my question and her clear, clipped accent went playfully husky. "George, my darling! Happy Christmas to you, a few days late. Where have you been hiding yourself, you handsome rogue?"

Then she switched to speakerphone and Serena joined in, her own Southern drawl warm like the honey on Flaco's *sopaipillas*.

"George, sugar, we haven't seen you in a month of Sundays. We're simply devastated you'd spend all day with that hard-headed granddaughter of yours and not come and see us. We've missed you!"

Grandpa's face lit up and turned a bit pink, making me grin. "Well, if it isn't my two beauties who know how to make an old man feel twenty-two again. I've missed y'all and your lying ways but good." Jo and Serena laughed with delight. They were a mutual admiration society if I ever saw one. "I'm in town visiting my beautiful *and* hardheaded granddaughter for the day. She brought me to see Flaco's new chef's table," Grandpa added. "It's a stunner, isn't it?"

My two best friends and my grandfather went on kibitzing like this until I cleared my throat, saying, "I'm sorry to inter-rupt, but did one of you beauties actually need something from me?"

Josephine laughed. "Yes, love," she said, using the same term of endearment Grandpa often did, but her London accent mak-ing it sound thoroughly chic and different. "Is there any chance you and that adorable granddad of yours could come to the office for a bit?"

"What's up?" I asked again. "Is something wrong?"

"Oh, not at all," she said. "Curtis called and asked if he could come do his end-of-year check of our office today instead of tomorrow. It's a long story involving his wife and her corn surgery—"

"Believe me, you don't want to hear it," Serena added.

"Too right," Josephine said dryly. "Anyway, Serena and I are both leaving to meet clients. I told him I could be back by four, but he's begging and can only come at half past two."

Curtis was our building superintendent, and was very serious about keeping the historic Old Printing Office running up to code. Grandpa was already giving me two thumbs up, and looking excited about the prospect, too.

"No problem," I told Josephine. Glancing at the clock on my dash, I said, "My adorable granddad and I have to, ah, pick up something at the archives, then we can be there. Tell Curtis two thirty will be fine."

There was another thirty seconds of my officemates doing a great job of making my grandfather blush again as they said goodbye, by which time I'd found a parking spot right outside the archives building. It was then that I noticed Grandpa looking a little tired. These days, he generally napped after lunch, so I wasn't surprised.

"You know, Grandpa," I said, making a last-minute decision. "All I'm going to do is put the microdot on one of the microfilm machines to enlarge it, then print out a few hard copies. It will only take me ten, fifteen minutes. Why don't you just stay here and relax? I'll be back in a jiffy."

"I wouldn't say no to a little catnap," he said, pulling out the little package he'd made from my business card. I left the keys with him, noting that his eyes were already closing even as I reminded him to lock the doors. I felt better about leaving him there when I saw the building's security guard, who understood completely when I told him Grandpa was ninety-two and said he'd keep an eye on my car until I came back.

After signing in and waving hello to a couple of staffers I knew, I took the elevator up to the second-floor Texas Family Heritage Research Center, where I was greeted warmly by the staff members.

Minutes later, I had a roll of microfilm that I chose at random, ending up with the 1922 to 1947 Washington County Tax

Roll, Series Three. Trotting downstairs to the little microfilm cubicles, I took my time attaching the roll to the machine, while one lady slowly packed up all her genealogy charts and painstakingly rolled up the last few inches of her own microfilm.

I was just feeling the need to scream when she finally walked away. After that, I moved quickly.

The first few images of a microfilm are usually blank pages, or title pages with lots of white on them. It was a title page to which I carefully attached the microdot and rolled it into position under the light. Part of me had wondered if my wild idea would even work, so I was pleased to see Hugo's list in all its dizzying glory.

Again, I felt goose bumps as I looked at the codes and the names, wondering who the people were and what their significance was, but relief spread over me when I saw the pigpen ciphers come up more clearly than they had upon our first try. I hastened to print three copies.

A few minutes later, I was walking back out to my car, the microdot back in its little paper package and my grandfather already coming out of his catnap, looking refreshed. I handed him the copies with a flourish. "Gotta love libraries. They always have what you need."

"That they do," Grandpa said, taking the copies eagerly.

As I drove to the office, each time we came to a stop, Grandpa pointed to the symbols Hugo had scrawled in the corner.

"See, each one of these symbols corresponds to a letter. This one"—he pointed to one that was a square box with a dot at the bottom edge—"stands for an 'N.' Without the dot, it stands for 'E,' but the others, I'd have to map them out." I realized he couldn't wait to get started on decoding Hugo's list.

"How long will this Curtis gent's inspection take?" he asked as we unlocked my office door at twenty minutes after two.

"Not too long," I said. "He just looks around for signs of foundation issues, leaking windows, and the like. We don't even need to do anything but be there."

Sure enough, as I was firing up my computer, Curtis showed up, sweat beading on his bald pate, breathing much more heavily from the stairs than my grandfather had and pulling up his khakis to a higher point under his impressive paunch. Never the most talkative man, after a polite handshake and "Pleasure to meet you, sir" with my grandfather, he began slowly walking the perimeter of our five-hundred-square-foot office, looking for any signs that the building was having issues.

I went to get us some waters, leaving Grandpa smiling down at my desk, running his fingers almost reverently over the large crosshatch that he'd so long ago carved into its wooden top so he and his reporter buddies could play tic-tac-toe for beer money when things were slow.

When I got back, he was marking on the crosshatch with a broken piece of chalk.

"Where'd you get the chalk?" I asked, setting a glass of ice water down on a coaster at the edge of my—Grandpa's—desk.

"Curtis," he said simply. I looked up to see Curtis with another piece of chalk, thoroughly oblivious to us, checking the wall behind Josephine's sophisticated black-lacquered desk. He was inspecting a wall seam that had bulged in the past, but I didn't bother asking if it was holding up or buckling again. I was too interested in what Grandpa was doing with the chalk.

The crosshatch formed nine separate sections, and I watched as he filled in each section with a letter of the alphabet. Working left to right and starting with "A" in the upper leftmost section, he got to letter "I" in the bottom rightmost section. Then he started over, adding a "J" next to the "A" and drawing in a small dot in the corner, where the crosshatch's lines came together.

In this same manner, he continued filling in the crosshatch again, adding letters and dots, until he'd reached the letter "R" at the bottom right corner. Then, to my amazement, he moved some papers on my desk above the crosshatch and felt around with his fingers. Finding what he wanted, he pulled out his housekeys and used one to scrape at something, which turned out to be a large, wide X. I stifled a gasp. I'd known it was there, but the cuts weren't half as deep as the crosshatch, so I'd thought it was an accident, or possibly even a bad first attempt at the tic-tac-toe area. Over the years, I'd added a little extra wood polish to it, letting the residue gradually fill in the shallow cuts.

Grandpa glanced up once, searching for Curtis.

"He's in the breakroom," I whispered, and we could hear Curtis moving the toaster oven aside to continue checking the walls. Grandpa nodded and kept working.

With the chalk, in the top of the X, he wrote the letter "S." Working counterclockwise, he wrote in "T," then skipped across to write "U." The letter "V" went in the bottom. The last four letters of the alphabet were added, each with a dot near the point that was formed where both lines of the X met in the middle.

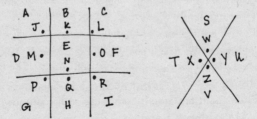

"This was never for tic-tac-toe, was it?" I hissed to my grandfather, just as Curtis came walking our way.

"Sometimes it was," Grandpa said with a grin. Luckily, Curtis was now looking up at the ceiling for issues and didn't notice when Grandpa moved some papers over his pigpen cipher key, feigning interest in his glass of water.

For the next few minutes, I pretended to check my emails and made idle chitchat with Grandpa while Curtis looked over the floors.

"I'll recaulk the windows after the first of the year, but that's all it needs," Curtis said amiably, then thanked me again for allowing him to come on such short notice, touched his hat to Grandpa, adding, "Nice to meet you, sir," and was gone. I forgot he'd even been there within seconds of locking the door.

"Any chance you feel Curtis isn't who he says he is?" Grandpa asked, one white eyebrow arched.

I was so startled I stopped for a second in my tracks, then relaxed. "Curtis came with the building and has been its caretaker for at least twenty years now. I've met his wife, and she's had trouble with her feet for ages. Plus, he's not exactly in tip-top shape. I think the chances are minimal at most."

Grandpa shrugged. "One of the most sinister people I ever met looked like the skinniest, most harmless man you've seen in your life. Absolutely timid when you talked with him. Spoke with this quavering voice and was always apologizing."

"What did he do that was so sinister?"

"Gouged out the eyes of his victims with a grapefruit spoon. After he tortured them, of course. We called him 'The Ophthalmologist.'"

I made about ten faces, shuddering with each one. "Thank goodness I've already had my eye checkup and Dr. Quayle said I didn't have to come back for two years. It's going to take me that long to even try to forget you told me that."

My grandfather chuckled. "Want to know what Hugo's message was?"

I stopped mid-shudder. "You already cracked it? But you barely looked at it."

Grandpa smiled modestly. "I just had to be reminded of the key, that's all." He used the chalk to tap the crosshatch. "On the internet or in a book, you'll see these written out in two crosshatches, one for the letters without dots, a second for those with the dots; same for the letters in the X, but I learned to do them all in as little space as possible. Out in the field, we often had only scraps of paper to write on, so combining them was essential."

"I was going to ask about that," I said, turning my phone to show him. "I pulled it up while you were working, but all the symbols were separated."

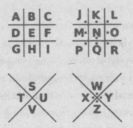

"Back before you could find the pigpen cipher all over the internet," Grandpa said, "it was harder to crack, because very few knew how to even create the key. Even after the war, we used them all the time—though only for simple stuff that was unlikely to come into enemy hands." He tapped the crosshatch again, careful not to mess up any of the chalk marks. "That's why I had this on my desk."

"And the X, though you never mentioned it," I said, trying hard to keep the accusing note from my voice, and failing.

Grandpa reached out and took my hand. His blue eyes held so many emotions, and I noticed for the first time that in the right lighting, they'd actually faded some.

"You know, my darlin', from the time you were about ten years old and helped me complete a crossword puzzle with words most ten-year-olds had never heard of, I had this feeling that you would be the one person I would eventually tell—outside of your Gran, of course. I'm so used to keeping it from the ones I love for their safety, though." He hitched one shoulder, the gesture not dismissive, but rather one of acceptance. "Well, it's been ingrained in me since I was eighteen years old."

He took a deep breath before saying, "I'd begun to think there would never be a good time and I'd have to leave you a letter to explain, and I didn't even know where to start such a letter. I've tried to leave you clues here and there over the years, and this was one of them," he added, gesturing to the crosshatch. "I knew it would make sense to you eventually."

He smiled, and there was such heartbreaking love in his face. "I know you're angry with me, but I hope you'll understand why I kept it from you. And I hope you'll realize how much it means to me to be able to show you a little of how I worked, instead of having to imagine it from nothing more than a letter."

Then Grandpa was holding out my box of tissues and letting me have a good cry, his eyes bright with tears as well. Finally, I waved my hand at the copy of the microdot's contents I'd made at the archives. Grandpa had circled Hugo's pigpen cipher, and had written the corresponding letter under each symbol. "Well? What does it say?"

He turned it so I could see.

"BUCHANS BEST, and then the Roman numeral for eighteen—XVIII."

NINETEEN

❧

I blinked my watery eyes at him, thinking it was rather anticlimactic. "Buchans Best? That sounds like the name of a scotch."

Grandpa grinned. "I'm betting he meant John Buchan, the author, and his best work. Are you familiar with Buchan's novels?"

Once again, my grandfather gave me time to let my mind have a go at figuring it out, and I nearly got there.

"Oh, it's on the tip of my tongue!" I cried, clenching my fists in frustration. Finally, I heaved a sigh. "Okay, just tell me."

"It's *The Thirty-Nine Steps*," Grandpa said, even as I groaned, "*The Thirty-Nine Steps*! I totally should have known that. It's a classic."

A beep from my phone told me I had a text. I looked to find one from Pippa. I read it, then typed out a quick reply.

"Another one from that pistol Serena?" my grandfather said with a twinkle in his eyes.

"No," I said, though I felt my cheeks heat up again at the memory. "It was from Pippa. She asked if I saw Chef Rocky before I left." I shrugged. "I told her I hadn't seen him. He mostly stays in the kitchens, so I've actually only ever met him once, when I first toured the hotel with Pippa after she hired me."

"This Chef Rocky," Grandpa began. "Is he the dark-haired, handsome gent with tattoos on both arms? Hair like he's been out in a windstorm?" He put his hands up to his head, fingers splayed, in a hilarious impression of the chef's artfully tousled hair.

I laughed. "That's definitely Chef Rocky," I said. "He was the one Roselyn Sutton was looking for when she came up to us earlier today in the hotel ballroom."

"That's strange," Grandpa said. "I saw Roselyn talking to him just before I came and found you. Or, rather, she was having a discussion with him, of the heated type."

"They were?" I said. "When was this?"

"It was when I arrived at the hotel and was being directed to the ballroom by that nice young bellboy. The chef and Roselyn were in the little niche that leads to the bathrooms." Grandpa cleared his throat. "I'm afraid I was hearing the call of nature, as I do all too often these days, which led me to ask the bellboy where I could find the loo, as the chaps in England would say. He pointed it out to me, saw the two of them, and got out of there *tout de suite*. I'm afraid I couldn't help but overhear, not that I knew who either of them were at the time."

"Interesting," I said. "What were they arguing about?"

Grandpa shrugged. "Sounded like a lover's tiff to me. Roselyn was saying something about meeting him later today at his place, and the chef was saying that he would rather come to her. He tried to romance her a bit—you know, pulling her close and kissing her—but she was adamant. Said she didn't want anyone to see. He eventually threw in the towel and said, 'Your choice, Rose. It's always been your choice.' When he stormed off, he looked straight at me, flung up his hands, said, 'I tried,' and kept going."

"Wow," I said, wondering if Pippa knew about her mother and the executive chef. "And did Roselyn see you?"

He shook his head. "Not that I could tell. I only saw the back of her the whole time. I noticed the blond hair and the color of her dress—only because it was so close to skin tone, and with my old eyes, I thought she wasn't dressed at all—but that was it. Then I went into the men's and didn't see her again until she came up to us later, looking like she would like to throw me bodily from the room."

"Weird," I said. "I wonder if Chef Rocky is MIA because he's had enough of Roselyn's dramatic behavior and has been off looking for a new job or something."

Grandpa canted his head. "That's a fairly good assumption for the set of facts I've given you."

I grinned. I was beginning to feel like Grandpa was giving me a field version of the CIA entrance exam and hoping I would belatedly follow in his footsteps.

"Do you know his last name?"

"Whose last name?" I said, my mind still musing on whether I would have made a good spy.

"Chef Rocky's."

I hitched a shoulder. "Haven't the foggiest. Why?"

My grandfather's expression was once again one of looking into his mental film reel of the past.

"He just reminded me of someone I knew in the war," he said. "It was in the way he did this—" Grandpa flung up his hands, mimicking Chef Rocky's frustration. "And also in his face, especially in this area." He made air circles to the area around his eyes and nose. "I'd bet my bottom dollar our chef is from Italian stock."

"I only met Chef Rocky once for about thirty seconds, but I wouldn't bet against you. He's got that hot-blooded Italian leading man thing down perfectly."

Grandpa rubbed his chin again. "I'll be the first to admit, I knew a lot of guys who were expressive like that and they came from lots of backgrounds. Still, his looks struck me as familiar."

I moved around Grandpa to my computer. "I'll look him up, then. I know he's on the Hotel Sutton website, so maybe it'll give us his last name."

I tapped around for a few seconds and found the page touting Eighteen Ninety-Five, the Hotel Sutton's restaurant. It was named for the year the mansion was built and featured New American cuisine mixed with classic Mediterranean specialties. Sure enough, there was a photo of Chef Rocky leaning casually against one of the prep counters, wearing jeans and a black shirt pushed up to mid-forearm so as to expose some of his tattoos. A bottle of red wine was at his hip, and he held a glass of it in his right hand, as if about to share a toast just with you. Underneath the photo, there was a short description detailing Chef Rocky's background. After a quick read, my jaw dropped.

"Grandpa," I said slowly, pointing to the text. "His name is Rocky *Zeppetelli*. That's why I thought it sounded familiar. I read it on the Hotel Sutton's website after Pippa first hired me."

I hovered my finger over the words, telling him, "It says here that Rocky is a native of New York City. He learned pasta making at his grandmother Fernandina's knee and the art of choosing the perfect wine to pair with any meal from his late great-grandfather, World War Two veteran and celebrated New York sommelier—"

"Angelo Zeppetelli," Grandpa read. "Well, I'll be dashed."

"So he *was* one of your spy buddies? Was he the one you knew?"

"He was," Grandpa said. "He was the guy I recruited for the mission. Angelo was one hell of a radio man, and truly a good man, too. Died, oh, a few years back."

"I wonder if Chef Rocky is actually Rocco Zeppetelli," I said, looking at Hugo's list of names, "or if Rocco is his father's or grandfather's name and Chef Rocky was named in honor of them." I drummed my fingers on the oak desk. "I think I'll try to trace his genealogy to find out. In fact, I'd like to trace all the people on this list."

"I'd like to see you work," Grandpa said. "Show me your process."

I pulled up Serena's rolling chair for myself and began explaining that there were several ways I could attack the issue, but I generally started with the simplest way first.

"Vital statistics, which are your birth and death records, are a great resource," I told him, "but each state is different as to what years they started collecting the data and what's the most recent year you can access data without being a direct relation. A lot of states, like Texas, keep the records private for seventy-five years, except when officially and properly requested by a family member."

Grandpa looked chagrined. "So my birth records are public now, being that I'm older than seventy-five?"

"Yep," I said dryly. "Fun, huh?"

He snorted.

I pulled up a website I used frequently. "Then there's the birth index, which, again, varies by state as to what years are available and published, but it's exactly what it sounds like, an index of births." I pointed to the example on the screen. "And, like any index, it offers only the basic information—the legal name of the person, their birth date, their parents' legal names, and the county or parish in which they were born. However, because it's just the basics, some states will publish more recent years, sometimes into the late 1990s. The birth index for England and Wales will even let you search from mid-1837 through the late 2000s. And, of course, the date range expands with each year that goes by."

"Time marches on, I suppose," Grandpa said with a wry smile. "So, can we use this birth index to find Chef Rocky?"

"We can't," I said. "We know he's a native of New York City and you can only find indexed birth records online up to 1965. Chef Rocky is in his thirties, I'd bet, so we have to take a different tack." I grinned. "We're going to hunt for Angelo instead."

I pulled up another bookmarked website and began typing in search fields.

"I can likely find Angelo's death record now that he's passed," I said. "I'll also search for his obituary, where you can often find a lot of good information."

I soon found Angelo Giuseppe Zeppetelli, who had passed away in New York City almost seven years earlier. Armed with that information, I found his obituary, which was extensive. Scrolling to the bottom, I looked for the paragraph that listed his surviving family members and those who'd already passed before him.

"Look." I pointed to the screen. "Angelo had four daughters and one son, Vincent, who passed away in the Vietnam War. He also had five grandsons . . ." I scrolled some more. "Okay, it only says 'numerous great-grandchildren and great-great-grandchildren. But wait . . ." I scrolled back up to near the top and exclaimed, "A-ha! There he is. It says Angelo's great-grandson, Rocco 'Rocky' Zeppetelli, gave part of the eulogy."

Though I hadn't done any fancy genealogy footwork, Grandpa looked mightily impressed.

"It doesn't surprise me Angelo had a big family," he said.

"Yes, he was a truly good man." Sitting back against my office chair, he picked up his glass of water and drank deeply.

I felt a pang of worry that bringing up all this from Grandpa's past was taking an emotional toll on him, and I didn't like it. Like most soldiers, World War II veterans had one level or another of PTSD, though it was understood and discussed much less in their generation. I knew Grandpa likely dealt with PTSD, what with all he'd seen in the war, but the only thing I knew for sure was that he often went to the local VA hospital and spoke to other soldiers. He'd told me more than once that it kept his spirits "even higher than normal to help others who'd seen the same, if not worse," but he'd never really wanted to discuss it more than that.

If he were having flashbacks, though, I knew he needed to be alone, for a while at least, just like I did when I was stressed. Grandpa and I were both willing to ask for help when needed, but mostly we got our strength from within ourselves.

"How about this," I said, checking the time. "It's ten after three. I have to get back to the Hotel Sutton fairly soon to interview one of Pippa's cousins, and you said the shuttle leaves back for Wimberley at three thirty. Whatever Hugo wanted us to know"—I made a sweeping motion over Hugo's list—"we can't prove anything more until we have a copy of *The Thirty-Nine Steps* to decode the last three names. How about I drive you to the shuttle pickup point and we can reconvene tomorrow? I have the whole morning free until early afternoon, when I have to interview another of Pippa's cousins."

Grandpa said, "That sounds good, my love, but if I'm reading Hugo's code correctly we need the eighteenth edition of the book specifically. It was published during the First World War and is still in print, so there could be any number of editions. I've read it, of course, but my copy is long gone."

"All right, then. How should we proceed, sergeant?"

That brought a grin to his face. "My little bookstore in Wimberley has a couple of vintage copies. Ronda, the owner, displays them right up front, so I see them every time I walk in. If Ronda doesn't have the right edition, I'm sure she can find it for me."

"That's a great idea," I mused, "but also likely to take time. However, there's nothing else we can do, short of—" I paused. I'd been looking at the copy of Hugo's list, focusing on where Grandpa had decoded the pigpen cipher.

> ꙮ   Λ Γ Γ Γ
> x   V I I I

"Grandpa, look," I said, pointing to the symbols that spelled out *XVIII*. "There's a significant space between the symbols for the 'X' and the 'V.' What if it doesn't mean eighteen at all? What if it means 'times eight'?"

I looked into his blue eyes. "You said there were eight spies." I tapped the lines of code. "There are eight groups of code here. What if the person who created all these ciphers used the same key text, but with eight different editions to further confuse anyone who tried to decode it?"

Grandpa took the page and was scanning it again. "By golly, I think you may be right. You noticed how Hugo's handwriting got worse with each decoded line. If one key text worked for all lines, there wouldn't be this much discrepancy amongst the decrypted names."

I said, "To me, that says Hugo may have had this list for some time but it's taken him a while to decode it because he had to find the right editions. Is that how it looks to you?"

I got Grandpa's proud face again. I was killin' it on the impressing-Grandpa scale today. "It does indeed look that way to me," he said.

Then, almost simultaneously, our faces fell.

I said, "That means we have to find the right three copies of *The Thirty-Nine Steps* amongst, what, possibly double digits of editions over the last hundred or so years?"

"I think," Grandpa said slowly, "that we may only need two right editions of the book."

I frowned. "Why is that?"

He pointed to the three lines of undecrypted codes.

"I've been thinking. Hugo told you to 'keep them safe.' There are eight lines of code, corresponding to eight different people. The operation I took part in had eight spies, one of which was Angelo Zeppetelli. His great-grandson, Rocky Zeppetelli, is on this list." He tapped the list of names again. "I think these eight people may be related to the eight original operatives of my 1944 mission."

"Okay," I said, nodding. It made sense. "And you're thinking these people might be in danger?"

"I am," he said. Then he began circling the last three groups of code. "And since I was one of the eight spies, then one of these ciphers is likely your name."

I was stunned at the thought. "But if I'm in danger," I said slowly, "then you must be, too. You're one of the original eight operatives. Maybe even the only one still alive."

"Odds are, it's very likely I'm the last one still alive," Grandpa said.

"That just proves my point," I said. "But furthermore, why would it be me on the list? Why not Dad, or Maeve?"

Grandpa shook his head. "I don't have the answer to that, but it's a hunch."

He took my hand and squeezed it. It felt reassuring. "Hopefully Ronda will have the editions of the key text we need and we can find out for sure. I'll try to go to the bookstore tonight. We could be completely wrong and this may be referencing a whole other operation that I had nothing to do with."

"Fingers crossed," I said, and Grandpa smiled.

"Now, my love, drive me to the shuttle and let's come up with a plan, including talking to Chef Rocky."

TWENTY

❧

"Where is everyone?" I asked Mrs. P. when I walked back into the Hotel Sutton a little while later. I'd expected to see a Sutton family member at every turn, but the place was as peaceful and quiet as always, except for the muted croons of Frank Sinatra coming from the direction of the bar. However, scenting the air was a heavenly mix of mint and chocolate, making me crave a peppermint-spiked hot cocoa.

After all the mental and emotional workouts I'd had today, plus worrying about the same workouts' effects on my grandfather, I felt like I could really use some time to chill out and process before I interviewed Pippa's cousin—maybe with that peppermint hot cocoa, which was sounding more divine by the second. Then I remembered Grandpa wanted me to find Chef Rocky, so chilling out and hot cocoa were probably not going to happen.

Speaking of Grandpa, it was only when his shuttle to Wimberley was driving off that I realized he hadn't told me the most important thing: the full story of the joint OSS–SOE mission involving him and seven other spies.

To be honest, I still had a feeling he didn't want to tell it, that he was hoping whatever mission Hugo had set us on would be resolved so quickly that he wouldn't have to divulge any of the secrets he'd kept so safe for over seventy-five years. I couldn't blame him if that were the case.

"Lucy? Did you hear me?" Mrs. P. said with a harried look from behind her station at the front desk. "I said most of them went shopping." She lowered her voice, glancing up the staircase to see if anyone was coming. "And heavens, I'm glad of it. With them all being family, they feel a level of comfort here that's, shall we say, a shade above your most demanding guest. I don't think I've ever answered so many calls for niceties in my years with the Sutton company. They've about run me off my feet."

I chuckled. "Thank goodness the whole hundred-plus family members aren't staying here."

"If they were, dear," she said wearily, "I'd have to invent a long-lost cousin who's suddenly become ill and ask for the week off."

"Or you could let me do your genealogy," I said. "I'm sure I could find you an infirm cousin somewhere." Angling my head to eye her dramatically, I said, "Pollingham . . . Are you sure it wasn't originally Pohlmann? Because I have a client named Frieda Sue Pohlmann who's a massive hypochondriac. I'm sure she'll claim you as a relative if you're willing to humor her that the heat in her forehead might be a severe case of bird flu, when she's actually just been gardening in the sun for an hour."

Mrs. P.'s eyes had been growing rounder, then her laughter burst out and she leaned on her desk, fanning her blotchy cheeks. "Och, Lucy, you *are* terrible, but you do make me laugh."

The sound of the front door opening made me turn, and the

newly married couple, who'd checked in yesterday just minutes after Hugo had been carried away by the ambulance, came into view. They were so wrapped up in each other, they could scarcely be bothered to give Mrs. P. more than a starry-eyed nod when she cooed, "Why, hello, Mr. and Mrs. Nguyen-Sobnoski. I hope you're having a relaxing stay."

"They took each other's last names," she said in an undertone when they'd passed by the front desk and, with a giggle that only honeymooners could make without the whole world rolling their eyes, began walking up the back staircase. "I think it's lovely, of course, but my, they'll be forever spelling it to people on the phone, won't they?"

I grinned. "True, but now they're officially one in a million—or even trillion—and that's pretty fun. Especially considering Nguyen is the most common Vietnamese surname in the world."

"So long as you want to be one in a trillion," Mrs. P. said dryly. "I happen to like being just another face in the crowd."

I rested my elbow on the front desk and grinned. "So, are you like Roselyn, then? Not wanting me to have a crack at your family tree?"

Mrs. P. grinned back at me. "No, little Miss Nosy Parker. It's because I already know. I was born in Florida, but my family is almost all English." Her accent, which had always had a trace of something not American, affected a working-class London accent that could rival any actor on the long-running English soap opera *EastEnders*.

"Me mum and me dad were about as far from being toffs as you could get. Hardly two shillings to rub between them their whole lives—though me dad always claimed he was the son of a peer. Mum never believed him, though. Told him if he were, he wouldn't have said, 'Cor blimey, you ain't half a corker, are you?' the first time they met and taken her to a Lyons' for tea and a bun on their first date."

This made me laugh so hard my eyes watered. Mrs. P. handed me a tissue. "And so how did they get to Florida?" I asked.

Her eyes were shining with mirth. "Mum won a lottery when she was barely pregnant with me," she said. "Wasn't much, a few hundred pounds, but it was during the winter; they were miserable and just wanted to go somewhere warm. Dad chose Florida, they went, and they ended up staying. Dad was great with cars and found a job working for a car company. Mum worked as a housekeeper at a hotel that became one of the Suttons' first outside of Texas." She shrugged. "They never had much money or a fancy house, but they were happy enough."

I was about to ask her how she decided to go from being a nurse to following in her mum's footsteps in the hotel business when Mrs. P. looked around, noted we were alone, and leaned across the front desk.

"So, how did it go at the police? Did they give you any news about our poor dead man?"

By forcing myself not to think of Grandpa's and my farcical subterfuge, I just managed not to blush. "Not even a bit," I said. "I got the impression they don't even know how he died yet because he's low priority."

"Och, how sad for the man," Mrs. P. said. "Low priority, indeed." She shook her head in dismay, then asked, "Were they pleased you found the fountain pen?"

I made a comical face as we heard the front door opening again. "All I know is they were ticked off with me that I accidentally wiped it off. I explained that it had been thoroughly Boomer-slobbered, but that didn't seem to make a difference."

"It would have if they'd ever had to clean Boomer's slobber off of anything," Pippa said, coming up beside me in blue running tights and a long-sleeved white athletic top, pink-cheeked from a midday run on Lady Bird Lake. Boomer himself was panting at her heels, though he still wiggled ecstatically when I went to pet him. He snorted and snuffled around my lower legs, no doubt picking up NPH's scent.

"I agree with that," Mrs. P. said. She looked at Pippa, affecting a casual tone. "So, what did Mr. Eason think of the Montblanc Lucy found? Is he already thinking of clients who might buy it?"

Pippa gave her front desk manager a look that was not unlike a preschool teacher playing referee between two squabbling children.

"Now, Mrs. P., I know you and Uncle Dave don't see eye-to-eye on a lot of things, but he really is knowledgeable about antiques. He's just had a stressful time of it, and sometimes it gets to him. I think you would, too, if you'd gone from being respected in your field to having no one who would hire you."

Mrs. P. sniffed in a way that said it was Uncle Dave's own fault, but didn't say anything.

"Boomer, stop that," Pippa chastised when she noticed him bumping my foot with his nose. "Oops, Lucy, I think you tracked in some chocolate mint."

Pippa pulled Boomer away and I bent to pick it up, but Mrs. P. was already there with handheld dustpan and brush.

"Och, no, I think it was my fault, girls. I was taking a stroll out in the knot garden after lunch and I must have brought it in with me. Everything sticks to these trousers, you know." She tugged on the leg of her black pants.

"So that's why I've been smelling mint and chocolate," I said, peering at the trampled, weedy-looking herb before Mrs. P. tossed it in her trash can. "Though I didn't know there was actually a variety of mint called chocolate mint."

"We have a ton of it in the knot garden," Pippa said. "Chef Rocky uses it for his famous chocolate mint–chocolate chunk gelato."

I was practically salivating. "Please tell me we'll be having some tonight."

"No doubt we will, if I can find him to confirm, that is." Pushing a strand of hair behind her ear, Pippa said, "He's been gone from the hotel since lunch and he's not answering my calls or texts. Has he checked in lately, Mrs. P.?"

Mrs. P. shook her head. "Though I was out earlier, running errands for the gala preparations, so I wouldn't have seen him if he came in during the lunch hours."

"Is that unusual? For Chef Rocky to not answer?" I asked, feeling a ripple of fear as the names on Hugo's list flashed through my mind. I'd been hoping Chef Rocky would have shown back up at the hotel by now and I could run down to the kitchen to talk to him.

Though what I would say would be another matter.

"Hi, Chef Rocky. I'm Lucy, your nosy resident genealogist. I uncovered a plot from World War Two and it's possible, but not for sure, that your life may be in danger. Thanks for the pasta carbonara last night, it was delish!"

Yeah, that sounded super sane and believable.

"Oh, it's hardly unusual," Mrs. P. was saying, to which Pippa mostly agreed, then splayed her hand and made a so-so gesture.

"If he leaves last minute like he did today, he's usually good about responding," she said, "but, yeah, if he's off duty, he's one hundred percent checked out and won't reply for hours." Pippa gave me a what-are-you-going-to-do shake of her head. "He's incredible with food, but he's your textbook definition of a mercurial chef. This time, though, I didn't get any kind of heads-up that he needed time off, and it's just not like him to ignore me."

I said, "Do you think he left a message on Roselyn's voice-mail by accident? I remember she was looking for him earlier. Maybe he called her instead?"

Pippa snapped her fingers. "That's probably it." She feigned wiping sweat from her brow. "Whew, thought I was losing it there. Thanks, Lucy. You're not just my favorite genealogist, you're a lifesaver."

"It's all part of my full-service package," I deadpanned as I caught the time on the mantel's nineteenth-century ormolu clock. "Speaking of, it's time for me to go set up for my interview with your cousin Catherine in the back parlor."

TWENTY-ONE

※

I t's the early 1970s and we'd just seen a rerun of *Them!*—it's a horror classic from 1954—completely silly now, but at the time, to three seven-year-old girls . . . ? Anyway, so there we were, Judy, Janie, and me, playing down in the ditch, right at the entrance to one of those huge concrete sewer pipes that was going in the ground. You could do things like that back in those days.

"So we're scared half to death, and daring each other to walk into the pipe. Finally, we plucked up our courage and got halfway in when, suddenly, there's this shadow at the other end and a huge *ROOAAARRRR!* Well, the three of us went tearing out of that pipe like our pants were on fire, screaming bloody murder, falling over each other and scraping our knees in the process. And lo and behold, if it isn't Gramps, belly-laughing so hard he could hardly breathe.

"Granny Nell came rushing out of the house at hearing our screams and was about fit to be tied! Oh my, but she did dress him down for scaring us. Made him doctor our knees up as we sat there on the porch steps, crying, and he just kept right on chuckling. After we calmed down, it was so funny we couldn't stop laughing, either, and it's been one of our favorite memories of our grandfather ever since."

Catherine's face was aglow with memories, and she pulled up her right pant leg to just under the knee. "See? I've still got the scar from that day, and it still makes me smile every time I see it."

After a couple of seconds where I held the camera on her smiling face, I made a fist, letting her know I was stopping the recording. It was just past five o'clock, over an hour after we'd started, and I'd gotten some great material to add into the family presentation. Even better, Catherine had already contracted me to draw up the other side of her family tree.

Outside the French doors, the rapidly darkening sky meant the landscape lighting was popping on, brightening the knot garden.

"I wish I'd known Sarah Bess," Catherine said, looking wistful. "She was one heck of a woman from the things we do know, and I'm glad the stories we've all been carrying around in our heads and hearts for so long are now being preserved in your wonderful video."

I felt like I'd been given a huge gold star and grinned like an idiot as I packed up my equipment.

Just before the interview started, Grandpa had texted me to confirm he was home safe and would be meeting his neighbor John McMahon for dinner. Then in less than an hour, I was to have dinner with Pippa and several of her family members, including Uncle Dave, though whether we were going to have a special meal prepared by Chef Rocky was another matter. By the time Catherine had arrived for our interview at four p.m., there had still been no sign of the chef.

Leaving my equipment in the corner, I slung my tote over my

shoulder and went to check with Mrs. P. I found her post empty, save for a bell and a small plaque she habitually left when she had to step away for a few minutes. *Ring Bell for Service. You Will Be Assisted Shortly,* it read. I knew the bell was electronic and would send an alert to Mrs. P.'s phone, sending her rushing back to help whoever had rung it. I felt it likely she was fulfilling some request for another Sutton family member. If so, I certainly didn't need to bother her.

I turned and strode into the bar, thinking the bartender or one of the bar staff would know if Chef Rocky had shown up.

Two steps in, I had to slow my pace. The bar was teeming with people and the staff was rushing to keep up. At the front of the bar, I glimpsed Uncle Dave laughing with a group of businessmen, all of them drinking Napoli old fashioneds. He was clearly starting the cocktail portion of our dinner early.

The swinging door to the kitchen was flung open by one of the waitresses holding a tray laden with hot appetizers, and she breezed past me before I could stop her.

"Okay, then," I muttered. "I'll just check for myself." Pushing through the swinging door, I walked down a short corridor to the kitchen.

The first time I'd ever been to the Hotel Sutton, Pippa had shown me around the entire former mansion, including the remodeled, state-of-the-art hotel kitchen where Chef Rocky had been gearing up to cook for a large luncheon being hosted in the ballroom. Pippa made introductions and Chef Rocky greeted me with a quick once-over and a flash of white teeth. Other than the fact he was clearly of Latin origin, with his slightly Roman nose, long-lashed brown eyes, and thick, dark hair expertly cut and styled to look like he'd just tumbled out of bed, he was moving at such speed around the kitchen that my best memory of him was of a sexy, dark-headed blur.

I recalled him being like an emperor surveying his kingdom, checking things at a frenetic pace and barking orders at his team while they sautéed, stirred, chopped, and mixed various things at their prep stations. His team called back, "Yes, chef!" at regular intervals and I noticed he paused longer at the station where a pretty brunette who looked just out of culinary school was creating garnishes. She turned scarlet and almost crushed the dainty edible flowers when he commented on her progress. Beside me, Pippa cast me an eye roll that was more indulgent than judgmental.

"He's a good guy, but also as bad boy a chef as they ever made them," she'd whispered, "which includes flirting with every woman over the age of eighteen and the full sleeve of tatts on each arm."

This was verified when Chef Rocky reached up to grasp a ladle hanging from a hook, which drew back the sleeves of his chef's whites and exposed a myriad of colors racing up his forearm.

"If he weren't so brilliant in the kitchen, and if I didn't know that he's got integrity underneath it all, I don't know that I would have brought him here from the Sutton Grand," Pippa added. "Pretty much everyone reacts like the brunette did, and he doesn't do much to stop it. Even Mrs. P. was flustered around him the first few times they met."

"You're kidding," I'd said. "Really?" I'd only just met Mrs. P. that day, but it was already hard to imagine anyone making her nervous.

"Really," she replied. "I hired him away from a New York hotel about eighteen months ago to work at the Grand. Mrs. P. had been on vacation in Europe at the time, so she didn't know about it. When I finally introduced her to Chef Rocky, she blushed nine shades of red and literally stuttered! She told me later she wasn't expecting to find our new chef so, and I quote, 'bloody handsome.'"

We'd both giggled all the way to our next stop on my hotel tour.

Expecting to see Chef Rocky and his stutter-inducing handsomeness, I pushed open another swinging door into his kitchen. There was a hum of activity, with an undercurrent of something else. I scanned every nook, but he was nowhere to be seen.

"Excuse me," someone snapped. "You're not supposed to be in here."

I turned to find the brunette who'd nearly crushed her flower garnishes the day I'd met Chef Rocky. She was holding a baking sheet full of cut root vegetables, ready for roasting in the oven. Under the cap holding back her dark hair, her face was shiny, like she'd been standing over a steaming pot.

"I'm sorry," I said. "I was just checking for Pippa—Ms. Sutton, that is—to see if Chef Rocky ever arrived." It was a lie, but hopefully she wouldn't know.

"Oh, Ms. Sutton is asking, is she? Are you sure it isn't *Mrs.* Sutton? She's the one usually sniffing around here looking for Rocky." The jealousy in her voice was as obvious as the slash of butternut squash puree across the front of her chef's whites. Her name was monogrammed on the left side. The jealous brunette was named Lacey Costin.

So, the kitchen staff knew about Roselyn and Chef Rocky, I thought. Not liking Ms. Costin's snide tone, I merely stared, letting my disdainful silence do the talking for me.

She didn't back down totally, but she did finally answer my question, her brown eyes flashing with annoyance.

"Fine. No, Chef Rocky hasn't come back, for your information. We don't know where he is, either, and now we're behind because of it, the selfish jerk." She made to push past me with her tray of vegetables. "And unless you're here to do the two jobs I now have since we're short a team member, please leave!"

It was then that I recognized the undercurrent in the kitchen as professional panic, and I didn't need to add to it. I left, and headed back upstairs to my room to get ready for dinner, feeling hopeful Pippa would have news on Chef Rocky by the time we met for cocktails.

Fifteen minutes later, I'd changed into a cherry red pointelle sweater and black cigarette pants. A few minutes with my hairbrush, some lipstick, and one more light coat of mascara, and I was good to go again.

Sliding my feet back into my wedges, I pulled out the faux-snakeskin clutch I kept inside my tote and checked that all my essentials were still there. Leaving my room, I was sliding my key card into my clutch when something hit my left shoulder and slammed me into the adjoining wall.

TWENTY-TWO

It was a moment before I realized what happened, and another before I breathed properly again. My door had shut with a soft pneumatic *hiss* and a secure-sounding *click*. My shoulder and the back of my head were smarting already as I stared, open-mouthed, at the figure who'd swung wildly around to face me. It was Uncle Dave.

Anger welled up inside me. What in the blue blazes was he playing at?

He swayed violently, and I realized he was drunk. So blitzed that he probably didn't even realize what he'd just done.

"That woman," he slurred, fishing around in his pocket for his key card as he lurched. He used the key card to point first at me, then in the direction of downstairs. "She's lying. I know she is." He stumbled sideways in the direction of his room, then pointed at me with his card again.

"I saw her, you know. That day—" He shook his head in disgust. "That damned day everything went to hell. I saw her looking at the Weems. She knew what it was worth." His key card dropped to the floor, and he put his face in his hands and moaned, "Why won't anyone believe me?"

He pitched forward, his own shoulder hitting the wall, his hands still over his face. Biting back annoyance at his continued feud with Mrs. P., I bent to retrieve his key card and took his arm.

"Come on, Uncle Dave, let's get you to your room." My tone was brisk efficiency, and I managed to guide him, stumbling and swaying, to his door. Using his key card, I opened the room and shoved him inside.

He didn't say another word. Just whimpered, weaved to his bed, and collapsed. He was passed out in seconds.

For a moment, I thought of Hugo and wondered if Uncle Dave had something really wrong with him. Screwing up my face, I reached out and put two fingers on his neck.

His pulse was there, strong and steady. So were his breathing and color. Exhaling in relief, I dropped his key card on the nightstand and walked out.

As his door shut, though, I held out my arm to stop it. Uncle Dave was part of Pippa's dinner party about to start downstairs at Eighteen Ninety-Five. Should I go back in and try to get him to sober up? Or call his sister Melinda? Then I decided doing so might create tension and embarrass Melinda and Pippa. I sighed; I didn't want that.

Thus, I consoled myself with shooting a dirty look at his door, hoping it would stick to it and he'd feel its intense heat when he came back out. Feeling better at this thoroughly juvenile mental image, I made for the grand staircase, surprising Pippa halfway down.

"Lucy!" she said on a gasp. She looked frantic, her eyes going around me and up the staircase. They were huge and worried.

"Pippa, what's wrong?" I said.

"I—I was looking for Uncle Dave," she said, fingering the zipper on the blue puffer vest she wore over a sweater the color of pistachios. "Um, my mom called and needs me to come get her. I was hoping he could come with me."

"I saw him go in his room," I said.

She was about to start up the stairs and I put my hand on her arm, saying quietly, "I think he might be drunk, though." I paused, then said, "In fact, I know he is."

Glancing down the staircase, the newlywedded Nguyen-Sobnoskis were walking in the front door. Pippa heard them, too, and, after mouthing a choice four-letter word, composed herself in a trice like only actors and people in the hospitality industry can do.

"Hello, you two," she said, her smile warm and friendly. "Did you have a good afternoon at the spa?"

Mr. and Mrs. Nguyen-Sobnoski stopped just long enough to give a glowing review of the day spa I would be enjoying in a couple of days with Serena and Josephine. I made a mental note to request the vitamin C facial, because Mrs. Nguyen-Sobnoski's skin looked like a million bucks.

Then I reminded myself that she was getting another regular dose of something I hadn't had in a long time, so the vitamin C mask was merely her skin's bonus elixir. My mind switched back to concern mode as soon as the newlyweds had continued up the stairs.

"Let me go with you," I told Pippa. "Uncle Dave needs to sleep it off anyway, and you and I can go get your mom. Come on, I'll drive."

Seeing Pippa's hesitant look, I peered down at the front desk to catch Mrs. P.'s eye. She'd have my back and encourage Pippa to go with me, I was sure. She was indeed back at her post, but she was turned away, taking a phone call while she tapped on the screen of her computer. I could just hear her saying, "Yes, that weekend is available."

"I don't know," Pippa was saying. Then she glanced at her phone as if hoping to see a text. There wasn't one.

"Then let me go get one of your other cousins," I said. "Maybe Aunt Melinda?"

"No," she snapped, then looked ashamed. "Forgive me, Lucy. I didn't mean to sound rude. Aunt Melinda is wonderful, but not who I need right now."

"Nothing to forgive," I said with what I hoped was a reassuring smile. Pippa was one step below me, putting us eye to eye. I saw her looking into my face, a realization coming over her features, and then got a sense that she'd made a decision.

"Yes," she said.

"Yes, you want me to go find Aunt Melinda?" I asked.

She shook her head, her blond hair tied back in a low, casual knot at the nape of her neck. "No, I mean, yes, I'd like you to come with me."

I held up my clutch with a smile. "Good thing I've already got my keys. Let's go." Then I remembered why I'd come downstairs. "But what about dinner with your cousins?"

"I've already texted a couple of them to reschedule for tomorrow. Told them Mom asked me to handle some last-minute errands for her for the New Year's party." Pippa's lips thinned into a line. "With how she's been lately, they won't be surprised. And with Uncle Dave being drunk, we were without one of the people who wanted to have dinner tonight in the first place."

I decided it was best to keep my mouth shut on both subjects. Pippa and I headed out the front doors in silence. If she wanted to talk, she would. She was staring straight ahead, though, her eyes concerned again, pushing her hair behind her ears every few seconds like a child might rub the edge of a stuffed toy's soft ear to soothe herself.

"Where are we going?" I asked as we buckled our seatbelts, trying not to show my growing worry at her state. My headlights illuminated a small section of Lady Bird Lake. As usual, runners were still out along the trail, and would be for some time.

She sucked in a breath. "Chef Rocky's house."

"Okay," I said, then gripped my gear shift. "Is Roselyn with him? Is she okay?"

Her voice finally cracked. "I don't know. I don't know where Mom is. But Chef Rocky isn't okay. Lucy, he's dead."

TWENTY-THREE

"How do you know?" I gasped.

"I've been looking for him since before lunchtime—I've been texting, calling," Pippa began, a flush on her cheeks. "When I couldn't get him to answer even when I said it was important, I finally decided to drive over to his house. He tends not to answer right away, yes, but he's never not responded for hours on end."

I was hoping she'd give me the quick explanation, but it was not to be. I reined in my impatience as I backed out of the parking spot.

"I went to his door and knocked, but he didn't answer," she continued. "Then this woman walked by with her baby in a stroller, looked at my car, and asked me what happened to my Tesla." Pippa was pushing her hair behind her ears again. "She told me she'd been wanting to ask how I liked it. She said she was going to ask me earlier today when she saw me, but I drove off too fast." Pippa glanced at me. "I drive an Audi, not a Tesla, so I realized she'd seen Mom and thought she was me."

"Did she say what time this was?" I asked as I drove out

of the hotel's parking lot, my mind reeling just like it had this morning with Grandpa.

Pippa shook her head. "No. But at this point, I didn't think anything was wrong, so I told the woman she'd seen my mother, not me, and that I was looking for Rocky." Pippa's voice was strained. "I didn't want to involve the hotel or start rumors, so I told her Rocky was our cousin. I don't think she believed me."

If she looked as furtive as she did now, I thought, I wouldn't have believed her, either.

"Did this woman say if she'd seen him?"

Pippa was now rubbing the space between her eyebrows with the tips of her fingers. "She said she saw him drive into his garage this morning around ten thirty, but hadn't seen him since."

After Grandpa saw him arguing with Roselyn, I thought grimly.

"Does he do that often? Leave and go home, I mean?" I asked, trying to breathe normally as I did my best to speed through the lit-up night toward our destination when I didn't really know where it was. Pippa had merely told me to head toward the West Austin dog park, between West Ninth and Tenth streets.

"Sometimes," she said. "The whole restaurant dining room had been rented out for a bridal shower during lunch, and that was mostly preprepared. He wouldn't be needed again until closer to dinner, so it was no big deal if he headed home for a bit."

"Okay," I said. "So then what happened with the stroller lady?"

She licked her lips. "I lied again and told her that Chef Rocky had hurt his back, and I was worried about him since he wasn't answering his phone. I told her I was going to try to look in the windows. I don't think she liked it, but her baby woke up and started crying, so she went back to her house. I knocked again a couple more times, and when Rocky didn't answer, I tried to look through his shutters." She frowned. "But they were all closed."

"How did you see in, then?"

Pippa was staring out into the night as we drove. "I was about to leave, then I decided to try one of the side windows, where Rocky's office is. When he first moved in, Mom and I went over one afternoon to help him organize. I had Boomer with me, and he jumped up onto the shutters trying to catch a moth. Two of the louvers broke, and I knew Rocky hadn't gotten them fixed yet, so I thought there might be a chance . . ." She sighed. "He hasn't told many people, but he's been working on writing a cookbook, so he's almost always in his office."

"And was he? You saw him clearly?" I was hoping against hope she was wrong.

She nodded, her hand going to her stomach, her voice a strangled whisper.

"He'd moved a plant in front of the broken louvers at some point, but I could just see him through the leaves. The light was on in his office, and Chef Rocky was on the floor. There was . . . an ice pick in his ear."

"Um," I said, hesitant to make her feel worse, but not seeing in my mind exactly what she meant. "How did you know it was specifically an ice pick?" Then I added, "And, where do I turn next?"

Pippa pushed her hair behind her ears once, twice more as she pointed out an upcoming street and told me to turn right. "It was a housewarming gift from Mom and me, part of a really nice bar set where all the handles were hand-carved in the shape of animals—I helped her find it. The ice pick handle was a leopard, carved from burled wood with real topaz for its eyes. It's beautiful and very distinctive."

"Okay," I said, making the turn and trying not to think how that added to the list of things that didn't look good for Roselyn. "And was the ice pick in the cartilage part of his ear? Or in his earlobe?"

"No," she whispered. "*In* his ear." She made stabbing motions toward her inner ear. "It was down in his ear canal."

I gave her a look of horror. "Are you sure?"

Her voice was a whisper. "I think he was stabbed all the way through the eardrum. I didn't know that could kill someone."

I didn't know it could, either, and I felt as sick as Pippa looked. I made myself take a couple of deep breaths, hoping that keeping my eyes on the road would keep my mind off the nausea.

"Are you absolutely sure he was dead?" I asked.

"I'm positive," she whispered, nodding with vehemence. "He was totally white and he wasn't moving at all. And the blood coming out of his ear . . . it wasn't, you know, running anymore." She made trickling motions with her fingers for emphasis.

I swallowed hard, but asked, "Did you call the police and tell them what you saw?"

She shook her head, staring out the windshield, but, I suspected, not seeing where we were going. "I don't know where she is," she said, and I knew she meant Roselyn. "I called her five times and she didn't answer. Texted her, too. She wouldn't respond. That's when I came back to the hotel."

"You were looking for Roselyn back at the hotel? Not Uncle Dave?" I asked.

"Yes, but then I went looking for Uncle Dave when I couldn't find Mom. I wanted someone with me when I came back here. That's when you met me on the stairs." Her expression went a mixture of mulish and frightened. "But I won't call the police until I know where my mom is. I'm scared she . . ."

She didn't have to finish the sentence. I was worried Roselyn might have done it, too. I wondered if Pippa knew about Roselyn's relationship with Chef Rocky. If she did, I bet Pippa could see her mother in a heated fight with the chef as clearly as it was playing out in my own mind.

Maybe the bar was near his office . . . Chef Rocky was becoming physical with Roselyn . . . She reaches out for a weapon and grabs the first thing her fingers close around . . . They struggle, twisting and cursing, until they're near the chef's office . . . Roselyn raises her arm high . . .

Oh, yes. With Roselyn's temper, height, and passion, I could see it all too vividly.

"Pippa," I said, keeping my voice gentle, "I really think we should call the police and have them meet us there. If Chef Rocky attacked Roselyn and she had to defend herself, then the police will find evidence of that."

Pippa's jalapeño-green eyes were suddenly as hot as the fiery chile pepper. Then they cooled just as quickly and her face crumpled. "I'm worried something is really wrong, Lucy. See, Mom and Rocky . . . they had a relationship a while back. It didn't last very long, but they still spend a lot of time together. Rocky's actually been very good for her, believe it or not, but Mom's been acting so weird lately. What if they did get into a fight and she killed him?" She looked at me imploringly. "Please tell me you'll help her if that's the case."

"But Pippa," I spluttered, as the dog park came into view, "I don't know what I could possibly do. I really don't know anything about law enforcement, and it's not good to meddle in police business."

But when Pippa put her face in her hands and I heard a strangled sob, I reached out to her once more. "We need to call the police," I said quietly but firmly. "I'll do it for you. I'll call them right now. They'll do their job and find out what happened.

And if there's a way I can help them and your mom, I'll do whatever I can. I promise."

Since I still had his cell phone number, I called Detective Maurice Dupart instead of emergency services. Probably it wasn't the way it was supposed to be done, but the detective shouldn't have given me his number if he didn't want me to use it, right?

"Good evening, Ms. Lancaster," he said, answering on the second ring, his deep voice coming through my car's speakers loud and clear. Evidently, my name was also still in his phone, and by his dry tone, he remembered me all too well. "What can I do for you?"

"Good evening, Detective Dupart," I said. "I'm so sorry to bother you, but . . ."

"Yes, Ms. Lancaster?" he said, a hint of wariness now creeping in.

"Well," I said, "I'm afraid something has happened and, ah, it appears someone is dead."

His voice sharpened. "Are you all right and somewhere safe?"

"Yes," I replied. "I'm with Pippa Sutton of the Hotel Sutton and we're driving to the house where her executive chef lives. He's been missing most of the day, and Ms. Sutton went to go check on him. She saw him through the window and it seems he's been stabbed in the ear with an ice pick. Down the ear canal, to be precise."

There was a brief pause. "Did you call nine-one-one?"

"Er, no," I said. "I called you. Ms. Sutton is traumatized and, well, she's positive he's been dead for a couple of hours at least."

Dupart swore under his breath. "Give me the address," he said. "And the two of you should stay parked on the street and not move out of your car until I get there. Is that understood?"

"Yes, of course," I said. I nodded at Pippa and she gave Chef Rocky's address, adding in the nearest cross street when he asked. She pointed out the last turn and we arrived at Chef Rocky's house moments later. I parked, with every intention of following Detective Dupart's orders.

Chef Rocky's street turned out to be a little enclave not far from the dog park, where a series of old and dilapidated 1950s bungalows were in the process of being completely overhauled into chic and modern 1950s-inspired bungalows. Chef Rocky's was near the end of the street, between one that was still being renovated and another that was for sale, making for three ominously dark houses all in a row.

But what if Pippa had been wrong? What if Chef Rocky was, by some miracle, still alive? Or what if it wasn't Rocky with an ice pick in his ear at all?

I glanced at my client. She'd just sent another text to her mother and was staring forlornly at her phone, looking like she was willing a reply to come in. I unbuckled my seatbelt and said, "I'll be right back."

I was out of the car and dashing in the cold evening air toward the space between Chef Rocky's house and the house that was for sale before Pippa could call out to me. Thankful I was in wedges instead of heels and it hadn't rained recently, I used the light from my phone to pick my way carefully over the uneven ground.

While the house next door was still waiting for its final touches in the form of greenery, Chef Rocky's bungalow looked to have been fairly recently landscaped in the uniquely Austin style that was a mixture of drought-tolerant grasses and succulents interspersed with Texas-loving greener plants like lantana, dwarf yaupon holly, and cast-iron plants for a lusher, less arid look.

Passing by the first set of windows, I noted young century plants beneath the sills. A member of the agave family, once grown, their long, spear-shaped leaves tipped with menacing thorns would add an extra layer of security to the house. For now, though, they were still small enough that I could easily slip between the plant and the house.

Shivering and wishing I had a jacket, I finally saw a pale shaft of light emanating from a spot midway up in the second set of windows. Sure enough, two louvers were missing. With the bungalows sitting on pier and beam, I was just barely tall enough to see through the space where the louvers should have been.

Peering through the top one, all I could see was the big, green leaves of a houseplant of which I could never remember the name. I bent lower and, bobbing around for a minute, found a small gap in the leaves allowing a decent enough view into Chef Rocky's office.

It was small, with what looked to be a stainless-steel prep station against one wall acting as a desk. On it was his keyboard, along with a large monitor sitting atop a handful of cookbooks as a makeshift riser. I could just make out a slew of yellowed and spot-stained papers on the desk, which I guessed were well-loved and often-made recipes from his family and life as a chef.

There were no photos on the wall that I could see, and no rug on the floor. His office chair, an old wooden barstool, had fallen over. And next to it, splayed in a grotesque pose that made him almost look like he was trying to run away, was Chef Rocky's inert form.

I hadn't intended to touch the side of the house and add my fingerprints to the crime scene, but I had to in order to steady myself when my eyes focused on the details.

The burled-wood leopard with glittering topaz eyes was sticking out of Chef Rocky Zeppetelli's ear all right, its sleek wood hiding a long, thin ice pick. It had been plunged deep into his ear canal, and blood had flowed out, seeping down his neck and onto the floor in rivulets that had long since dried.

There was no doubt about it. Chef Rocky was dead.

TWENTY-FOUR

❧

In the back of my mind, I'd heard the sirens in the distance. What I hadn't counted on was Detective Dupart being sneaky enough to arrive in an unmarked vehicle well before the rest of his APD posse did. Nor did I consider that he might be dressed in dark colors and hide himself in a particularly deep shadow that had me jumping back with a scream when he moved to block my path.

"Jesus, Mary-Louise, and Joseph!" I exclaimed, hand over my thundering heart. "Why on Earth did you do that, Detective?"

He snapped on a flashlight, holding it high so the beam angled down at me. "And why in the name of all that is holy did you disobey my request to not leave your car, Ms. Lancaster?" His dark Creole eyes were narrowed and glittered like ebony beads in the residual light. "Do you think you're more experienced in law enforcement than the Austin Police Department?" he growled. "That since you helped in a minor way with one crime, you suddenly have the skills to handle a sensitive and potentially dangerous situation? What if there'd been someone still in the house willing to kill you so they could get away? What then?"

His words felt like I'd just been pushed onto a bed of century-plant thorns, and I winced with the pain of knowing I deserved every word.

"You're absolutely right, and I'm sorry," I said. I glanced at my car, where I could just make out Pippa's worried face.

Then I had to shout to be heard above the multiple sirens sounding like they were just around the corner. "I was afraid Pippa—Ms. Sutton—might have misinterpreted what she saw. Or possibly not have seen it at all. I realized I called you without confirmation of it, and I wanted to make sure it wasn't a false alarm."

I was right about the sirens. Suddenly, the street was lit up with the flashing lights of an ambulance and a black-and-white APD patrol car. I shivered again with a sudden gust of cold wind.

"Well?" Dupart shouted. "Was it a false alarm?"

I shook my head, yelling, "He's in his office, dead, with a leopard-handled ice pick in his ear," just as the sirens cut and silence filled the street.

It was over two hours later before I was allowed to go back to the hotel. Pippa and I were interviewed individually and kept separate, with Pippa asked to sit in Dupart's car while I was allowed to sit in mine.

Dupart had used a handheld steel battering ram to break down Chef Rocky's front door so he and his men could confirm that Rocky was indeed dead and no one else was in the house. After that, Dupart had to secure a search warrant before his team could begin collecting evidence, but he managed to do so in record time. Chef Rocky's porch lights were turned on once the police got into his house and portable lighting was set up to illuminate the yard. The added light also allowed me to see Pippa's increasingly stressed-out expression every time she turned her head as she waited in Dupart's cruiser.

The neighbor Pippa had spoken to earlier, an athletic-looking redhead in her twenties, came out of her bungalow, which was three houses down, and once she found out Chef Rocky was dead, she loudly told the police officers she had information to give. I thought about trying to slip out of my car and eavesdrop on her interview, but Dupart must have known such shenanigans might cross my mind because he sent me a stern look and then walked the redhead up to Chef Rocky's porch to take her statement.

Finally, just when Pippa looked close to tears and was minutes away from being taken to the APD for more formal questioning, I heard her phone ring. The window of Dupart's cruiser had been cracked and when I opened my own door, I could hear her answer with a strangled, "Mom! Where are you? Where have you been? I've been calling and texting you. Chef Rocky is dead!"

After that, Detective Dupart asked to speak with Roselyn, and there appeared to be a very civil conversation, with Dupart nodding every so often. I could just make out him giving Roselyn the address for the police department, saying, "I will see you there in twenty minutes, Mrs. Sutton."

Dupart walked up to me, and I got out of my car, wrapping my arms about my chest in the cold air. He didn't look any happier than he had earlier.

"Ms. Lancaster, I just have a couple more questions for you, then you're free to go home." He rubbed his brow, and I noticed belatedly that he'd changed the shape of his goatee so that it was thinner, better defining the strong lines of his face.

"I understand Roselyn Sutton and Mr. Zeppetelli were in an on-again, off-again relationship," he said. "Did you know of any tension or issues between them?"

Though relieved Pippa had been up front with the detective about her mother's relationship with Chef Rocky, I hated to add my thoughts—but, annoyingly, the urge to tell the truth was strong inside me.

Really, I would have made a terrible spy, despite Grandpa's faith in me . . .

"I know Roselyn and Chef Rocky had a minor argument this morning," I said. "Something about her wanting to come here, to Chef Rocky's house, and he wanting to go to her place." I lifted my chin. "For what purpose, I don't know, but I can tell you the argument ended without any hint of violence whatsoever."

Dupart's face remained impassive, but I knew what he was thinking: the violence had waited until Roselyn got Chef Rocky back to his place.

He shifted and I could see Pippa looking wiped out, like she couldn't take too much more. I gave her what I hoped was a reassuring smile.

"Ms. Sutton asks that you go back to the hotel and ask a Mrs."—Dupart checked his notes—"a Mrs. Pollingham to contact a Chef Cardo, who apparently used to work for the Suttons at another location and is now retired. Ms. Sutton would like Chef Cardo to oversee the hotel's kitchen until a suitable replacement can be hired. Two of our deputies have already been dispatched to the hotel to talk to Mrs. Pollingham, as well as the rest of the kitchen staff who are still on duty this evening. I'll be sending two more deputies over to interview the other members of the staff tomorrow."

"I'll give Mrs. P. the message."

He nodded and was about to walk away when another officer walked up, doing a double-take as he saw me.

"Hello, Officer Carr," I said, dread stealing over me.

"Well, well," he said, "if it isn't Ms. Lancaster. Is your grandfather here, too? Planning on pilfering evidence from this crime scene as well?"

"Is something the matter, Officer Carr?" Dupart asked, arching one eyebrow.

"Yes," he said, a note of venom coming into his voice. "Ms. Lancaster here and her grandfather came in this morning, supposedly to hand over evidence on the guy who died at the Hotel Sutton. Instead, they put on a pity show to get a look at the vic's personal possessions. Her grandfather acted like some dementia-addled old fool and got an evidence bag stuck in his coat zipper so he could open it."

Officer Carr turned to me. "We saw on the footage that your grandfather took something off the theater ticket. I've been told to stand down about it, but if you ever play me like that again, Ms. Lancaster, I'll make sure you or your granddad are charged with tampering with evidence." He bared his teeth. "Or better yet, both of you."

"I think that's enough," Dupart said, but Officer Carr wasn't quite done.

"One other thing, Ms. Lancaster. The victim who died at your feet? It seems he had some underlying health issues, but that wasn't what killed him. He was poisoned, and it's unlikely it was accidental."

I stared at both men.

"Poisoned?" I said. "I mean, the hotel's front desk manager saw symptoms that made her think he'd been sick, but . . ." I trailed off, my shock all too real.

Officer Carr seemed unmoved. "He was poisoned all right,

Ms. Lancaster, and with radium chloride. Do you know what that is?"

I'd heard about radium chloride somewhere . . . The history geek in me also had a science-nerd side and both were working together, opening mental filing cabinet after mental filing cabinet. Then I snapped my fingers.

"It was used to make things glow in the dark, right?" I said.

"Good for you," he said, though he hardly sounded proud. "Early in the last century, it was used for luminous watch dials and some quack health remedies. People who regularly handled it had all sorts of nasty things happen to them."

I sucked in a breath. "Holy cow, is that what his symptoms were? The hair loss? The broken tooth? It was radium chloride poisoning?"

Officer Carr was nodding, but I was remembering Grandpa's reaction when I'd told him of Hugo's symptoms. He'd recognized them as being the effects of radium chloride.

"Oh, how horrible," I said, pity filling me for poor, harmless Hugo. "How would someone even get radium chloride these days?"

Dupart took this one. "It's highly regulated now, so generally only scientists and medical research companies have access to it."

Companies. The word made me think of Hugo's job and how he enjoyed taking down white-collar criminals.

"As I understand it," I began, "Mr. Markman was a forensic accountant. Are you checking to see if he investigated any medical research facilities? Maybe someone had it in for him at one of the companies he took down."

"Don't tell us how to do our job, Ms. Lancaster," Officer Carr snapped.

Dupart shot his officer a look and said, "I'll take it from here, thank you."

Officer Carr stalked off, still looking huffy, and Detective Dupart turned to me with a look of resolute calm.

"Ms. Lancaster, it's worth asking. Do you have any reason to suspect the death of Mr. Markman and this death tonight of Mr. Zeppetelli have something in common?"

Hugo's partially decoded list with Chef Rocky's name on it practically swam before my eyes. But the two men had been killed in such different ways, and both could have had people who wished them harm.

Hugo most definitely could've had enemies that had everything to do with his job and nothing to do with a spy operation from 1944. And I already knew Chef Rocky had made more than one person upset. I thought of Roselyn and their argument, of the jealous prep cook named Lacey, and of the fact that the handsome, bad-boy chef never did much to discourage his coworkers from crushing on him.

Plus, Grandpa and I were still trying to make sense of what we'd found earlier today, and I didn't even know all the details about the joint OSS–SOE mission to begin with. If I could barely explain what I did know thus far to myself, how would I explain it to Detective Dupart?

"Ms. Lancaster?"

Time to tell the truth. Or at least part of it.

"I'm afraid I'm at square one just like you, Detective. But if I do suspect anything, I'll let you know."

TWENTY-FIVE

✌

When I arrived back at the hotel, I was met by one of Dupart's officers. Explaining who I was, I asked to speak with Mrs. P., telling him I had a message to deliver about contacting a replacement chef. The officer explained Mrs. P. was on her way back into the hotel to be interviewed, as she had already gone home for the evening when the deputies arrived.

"Oh, of course," I said, finally noticing it was after eight o'clock. Though Mrs. P. often stayed late, she technically got off work at six p.m. She seemed such a ubiquitous part of the hotel, I'd forgotten she actually had a home life.

By this time, I was exhausted and starving, so I wrote a quick note to Mrs. P. asking her to call Chef Cardo. The moment I handed it off to the deputy, I was sending a group text to Josephine and Serena, asking if either of them were up to meeting me at Flaco's. I told them I'd been involved in some high drama and needed to vent.

Their replies were almost instant. Serena's said, *High drama? I'm SO in.* Josephine's was a series of emojis that included a girl raising her hand high in the air, a smiley face with its mind being blown, and, of course, several tacos.

I ran upstairs, changed into jeans and a pair of booties, grabbed a jacket, and flew back out the front doors of the hotel, relieved to not run into anyone as I did so. I needed food and my friends to help me think clearly again, and I needed a drink to take my mind off the image of Chef Rocky with an ice pick jammed down his ear.

"A top-shelf margarita, please," I told Ana when I slid into the corner booth beside Serena. "On the rocks, with salt." Internally shuddering at the thought of ice, I said, "Make that frozen instead."

Serena and Jo looked at each other, then back at me.

"This must be big drama if you're going top shelf," Serena said.

"And something must be really wrong if you're forgoing rocks for frozen," added Josephine. "You told me last time that slushy drinks should only have low alcohol content so you can drink more of them and crunch on all those lovely little bits of ice."

"Ohhh, don't say 'ice,'" I groaned.

Ana, seeing that something was amiss with me, brought me an order of guacamole and chips before the other table of four guys who'd ordered ahead of us.

"Hey," one guy complained as I scooped up a liberal amount and practically stuffed it into my mouth, "we ordered ours five minutes ago."

"You have your choice," Ana replied, leaning casually on their table with one hand. "You can wait until I get yours, or you can try to take that one away from Lucy." A broad smile with just a touch of challenge spread across her face. "Go ahead, I would like to see what happens. Lucy may be *pequeña*, but she is—" She turned to Josephine and me, and said, "*¿Cómo se dice 'poderosa' en inglés?*"

"'Mighty,'" Josephine replied at once with a laugh.

"Small but mighty," Serena said, giving me grin. "Yep, that about sums you up."

The guys at the other table gave us sullen looks mixed with a little fear and didn't attempt to take my guacamole. Which was good, because we would have had a second stabbing that night if they'd tried.

"Now," Josephine said when Ana left with our order and the four guys weren't paying us any attention. "Spill the tea."

"Huh?" I said through a mouthful of guacamole-loaded tortilla chip.

She turned to Josephine. "This is what happens when you're besties with someone who spends so much time with their head in the past. They know archaic phrases like 'Bob's your uncle' and 'the bee's knees,' but they're woefully undereducated when it comes to modern slang."

"Darling," Josephine replied, "that's what she has us for. To drag her into the twenty-first century." She grabbed my non-tortilla-chip-holding arm and pretended to yank on it.

"Very true," Serena said, eyeing me like she had quite a bit of dragging me into the current century to do before she'd be confident I was at one with the times.

I gave my friends a haughty look, which I was totally up to doing now that my blood sugar had resumed normal levels. "May I actually spill some tea now, ladies, or are you going to continue to blather until our food comes?"

"*Blather*," Serena said. "See what I mean? She belongs in another era."

"I take that as a compliment," I said.

"Of course you do, darling," Josephine said with a grin. "But please do spill. We've been on pins and needles since you texted us the words 'high drama.'"

I glanced over at the table of guys next to us. Ana had brought them their guacamole—a very generous scoop, I noticed—and they attacked it with gusto, paying us absolutely no mind.

"I just came from being interviewed by the police. The chef at the Hotel Sutton was killed today. Someone stabbed him in the ear canal with a leopard-handled ice pick."

Josephine gave a horrified gasp. Serena sat back, nodding at me like the proud mother of a certified gossip monger. "Now *that's* some tea."

Two fish tacos later—one fried in Flaco's special tempura-style batter because I was feeling naughty, and the other grilled because I was trying to be good, and both with an extra spoonful of Flaco's delicious lime crema and a good layer of pico de gallo—I drove back to the Hotel Sutton. Thinking of Grandpa's earlier words about being watched, I took a roundabout way, checking to make sure I wasn't followed. I felt a bit safer when I found that Mrs. P. or someone had locked the hotel's front doors earlier than normal, making guests like me have to use their access key to get in.

Standing at Mrs. P.'s desk was Terrence, the relatively new night porter, whom I'd heard Pippa and Mrs. P. refer to, but had never met until now. I introduced myself and asked if Mrs. P. was still around.

"No, ma'am, she went home with a headache after being interviewed about Chef Rocky," he said, his voice somber. "She was mighty broken up, as we all are. It's shocking, that's for sure."

"It definitely is," I said. I was about to thank him and go upstairs, but instead I asked, "Did you know Chef Rocky well?"

Terrence stood about six foot four and had some impressive muscles showing underneath his hotel uniform of a white shirt, black vest, and black pants. I recalled Pippa calling him a gentle soul, even though he'd worked as a bouncer before coming to the Hotel Sutton, where he doubled as extra security. He shook his head.

"Not really. I've only been working here since Thanksgiving, and Chef Rocky has always been busy in the kitchen for the dinner rush when I came on duty. Fact is, I've barely even had a conversation with him—not a real one, at least, because he was always working. When he was done for the night, he never stuck around, either. He was out the back doors and gone in that sweet black Porsche of his."

Then Terrence screwed up his face. "Come to think of it, he did come talk to me once, a few days after I started here. He asked me if I ever did any personal-security work." He made a fist and softly hit it on the desk in consternation. "Damn, I forgot to mention this to the cop who interviewed me."

Though I was exhausted, I perked up at his words. "Personal-security work? Was he worried for his safety?"

"Nah," Terrence said. "He said it was for a friend of his. I gave him my card and told him to tell the guy to contact me, but his friend would've had to pay really well to get me to leave this job." He shrugged his big shoulders. "I never heard from the friend, so I forgot all about it."

"Any chance you think Chef Rocky could have been lying, and he really needed protection for himself?" I asked.

Terrence gave me a hint of a sad smile. "At the time? No ma'am, I was sure." His expression sobered again. "Though now I wonder what he could have been mixed up in. An ice pick in the ear is no joke, and not a random act, either. You'd need black ops training or doctor training to get that right. I've heard of contract hits like that and I gotta say, someone must've hated Chef Rocky real bad."

On that unpleasant thought, I thanked Terrence and went upstairs.

I showered and crawled into bed, my mind still whirring. I hadn't told my best friends that Grandpa knew the man who'd died at the hotel yesterday, and I definitely hadn't mentioned that my grandfather was a real, honest-to-goodness spy. Or had been for many years, at least. That information was just now truly beginning to sink into my brain and my heart.

I thought about the things Grandpa had said to me over the years, the stories he'd told me of his life, of his work, and of his dreams when he'd been younger. Were those stories, those dreams, real? Or were they fabrications of a man taught to lie when lying was a skill he'd needed to survive—to help us win the war, for pity's sake—and who had never quite gotten used to being able to live a life where he needed nothing but the truth?

It was nearly an hour later that I finally fell asleep, but I did so with a lighter heart. Grandpa had never given me cause to doubt him and, in the end, I decided I had two choices. I could either question everything Grandpa had ever said to me, or I could believe him when he said that he only lied when absolutely necessary, and to protect others.

I decided to believe.

TWENTY-SIX

I n my dream, I was in a baseball game. It was my turn at bat. The pitcher kept throwing the ball, which turned into a palm frond, each time falling short of my bat's reach. I kept swinging, becoming more and more frustrated. And with the last two throws, a bee was buzzing around me.

"You're not close enough, Ms. Lancaster," came the voice of the catcher behind me. "And yet you're too close. You're always too close."

I knew that voice, and turned to see a pair of blue eyes with green around the pupils looking out at me from the grill of a catcher's mask. I wanted to ask him why he hadn't called me, but the words wouldn't come out of my mouth.

The bee buzzed again and the umpire yelled, "Strike!" I sat up, breathing heavily, blinking at the clock by my bed. It wasn't even midnight; I'd barely been asleep three hours.

Bzzzz. My phone, on vibrate, signaled a voice mail. It was an unfamiliar number, but it had called twice, leaving a message each time. This had been the bee in my dreams.

My eyes too bleary to read the transcription of the message

that came up in my voicemail, I played the message back. I was out of bed and searching for my jeans as soon as I heard the words, "Ms. Lancaster, this is Dr. Kristen Brozo from Austin Regional Medical Center. Your grandfather will be okay, but he's been badly hurt in a car accident. We were given your number to call. Please call us back at the following number . . ."

I got ahold of the nurse as I tore out of the hotel's parking lot. All she could tell me was that my grandfather was in intensive care, but was in stable condition at present. The doctor, I was told, would explain things when I got to the hospital, as they could not give out any other information over the phone.

Despite the late hour, parking in the hospital garage seemed to take forever and I uttered a long stream of blue words every time my forward motion was impeded. Then finding my way to the right desk nearly had me in tears, until a nurse looked at my stricken face and escorted me to intensive care.

I asked for Dr. Brozo, and after a few agonizing minutes, a blond beauty who could have been Pippa's sister walked up and introduced herself. She wore teal-colored scrubs under her white doctor's coat, and the requisite stethoscope hung across her shoulders. Her hair was parted on the side and tied back in a low ponytail and her eyes were an ice blue. Though instead of being cold, they were kind and sparkling with intelligence. I felt her confident and calming presence on my frayed nerves and was grateful.

"Is my grandfather still okay?" I asked, wiping tears away from my face with the sleeve of my sweater. "Please tell me he's still okay. And when can I see him?"

Dr. Brozo led me around the nurse's station to a little alcove with a water dispenser. "He'll be all right, Ms. Lancaster. Your grandfather got really lucky. But he's banged up and in a lot of pain from a few broken ribs. He'll need to stay here for a couple of days at least. However, he was alert and able to talk when he came in. He knew his name and the year, and he asked after you." Her lips curled up into a pretty smile. "In fact, he seemed more with it than some of our patients half his age."

"He is," I said, anxious for her to know my grandfather wasn't your typical ninety-two-year-old man. "I was with him all today, and I was with him at his most recent checkup not too long ago. He's healthy in mind and body."

She smiled again. "Good. We have him sedated right now, so he's asleep. You can see him after we talk, but he'll likely sleep until the morning."

I nodded, feeling like I was going to ugly cry if I said a word. She handed me some cool water in a paper cup and I sipped it, letting it soothe my throat.

"What happened?" I finally asked. "How was Grandpa involved in a car accident? He barely drives these days, and almost never at night."

"This is what I know, Ms. Lancaster," Dr. Brozo said. She checked her notes, then nodded to herself that she remembered the details correctly.

"Your grandfather was driving in a residential area of Wimberley around seven fifteen this evening. At a crossroads, your granddad had the right of way and was driving through when another car blew through the stop sign, hitting the tail end of your granddad's car and sending him into an embankment. The other driver drove off without stopping. A good Samaritan was about fifty yards away and saw the accident, but couldn't get the driver's license plate. He only got a brief look at the driver and could only say the person looked elderly as well. The gentleman immediately called nine-one-one and checked your granddad's vitals. He stayed with him, talking to him, until the ambulance came."

"But then how did Grandpa get here?" I asked, pointing at the floor. "To Austin Regional?"

Dr. Brozo said, "Due to his advanced age, it was felt that he should be brought here, just in case. Also, apparently your grandfather was lucid enough to ask the gentleman to write down your name and phone number, saying that you specifically should be called." She pulled out a slip of paper from the pocket of her doctor's coat.

"There's also another word on here," Dr. Brozo said. "Is your grandfather a bird watcher?"

I frowned. "No, why?"

She gave me the paper, which was folded in half. Inside, I saw my name and number written in a neat, masculine hand. Underneath it, in all caps, was the word *GREENFINCH*.

"Could it be his address?" Dr. Brozo asked. "Or possibly the name of the street where he was going in Wimberley?"

"Not his address," I said. "I couldn't tell you if there's a street in Wimberley called Greenfinch, but I'll look it up later. Thanks for this." I tucked it into my wallet for safekeeping. Now that I knew Grandpa was going to be all right—in time, at least—the anger that had accompanied my fear was taking center stage.

Someone, even if it were an elderly someone, ran into my grandfather and took off without even stopping. Grandpa could have been killed!

Even the objective side of me, who knew Grandpa's area was filled with elderly citizens, didn't make me feel any better. I was growing livid, but I strove to stay focused on the positive.

"And what about the gentleman who found my grandfather? Do you have his name? I'd like to thank him."

"You'll have to check with the police on that," Dr. Brozo said. "To my knowledge, he didn't give his name. As I understand the report, he gave his account of the accident and this paper to the EMT technician and then left." She then motioned for me to follow her. "Come on. Your grandfather's asleep but you can go see him now."

I began to follow. I was feeling calmer, but anxious to see Grandpa for myself. Then the events of earlier today caught up with me, and I remembered one big detail. My grandfather was a spy, and keeping his lips from becoming loose was of the utmost importance to him. I stopped in my tracks. "Dr. Brozo?" She turned and walked back to me.

I looked around and didn't see anyone watching us. Still, I lowered my voice. "Look, my grandfather was in World War Two." I paused. "Specifically, he worked in intelligence. I know he'll be concerned he might say . . . you know, things he probably shouldn't while sedated, and it will stress him out to think that he might have spoken about . . . you know, whatever things he knows and has never spoken about. Is there a way we could put him in a private room?"

I was also already thinking about hiring a private nurse for him, one who could keep her mouth shut about any ramblings about "V for Victory," palm fronds, microdots, and Montblancs, to say the least, so it took me a second to realize what Dr. Brozo just said.

"I beg your pardon?" I said, blinking.

"It's already been done, Ms. Lancaster," she said. "In fact, he has a guard on his room. Within minutes of your granddad showing up, I received a call from one of my hospital administrators saying that your granddad should be kept private, and someone would be arriving to stand outside his door. The dude was there when we wheeled your granddad into his room, matching the description I was given. Big guy. Not half bad-looking, either, if you like the strong-jawed and silent types."

Her eyes were twinkling, but mine narrowed. "Who made

this call to put a guard on him?" I asked, not caring that I sounded suspicious.

Dr. Brozo hitched her shoulders. "I'm afraid I don't know. It's above my pay grade, as they say." She looked around, then lowered her voice to just above a whisper. "Though I've only seen a guard like that once before, and we knew he was, shall we say, government-issued. No one is getting to your grandfather, that's for sure."

She smiled at me again when I still looked hesitant. "Look, my great-grandfather was World War Two as well. Worked on the atomic bomb, and died as a result of Agent Orange. The point is, I get your concern, and so I've assigned him Nurse Angelique, who was a former army nurse. She'll work with your granddad until we know he's off any meds that might make him loose-lipped. And if the guard is for any reason not on the side of the angels, Angelique will find out and send him packing, believe me."

My eyes welled up again in gratitude. "Thank you," I whispered, unable to say it louder.

"Don't mention it," she replied, turning to lead me to see Grandpa. She and I both had to show our IDs to the guard, who was about six-three, bald, square-jawed, and had the Fed Face down to a science. Once he checked us both off, I introduced myself and asked him who had sent him. It would be the only time I got a hint of a smile from him. "'Fraid I can't tell you that, Ms. Lancaster."

"You can't tell me, or you won't?" I asked.

"Both, Ms. Lancaster," he said. "But the hospital administration is aware of the situation."

"Right," I replied. Dr. Brozo had just told me as much. "Thank you for keeping my grandfather safe, then."

He nodded and held the door open for me with one long, muscular arm, and I rushed in to Grandpa's side.

TWENTY-SEVEN

❧

I slept in a chair by Grandpa, holding his hand, and woke with a start when I heard him croak, "Lucy, my darlin'."

Nurse Angelique and Dr. Brozo were in the room in moments, checking him over. The pain quickly overwhelmed him, though, and he was given more medications to make him sleep. In the brief moments I had with Grandpa alone while he was conscious, I promised him his friend John McMahon was taking care of his cat, Bertie, that he was being guarded, and that he hadn't spoken while under the influence. This made him more restful as he started to drift back off.

When he'd been sleeping earlier, it had occurred to me that he might have been driving to his local bookstore to find copies of *The Thirty-Nine Steps* when his car was hit. "Were you going to the bookstore?" I asked before his eyes closed.

He gave me one brief nod. After that, he only was able to get out one word before the medications took hold again.

"Greenfinch," he whispered.

"Copy that," I responded, and squeezed his fingers twice, hoping the military talk would further add to his comfort. He nodded with his eyes closed—which was good, because mine were filling with tears.

I still had no idea what "Greenfinch" meant, though. I stayed with Grandpa until he was sleeping peacefully and Nurse Angelique had promised me three times that she would guard him and get him well again. Through the windows, morning twilight was just nudging the blackness aside as I finally agreed to leave and get some rest.

At the elevator bank, I was in my own little world, trying to think what the heck "Greenfinch" might mean. Could it be someone's last name? Bird names were often found as last names. Hawk, Swan, Crane, Starling—bird-related surnames were all over the place, and in multiple languages, too. Finch itself was certainly one, and I happened to know the German surname Stieglitz meant "goldfinch," so while I hadn't heard of Greenfinch as a surname, it wasn't impossible for it to be one.

Or was Greenfinch a company name? Or maybe, like Dr. Brozo suggested, a street name? I stood up straighter. Could Greenfinch be the street where Hugo Markman lived? Was Grandpa telling me to go there and find something of importance at Hugo's house?

The elevator dinged. A car going down opened and I got in along with a nurse who looked to have just gotten off shift and a mother holding on to the hand of a little boy. I pulled out my phone and turned around to face the closing doors, ready to search for Greenfinch Street, just as another elevator opened across from us and my breath caught.

He was looking at his phone and didn't see me as I silently mouthed his name. Ben?

Then I exhaled as I took in the whole picture of the guy. He was the same height and build as Ben, and, well, it was hard not to stare. If my Ben looked uncannily like Harrison Ford as buttoned-up Professor Jones in the *Indiana Jones* movies, this guy was channeling Harrison Ford as Han Solo circa the cantina scene in *Star Wars*. Brown hair that hung down past his collar, a white shirt unbuttoned at the throat, dark leather jacket that hit at his hips, well-worn jeans, and beat-up motorcycle boots. A day's worth of scruff was only adding to the overall rugged look of him.

I'll admit, the words, *Oh, hot damn* . . . came to mind. I was never one for bad boys in practice, but I couldn't deny the visceral attraction to them in theory. Then I chastised myself for my earlier thought. *My Ben. Come off it, Luce. He was never your Ben.*

But the nurse next to me with her dozens of tiny braids tied back at the crown and her purse slung over her shoulder saw him, too. In fact, she'd craned her neck to watch him walk away, with appreciation written all over her face.

"You know him?" she asked.

I gave a half snort. "No. I'm not sure the guy I know would ever look like that." *Unfortunately*, I didn't add. Ben would have made a smokin' Han Solo for Serena's next Halloween party.

She raised her eyebrows and went for one more look as the elevator doors closed.

"Too bad, honey. That's one nice-looking man."

As we rode down to the parking garage, I was starting to feel overwhelmed with emotions—worry, anger, tiredness, fear, general stress—none of which were helped by seeing Ben's *caliente* Han Solo bad-boy doppelgänger.

I let out a frustrated huff as I made for the parking garage, not realizing the nurse from the elevator was walking next to me.

She nudged my shoulder briefly with hers and said, "Honey, you look like you've got the weight of the world on these skinny things. You need to phone a friend, go get a drink, and talk things out."

She tilted her head back toward the hospital again and gave me a broad grin. "Or better yet, go find that hunk of a man, get a drink with him, and let him take you for a ride as you tell him all about it. The point is, do yourself a favor and halve your problem by sharing it with someone."

"You're right," I said, returning her grin. "Thanks for the reminder."

It was true, I needed some help. I started my car, thinking hard, but my brain kept going back to the guy from the elevator. Part of me wished furiously it had been Ben, but then I knew I probably would have been so frustrated with him that I wouldn't be able to even speak to him properly at best, or I'd say things I didn't mean at the worst, and I didn't want or need either at the moment.

"Face it, Luce," I muttered as I caught my reflection in my rearview mirror. "The cards were stacked against you. So for the love of Pete, think of something useful!"

And just like that, I remembered my ace in the hole. His name was Sean Nelson, but he wasn't some shadowy contact like in Grandpa's world. In fact, Sean worked for the National Archives, but I knew he had contacts in a lot of worlds that were shadowy-adjacent at times . . . if that were even a thing.

Then I stopped, with my finger hovering over his name in my contacts. If I talked to Sean, I would have to give him information about my grandfather that Grandpa hadn't authorized me to give. I bit my lip. Would Grandpa allow me to tell his secret?

I thought of Hugo Markman and Chef Rocky Zeppetelli. Then I thought of the other six people on the list Hugo had left me. I had to do my best to save them from whatever was going on, and I had to believe my grandfather would want me to save them, too. If that meant giving away his secret in order to do so, I felt sure Grandpa would give me the go-ahead.

The only thing I can do is try, I thought. And my friend Sean was about as trustworthy as they came, so if I had to tell Grandpa's secret, at least it would be in good hands.

As it was so early, I called Sean's work line and left a lengthy message, but without giving away Grandpa's past just yet. Still, I was already feeling like my problem was being halved as I drove out of the parking garage and headed back to the Hotel Sutton.

TWENTY-EIGHT

❧

The sun had barely started to rise when I trudged back into the hotel. I slipped through the doors just in time to hear an angry male voice talking without any attempt at modulation.

"There's no way we're going to stay here when people keep turning up dead."

"That's right," came a shrill feminine one.

Mrs. P. met my eyes and gave me a strained smile. A couple I recognized as Mr. and Mrs. Carverson were standing, stone-faced, at the front desk. Their luggage was at their feet.

"Can you imagine how unsafe we felt when we woke up this morning, turned on the TV, and heard what happened to your chef?" Mr. Carverson was saying, his protuberant dark eyes flashing and mustache wiggling like a fluffy slug attached to his upper lip.

Mrs. Carverson, who was petite and thin, with red hair a half shade too orange for her coloring, finished her husband's thought, echoing his tone and expression. "And Roselyn and Pippa Sutton, the very owners of this hotel, are under investigation! What kind of place are you running here?"

I gave Mrs. P. a sympathetic wave and headed upstairs as she was telling the couple, "Of course, I do so understand," in patient tones mixed with the right amount of concern and remorse. "We'll be happy to refund your last two nights. Let me get that done for you right now."

I felt for Mrs. P., and for Pippa and the whole staff—though with the exception of one other room currently occupied by the newlywedded Nguyen-Sobnoskis, the rest of the hotel was filled by Sutton family members through New Year's Day. Thus, there wouldn't be a mass exodus of guests that could look bad for Pippa's fledgling hotel. They would weather the storm and be fine.

Making my way to my room, I saw a waiter at Uncle Dave's door. Uncle Dave himself had stuck his head out of his room, hair wildly disheveled and cheeks blotchy, and was blearily eyeing the waiter, who was holding a breakfast tray with a French press full of coffee, a cup and saucer, a pitcher of cream, and something underneath a stainless-steel food cover.

"Miss Pippa thought you might like this, sir," the waiter said. "It's plain toast with a side of marmalade. Thick-cut, your favorite. May I come in to leave the tray?"

I heard a grunt of thanks, then the waiter stepped inside Uncle Dave's room.

At least he was alive, I thought with relief, closing my door. That was one good thing that had happened in the last twelve hours.

My room was dark, the blackout curtains still closed from when I'd fallen asleep last night. My bed looked more inviting than ever. And yet I was strangely awake and full of energy. I threw open the curtains to reveal a beautiful day in the making, but with hints that the temperatures were going to stay colder than they had been for the previous few days. Since snow was predicted for late on New Year's Eve, I wasn't surprised.

Looking out over the lawn, I saw Boomer cavorting around, finding just the right bushes on which to do his morning business. That meant Pippa was awake. I decided to go see if she and Boomer wanted to take a walk with me. I figured we both could use some fresh air.

Changing into workout gear, I took the back stairs instead of the grand staircase, just in case the Carversons hadn't left and were still doing everything they could to win Annoying Guests of the Year.

Instead, it was Mrs. P.'s and Roselyn's voices I heard. In my running shoes, I barely made a sound on the stairs, so it didn't surprise me they hadn't heard me approaching.

"Did Rocky say something, do you think?" It was Mrs. P., speaking in low tones.

"I don't know," snapped Roselyn, stress giving her voice a knife edge. "I had other things I wanted to discuss."

I froze on the stairs. I couldn't tell where they were.

"I'll bet you did," Mrs. P. replied in knowing tones.

My eyebrows shot up. I wouldn't have expected Mrs. P. to talk like that to her employer, even if they had known each other for years. Roselyn, however, seemed to be so much in her own head, she either didn't notice or didn't care that Mrs. P. had made a crack at Roselyn's friends-with-benefits relationship with Chef Rocky.

"All I care about is that he didn't tell Pippa or that annoying little genealogist," Roselyn said. "God, she irritates me. Always has a factoid to roll off her tongue about history or genealogy like a pert mynah bird. The past is the past! And who cares where you come from anyway?"

"Pippa, for one," Mrs. P. said, though mildly. Again, Roselyn seemed not to hear. I wished I hadn't been hearing this myself. Every word from Roselyn was like a stab to my heart.

"And because she has some contact at the APD, she let loose the hounds before I had a chance to talk to my daughter and call them myself."

"Were you going to call them yourself?" Mrs. P. asked, sounding almost amused.

"Eventually, of course," Roselyn said in a sniffy voice. "But I didn't kill him, so that's not the point here."

Mrs. P.'s voice went ghoulish. "Do you know who did? Do you think *they* did?"

Roselyn's voice broke and she cried out in a tearful voice, "I don't know. I just don't know!"

I heard Mrs. P. soothing her and saying she would go to the sitting room and get her a nice warming cup of tea. I realized the two were directly below me, in a hall near the back parlor. Hurriedly, I tiptoed back upstairs before Mrs. P. could walk across the hall and notice me. Then I waited upstairs for a full five minutes—mostly to compose myself in case I happened to see Roselyn—and went down the grand staircase and out the front door instead.

Though it was cold, the sun's rays were blinding. I'd planned to warm myself up with a light jog to Pippa's, but I was so angry and hurt, I sprinted the entire way. Boomer, who'd been sniffing around some dormant rosebushes, raced to catch up with me, making it up the stairs to Pippa's porch several strides before I did.

Panting as hard as Boomer, and with a stitch in my side, I knocked on Pippa's door. A good thirty yards away was Roselyn's cottage, but thankfully I could no longer see it due to a tall hedge that served as a privacy barrier between the two homes.

Suddenly, I couldn't wait for my time at the hotel to be up so I no longer had to see Roselyn Sutton at all.

Then the front door was flung open and Pippa was rushing forward to envelop me in a hug.

"Lucy, where have you been? I've called you twice this morning. After last night, I've about been going crazy with worry!"

Sure enough, two calls from Pippa had come in while I'd been changing, but I hadn't heard them since my phone was still on silent. After a wholehearted apology, and the ceremonial flipping of the switch on my phone that turned the ringer back on, I told Pippa about my grandfather.

"He'll be okay, though. Really," I said as Pippa clasped her hands on top of her head and exhaled slowly, walking around her living room like she couldn't take much more stress. In contrast, Boomer snuffled happy circles around me, his tail literally whipping the nearby sofa.

I'd been in Pippa's house a few times over the weeks of our working relationship and never failed to find it warm and inviting—and not anything like how she'd decorated the Hotel Sutton.

Her three-room, open-floor-plan cottage was decorated in soothing neutrals, with cool white walls, ivory-toned sofas, and an oversize square ottoman in a sandy-brown giraffe print. Color was used sparingly, but well, with the biggest swath coming from a sofa-size daub painting in primary colors in Pippa's office. Since her office door was a wide, sliding barn door that she rarely needed to close, the huge painting added almost enough color to brighten up the entire home.

"I'm so glad your grandfather will be all right," she said, then gestured for me to follow her. "Come on back to the kitchen. Have you eaten breakfast yet?"

I admitted I hadn't, except for a granola bar at the hospital when Grandpa was being checked over by Dr. Brozo and her team while I stood outside with Grandpa's government-issued guard.

After offering my help and having it refused, I relaxed in Pippa's cozy little breakfast nook while she fixed us some scrambled eggs on toast with slices of avocado and made some chicory coffee in a French press, serving it with warmed milk for cafés au lait.

"Do you know who took this photo?" I asked, pointing to a framed, poster-size print of what looked to be an abandoned stone temple. "It's really lovely. Looks like the temple is about to be reclaimed by the woods at any minute."

I'd been entranced by the photo while Pippa cooked. Beams of slanted light were filtering through the tall trees, hitting the temple's golden blocks of stone, one strong beam passing through the middle of the four decorative columns to illuminate the floor within and banish the shadows. It was an amazing shot at the right moment.

"I did," Pippa said. "It's actually a folly designed in the early 1900s for Sarah Bess so she had somewhere cool to go in the summers. It's made out of Austin limestone and had been unused and neglected for, oh, about twenty years when I discovered it as a child. I've had it restored and I still go out there when I just need some peace and quiet."

"So this folly is on the grounds somewhere?" I asked.

Using her spatula, Pippa pointed out the window, past her back porch that stepped down onto an Italianate patio, and just over a wrought-iron gate covered in evergreen vines. "It's back there, in the woods. There's an almost-hidden pathway just off the side of my place. It winds back into the woods for, oh, a minute or more. You hook around a last curve and it's right there."

"Do you ever get any random hikers or other hotel guests finding it?"

She shook her head. "No, for liability reasons—and for somewhat selfish reasons of my own, because I think of it as my special place—we don't tell the guests it's there and don't encourage them to go back into the woods. If someone gets hurt back there, they could scream and yell and it'd be unlikely someone would hear them."

"Are you serious?" I said.

She nodded. "It's six acres of pretty dense woods. When I was fifteen, I tripped out there and broke my ankle. I yelled at the top of my lungs for nearly an hour and no one heard me. Mom finally came looking for me when it was time to go to dinner. She figured I'd be sitting in the folly reading the Harry Potter series for the tenth time, not lying in the dirt with a busted ankle."

Her phone dinged with a text message as she plated our breakfasts. She read it with a wry smile.

"Uncle Dave," she said. "He says he's got a raging hangover."

"Poor guy," I said, and told her about seeing the waiter bringing him the toast and marmalade she'd sent. "He seemed to appreciate it as much as he could."

"I'm sorry you had to see him like that," Pippa said, shaking her head in frustration as she placed a plate in front of me and added two links of chicken-and-apple sausage, still spitting from the skillet. She went round the other side of the banquette and slid in next to me. Boomer laid down at her feet. "He's lost without his work. I honestly don't know that I'd fare any better if I were in his shoes."

"Really? You're impressive and strong; I've no doubt at all you would," I said, and she gave me a grateful look. For all of Pippa's wealth, beauty, and business acumen, I got the impression she could have used a truly supportive confidante in her daily life, like a sister or a brother. Or even a mother who was less flighty and more nurturing.

I picked up my coffee cup. "How are you doing after last night?"

I'd noticed that while she'd made a delicious breakfast, she was really only nibbling at it while I was plowing through mine and trying to stop myself from eyeing her two as-yet-untouched sausage links.

She gave a piteous little moan, leaning her head back on the backrest. "Oh, Lucy, it's just so hard to believe. I can't stop thinking about it, and at the same time, it's impossible to imagine Chef Rocky is dead. I feel like I could just walk into the kitchen and find him joking around with the kitchen staff, but it's not going to happen." Meeting my eyes again, she said, "But right now, my worries for my mom are taking precedence over anything else."

I pounced on the opportunity. "How is Roselyn? What happened after you went to the police station?"

She sighed. "Mom's a person of interest, apparently, but hasn't been formally arrested."

"Did she say anything to you?"

Pippa shook her head. "She was too broken up over Rocky to say much," she said, a bit stiffly. "Though she must have said a lot to the police or our lawyer, because they were satisfied enough to let her go home. She's not supposed to leave the city, however."

I wasn't surprised. "And you?" I said. "I don't think I even asked if you had an alibi for the time frame. I just trusted you were innocent."

Pippa gave a hint of her throaty laugh and speared one of her sausage links, putting it on my plate. Obviously I hadn't been so subtle.

"Thank you for believing in me," she said. "I wish I'd felt the same vibe from the police, though I get that they're just doing their job." She sipped her coffee. "I have a cast-iron alibi, with security-camera proof, no less. I was at the hotel with family in the morning, at lunch with more family after that, and then I gave tours to two prospective brides"—her voice briefly darkened—"since Mom wasn't available."

Boomer had sat up hopefully, and she gave him half of her other sausage link. "Anyway, the only other time I left was around five thirty, to go to Chef Rocky's house. When I saw what had happened, I immediately came back to look for Mom, then for Uncle Dave. I found you instead, and you know the rest."

"Did the police say when Chef Rocky died?" I asked.

Pippa's mouth turned down. "We don't have an exact time frame yet—or not one we've been told."

"Do you know if any of the staff said anything of interest when they were being interviewed by the police?" I asked. I then told her about my conversation with Terrence, and how he'd forgotten how Chef Rocky had asked about hiring personal security for a friend.

The frown lines between Pippa's eyes deepened over this. "Detective Dupart has checked a few facts with me, but nothing remotely suspicious. Mostly about a handful of employees' whereabouts, like confirming Ysenia, Chef Rocky's sous chef, had been cleared to come in late; that Mrs. P. had been asked by my mom to run some errands for the New Year's Eve gala; and one of the groundskeeping staff, who didn't show up for his shift on time, had called to say he'd blown a tire and was at a tire shop getting a new one."

On her kitchen island, her phone began ringing and she got up, adding in a determined voice, "I'll definitely make sure

Terrence tells his story to Detective Dupart, though. If Chef Rocky was involved in something shady, I want the detective to find out what it was so that we can make sure the hotel won't be touched by it further."

"Good idea," I said, as Pippa picked up her phone.

"It's one of our suppliers for the gala. I'll be just a minute. Help yourself to more coffee."

TWENTY-NINE

❦

Pouring myself another cup, I half listened to Pippa discussing details of a shipment of extra chairs and table linens and felt an inexplicable relief at knowing that my client had such a tight alibi. Remembering how I'd overheard Roselyn saying she hadn't killed Chef Rocky, I hoped against hope that her assertion of innocence was true.

And yet . . . there was a part of me that kept musing on how Pippa was so protective of her mother, constantly giving Roselyn leeway on her bad behavior.

What if Roselyn were indeed guilty of Chef Rocky's murder? Could Pippa, out of filial loyalty, have been involved in some way?

It made me heartsick to think that way about Pippa for even a second, so I made myself concentrate on other possible suspects. I had one in mind as soon as Pippa sat back down.

"What do you know about one of the kitchen staff, Lacey Costin?" I said.

"The brunette prep cook? What about her?" Pippa said, sipping her coffee.

I explained about going down to the kitchen to find Chef Rocky, but meeting Lacey and her pan of root vegetables instead.

"She made it quite clear that she, and probably the whole kitchen staff, knew about your mom and Chef Rocky's relationship. Her jealousy was such that the kitchen staff likely knew about her crush on Chef Rocky, too."

Pippa's eye roll was both frustrated and resigned. "I can't say I'm all that surprised. When Mom and Rocky first started seeing each other, they were never exactly unprofessional, but they also weren't as discreet as they should have been."

"Why did they break up?" I asked.

She shrugged. "Mom said it just burned itself out—that they were better off as friends who enjoyed each other's company when they felt like it." She reached down to pet Boomer's head. "While there was an age difference between them, yes, there was also something, I don't know, deeper with them, like a truly solid friendship. Rocky was actually a good friend to her, you know. He called my mom out when she needed it, but also made her feel good about herself. They seemed to enjoy spending time with one another."

I said, "Okay, so with your mom still very much in the picture in one way or another, and more women waiting in the wings, do you think Lacey Costin's jealousy could have led her to do something stupid?"

"I don't know," Pippa said slowly, then narrowed her eyes. "Come to think of it, Lacey was written up a couple of weeks back, though I don't remember why. Chef Rocky and his sous chef, Ysenia, managed all their staff themselves, but I have all the HR reports. Come on. Let's go into my office and check the files."

A few minutes later, we were reading the report on Lacey Costin, who'd been written up for having a verbal altercation with one of the female pastry chefs. The pastry chef claimed Lacey said things she considered to be threatening, but refused to detail exactly what had been said.

"Do you know this other staffer?" I asked, scratching Boomer behind the ears.

Pippa made a kinda-sorta motion with her hand. "Incredibly talented with pastries, but don't know her personally." She picked up her cell phone. "But Mrs. P. knows most of them, and those she doesn't know, she hears about. Let me check with her."

While Pippa left the room to get intel from Mrs. P., I looked around her elegantly minimal office. There was a sitting area with two comfortable armchairs and a rug that spanned most of the room. Her desk, an electric sit-stand model with a glossy bamboo-wood top, held decorative bins for her pens and sticky notes. Two dome-shaped glass paperweights held down various papers.

I picked up the smallest paperweight, which held a photo of Boomer under its glass. Underneath were torn-out magazine pages with party favor ideas for the New Year's Eve gala. One used twisted satin cording to tie a sachet containing Texas wildflower seed "bombs," which guests could later toss wherever they wanted wildflowers to grow. The other page showed handmade chocolate-covered caramels in a pretty little box. A sticky note on the top page in Mrs. P.'s handwriting reminded Pippa to pick up the seed bombs and caramels so that she, Mrs. P., could assemble the sachets.

What made me smile, though, were the framed photographs on the wall between two large windows, and I locked on to one Pippa had scanned and sent me weeks ago. It was a photo of her great-grandfather James and his wife, Nell, taken on V-E Day in 1945, not long before they were married. They were both in uniform—his British, hers American—and looked so in love.

Pippa came back in and sat down. "Mrs. P. said the pastry chef got along like a house on fire with Chef Rocky, but there was never any romance."

"Did she say anything about Lacey?"

"Yep. A few weeks ago, the kitchen team was out for drinks after work and Lacey became aggressive with a woman who had flirted with Chef Rocky. Lacey actually had to be carried out in a fireman's hold by one of the other kitchen staff because she was so riled up. Mrs. P. described her as impetuous and hot-tempered. She also said that Rocky had been staying well away from Lacey in recent weeks, which had likely made Lacey even more upset."

"Did she know if Rocky and Lacey had a relationship?" I asked.

"Apparently they flirted a lot, but that was it."

"Lacey might have seen much more into that flirting, though," I said.

"Should I call Detective Dupart and ask him to check her out?" Pippa asked, uncertainty in her voice. I could tell the thought of accusing one of her employees without a really good reason was not what she wanted to do, and I didn't blame her.

"How about this?" I said. "Let's check the security footage first to see if she was on the premises during the hours Chef Rocky would have been murdered. If she wasn't here, or we see anything suspicious, then we can call Dupart."

She agreed, and we began going through yesterday's security footage from the kitchen. It was strange seeing Chef Rocky alive and well in the morning, knowing what would happen to him just a few hours later. The kitchen staff went about their business, including Lacey. However, a few minutes into the footage, she beelined it to Chef Rocky, cornering him by the stove. We couldn't tell what they were saying, but Rocky shook his head vehemently. Lacey kept talking to him, at one point reaching out to him, but he moved smoothly away from her. Seconds later, he was walking out of the kitchen, Lacey glaring after him. Then she stalked over to her prep station and began angrily cutting up potatoes.

"Check the footage for outside the ballroom, near the bathrooms," I told Pippa, explaining about Grandpa seeing Chef Rocky and Roselyn.

Sure enough, they were there, and Grandpa could be seen passing Rocky as the chef threw up his hands in irritation. Grandpa then went into the men's room, while Roselyn disappeared into the ladies'. We followed Rocky's path through the hotel, his body language giving off waves of frustration. At one point he strode past Mrs. P., who said something to him. Chef Rocky responded without looking at her, but had been so close to the camera we could read his lips.

"It looks like he said, 'I'm going home,'" Pippa said, and I agreed. Moments later, we saw Chef Rocky striding out to the staff parking lot in back and then driving off in a black Porsche.

"Check the kitchen again, please," I said. "We need to see if Lacey is still there."

We watched the footage for several minutes, and no Lacey. Pippa fast-forwarded the kitchen footage, and Lacey was seen arriving again at 5:23 p.m. She didn't speak to anyone, but began pureeing some roasted butternut squash. We stopped the footage seconds after she yanked the immersion blender out too fast and a slash of orange squash puree ended up across her chest.

It was the angry outburst we witnessed afterward that made Pippa call Detective Dupart. She was careful not to accuse Lacey, but laid out the facts and suggested his officers question her on her whereabouts.

"Will do, Ms. Sutton," I heard Dupart say, adding that he wanted to see the security footage.

Pippa told Dupart she would make the footage available to him whenever he needed it.

"I can't say I want Lacey to be guilty," Pippa told me after hanging up. "I want someone I don't know to be behind this. Someone evil and easy to despise. But if telling Detective Dupart about anyone who might have had a motive to kill Chef Rocky helps to clear my mom's name, then it's worth it."

"I feel the same way," I said.

Pippa was quiet, picking up her coffee cup, holding it between both hands like its warmth could soothe her frayed nerves. "My mom . . . she can be selfish, vain, unthinking, petty, and neurotic, but she's not like that when it comes to me. To me, she's smart, hardworking, warm, funny, generous, kind"—she let out a frustrated laugh—"and only occasionally selfish and neurotic. I don't believe she'd hurt Chef Rocky, Lucy. I just don't believe it."

Outside her office window, a blue jay landed on the sill and flew away just as quickly. I squeezed her fingers. "I don't believe it, either," I said, which I realized was the truth in my heart. "I'm hoping I can help prove her innocence, too."

Pippa sat up straighter. "How?"

I hesitated, thinking of Hugo's list. I still had so little to go on, and I hadn't proved anything yet.

"I can't tell you right now," I said. "Just give me a little bit of time to look into it. I wouldn't want to be wrong and get your hopes up."

Pippa surveyed me for a long moment. Then she said, "Whatever this is, have you told the police? Do they know what you're thinking?"

"They don't," I said, then hurried to add, "and nothing I will be doing will interfere with their investigation at all. If I find something of note, though, I will absolutely tell them."

Pippa waved that off with a dismissive noise. "Hell, honey, interfere away if it clears my mom's name and helps find Rocky's killer. I don't care."

I laughed, and put my hand on her shoulder. "You are *so* much easier to convince than a federal agent."

Pippa laughed, too, finally, and then her phone beeped. She looked at the screen, tapped on a notification, then groaned. "I think I need to temporarily unsubscribe from the news alerts I get. I used to like staying current, but now I feel like I only see negative stuff."

She turned the phone toward me, and I saw a photo of a smiling, gray-haired woman.

"Some poor woman from England was found dead on the other side of Lady Bird Lake early this morning." She swiped the news story away, but not before I saw the caption under the photo.

Penelope Frances Ohlinger, 74, of Tunbridge Wells, Kent, England.

Another name from Hugo Markman's list.

THIRTY

❧

I don't think I breathed properly until I left Pippa's cottage and ran back to the hotel, all thoughts of a morning walk forgotten, and only barely aware of Pippa telling me our dinner with her family was rescheduled for tonight at Eighteen Ninety-Five.

Once in my room, I practically lunged for my iPad on my bed. I'd noted the web page Pippa had shown me; it was for the local news station. I brought it up and scanned the short accompanying story.

It appeared that Penelope Ohlinger's body had been discovered by an early-morning jogger on the south side of Lady Bird Lake, in a protected area where grasses grew high and thick in the winter and would house native wildflowers in the spring and summer. At present, the grasses were very tall and her body had not been noticed for several hours after her death, until the jogger's dog began barking at the grass. The jogger initially thought his dog had detected a snake or maybe an armadillo, and had been shocked to find a body.

I read on. Mrs. Ohlinger, a widow, was reported to be on vacation and had been a guest at the nearby Carlingford Hotel, which had a path leading down to the lakeside trail. She had traveled to Austin on holiday to meet up with a friend. Initial toxicology reports were forthcoming, but her two adult children said she was on medications for a heart issue and hadn't been sleeping well due to jet lag. The article ended by saying the death was being treated as accidental at this time.

Hugo Markman's raspy last words were in my ears.

Keep them safe.

I felt wretched for this woman I had never known and would never meet, and my gut was telling me the chances her death had been accidental were slim.

I was hardly doing a good job of keeping anyone safe thus far, was I? Time to remedy that.

I had my laptop with me, which had all my genealogy programs on it. My iPad did, too. But I felt like I needed the big guns for this. I needed my two big computer screens and the power of the super-fast internet we enjoyed at the office.

I changed into jeans and a Fair Isle sweater. Grabbing my coat and my tote, I was halfway down the back stairs, hoping I wouldn't run into Roselyn, when my phone rang. I'd already put in my wireless earbuds to call the hospital and check on Grandpa, but when I saw the contact photo of a man with a kind face and smiling blue eyes, I grinned. It was just the man I had been waiting for.

"Sean, hi! It's so good to hear from you."

"Well, if it isn't my favorite scrappy genealogist," Sean said, greeting me warmly like the pseudo older brother he'd always been. "Hot on the trail of another ancestry investigation, from what it sounded like in your message."

I had to laugh. Sean and I had worked with each other during a sixteen-month period between the years I worked at the Hamilton American History Center and the day I finally hung out

my shingle as a fledgling but fully trained and accredited professional genealogist.

The job was at a university library in Houston, and the only
reason I didn't love it was because of three female coworkers
who could have shown NPH and Bertie a few things about being catty.

Through that period, my saving graces had been in the form
of two people: a lovely genealogist named Ginger, and Sean,
who was our head librarian before moving up in the world and
over to Washington, DC. Being as his own personal research
passion were the two world wars, once he found I had an equal
passion for hearing about them, we'd often have lunch and talk
World War history.

Or, rather, he would give me a professorlike lecture on some
aspect of one of the wars, and I would eat my lunch and listen
in thoroughly focused silence.

Now, as I drove out of the hotel parking lot and my phone
connected with my car speakers, Sean and I spent a few minutes
catching up on each other's lives. I asked him about his lovely
wife and young son, both of whom he absolutely adored, and
I could practically see his face lighting up with joy as he talked
about them.

Through the phone I heard a knock, a man's voice saying,
"Meeting still in ten?" and Sean replying in the affirmative before the door closed.

"Now, my friend," Sean said, "you know I'd love nothing
more than to keep talking with you, but as you probably heard,
I have a meeting in a short while. Can you speak freely?"

"I can," I said. "Sean, do you think you can help me confirm
the identities of some OSS and SOE operatives if I give you a
set of potential names? As we speak, I'm heading to my office
to trace the wartime ancestors of the list of names I told you

about. There's already been a second death, both of whom are on this list."

"Are you serious?" Sean said, aghast.

"More so than I'd like to be," I replied. "And to make a credible case for the police, I need records assistance, but I need it quickly. Any chance you can help?"

Sean hesitated, which was unlike him. In the past three years, I'd only asked for his help a handful of times, and he'd always jumped at the chance, especially if it involved anything surrounding the World Wars. In fact, he'd metaphorically broken down doors for me a couple of times to get information I needed for one of my clients. Though, admittedly, nothing had ever been of a clandestine nature, and I'd always been able to give him several weeks of lead time to begin with.

"Look, Luce, if all you needed were names, that would be a better possibility," he said with a note of chagrin in his voice. "I could even call in a favor at A-Two if I had to," he added, referring to the National Archives at College Park, Maryland, often referred to as the Archives II building, or just "A2," as they were specialists in handling these kinds of military records. "But you also need me to link these names to a specific mission, and that makes it much harder."

"I know," I said as I pulled into my parking spot at the Old Printing Office and put my earbuds back in. "But you know you're my personal archives wizard, Sean, and I hoped it would sound important enough that you could work some extra magic for me."

"I, of course, think it's important, and I'd love to help," he said. "I'm practically champing at the bit to do this, actually. However, unfortunately, the only way I could get you information quickly is if you could give me the mission's code name. Otherwise, I could still look into it, but it would take weeks, months, or even longer to find the right mission—and that's if it's even able to be found in the first place." He lowered his voice. "Some of these missions are still potentially the proverbial hot potatoes, if you know what I mean."

I knew all this, of course. It took weeks to get even nonclassified military service records for a deceased family member who had served in a past war. Asking Sean to try to find operational information from an OSS mission during World War II could take ages. Honestly, I didn't know what I was thinking.

I unlocked the door to my building—after my fiasco in the fall, the tenants had unanimously voted to keep the doors locked at all times—and as I grasped the door handle, a jewel-bright bird flying past was reflected in the window. It was another blue jay, landing in the tree outside my building. He looked around with lightning-fast head movements and then flew away again, just like his avian relative had earlier at Pippa's cottage.

I stepped into the small, quiet foyer of my building and the door shut, locking me in. Then I froze and my voice went breathless.

"Sean, I know. I know what the mission's name was."

Grandpa had told me, twice. I found my wallet and pulled out the piece of paper on which a good Samaritan had written one word under my own name and phone number.

My heart sped up, and the excitement in Sean's voice matched mine. "Don't leave me in suspense, Luce. What is it?"

"Greenfinch," I said. "Operation Greenfinch."

THIRTY-ONE

※

"Well, well, fancy seeing you here amongst the peasants who can't afford a four-star hotel," Serena teased as I breezed in the door to our office.

I stopped in my hurried attempt to boot up my computer to give my friends a regal nod.

"Hello, love," Josephine said, blowing me a kiss. "What's with all the rushing about?"

"I have a genealogy emergency," I replied as I tapped my foot impatiently, willing my computer to hurry up. Sean had told me to get him the ancestors of the people on Hugo's list as fast as I could.

Then I really did stop, remembering I had a second quest. I still didn't have the right copies of *The Thirty-Nine Steps* that would allow me to decipher the last three names on Hugo Markman's list.

I put my head in my hands and groaned.

There could potentially be dozens of editions out there, some from different publishers and some from the same publisher, just reprinted for one reason or another. The task was daunting, and I practically wilted into my office chair. "Actually, I have two emergencies."

Behind me, Serena addressed Josephine. "Did you see that? Sometimes I think our girl could have been an actress."

"Very *La Dame aux Camélias*," Jo agreed.

"Anything we can do to help, Camille?" Serena asked with amusement.

When I didn't answer, but instead stared down at Grandpa's crosshatch, now wiped free of all chalk marks except for hints of white stuck in the crevices, my friends stopped teasing me.

"Everything okay, Luce?" Serena asked. "You know we're just messing with you."

"Yes, darling," added Josephine. "What can we do?"

"What?" I said, looking over at them. "Oh, no, I wasn't upset. I'm just trying to figure out how to do everything I need to do before two o'clock, when I have to be back at the Sutton to interview another relative."

I then decided they should know about Grandpa's accident, just in case. They were out of their chairs and at my desk as soon as I said the words, "Girls, you should know Grandpa was in a car accident last night."

They hovered protectively around me as I told the story of what had happened and how Grandpa had been saved by a good Samaritan.

"Then let us help you with one of your emergencies," Josephine said.

"Only it probably should be the second one, as we can't do much about the genealogy stuff," Serena said.

I looked up at my friends in gratitude. I wouldn't tell them about my grandfather being a spy unless things became absolutely necessary, though. Until then, it wasn't my secret to give, so I had to choose my words carefully.

"Okay, Grandpa set me a task before he got hurt," I began. "He was looking for copies of a particular book. It's an espionage mystery first published in 1915 that has never been out of print, so there's lots of editions out there. And I, uh, need every edition I can find."

I had one set of blue eyes and one set of hazel eyes flecked with gold blinking at me like they weren't sure they were hearing me correctly.

"Which could be upwards of how many?" Serena asked.

I turned my palms up. "I'm not sure. Three? Fifty? Somewhere in between?" I bit my lip for a second, then said, "Girls, would you trust me if I told you that this isn't just a whim or something to cheer Grandpa up? This is really important. I need the books to figure out something he was working on. I promised him I would, but I also promised him I'd do this." I gestured to my computer, and I didn't have to explain further.

Josephine had gone back to her desk. Pulling her wallet out of her purse, she said, "I've got my library card and I can check their online catalog." She looked at Serena. "Let's divide and conquer. Why don't I go to the library and you go over to Book-People. We'll talk and compare editions. Whatever we don't find at both places, we'll see if the chain bookstore or one of the other independent bookstores has it."

"Excellent plan," Serena said. She had her purse in hand and met Josephine at the door. Then she turned back, giving me a look of feigned impatience.

"Well? Are you going to tell us what book we're hunting or not?"

I grinned. My friends were the best.

"*The Thirty-Nine Steps*, by John Buchan."

They were already out the door as I called out my thanks to them, Josephine telling Serena that there'd been a "brilliant PBS movie version" of the book that had come out a few years back with a "rather dishy actor as the lead" and that Serena would like him because he was tall, lanky, and blond like Walter, Serena's boyfriend.

"Hot damn, I'm always up for trying a new dish," I heard Serena say as I locked the office door. I was still smiling as I pulled up my favorite genealogy apps and started eight different files. I named the first five with the five decoded names from Hugo Markman's list. The last three were titled "Unnamed Person in Possible Danger."

I'd been thinking on how to attack things while I'd changed clothes earlier. If there were a connection between these eight names and World War II, then I only had to trace each name back to their ancestors who would have been of military-service age in the 1940s. For the five already decoded names, that likely meant going back to their great-grandparents at most, unless one of the people listed was particularly young.

The one bit of relief was I already knew the spy associated with Chef Rocky Zeppetelli was his great-grandfather Angelo. I filled out the ancestor chart for Rocky first.

One down, seven to go. If the right key texts to decipher the last three names could be found, that was.

I started ancestor charts for the four names I already had—Alastair Newell, Penelope Ohlinger, Fiona Keeland, and Naomi Van Dorn—and tried not to think about what would happen if I couldn't properly trace them. I'd still go to Dupart with the knowledge I had, but would the detective take me seriously?

Then I reminded myself harshly that two on the list were already dead and, once I showed the list to Dupart, he would see a connection and would have to take it seriously. Short of there being a credible threat Dupart and his team could act on quickly, though, it would come back to the connection being somewhere in the past—the World War II–era past, to be specific. And who better to research that than a genealogist?

Yes, I thought, Dupart needed my help with this, even if he didn't know it yet.

Glancing at the time, I saw that I had nearly four hours before I had to go back to the Sutton for my two o'clock interview session with Pippa's cousin Ginny. Until then, I had to pin down as many ancestors as I possibly could.

THIRTY-TWO

I was so engrossed in my searching I barely heard our office door unlocking sometime later. Serena and Josephine came in, carrier bags in their hands, their faces alight with triumph.

"Oh, *honey*," Serena said, stopping short at the sight of me.

I sat back and took stock of myself. My reflection in the window told me I looked like I'd been out camping in high humidity on a bed of ancestral charts and neon-hued sticky notes. My hair was haphazardly pulled up into a knot on the top of my head, my face shiny and greasy feeling. I'd long since rubbed off my lipstick and had been concentrating so much I hadn't even pulled out one of my many lip balms. I'd also kicked off my booties, one low-cut sock was threatening to come off my heel, and somehow I was sitting on my discarded overcoat.

Serena came over to my desk, pulled open the top drawer, and rummaged among my various lipsticks, glosses, and balms until she found one that moisturized and added some sheer color. She handed it to me, but refrained from any other commentary. Serena knew when to leave my overall appearance alone to, as she put it, "hunt down dead people," but that didn't mean she'd let me do it with dry, colorless lips.

As I applied the rosy-hued balm, Serena deposited two carrier bags on my desk.

"Jo found a copy at Austin Central Library, and I found two different editions at BookPeople, but we decided to cover all our bases. We went to every bookstore we could find, indie or not."

Josephine added two more bags to the pile, and put down the library copy of *The Thirty-Nine Steps* right over Grandpa's crosshatch.

"Yes, we agreed that if we happened to miss a copy, and it was the one you actually needed, then it would just set you back. In all, we found nine separate copies of the book, all from different publication dates. Can you believe it?"

"You two are wonderful, brilliant, and gorgeous to boot," I said, taking out the copies to lay them on my desk.

"We are, aren't we?" Serena said to Josephine, who replied, "Darling, was it ever in doubt?"

Serena snapped her fingers. "Nearly forgot. The girl who checked us out at the chain bookstore said there'd been two other people asking for multiple copies of this book. One was a couple of weeks back, but the other was a while ago."

My head snapped up so fast, it gave me whiplash, and my hair started to tumble down from its knot. One of those people was undoubtedly Hugo, but as for the other?

Weirdly, it hadn't fully sunk in until that moment that there was a real, breathing, and possibly evil person out there who'd created this list and had treacherous ideas when using it. Yet there had been, and someone had seen him or her.

"Did the employee remember who it was?" I asked, redoing my top knot.

"She said she never saw either of them," Serena said. "She only remembered hearing about it because you don't get a ton of people searching for *The Thirty-Nine Steps* anymore, do you?" She seemed to anticipate my next question by saying, "And apparently the staff member who mentioned it is currently on vacation."

I felt my shoulders droop.

"She said she'd be happy to email the coworker if it turned out to be that important to you, but she probably wouldn't get a response until after the new year," Serena added, pulling out a business card and handing it to me.

I gave my friends a grateful look, then Jo leaned in to give me an air kiss. "Must run, love. Ahmad called while we were tearing around Austin looking for your books. He got back in town early from his work trip and wants to treat me to a movie and dinner."

"Methinks the 'movie' part might be a euphemism," Serena drawled. Josephine gave a cat-with-cream smile and didn't contradict her.

"High-five to that," I said, holding out my hand to my beautiful British friend. She slapped my palm and strutted out the door to Serena's catcalls.

"I actually have to run, too," Serena said.

"Walter wanting a little bit of afternoon delight as well?" I asked with an arched eyebrow.

Serena batted her eyes at me while fluffing up her blond hair, which she'd recently cut in a chic bob that ended a couple of inches below her chin. "You know me, my friend, I'd rather have a lot of an all-nighter. Right now I need to go meet a client who called with a fashion emergency. She ran into her ex-fiancé's new fiancée, who invited her to their wedding on New Year's Day, if you can believe it."

Then she, too, blew me a kiss and was out the door, leaving me in the quiet of our office with my thoughts.

I picked up one of the copies of *The Thirty-Nine Steps*. *Should I start trying to decode the last three names*, I thought, *or take what information I already have to Detective Dupart?*

I decided to go with my gut. I called Dupart and he answered immediately.

"Hi, Detective, it's Lucy Lancaster."

"Ms. Lancaster," he said. "What can I do for you? And please tell me you haven't found another dead person."

"Dead person? Oh, I found several," I quipped, trying to lighten the mood.

"What?" Dupart said sharply. I heard a sound that may have been propped-up feet hitting the floor.

"Ancestrally speaking, of course," I finished.

After a moment where he took this in, he snapped, "I'm not in the mood for my time to be wasted, Ms. Lancaster."

"I don't intend to do so," I replied, my already frayed nerves not enjoying his tone. "I do, however, have some important information, and I'd like to meet with you as soon as possible to go over it."

"Why?" Dupart asked. "So you can tell me Rocky Zeppetelli had a five-times-great-grandfather who may have been murdered with an ice pick somewhere in Venice in 1905, and now you think there's someone targeting the ancestors of the Zeppetellis di Venezia, determined to finish them off one by one with their signature leopard-handled ice pick?"

Dupart clearly had not picked up on my More Snark Is Not Appreciated Right Now vibe.

"For one thing," I said, the chill in my voice nearing the stage where it would need an ice pick itself, "Chef Rocky's fifth great-grandfather would have lived closer to 1805 than 1905. Next,

Venice is in the north of Italy, and the name Zeppetelli originates from the southern parts, likely near Naples. And lastly, it would be the *descendants* of the Zeppetellis *di Napoli*, not the *ancestors*. But that would make a good mystery, wouldn't it?"

Dupart muttered a string of oaths under his breath in what sounded like Louisiana French Creole.

"Whatever you have for me, Ms. Lancaster," Dupart finally growled, "it had better be damn good. I'll be here until four o'clock, and not a second longer."

"It is damn good," I replied. "And I'll be there in twenty minutes."

THIRTY-THREE

Detective Dupart was holding up a copy of Hugo Markman's list. He was leaning forward across his desk, and his eyes were so narrowed, the right one was actually closed and the left was merely a slit with enviously long lashes.

"You're really trying to tell me the guy who croaked at the Hotel Sutton had a microdot viewer hidden inside a World War Two–era fountain pen? And the viewer was used to read a microdot left on a theater ticket? And that all these names were on the microdot?" He shook Hugo's list.

"And that they're the descendants of eight World War Two spies, yes, some of whom were with America's Office of Strategic Services, or OSS, and the others with England's Special Operations Executive, or SOE."

"You're kidding me, Ms. Lancaster."

The list he held was only inches from me, the names and the three unbroken ciphers now as familiar to me as my own name.

I pointed at two of the names, my voice growing insistent.

"Two of them—Rocco Zeppetelli and Penelope Ohlinger—are already dead, Detective. And you were there when Officer

Carr said Hugo Markman—the guy who croaked at the Hotel Sutton—was poisoned with radium chloride. How can you think I'm kidding you when I'm bringing you irrefutable proof that these people are somehow connected and the others are in danger?"

Dupart lowered the list. "Ms. Lancaster, you have to realize how absurd this sounds. How do I know that Hugo Markman wasn't some crazy, overzealous conspiracy theorist who licked the glow-in-the-dark stuff on one of his old clocks to commit suicide? Then when he knew he was dying, he found some names of people with war-era relatives, made this list, and happened to get, for lack of a better word, lucky that he picked two people who ended up getting killed?" This time it was he who jabbed at the list, indicating the three undeciphered codes. "Plus, these three we have no proof are names at all. He could have written gibberish, for all we know, just to give it extra drama."

"But he didn't. Hugo didn't," I said, but my voice was small. I'd never considered that my evidence wouldn't be taken seriously—and frustratingly, I could see Dupart's point.

What was worse, a part of me was being traitorous and wondering if my grandfather's mind really was going on him. That he, like Hugo, may have created something out of nothing. The very idea I was even entertaining such a thought made me weak with shame and fear. Dupart seemed to sense my lack of conviction and used a pen to put a mark by Penelope Ohlinger's name.

"Look, there's no proof Mrs. Ohlinger was murdered to begin with. She'd had three small strokes already in the last two years and was on some pretty intense heart meds. The toxicology tests are still pending, but in all likelihood, she just had a heart incident and happened to fall into the weeds when she was out walking in the dead of night while suffering from jet lag."

I looked at Dupart and realized that, while he wasn't being

a jerk, he was wondering whether I was being played as a major fool by someone. And he was possibly suspicious about my overall state of mind, too. He was treating me like the CIA had treated Hugo Markman: like a harmless nutter.

I bit the inside of my cheek for a moment, then lifted my chin and sat up straight. I hadn't met Hugo, but I had faith in him, and I had ten times that amount of faith in my grandfather. I was determined to proceed. Pulling out a folder bulging with papers, I turned it around to Detective Dupart and slid it to him.

"Here are copies of the research I've done on the people on Hugo Markman's list," I said. I pointed to the tabs I'd created out of pink sticky notes. "I've traced the World War Two–era ancestors of Rocky Zeppetelli, Penelope Ohlinger, Naomi Van Dorn, Alastair Newell, and Fiona Keeland."

I separated out two ancestral charts. "Though as for the name Fiona *Keeland*, I strongly believe she is actually either forty-two-year-old Fiona Pulleyn Kenland of York, England, or fifty-four-year-old Fiona Jameson Keyland of Lexington, Kentucky. I could find no credible instances of the surname Keeland and I truly believe it was an error made by whoever created the cipher that Hugo found and partially decoded. It's also possible the cipher creator took the name based on Soundex."

At Dupuart's furrowed brow, I explained. "Soundex, in the simplest terms, is an index of surnames that are grouped by the way they sound instead of the way they're spelled. It's meant as a system to help you find your ancestor if their name was unintentionally misspelled when it was recorded."

Before the detective could respond, I took a breath and continued. "Regardless, I made ancestral charts for both women, as they each had had grandfathers in World War Two and, at one point or another, posted something on social media about their respective grandfathers being honored for their service."

Dupart took the folder without any hint of sarcasm. "Thank you, Ms. Lancaster." He seemed to be aware my feelings were bruised, and this almost made it worse. I kept talking.

"You should know that Alastair Newell is in bad health in England. He was in an accident during a vacation and has limited walking abilities now. I found a small news article from his village in the Cotswolds that said his injuries were a result of a hit-and-run during a vacation to Germany about a year and a half ago." I reached over, opened the folder, and showed him the article I'd printed. "It makes me wonder if he was the first target and the killer didn't succeed."

Dupart's eyes silently scanned the short article, which was about a fund-raiser to help Alastair pay for a wheelchair ramp at his house, but he said nothing.

I said, "Then Naomi Van Dorn—or, rather, Naomi Marie Cogswell Kostopoulos Liebovitz Van Dorn—has a blog where she writes about her marriages and various other things. She wrote three separate posts dedicated to her search for her paternal grandparents, both of whom were in World War Two. Her grandfather died just before D-Day and her grandmother died from complications of childbirth just after Naomi's father was born."

Again, I pulled out a two-page printout. "In the third post, Naomi said she'd been contacted by a woman in England who claimed to be her half aunt. The woman claims Naomi's grandfather Robbie Cogswell had a wartime romance with this woman's mother, who was one of England's Land Girls, and got her pregnant just before his outfit was moved. This woman is claiming Robbie had boasted he worked with the OSS."

I'd highlighted the sentences, and Dupart's eyes darted to them as he rubbed his goatee with one hand.

I said, "You'll see that she and the half aunt were planning on meeting up around the holidays, though she doesn't say where or when. If you recall, Penelope Ohlinger was also here in Austin to meet up with an old friend she'd recently reconnected with. Were you able to contact this supposed friend, Detective?"

Dupart looked at me, his jaw tight, his eyes still doubting, but didn't answer directly.

"Ms. Lancaster, this information is interesting, but what motive would anyone have to want to kill off descendants of some OSS and SOE spies after all this time? And why *these* specific descendants and not others? Surely all these spies have multiple descendants."

"You're right, they do," I said. "I've thought about it a lot, and I believe the killer isn't trying to wipe out whole families— that would take too much time. He just wants to hurt or kill someone from each family for some sort of decades-late retribution. An eye-for-an-eye type of thing, possibly."

"How is this person deciding on their victims, then?" Dupart asked.

"Well," I said, "after tracing each of their lineages, I think the people on this list are being targeted for a couple of reasons. One, they either look like or are named after their OSS or SOE parent, grandparent, or great-grandparent. The other option is because they had a particularly close relationship with that relative."

I took back the file and selected Chef Rocky's tab. One of the little extras I often did for my clients, especially those who cared very little for their family histories and didn't see much to get excited about, was to create a photographic side-by-side comparison of my client and one of their ancestors. I used it to point out the little visual signposts that linked them to their familial past: the shape of their eyes, ears, or nose. The fullness of their lower lip. The way their jawline curved or their eyebrows arched.

Or sometimes it was in their expressions or their facial measurements, meaning the distances between certain parts of their faces, such as from the hairline to between the eyes, or between the base of the nose and the chin. I'd never failed to help someone discover the magic in themselves as a portal to the past, even if they continued to struggle with finding their family history interesting.

Within the file, I pulled out the side-by-side I'd created of photos of Rocky and Angelo Zeppetelli at around the same age. "For example, as you can see, Rocky Zeppetelli and his great-grandfather Angelo didn't greatly resemble one another, except for in this area." I used my fingers to circle Rocky's and Angelo's eyes and nose, where the similarities were striking. "Also, Rocky stated more than once in interviews and on the Hotel Sutton website that he revered and was very close to his great-grandfather, who I already have confirmation was in the OSS."

"How do you know for sure?" Dupart asked, his eyes narrowing again.

"I have a source," I said, unwilling to let loose Grandpa's secret just yet.

Dupart's eyes narrowed further, but he didn't challenge me. I figured he was thinking that, along with having a screw loose, I was also embracing my inner amateur sleuth a little too much again.

Inwardly, I sighed, but continued. I was determined not to leave until Dupart had the information he needed. I would do my part to protect these people, even if I would never meet them and got branded by the APD as a genealogist who was a taco short of a combination plate.

I located another chart. "Alastair Newell is one who was named for his father—though we don't know if his father was the spy or not."

I found another printout, this time of a Facebook post. "Then Penelope Ohlinger posted on her public Facebook page that she was her father's favorite child and was named for her father as well. His name was Francis and her middle name is the feminine form—Frances, with an 'e-s' instead of an 'i-s.'" I pointed to a second printout. "She also hints in another post that her dad did 'hush-hush' work during the war."

I went back to Naomi's information, pulling out yet another blog post. "Then, as you'll see on Naomi's blog, she's posted a photo of her grandfather next to a photo of her, and she's nearly his feminine spitting image."

"And all this information you found on social media?" Dupart asked, waving a hand over all the papers spread out over his desk.

I nodded. "Researching people's family history means I use every tool at my disposal, and social media is one of the best ones there is. You'd be surprised what personal information people put out there, not realizing it will never disappear and it can be found by nearly anyone."

"Actually, I'm not surprised," Dupart said dryly. "You have no idea how many criminals I've busted based on their social media posts."

He began rifling through the other information in the folder, but didn't ask me anything further. I stood up, slinging my tote over my shoulder. I was exhausted now and I had to get back to the hotel to interview Pippa's cousin Ginny.

"You'll see I've given you ways to contact all these people. I'm especially worried about Naomi Van Dorn. The potential half aunt she's been talking to may be legit or may not. If she isn't, Naomi could be the next one in danger. She may be making plans to meet with the woman at this moment."

"Or this person could be a man, posing as a woman," Dupart said.

"Exactly," I said. I paused, then added, "One last thing, Detective. As to the reason why this person is targeting descendants of these particular eight spies . . ."

He looked up. "Yes, I was wondering about that."

"My source believes it's because of a specific joint OSS–SOE operation during the war, but as of yet I have no other details, except for one. My source has given me the operation's code name." I gestured to the folder in his hands and said, "I also have another source, one at the National Archives, who's going to help me find the names of those involved in the operation, assuming it's been declassified. He has the code name and I've sent him all the information you have here. He's working on cross-referencing Hugo's list and the ancestors I've found with what he uncovers about the operation to see if there's any matches."

Dupart ran a thumb along the edge of his goatee, seemingly weighing whether to give my assertions any credence. Finally, he said, "And what about the last three potential names?" He pointed to the ciphers at the bottom of the page.

I gave him a wan smile. "With a little help from some friends, I've gathered nine different editions of *The Thirty-Nine Steps*. I plan to try to crack the other codes tonight. I'll let you know what I find."

I didn't tell him that my name could be one of them. That would give Grandpa's secret away, and I still wanted to hold off on that if I could.

Before he could reply, I said, "Thank you, Detective. I hope you won't dismiss what I've given you without at least looking into it first," and turned and walked out of his office, proud of myself for keeping my composure.

THIRTY-FOUR

❧

On the way back to the Hotel Sutton, I called the hospital again to check on Grandpa. If he was awake, I'd make a beeline to his side. Instead, Nurse Angelique told me he was still asleep, but she'd been checking on him regularly for signs of any issues.

"He seems to be doing good, Lucy. Sleep is the best healing medicine he could get right now, but I expect he might wake up in a couple of hours."

I thanked her, telling her I'd be by in the late afternoon, after my interview. I hung up as I pulled into the hotel's parking lot and hauled out a large paper carrier bag holding all nine copies of *The Thirty-Nine Steps*. Walking up the pathway, I felt the bag's handles strain with the weight, so I hoisted it up into my arms as I struggled to open the hotel's heavy front door.

Inside, a gaggle of Sutton family members were crowding the foyer. Some were on the grand staircase, taking photos. Others spilled into the bar area, and a few more were in the front room, including little Claire and Marilyn, who were sitting on one of the emerald-green sofas, giggling with each other and swinging their feet to their own made-up rhythm. They sat almost directly under the portrait of their ancestor, and I felt like Sarah Bess was benevolently watching over her young descendants.

From a few steps up the staircase, Pippa waved to me in between photos with her various other cousins. Roselyn was standing next to her daughter and, while smiling dutifully at the camera, she wouldn't meet my eyes and looked strained.

Pippa glanced at her mother, then back at me, mouthing, "*I'll see you at dinner*," when the other cousins were switching around for a different lineup or checking the photos to see how they looked.

I sent her a grin, then I sidled left around another cousin while aiming for the back staircase, and nearly bumped into Uncle Dave.

"Oh, hello, Lucy," he said. He was holding a bottle of water and looking uncomfortable.

"Hello," I said, feeling a tad uncomfortable myself.

He cleared his throat. "I feel like I was the world's biggest idiot yesterday, and I'd like to apologize," he said. "Both for behaving as I did in front of your grandfather, and for—" He broke off and ran a hand over his hair, which was once more neatly brushed back. "Um, I'm not exactly sure what I'm apologizing for last night, since I can't remember much clearly, but I feel like I might have accidentally run you over." His blue eyes, so like Pippa's father's, looked at me with almost boyish embarrassment.

I grinned. I no longer felt the need to take him to task. "You did, but just a little."

His face flushed for a moment. "I'm thoroughly mortified, Lucy. I think it was those old fashioneds the bartender was serving me. I usually can handle my bourbon, so I don't know what happened."

"What happened was that they were Napoli old fashioneds," I told him, rocking up on my toes in amusement. "They were spiked with *arancello*—Italian blood orange liqueur. Two doses of high-octane booze in one tasty drink."

"Good grief," Uncle Dave said. "No wonder I felt like I'd been hit by a tractor this morning. I'm only now starting to feel somewhat human again, and that's only because Pippa took me to this fantastic little taqueria for some lunch."

I grinned. "Big Flaco's Tacos?"

"Yeah," Uncle Dave said, his smile growing. "You know it? Big, scary-looking guy runs the place. There's a huge velvet portrait of him on the wall, looking like Elvis in *Blue Hawaii*, only holding a cast-iron pan instead of a ukulele."

"That's Flaco," I said with a laugh. "And that place is practically my second home."

"I can see why," he said. "Fantastic food. Pippa told me that something called menudo is a good cure for a hangover. It looked like it had some funny stuff in it, but I ate it and felt a ton better. Had a couple of tacos, too, once I felt the clanging in my head subside. I may have to go there a few more times while I'm in town."

I grinned, decided not to tell him he'd consumed the lining from a cow's stomach in a spicy broth, and excused myself, telling him I had to go set up to interview his cousin Ginny.

"She's got some stories, that one," he said cheerfully. "Ask her about the time she convinced our grandfather to let her drive his brand-new Cadillac. It's one for the books, no doubt."

I promised I would, and wended my way around another group of family members, sending a wink to Claire and Marilyn, who started giggling again, and breezed by Mrs. P. at the front desk. She gave my bag full of books a curious look, but waved me on with a smile as I said, "I'm on a mission—have to get set up for my interview." I was two steps into the hall, my head still turned toward the front desk, when I crashed into someone coming the other way.

My bag of books toppled, and three paperback copies of *The Thirty-Nine Steps* crashed to the floor with a fluttery *fwump*.

"Oh, I'm so sorry," came a feminine voice with a hint of a Hispanic accent. "Let me help you."

As I fumbled to keep the other books from falling, I saw a petite woman about my height bend to pick up the two nearest books. She was wearing chef's whites, with her hair covered by a baseball cap. She held a bunch of greenery in one hand, along with a pair of garden shears, and I once again breathed in the delicious mixture of mint mixed with a hint of chocolate.

"Is everything okay, Lucy?" Mrs. P.'s voice came from behind me. Then she started chuckling, stooping to pick up the third book. "We can't leave you alone for five seconds put together without you getting into some kind of trouble, can we?"

I grinned. "You may be right, Mrs. P." I addressed the chef, thanking her for picking up my books, and asking, "Are you all right? I hope I didn't hurt you with my bag of books. I'm Lucy, by the way—the genealogist. I don't think we've met."

"No, no, I'm fine," she said, adding the two books back into my paper tote. "I'm Ysenia, the sous chef."

Mrs. P. was looking down at the book in her hand, then at the same titles in Ysenia's hand. "What are all these for, Lucy?"

"For my grandfather," I said, thinking fast and trying not to blush. "He's always loved *The Thirty-Nine Steps* and collects various editions of it."

"Miss Pippa told me he was in the hospital after some sort of accident," Mrs. P. said, searching my face. "I'm so sorry, my dear." She perched the book on top of the others. "Is this something to make him feel better?"

"Thanks, Mrs. P.," I said. "He's doing okay, yes, thank goodness, but I'm hoping the books will help perk him up."

A booming voice from the foyer that I recognized as Great-Aunt Tilly's called out, "Mrs. P.?" I heard rather than saw Mrs. P. hurry back to her post at the front desk. I used my chin to gesture toward the bunch of herbs in Ysenia's hand. "Is that for the famous chocolate mint–chocolate chunk gelato I've been hearing about?"

She flashed me a smile. "It is. I just cut some from the knot garden. Since it hasn't been too cold this winter, it's still growing." She paused, then said, "It was Chef Rocky's special recipe, actually. He grew mint himself and experimented for a good year with the recipe at home before he started making it at the Sutton Grand, where we both used to work before coming here." She paused again, and there was a sheen of tears in her brown eyes. "It got to be that he smelled like chocolate mint so much that we called it his signature scent."

"That's a lovely memory," I said. "I think he'd like being remembered that way."

She sniffled, but managed another smile. "Yeah, Chef Rocky would test his batches on anyone who was willing. There was this one older guy who was living at the Grand at the time, and I think he tried every last batch of it."

She glanced over my shoulder, then leaned toward me, lowering her voice. "In fact, we all thought the guy had a thing for Mrs. P. because he was always inviting her to have gelato with him when she went off duty." Her voice went to a whisper and she added, "I think she liked him, too, because she almost always accepted."

"You don't say," I said with a conspiratorial grin.

Ysenia nodded. "They'd sit at this little corner table near the kitchen doors and talk about history. It was really cute."

My smile went bigger. I could totally see Mrs. P. doing that.

Ysenia glanced over my shoulder, then leaned in again, whispering, "And I hear that eventually it led to drinks and more. Chef Rocky actually saw them out on a date one night."

"That's so sweet," I whispered back. "Are they still seeing each other?" In the weeks I'd been in and out of the Hotel Sutton, I'd had many a conversation with Mrs. P., and she'd never mentioned a boyfriend. Not that I'd ever asked, I realized.

Ysenia shrugged. "She moved over here to help with the hotel's opening and Mr. H.—that's what we called him—came to the dining room less and less. Then Chef Rocky and I moved over here, so . . ." She shrugged again. Sometimes you lost touch; that was the way the cookie crumbled.

"And you've never asked her?" I said, nodding back toward the front desk.

Her eyes widened and she shook her head. "You don't ask the Force of the Front Desk personal questions. She doesn't like it."

Huh. Mrs. P. had always seemed so open to me—but then again, I wasn't a member of the hotel staff with whom she had to work every day. I could understand her not wanting to overshare.

"Anyway," Ysenia said, holding up the chocolate mint. "In honor of Chef Rocky, you'll get some of his chocolate mint–chocolate chunk gelato tonight, plus about ten other of his favorite dishes, so bring your appetite."

I told her I couldn't wait, and the sous chef and I went our separate ways. When I reached the stairs and made it up the first step, however, I realized I'd been feeling a prickle between my shoulder blades the whole time. It was that same feeling I'd had the other night in the back parlor, when I thought someone had been watching me.

My arms still full of books that were getting heavier by the second, I silently moved backward down to the hallway again, turning my head first toward the French doors, then back toward the front desk area. Mrs. P. and all the Suttons were in the front room, but no one looked like they'd been watching me. Then, from under the portrait of Sarah Bess, Roselyn turned and met my eyes. Her expression was icy cold, leaving me with the distinct impression she'd send me packing this instant if she could.

In contrast, my eyes shifted to a tall woman about the same age as Roselyn, who was approaching me with a warm smile. It was Ginny, Pippa's first cousin, once removed.

"I'm so excited for my interview, Lucy," she said, clapping her hands together.

I smiled, telling her I was as well, and we could start as soon as I had my equipment set up. "I'll be down in ten minutes," I assured her. With that, I hoofed it upstairs with my books and made for my room.

THIRTY-FIVE

I packed up my equipment as soon as I finished interviewing Ginny, who was indeed a firecracker who kept me enthralled with stories for the whole ninety-minute interview.

The dark-haired beauty had me laughing so hard at one point, I had to stop the recording for fear I wouldn't be able to successfully edit out my laughs. Especially when she told the story Uncle Dave had mentioned, how she'd driven her grandfather James's "brand-spanking-new" Cadillac all the way to the Mexican border in the early 1980s, picking up her cousins Bracewell and Dave along the way, just to have dinner at the famed, though now defunct, Mrs. Crosby's restaurant in Acuña, Mexico.

She said, "We made it back to Austin at six the next morning and drove back into the garage—me wearing only my undies and a serape, Bracewell in a big, black sombrero, no shirt, and a pair of castanets on each hand, and Dave in nothing but his boxers after losing his Levi's and his Ralph Lauren polo shirt in a strip poker game with two of the barmaids.

"So I pull in and Gramps is standing there with his hands on his hips, looking like he was about to kick our rumps into next Tuesday, but only after tanning our hides shiny first. Then he comes over, opens my door, and holds out his hand for the keys. When I gave them to him—my hands shaking from a combination of fear and the tequila DTs, of course—he leans over, stares each of us down like a vulture deciding whose eyes to peck out first, and says if we ever did that again and didn't invite him along with us, we could consider ourselves out of the will."

She'd winked at the camera and said, "That was when I realized I'd come by my crazy streak honestly." Then she'd looked up toward the heavens and said with a huge grin, "Thanks a million, Gramps."

Despite the other things on my mind, I couldn't wait to go through and edit Ginny's and Catherine's stories into the video. They'd added another layer of color and insight into Pippa's family that you couldn't get with documents and photos.

Pippa was going to be ecstatic with the final video, I thought, as I left through the hotel's back doors to head to the hospital. I didn't want to run into any Sutton family members and miss the chance to catch Grandpa awake.

I was rolling slowly out of the parking lot, digging in my tote for more lip balm and a mint, when a red Tesla Model S passed by, Roselyn at the wheel. She was talking emphatically and gesturing wildly, but no one else was in the car. It was clearly a phone call, and whoever she was talking to was stressing her out.

I was just about to follow her when I saw Pippa and Boomer walking the opposite way, coming in from an afternoon walk. I watched as she tried to flag her mother down, but Roselyn just kept going.

"Mom!" Pippa yelled after her mother, but Roselyn didn't stop. I pulled up alongside Pippa even as Roselyn made the light at Cesar Chavez and turned, heading east.

"Something's not right, Lucy," Pippa said, echoing my own thoughts as I rolled down the window.

"Get in," I said.

She opened the back door and Boomer happily hopped in and flopped down on my back seat, panting lightly. His human was in the passenger seat in seconds, and I tore off after the Tesla.

"Are you sure she doesn't just have an appointment with the caterer for the New Year's Eve gala or something?" I asked.

"No, she's totally free this afternoon," Pippa said, then held out a calming hand. "But slow down. Don't let her see you following her."

Traffic was light on East Cesar Chavez, so we could see her accelerating, the Tesla smoothly zooming forward.

"Why?" I asked, ready to gun it through the light, but I braked to a stop instead. "We'll lose her and won't know where she's going."

Pippa was sliding her phone from the pocket of her running vest. "Oh, we'll know where she goes. I put a tracking app on her phone last night without telling her."

I briefly lifted up my sunglasses so she could see me goggling at her.

"Mom was kept at the police station longer than me," Pippa explained, tapping an app within her phone, "and they didn't allow her to have her phone or other devices. She'd given her phone, iPad, and smartwatch to our lawyer's second in command, but then that dude was asked to run back to the office, so he handed all Mom's devices to me."

She turned her phone so I could see a little blue dot crossing over Guadalupe Street.

"Since I already know her passcode, I downloaded the app while I waited for her, then verified permission to track her and erased any messages the system sent to her other devices to let her know what I did."

Pippa looked sideways at me with a stealthy half smile. "She's got at least four pages of apps, and I hid it on the page she hardly ever uses."

I held out my hand, eyes still on the road. "High-five, sister."

She gave me an enthusiastic high-five, but added, "Now all I've got to worry about is what she's doing that's causing her to freak out like this."

"We'll figure it out," I said.

Pippa's voice quavered. "Mom's scaring me, Lucy. I've been trying to follow her for the past two weeks, but she always manages to leave when a client is scheduled to come in, which forces me to stay at the hotel. I asked Chef Rocky about it once, thinking like you did earlier, that they were having troubles. He said I shouldn't worry. He said he was taking care of things and everything should be all right, but he didn't explain what that meant."

She pushed a loose tendril behind her ear. "I kept meaning to check back in with him about it, but we had the New Year's Eve gala to plan, all the family was coming in, and"—she gestured to me—"you've been finishing up the project I hired you to do, and doing everything brilliantly, I might add. But basically, other things kept getting in the way of talking to Chef Rocky again." Her voice choked up. "And suddenly, I had no more chances."

I gave her a sympathetic glance. Before she let herself go teary, though, she straightened her shoulders, gave her head a little shake, and checked her tracking app for Roselyn's progress.

"She's coming to Congress Avenue . . . nope, she didn't turn. She's still on Cesar Chavez."

There was something about Pippa's calm, though, that had me thinking she knew more than she was letting on. .

"Pippa," I began as we made the light at Guadalupe Street and cruised toward Congress Avenue. "I have a feeling that you know in your heart what's going on with your mom already—or you have a pretty good idea—but you're just not saying it out loud." I glanced at her, but when I didn't see any signs of anger, I said, "Look, I was recently reminded that a problem shared is a problem halved, and so just know I'm here if you need to hand over a half to someone else."

Pippa nodded, but kept watching her mother's progress in silence. Then, just when I thought she was shutting me out, she spoke.

"I think she's gotten in with some bad people."

"Okay," I said when she went silent again. "Bad in what way?"

"I don't know, because I don't know who they are. But I went through her phone last night." This time she flashed me a guilty look. "I was desperate."

I was already slowing for the light at Congress Avenue. "Hey," I said, holding her gaze and sounding like a stern older sister. "I am *not* judging you. You've given your mom ages to come to you and come clean about what she's been up to. She may be doing something that affects the hotels, for Pete's sake. You're only doing what you have to do and I know that."

"Thanks, Lucy," she said, "but I didn't find out much. I didn't see any weird emails or text messages. The only thing I noticed was she'd gotten a bunch of phone calls from a guy named Brent Embry recently, but there weren't any voice mails or texts from his number. Only calls."

"Did you google or call the number?" I asked.

She shook her head. "I spent too much time looking around her devices last night and I either haven't had the time or the guts to call it so far." She pushed another loose tendril of blond hair back behind her ear. "I think I've been too scared to as well."

I could understand that. "Did you check her texts and voice mails from Chef Rocky?"

"I did," she said. "There were a couple of texts that alluded to something going on, but nothing specific. One text said, 'I screwed up,' and he replied, 'Again? You're going down a big hole, Rose.'" Pippa sniffed. "He always called her Rose or Rosie. I always thought it was sweet. Regardless, I'm worried she may be addicted to something, and she can't kick the habit."

My mind immediately went back to the Hotel Sutton ballroom, where Roselyn came up on Grandpa discussing addiction and looked like she was about to explode. I wondered if Roselyn thought she'd been found out and we were discussing her.

Before I could reply to any of this, however, Pippa pointed ahead and said, "She's turning right on Red River."

I knew Red River dead-ended quickly in that direction, becoming the gateway to Rainey Street, a formerly residential street that had been transformed in the early 2000s to a hotbed of food trucks and hip, eclectic bars and restaurants, mostly housed in the street's renovated bungalows.

"Maybe she's heading to Rainey Street?" I said.

"I think you're right," Pippa said, her eyes fixed on the moving dot on her screen. "She just pulled into that pay-to-park lot at the corner of Red River and Cesar Chavez."

"I'll do the same, then," I said.

I navigated through three more lights to Red River and pulled into the parking lot. Pippa clipped her lead to Boomer's collar and used her credit card to pay for the parking meter. I grabbed my tote and we started walking across the crushed-limestone parking lot.

"She's at the Boarhound," Pippa said, looking at her phone. She screwed up her face. "Is that new? I haven't heard of it. But then again, I haven't had time to date or even go out with my friends in ages, so I'm way out of the loop."

"It's been around a couple of months now," I said, buttoning up my coat as we walked, Boomer trotting happily at Pippa's side. "It's dark and pubby-feeling, with a couple of bigger rooms and some smaller ones. Jazz music, mismatched furniture, lots of craft cocktails, that sort of thing."

We crossed over one small side street, and it was immediately like entering another world, going from residential normality to a street full of vibrant bars and restaurants, its sidewalks teeming with people. And because this was Austin, Boomer was hardly the only dog on Rainey Street. He was, however, one of the best behaved, proving Mrs. P. wrong that he hadn't learned anything in all his weeks of training.

Rainey Street was technically only one block long, and the Boarhound was on the east side of the street, abutting an area left open for food trucks to park. We set off, and I realized we hadn't formulated any plan for when we actually saw Roselyn. However, there was something I needed to ask first.

"Pippa," I said. "What kind of addiction do you think your mom has?"

"I don't know," she said. "She hurt her back last year, so I've been wondering if it's prescription painkillers, but I've never seen any in her house or in her purse. So, to answer your question, I really have no clue."

"Okay," I said as we neared the Boarhound. "Then the only thing I have left to ask is this." I gestured to the pub, which was up ahead and housed in a bungalow painted the color of blackberries with white trim. "Whatever we find in there, no matter how bad and embarrassing or scary, are you willing to help her deal with it and get help? Because if not, I'll go in there alone and talk to her. One of my cousins is an addiction counselor. I can call her for recommendations once we know what's going on."

Pippa looked me in the eyes. "I'll do whatever it takes to help my mom, Lucy. I'll pay whatever, do whatever—it doesn't matter. I'll keep helping her no matter what."

I nodded with satisfaction. I knew that Roselyn had to want to get help before Pippa could do anything else, but we didn't have time to discuss that now. I smiled bravely and she gave me a wobbly smile back.

"Let's go," I said.

THIRTY-SIX

It was Pippa who stopped. "Wait, we don't even have a plan. What are we going to do? Just rush in, interrupt whatever conversation she's having, and haul her out of there?"

I opened my mouth, then closed it. Finally, I said, "Why don't we try to go in and see if we can hear their conversation first? Then we can make rushing over, interrupting, and hauling out our plan B."

Pippa looked down at Boomer, who was watching us with his ears perked, like he knew something was up. She bit her lip, leaning sideways to stroke his forehead. "I'm worried he might give us away."

"He's a little obvious," I agreed. "Okay, how about I go in first and scope the place out? I'll find out where they're sitting and see if we can get close enough to them to listen. Because if not, we may very well have to go to plan B."

Then I gestured up and down at her with a grin. "And since you're the spitting image of your mom and a sporty blond goddess, I think you'd be noticed if you went to do the scoping."

Pippa blushed, but nodded. "Okay, good plan."

I dug into my roomy tote and came up with a slouchy, newsboy-style knit hat and the glasses I wore to drive at night. As usual, a hair tie was already around my wrist. I wrapped my long hair into a low knot, put the newsboy cap on, and added my glasses. "What do you think?"

Pippa nodded. "It's good. Mom will have to look hard to recognize you."

"Excellent," I said. I looked at the time. "Give me at least five minutes. And text me before you try to come in." I turned to leave, then spun back around. "And don't go near the pub while I'm scouting. They might be sitting by a window."

Pippa suddenly grinned. "You know, sometimes I think you're actually a Jason Bourne–style operative masquerading as a mild-mannered genealogist."

"Honey," I drawled. "I might be nice, but I was never mild-mannered."

She laughed. "Truer words were never spoken."

I flashed her a toothy grin. "All right, I'm going in."

I walked with purpose to the front lawn of the Boarhound, where stood two picnic tables with patrons enjoying their drinks in the late afternoon sunshine. I trotted up the steps to the porch, past a guy in sunglasses and a baseball cap leaning casually against a pillar with a beer in his hand, and sailed through the open doorway. I felt like the guy might have done a double-take, but beyond noticing he had one heck of a great physique, I didn't recognize him, so I didn't care.

Luckily, I'd been in the Boarhound before, so I was familiar with the layout: three rooms to my right, two to my left. On both sides, the bigger, more communal rooms were the first ones I passed.

I'd also been thinking about where Roselyn could be having a private conversation with someone shady—if, in fact, that was what she was doing—and knew it would have to be in one of the three smaller rooms. The other two held too many people, so they were likely out. And if I had to bet on which of the three smaller rooms it would be, I would choose . . .

As a waitress strode past me toward the bar and two guys ambled toward the exit, I made for the room that had probably been the house's study. I'd just craned my head around the open doorway and seen three people in deep conversation—Roselyn, a well-dressed older man, and a third person I was trying to make out—when someone grabbed me by the arm, spinning me around.

"Lolo, *querida*!" he exclaimed. He wrapped me in a big bear hug that pinned my arms to my sides, picked me up, and spun me around twice as he said in English heavily accented with Spanish, "I found you! You rush right past me, *cariña*. Come, I take you to our table."

The pub was so small, he'd danced me back to the front door before I'd even had a chance to struggle. I looked in complete shock at his face, which was grinning charmingly at me, though his eyes were obscured by his sunglasses. The weird thing was, there was something familiar about that grin.

He let me down out on the porch just as fury raced through my bloodstream. "I'm not Lolo," I snapped, jerking my fallen tote bag back up on my shoulder. I felt like I'd been accosted and I wanted to lash out with some of my newfound self-defense moves. "And how dare you," I began, raising up my bootie-clad foot. I was going to smash his instep, and he would *not* like it.

The guy seemed to know what I was about to do and backed up a step, while leaning down at the same time to speak in an undertone laced with anger.

"You're poking your nose into something dangerous, Lucy.

So for once in your life, do as you're told and get out of here. Now. And take Ms. Sutton with you."

Then he brushed past me and went back inside.

All traces of an accent had gone when he spoke, and I must have looked like a weird, tote-bag-hugging version of the Karate Kid with my foot raised up and at the ready.

My gritted teeth dropped into a gape. I knew that voice. The hair was longer and darker, the physique was slimmer and more muscular, the jawline tighter. But I knew that voice, and that charming smile. They belonged to a ghoster. They belonged to Ben.

I turned and was down the porch steps and on the sidewalk before I could process what had happened. My heart was pounding and I knew my cheeks were flushed.

"We need to go," I said to Pippa, pulling off my knit cap and glasses. "Follow me and I'll explain."

I must have looked like I could chew through nails, because she turned around with Boomer and followed me in silence.

I was still steaming as we reached my car, but between taking Ben's name in vain a couple of times for preventing me from spying on Roselyn, telling me off, and ordering me out of the pub, I'd managed to give Pippa the facts of my botched mission.

"He's an FBI agent, this Ben guy?" Pippa asked for the second time. "Are you serious?"

"I'm serious," I said. "He's the one I told you about."

"Wait, he's *your* Ben?"

"Hardly," I said, feeling my heart give a twist despite my anger.

"But what could Mom be doing that involves the FBI? Does she know? Is Ben looking to trap her and put her in jail?"

I couldn't answer any of those questions and, needless to say, Pippa and I were both frustrated and angry when I drove out of the parking lot. In my state, I punched the accelerator and we flew up Cesar Chavez, somehow making most of the lights, neither of us saying anything as the heavy feeling of unanswered questions and worry filled the car like some noxious gas.

Even Boomer seemed to notice it. When I glanced back in the rearview mirror, I saw he had his head on his paws, but his brown eyes were worriedly shifting back and forth between Pippa and me.

The look on his sweet face made me embarrassed to be acting so childishly and ashamed for being angry at Ben, especially now that I was finally admitting to myself he was just doing his job, whatever it was. It had to be something undercover, from his continued Han Solo look.

And his brusqueness? My cheeks heated. Ben was protecting me, again, and had risked putting his undercover work in danger for me.

Now the only question was whether the FBI was setting Roselyn up for something, or if she was somehow merely in over her head and would be caught up in the arrests when Ben and his team made their bust.

Glancing at Pippa, I saw that she was wiping a tear from her cheek. I pulled my foot off the accelerator, letting my car slow on its own as we approached our turn. My blinker on, I pressed the brake, then made a left onto Delta Drive.

"Whoa," Pippa said, even as Boomer's collar tags jingled when he slid on the back seat.

"Oops," I said. "Sorry about that. Didn't slow enough." I pressed the brake pedal, but my car didn't respond like it should. I pumped the brake again, twice, and felt the mushiness give way to nothingness.

Frantically, I slammed my foot on the brake one more time and felt the sudden horrible, stomach-clenching thrill of being out of control as the brake and my foot went all the way to the floor.

"Lucy, what's wrong?" Pippa said.

"My brakes," I said, trying to remain calm. "They're not working."

"Oh God," Pippa said. Then she swiveled around to look at Boomer. "We have seatbelts, but he doesn't."

"It's going to be all right," I said, even though I was hardly sure of it. "We're only going twenty and we're off the main road."

"Downshift to a lower gear," Pippa urged as we continued to roll onward down the road.

"Good thinking," I said, grasping the gear shift and shoving it down to low. My car slowed further to eighteen, then seventeen miles per hour. Better, but not enough.

"I'm going to push on the parking brake," I said. "I don't know how hard the car will jerk, so brace yourself. And while you're at it, look for somewhere good for us to crash, if we need to."

"I don't like the thought of 'a good place to crash,'" Pippa said, but pointed up ahead, saying, "There, aim there."

She was pointing to the line of tall, conical juniper trees stretching from the road all the way down to Lady Bird Lake Trail.

I nodded. We'd slowed down to twelve miles an hour. Pippa shot a worried glance back at Boomer and then pushed herself back in her seat. "Hold on, buddy," she said to him as I used my left foot to step on the small parking-brake pedal, pushing it in until I heard the rapid metallic clicks.

My car lurched, then slowed even more. Eight miles an hour, then six. I aimed us toward the junipers. We were drifting at four miles an hour when my car hit between two fluffy trees in a *whoosh* of scraping sounds, finally coming to a halt with a still-sickening jolt. We heard Boomer slide forward in a heap, but when I glanced back, he was standing, uninjured, between the back and front seats. I turned off my car and Pippa reached one hand out to me and the other back to her dog. We sat for a few seconds in silence, breathing heavily.

"You know, my great-grandfather planted the original set of junipers," Pippa said. "He liked the way they looked soft, but were still very imposing and sturdy." She gave a shaky laugh. "Glad to know he was right."

My mind whirled. Above us, a small flock of birds was flying toward the water. I saw Grandpa's face, heard him whisper, "Greenfinch." I looked at the juniper bushes we'd crashed into and thought of James Sutton, Pippa's great-grandfather. One man was OSS, the other was SOE.

I couldn't believe I hadn't made the connection yet. Was it possible? Could Pippa—the great-granddaughter of an SOE agent—be one of the still coded names on Hugo's list? Could Pippa and I *both* be on the list?

"I'll call up to the hotel for help and get Mrs. P. to call a tow truck," Pippa said, releasing my hand. I clamped down on her fingers.

"Wait." I shifted in my seat. "Would you be okay with not telling anyone that my brakes went out? At least, not yet? Can we just tell them I swerved to keep from hitting a squirrel or something?"

Pippa's brows knitted. "Okay . . . but why?"

She was strong, intelligent, and I trusted her implicitly, but I didn't want to scare her quite yet. Then the faces of Hugo Markman, Chef Rocky, and Penelope Ohlinger swam before me, and I was again harshly reminded of my duty to them, and to Grandpa. I hoped like crazy that Sean was making some headway with the information I'd sent him.

"Because I just don't want the fuss," I said finally. "You, your mom, and the staff are all still mourning Chef Rocky, and I don't want to add to anyone's stress. Plus, I haven't had my car checked in ages. It's possible the brakes were just worn down or something."

This wasn't true, of course. I kept my car regularly serviced, but it was the best stall for time I could think of at the moment.

"I'll have Frank look everything over," I assured her. "Frank's my service guy. We can tell people as soon as I know for sure."

After a few seconds, she nodded. "All right. I'll get Mrs. P. to call for a tow and we'll go with the squirrel story for now."

She called to the front desk, but got the bellboy, who said Mrs. P. was on the other line assisting one of the guests. After Pippa assured him that we were perfectly all right, he said he'd call the tow truck immediately. We then assessed our ability to get out of the car, seeing as we were surrounded by junipers. "We're crawling out the back, then," I said, popping the trunk of my SUV. Boomer leapt out, tail wagging. Pippa and I hopped down with less joy.

"Well, it's been one hell of a day," she said. "And we still have dinner with my family in"—she checked her watch—"oh, about an hour. If you're still up for it, that is."

"Of course," I said, with more enthusiasm than I felt.

Practically on cue, the sky changed hues from a pale blue to a dusky purple. The fairy lights at the hotel would be popping on at any minute.

"Pippa," I said as we sat on my tailgate. "May I ask a very weird question?"

Her look was amused. "With all the weirdness you've been

witness to in the last couple of days, I don't think you could shock me, Lucy."

"True," I said. "Um, okay, how should I put this? Have you had anything strange happen to you recently?"

She cocked her head to one side. "Strange—as in alien-abduction strange? Or strange as in my ex-boyfriend calling me out of the blue and trying to get back together with me strange? The former has never happened, and the latter did about a week ago. I told him thanks, but no thanks."

I grinned. "Somewhere in between." I gestured to my car. "Something like this kind of strange. Where you might have been hurt under the right circumstances. Or something completely different, but still odd. Like having someone be unduly interested in you, asking questions about you and your family for no apparent reason."

Pippa was looking at me like I was strange now. "Not that I can think of," she said. "Why?"

Headlights flashed, and we saw a tow truck rumbling our way. At the same time, we heard our names being called. It was Mrs. P., rushing toward us.

"I'll tell you later," I said. "Why don't you head Mrs. P. off at the pass and go inside while I get my car situated?"

Pippa jumped up and called Boomer to her side. I heard her repeating the squirrel story to a concerned Mrs. P. as the tow truck driver backed the truck up to my car.

THIRTY-SEVEN

❧

Yeah, I know Frank's Repair Shop," the tow truck driver said as he handed me paperwork to sign. "I'll take it there right now and have him give you a call." Then he touched the brim of his cap and drove off, hauling my scraped-up car.

A small wave of unsteadiness washed over me as I walked to the hotel in the rapidly darkening evening. I recognized the combination of low blood sugar and fading adrenaline. Digging in my tote once more, I came up with a peppermint and popped it into my mouth. I had so much to think about, not to mention three lines of code to break and a Sutton-family dinner to attend. First, however, I needed to check on Grandpa.

Nurse Angelique assured me he was doing better, had eaten well, and was sleeping again, and the relief made me feel better. "Shall I tell him you'll visit first thing in the morning?" she asked.

"First thing, absolutely," I said.

I was almost upon the sign for the Hotel Sutton, which had been decorated for the holidays with lots of garland and shiny ornaments. I thought about Roselyn, how she'd glared at me earlier, and how Pippa thought she might be in with some bad people. I wondered if, just maybe, Roselyn was so scared of having her secret discovered by me that she would try to kill me—or get someone else to do it for her.

Somehow, it didn't seem right. I couldn't pinpoint why, but it just didn't.

When I made it through the hotel's front doors, Mrs. P. was once again helping out the Nguyen-Sobnoskis. When she glanced up at me, I pointed to myself, flashed a thumbs-up, and smiled. She nodded, though still looked concerned even as she put her focus back on her guests.

A half hour later, I found myself seated next to Uncle Dave at dinner. He held up his wineglass. "No Napoli old fashioneds for me tonight, no way. Sticking to good ol' wine."

He was looking abashed again, so I clinked my wineglass to his. "To a delicious meal, good wine, and wonderful friends and family," I said. Pippa, who was on my other side at the head of the table, seconded our toast as a team of waiters put our first course in front of us, a teaser of Chef Rocky's famous hand-made butternut squash gnocchi with sage butter sauce.

Uncle Dave attacked his with gusto, and I leaned in toward Pippa. "Speaking of butternut squash, any word from Detective Dupart about a certain kitchen staffer?"

She shook her head, then stopped when Mrs. P. came up to her shoulder and whispered in her ear.

"Oh, of course," Pippa said, clapping one hand to her cheek. "I'm so sorry, Mrs. P. I brought Mr. Naveed's check, but I must have left it in the kitchen when I was checking in with Chef Cardo. Hang on and I'll go get it." She was up and striding away through the kitchen doors before anyone could even ask what was going on.

"Mr. Naveed is doing the flowers for our New Year's Eve party," Mrs. P. explained, casting a smile around the table. Her expression cooled into barely concealed dislike when she got to Uncle Dave, who was unfolding his napkin and putting it in his lap. I could almost see his hackles rise when he caught the look on Mrs. P.'s face.

Taking up his wineglass, he drawled, "So, Mrs. Pollingham, how is that boyfriend of yours? Has he shown up here for any gelato lately?" He brought the glass to his lips, not quite hiding his smirk.

I turned to see the pink spots in Mrs. P.'s cheeks deepening into a flush.

Aunt Melinda said, "Why, Mrs. P., I didn't know you were seeing someone. How wonderful!" She clapped her hands together. "What's his name? How did you meet him?"

Mrs. P. opened her mouth, but Uncle Dave answered for her.

"He's some accountant staying at the Sutton Grand for work. He moved in while I was working there. Took one look at our Mrs. P. here and I thought I was going to have to attach his jaw to my fishing reel and crank it back up into place." He mimed reeling something in and guffawed. His relatives grinned, giving Uncle Dave the encouragement to continue.

"They were the toast of the hotel for the rest of the time I was there, ol' Mr. H. and Mrs. P. He was always asking her to go have gelato with him. They'd sit close together, talking history and their grandparents who'd lived through the war." He sent her an exaggerated wink, the tail end of which he slid my way. "And on more than one night, I saw her sending a whiskey up to his room as a nightcap. The good stuff, too, not a blend." He clapped one hand to his heart. "Oh, the signs of true love."

Mrs. P.'s blue eyes were now bright with frustrated anger, but no one seemed to notice. I could tell the rest of the table was genuinely happy for her. It was only Uncle Dave who was doing his best to needle her. Luckily, Pippa came back at that moment with an envelope.

"Here you go, Mrs. P. Please tell Mr. Naveed thank you for coming to pick up his check tonight."

Mrs. P. took the envelope, giving the table a stiff but courteous nod of her head. "Enjoy your evening, everyone."

"David," Aunt Tilly admonished when Mrs. P. had gone. "You shouldn't have teased her like that in front of everyone. She's a woman of a certain age, and probably didn't want to talk about her love life."

"What's this?" Pippa asked, sitting down again. "What happened with Mrs. P.?"

Uncle Dave had swallowed another mouthful of wine and said, "Oh, it was no big deal. I was just asking Mrs. Pollingham about her boyfriend, that's all, and she got offended. Like she always does when I ask her anything."

"Oh, Uncle Dave, you didn't," Pippa said, despair coloring her voice.

He gestured with his wineglass, becoming defensive. "I mean, who cares if we know? I was trying to be nice. They made a cute couple."

Pippa pulled her lips in for a moment, as if trying to keep them from cutting her cousin down to size. A waiter came around to refresh everyone's wineglasses, and she held hers out, looking like she needed it.

I drank, too, but I was feeling queasy. The man both Uncle Dave and Ysenia had referred to as "Mr. H." wasn't just a hotel guest, but an accountant who was staying in Austin for work purposes. Could he have been Hugo?

When Pippa was discussing the New Year's Eve gala with her cousin Ginny, I turned to Uncle Dave and said with as casual a tone as I could, "It is kind of cute—Mr. H. and Mrs. P., both going by the initials of their surnames. What did the 'H' stand for?"

Uncle Dave was happy to oblige. "Actually, it was his first name, but I can't remember exactly what it stood for. Hubert or Hugh, something like that." He speared his last gnocchi and popped it into his mouth. "Can't say I ever knew his last name."

I made myself ask the words. "Would Pippa?"

"Doubt it," Uncle Dave said. "She was always over here, supervising the renovations. Roselyn would, though. She and I used to rib Mrs. P. about him and their gelato dates all the time. That woman is so damn easy to rile up."

I realized I'd been holding my breath, and I sipped more wine to cover up my shock. Mr. H. had to be Hugo Markman. But if he had indeed been Mrs. P.'s boyfriend, how come she had acted like she didn't know him? And for that matter, how come Roselyn had acted like she'd never seen him before, either?

I thought back to the night Hugo had died. Roselyn had stared at his body, horrified, but she'd never actually said she'd never seen him before, had she?

Something was fishy, and I was growing more and more anxious to know what it was. I remembered how Roselyn had stared at Hugo, clutching her pearls as he lay on the ground. And how Mrs. P. had sought to calm her and had removed her from the scene quickly. Did Hugo have something to do with whatever was going on with Roselyn, and was Mrs. P. shielding her? Was that why Mrs. P. had acted like Hugo was a stranger to her?

Then I remembered Hugo Markman wasn't just any accountant—he was a forensic accountant, skilled in locating accounting fraud within companies.

I glanced at Pippa, anxiousness mounting in me. She was

the sole owner of Sutton Inc., and highly educated. Yet at only twenty-four years old, she was still a young and relatively inexperienced business owner.

A potential theory took shape. I thought I might know what was going on with Roselyn and her mysterious absences, and I needed to find out if I was right.

I was about to excuse myself to go in search of Roselyn when the table seemed to remember I was there, and that I was a professional genealogist. Aunt Tilly started off by asking me how long it took me to trace the Sutton family line, and from there, the questions snowballed.

Course after course of delicious food was served, all an homage to Chef Rocky's talents and tastes, but it was I who'd become the center of attention. Pippa's cousins were genuinely interested in their family history and how I'd worked to flesh it out. Even Uncle Dave switched to sparkling water and asked me some interesting questions, none of which had anything to do with the cost of any Sutton family heirlooms.

Before I knew it, Chef Rocky's signature chocolate mint–chocolate chunk gelato was being served along with fresh coffee. It was utterly scrumptious, and we all sent up a toast to Chef Rocky. A half hour later, it was nearly ten o'clock, and the dinner was finally breaking up.

By this time, the past twenty-four hours had come down hard on me. I practically drooped in my chair with tiredness and stress, my jaw hurt from smiling and talking so much, and a tightness had spread up my shoulders and neck that was not helping the dull headache I'd been feeling since the fourth course was served. I looked over to see Pippa drooping as well, one hand massaging the back of her neck.

She leaned in and whispered, "Despite our slow crash, I think I have a bit of whiplash."

"I do, too," I said, realizing the tightness in my neck and shoulders was just that. "I'm so tired I can't even see straight," I added, and tried to ignore the stab of guilt and worry that came with saying the words. There was no way I'd have the brain-power to delve into multiple copies of *The Thirty-Nine Steps* to find the remaining key texts for the last three names on Hugo's list. However, I was clear-headed enough to realize I could use some help when I did.

"Pippa," I said as we walked out of Eighteen Ninety-Five and made our way to the front foyer. "Would you have time to help me with something tomorrow?"

"Of course," she said, then added with a laugh, "but as long as it's tomorrow. I'm absolutely beat."

I told her I'd be visiting Grandpa in the morning and would bring my project over to her cottage after that. Then I gave her a hug good night. Boomer, who'd been sleeping in the front par-lor, jumped up when he heard his human. I was grateful that he would be with her as she went back to her cottage.

Mrs. P.'s little *Please Ring Bell for Service* sign was up, though any requests at this hour would no doubt be handled by Terrence. Despite my tiredness, I would have liked to ask Mrs. P. a few questions. I was just thinking my talk with Roselyn and Mrs. P. would have to wait until tomorrow when I heard the French doors at the back of the hotel open. I looked around the front desk and saw Roselyn. We both froze.

THIRTY-EIGHT

oselyn," I said, striding toward her. "You and I need to talk."

She'd stopped level with the back staircase, glancing up at it like she might use the stairs as an escape route. In an instant, her desire to get away from me made all my tiredness and aches disappear.

As I neared her, I saw redness rimming her eyes. Her face, a slightly haughtier version of her daughter's that weirdly made her slightly more beautiful, was set like stone.

"I'm very tired, Lucy," she said. "It's been a long day. Could I schedule some time with you tomorrow?"

I gestured toward the little sitting room. "I'm afraid not, Roselyn, and I think I could pit my long day against yours and come up equal, if not the winner. For that matter, so could Pippa. So can we talk?"

"Pippa?" she said, her full lips turning down. "What's wrong with Pippa? What happened?"

"She's fine," I said. "Other than being worried sick about you." I held up my phone, showing her my contact for Detective

Maurice Dupart. "Now, please. Let's talk, or I will have to call my detective friend and tell him what I suspect."

I figured Dupart would laugh at my use of the word "friend," but I didn't care if it got Roselyn to talk. She stared at his name for a moment, then turned and walked into the sitting room.

I closed the door behind us, and we faced each other.

"Roselyn, I'm exhausted, so I'm going to get straight to the point," I said. "Was Hugo Markman investigating you and/or Sutton Inc. for embezzling funds, or for the misuse of funds? Is that why you've been acting so squirrely these past weeks, leaving Pippa to constantly take up your slack?" When her lips parted in shock, I decided to add to it. "And did you and Mrs. P. poison Hugo Markman with radium chloride to keep him from discovering what you'd done?"

Her face had gone absolutely white. A part of me felt triumphant. The other part of me was sinking with the horrible knowledge of being right for the wrong reasons.

"How did you recognize him?" she asked, beginning to pace the room. "How did you even know Hugo? You said you'd never seen him before."

"I hadn't," I said simply. "I've just found out a few things over the past couple of days."

She gave me a look of such irritated disgust, I almost felt slapped.

"God, you're such a perfect little nosy know-it-all," she said. "I knew you'd be trouble for me the moment Pippa introduced us."

"There's no such thing as perfect, Roselyn," I snapped. "I screw up all the time, and I've done things I'm not proud of, too. I make mistakes every day, but at least I try to learn from them."

I paused, then said, "I am somewhat nosy, though, I admit

that. I have more factoids in my brain than I know what to do with sometimes, so I spit them back out at others. However, I don't apologize for loving learning and information. I'm smart, I'm good at my job, I work hard, and I'm proud of it." I clasped my hands in front of me. "But if I come off like a know-it-all, then I apologize, and I'll try to be better about it."

Roselyn's face was stony, and I braced for her to go off on me. But she surprised me when she walked to the chair I'd occupied just two nights earlier when Officer Carr had taken my statement and sank down heavily into it.

"I've never touched a cent of Pippa's or the Sutton Inc. money." She covered her face with her hands, bringing her palms down together to cover her mouth as if in prayer. I sat down in the chair across from her.

"You didn't?"

Lowering her hands, Roselyn shook her head. "I only . . . I only misused my own money. Repeatedly."

She'd said it in just above a whisper, and it took a beat for her words to sink into my tired mind, and for my mind to get the meaning behind them.

"Wait. Are you saying you have a gambling problem?"

She nodded, her eyes filling with tears. "Hugo Markman was investigating another company, but he overheard a conversation I had with . . . a man . . . a very bad man . . . one night at the Sutton Grand. Hugo recognized the signs that I'd gotten in over my head, financially speaking. Mrs. P. and Chef Rocky were the only other people who knew. Mrs. P. found out a couple of years ago when I got in deep. She loaned me some money." A tear fell and she wiped it away. "When—when Hugo realized what was happening, I told him Mrs. P. knew about my gambling."

"And Chef Rocky?" I asked.

"He had addiction problems in college, so he understood.

He was wonderful and was getting me help. The day he died, Rocky was going to introduce me to a counselor." Roselyn's voice broke. "Hugo was such a nice man, too, and was trying to help me as well. He *was* helping me. He set me up with some people in law enforcement who could use me to get evidence that could put this guy away, and—"

I cut in. "Wait. Roselyn, are you working *with* the FBI?"

Her eyes went wide. "How did you know?" Then she rolled her eyes, but it was without malice this time. "Don't answer that. You're quicker than anyone gives you credit for, so I shouldn't be surprised."

I sat forward in my chair. "Roselyn, if you knew how long it took me to figure that out, you wouldn't be saying such things." I shook my head and thought about Ben, feeling even more ashamed now than ever. He hadn't ghosted me at all, and he wasn't setting Roselyn up for a sting. They both were part of a sting, and I'd nearly ruined everything today with my snooping at the pub.

Roselyn went to say something, then she was sobbing. I got up and went to the silver urns that would stay filled with hot water and coffee until midnight. Selecting a decaf Earl Grey, I made her some tea in a Burleigh mug in a peacock pattern. While it steeped, I brought her a box of tissues.

"Thank you," Roselyn mumbled, taking the box from me. She dabbed at her eyes, then looked up imploringly at me. She was ready to talk, and she wanted me to understand.

"When I saw him—Hugo, I mean—dead on our lawn, I thought *he* was responsible. I thought he'd killed poor Hugo."

"He . . . you mean the very bad man?" I asked. I added some honey to the Earl Grey, and handed it to Roselyn.

She nodded, clasping the mug gratefully. "I thought he'd found out that I was getting help and he wouldn't have power over me anymore. I thought he'd killed Hugo in response."

I had a surge of hope that her idea might be true. That there was some horrible Very Bad Man who preyed on those with money problems and it was he who'd killed Hugo, and Chef Rocky, too. That Penelope Ohlinger really did die of heart complications. That none of this had anything to do with Grandpa and a set of World War II spies.

"But my contact at the FBI assured me this man had nothing to do with Hugo's death. In fact, they believe Hugo was so adept at being invisible that he wasn't even on the man's radar."

My hopes popped like a balloon landing on the thorns of a century plant.

"What about Chef Rocky?" I asked. "Did this man kill him?"

Roselyn shook her head, tears brimming in her eyes once more. "I thought he might have. That's why I freaked out and disappeared after going to Rocky's house and finding him dead. My contact won't give me details as to why they're so sure, though." Her fist went up to her lips as she tried to keep from crying again. "I still have no idea what happened to Rocky. I was wondering if he had gotten back into the drug world, but there isn't any evidence of it. My lawyer called me earlier and told me they have other leads, though."

I wondered if the leads had anything to do with Hugo's list and the file of names I gave Dupart earlier today, but I'd have to wait until tomorrow to call him.

"What about Pippa?" I said. "When will you tell her all of this?"

Roselyn sipped on her tea, then sighed. "I need a few more days. I'm told we've almost convinced this man to take the bait, but the longer Pippa can act confused and worried about me, the more stressed out I am, and the more flighty and scared I seem to him"—she gave a harsh laugh—"and for some reason, the more he trusts me. It's been horrible acting like this around my daughter, but the FBI assures me this is the best way."

"Say no more," I said. "I've had a little bit of experience with the FBI. I won't tell."

Roselyn nodded, then went to get up.

I stood, too. "You'll want to fix your eyes," I said, and handed her another tissue. From my tote, I pulled out a mirror, and she wiped away the signs that she'd been crying.

"Thank you," she said. She straightened her posture and shook her hair back. "Presentable?" she asked.

"More than," I said with a smile. "Though may I ask you one other thing?"

From the look on her face, I had a feeling she knew what I was going to ask, but I said the words anyway.

"Why are you so averse to having your genealogy traced?"

She took one last drink of her tea, then set the mug down on the tray, and we walked to the door. She grasped the lock, then turned back to me.

"Lucy, I don't want my genealogy done because I already know who I am," she said softly. "I'm the granddaughter of a traitor. Of a German American soldier who tried to sell secrets to the Nazis. He was caught and shot—by the Nazis, in fact. He was double-crossed."

I thought she was going to cry again, but she reined it in with a deep breath and met my eyes once more.

"Pippa comes from heroes and good, hardworking people on her father's side, and traitors and gambling addicts on her mother's side," she said. "I don't want my daughter to know my side because she's *my* hero, and I don't want her to ever associate with anything other than the heroic side of her family."

With that, she turned the lock, opened the door, and walked out.

THIRTY-NINE

❧

I intended to be up at dawn to go see Grandpa, but my exhausted body said otherwise. It was nearing nine o'clock by the time I found myself downstairs waiting for my ride-share.

It was December thirtieth, the day before New Year's Eve. The weather was a relatively balmy fifty-five degrees, but it was due to turn ugly, rainy, and twenty degrees colder before possibly getting cold enough to snow. I was in jeans and booties yet again, but I'd put on a cheerful color-block sweater to hopefully counteract the increasingly gray day.

I settled myself on one of the emerald green sofas with a cup of coffee as Mrs. P. came in from directing teams of men delivering extra chairs, tables, and linens for the gala. In preparation for the weather to turn cold and wet, she was wearing a pair of black, ankle-high rubber boots and a chunky turtleneck sweater in marled gray tones. Her black pants were slimmer than she usually wore and had cargo pockets on the thighs. I watched as she pulled a pen from one of her pockets to check off something on a clipboard.

"I like your work outfit today, Mrs. P.," I said. "You look like a cute and stylish general."

Mrs. P. let out an amused snort. "Thank you, dear. I've got lots of work to do outside today, so I came prepared."

My phone rang and a photo came up on the screen of a man in a trucker cap with a weathered face and bulldog-baggy cheeks. It was Frank, who'd been servicing my cars since my days in grad school at UT.

"Frank, good morning. How's my car?"

Frank's thick drawl came through my phone. "Lucy, I found somethin' that's right suspicious."

"How so?" I asked. My other hand clenched around my coffee mug.

"Well, it looks like there's a hole in yer brake line. Not a big 'un, mind you. It's barely noticeable. Heck, I darn near missed it. It also looks like there mighta been tape of some sort over it, too."

"Tape?" I repeated, watching Mrs. P. measure out a length of silvery, twisted satin cording I recognized as being the same type she'd asked Pippa to buy for putting together the gala favors. She then used it to tie a bow onto a sachet containing three wildflower seed bombs.

"Yep, tape. It's to keep the brake fluid from leakin' too fast. As you drive, all an' sundry heats up under your car, which would eventually make the tape come off and the fluid start to leak. It'd be so yer brakes stopped working somewhere far away from where the brake line was tampered with."

"Oh?" I said, my voice faint. I saw Mrs. P. glance at me, then measure out another length of cord.

"Someone knew what they were doin', all right," Frank continued. "Lucy, I'm gonna send you a video of what I found. You should send it to yer insurance guy, and go to the police." He pronounced it in two distinct syllables, *po-leese*.

"Will do, Frank. Thank you so much."

"You be right careful, Lucy," he said. "I don't want nothin' happenin' to you."

"I will, I promise," I said, and hung up, feeling a cold all over that had nothing to do with the weather.

So, it was true. Someone had tried to kill me.

"Was that your car man, Lucy, dear? Was it your brake line, like you thought?"

My phone pinged. Frank had sent the video. I looked up from my daze. "I'm sorry, Mrs. P. What did you say?"

A slightly guilty flush came over her cheeks. "Miss Pippa told me this morning," she said, loosely rolling up the satin cording. "I never believed that story about a squirrel. Och, you poor girls. That must have been scary."

"It wasn't fun, I'll tell you that," I said, but to myself I was thinking "scary" was the right word. I was feeling downright scared and unsafe. My phone pinged again; my ride was near. I stood up on autopilot and put on my down vest and a scarf, adding, "But we're both all right, and that's what matters. I'm picking up a rental after visiting my grandfather."

"Oh, you're seeing Mr. Lancaster? Wait here, then," Mrs. P. said. She bustled off and was back in a few seconds holding a small white box sealed with a sticker featuring a drawing of the Hotel Sutton. From her desk, she pulled a roll of wide, stiff ribbon. Cutting a length, she tied it around the box, fashioning it into one of those gorgeous, perfect bows I could never seem to make.

"Here," she said, crossing to me. "These are the homemade caramels for all the guests at the gala. A little shop not far from here makes them for us. Take them to your grandfather with my compliments."

"Ooh, Grandpa and I both love caramels. I might have to sneak one and just tell him there was always one missing."

Mrs. P. winked at me. "I think you should do that, Lucy, dear. You deserve one, for sure."

"Thanks, Mrs. P." My phone signaled that my ride was in the parking lot, and I dashed out, ready to see my grandfather and feel safe again.

But my late start to the morning ruined my chances of catching Grandpa awake. He was sleeping peacefully again when I got to his room, but I nevertheless stayed with him for a while in case he woke up. I wanted to talk to him, to have him tell me what to do, to reassure me that everything would be okay. However, Nurse Angelique said he'd been given some pain meds and would probably sleep for hours. "He's improving markedly, though." She smiled. "And his lips are still zipped."

I thanked her for all she'd been doing and asked if I could leave the caramels for Grandpa. "I know he'll share with you," I said. "So feel free if you'd like one."

When I left Grandpa's room, his tall, bald, silent guard stood up again. "All quiet?" I asked.

"All quiet," he replied. "You?"

"All good," I said, then stopped myself. "Actually, no. Someone tampered with my brake line last night. I got lucky, but keep an extra-special eye on Grandpa, would you?"

His jaw tightened. Then he ripped off an edge of the paper from his clipboard logging Grandpa's visitors and wrote a number on it, along with a name.

"Please only use this in an emergency, but use it if you need to."

I looked at the name, then smiled. "Thank you, Tom."

He nodded, and I left the hospital, catching a call from a

yawning Pippa as I slid into the back seat of another ride-share.

"Man, I was worn out from yesterday," she said with a groan. "I just woke up about a half hour ago, if you can believe it, but I'm ready to help you with whatever you need."

"Oh, thanks," I said. "I'm being driven to the rental car place. I should be back in about an hour."

"Sounds good," she said with another yawn. "Oh, and I remembered something strange," she added. "Meaning, something that happened recently that was strange." She amended this by saying, "Well, it could be nothing, of course. Or simple coincidence."

"Even so, spill the tea," I said, a tad impatiently.

Pippa chuckled. "Okay, so a couple of weeks ago, I'd been out running errands and picked up some take-out from my favorite Chinese place. I brought it back to the hotel and ate half of it, but Mom had disappeared again and I had to show a potential client around last minute. Anyway, the rest of my food got cold—it was crispy shrimp and vegetables, so, you know, it's fried in that puffy tempura batter that's so good when it's just made and hot but disgusting when it's cold."

"And impossible to reheat well," I said.

"Exactly," Pippa said. "So when I was done with the tour, Mrs. P. brought me my leftovers, telling me I hadn't eaten enough and I should finish my lunch. I knew it wouldn't taste good, so I went to throw it away, and that's when one of the gardeners asked me to look at something in the knot garden. When he saw me about to trash my leftovers, he asked if he could take them to his chickens."

"Chickens eat Chinese food?" I said.

"Yeah, apparently they're carnivores and will eat almost everything except for a few things that are toxic to them, like uncooked beans and avocado," Pippa said. "Anyway, the next day the gardener came up to me and asked if I'd gotten sick from my food. When I said no, he said that two of his chickens had died within minutes of eating my leftovers. He took the scraps out before the rest of them could get to it, but still. Until today, I've been thinking there was simply something toxic to the chickens in the recipe. Now, though . . ."

"It definitely qualifies as a little strange," I finished. "Especially because the chickens died within minutes of eating the leftovers." Something was definitely not right. "Does Mrs. P. do that a lot?" I asked, grasping at the nearest straw.

"Make me eat?" Pippa said with a laugh. "Yeah, *all* the time. She could put a worried grandmother to shame."

I remembered her bringing me a cup of hot, sweet tea after Hugo had died. Yeah, Mrs. P. was definitely the mothering type.

"Did anyone else know you were ordering from that restaurant?" I asked.

"No, but I did eat it in the kitchen. I often do."

The kitchen. "Was Lacey Costin there that day?" I asked.

"Wait, are you thinking she tried to poison me?" Pippa asked. Then, before I could answer, I heard a distant knock and Boomer barking in response.

"It's Mrs. P.," Pippa said, "bringing me the invoices for the gala. Look, I'll check and see if Lacey was scheduled to work that day. If she was, I'll check the security tapes."

"That's a good plan. As soon as I'm back, I'll bring my stuff over. I shouldn't be long."

I was worried about Pippa nevertheless, and it made me antsy to get back to the hotel. As predicted, the temperature outside was dropping fast. Once in my rental car, I turned on the heat and drove off the lot.

I heard my phone ring from inside my tote bag as I navigated onto I-35. *What if it's the hospital calling about Grandpa?* I thought worriedly, wishing I'd connected my phone to the car's Bluetooth. Austin traffic was notoriously bad, and today it was crazier than ever, so I kept both hands on the wheel, glad my exit wasn't too far off. Once on Cesar Chavez, I grabbed my phone at the first stoplight.

It wasn't the hospital, though. It was Sean Nelson.

Excitement buzzing inside me, I played the message from my phone's speaker as the light turned green.

"Lucy, it's Sean. Look, I'll be out of pocket almost all afternoon, but I wanted to let you know right away that your theory was right. The names on your list are indeed the descendants of the Operation Greenfinch spies."

I gasped so loud, I almost didn't catch what he said next.

"And my source tells me there's at least two other people who have searched for information about this mission, though I don't have their names yet."

Hugo Markman was likely one of them, I thought. The other person had to be the killer.

Sean continued. "As for the agents' names, I've only got their first initial and surname, along with their code name. I can explain everything further later, but here's the gist: Operation Greenfinch happened because a female American OSS agent, codename Judith, discovered an SOE operative was acting as a double agent. Judith's real name was H. Davis."

Hitting the brakes, I took a fast turn onto a side street, causing honking behind me even as Sean's message continued to play.

"So, this double agent was a former German aristocrat who'd lost his lands and title. He'd then married an Englishwoman and had been living in England for more than ten years. Unhappily so, it appears. His is the only full name I have. The double agent's code name was Anthony, but his real name was—" Then Sean, who'd studied German, pronounced a name that sounded something like "*von Pole-mah-ha*," adding that the man's first name was Reinhard.

As if he realized I wouldn't see the name correctly in my mind, he spelled it, letting me know the "o" had an umlaut. The double agent's name was Reinhard von Pöllmacher.

I pulled alongside the curb and put the car in park.

Sean was saying, "Now, I don't know the full details, you understand, but it appears this double agent named von Pöllmacher was giving the Germans information about plans for D-Day in return for regaining his stature, lands, and bank accounts in the fatherland. OSS Agent Davis helped set up a mission to reveal von Pöllmacher's deception, and that mission was Operation Greenfinch. It involved four OSS agents, Ms. Davis included, and four SOE agents."

I was holding my phone nearer to me, feeling like the information wasn't coming fast enough, and also like I was desperate for Sean to speak every word slowly so I wouldn't miss a syllable.

He said, "Apparently von Pöllmacher was really good at seeming loyal to Britain, the SOE, and the Allies, as well as hiding his association with the Nazis. The mission to force his hand was fairly elaborate, with microdots, misinformation, and Montblancs, just like you mentioned in your first voicemail to me. Lucy, it sounds like stopping this guy was instrumental to the Allies succeeding on D-Day and, eventually, winning the war."

"Holy wow," I breathed. "And Grandpa was part of it." Goose bumps were popping up all over my arms at the thought.

"The point is, the eight agents were successful in catching von Pöllmacher at his own game. He was killed before the D-Day plans could be ruined. However, of the eight agents involved, three were killed. Two of them—R. Cogswell, an American, and

A. Newell, a Brit, codenames Ted and Jarvis, respectively—were exposed by von Pöllmacher and killed by the Nazis."

Naomi Van Dorn's grandfather and Alastair Newell's father, I thought.

Sean added, "A third, whose name was E. Weissman, was an American, but there's some confusion as to whether he was working for the SOE or OSS. Regardless, he was killed by von Pöllmacher himself when von Pöllmacher began to suspect him. His code name was Rupert."

I wondered if E. Weissman was Hugo's grandfather. Then I gasped again. That's what Grandpa had meant by Rupert's life-ending bravery ensuring the mission's success. Holy wow indeed.

If the spy codenamed Rupert was indeed Hugo's grandfather, then Hugo was on his own list. Did he know it? I had to believe he did.

Sean's voice was as excited as my thoughts. "Okay, my friend," I heard him say, "I hope you have a pen ready and I hope you're sitting down, because here are the names of the other operatives, plus their code names. However, Ms. Davis and Mr. Weissman don't match up with any of the names you sent me, which tells me they're the ancestors of one of the three names you haven't yet decoded." Sean cleared his throat. "There's also a third name that doesn't match up with any of the names that are already decoded. Lucy, that name is G. Lancaster."

I'd hastily pulled out a copy of Hugo's list. When I heard him say Grandpa's name, I paused Sean's message. I needed a moment to breathe.

I was filled with pride, fear, wonderment, and about ten other emotions all mixed together at hearing Grandpa's name. And yet it was still surprising to me that he hadn't been targeted ages ago. He should have been the very first target. So why had it taken so long for the killer to set his sights on my grandfather?

I still didn't have the answer to that, so I hit play on Sean's message again, and heard his voice go serious.

"Lucy, if the 'G. Lancaster' is your grandfather, then that means you're in danger. Please, please be careful, my friend. Text me to let me know you got this and you're safe. And keep the texts coming until all this is figured out, okay? You sent me the number of that Detective Dupart in Austin. Just know I won't hesitate to call him if I don't hear from you on the regular."

I smiled, thinking what a good friend Sean was, then started scribbling names, matching the spies and their code names with their descendants on Hugo's list, as Sean named them:

Descendant	Spy + Nationality	Code Name
Alastair Newell	A. Newell, British	Jarvis
Fiona Kenland	L. Pulleyn, British	Nigel
Penelope Ohlinger	F. Whitcross, British	Charles
Naomi Van Dorn	R. Cogswell, American	Stanley
Rocco Zeppetelli	A. Zeppetelli, American	Louis
UNKNOWN (Hugo?)	E. Weissman, American	Rupert
UNKNOWN	H. Davis, American	Judith
UNKNOWN (Me?)	G. Lancaster, American	Robert

At the bottom, I added in an extra line for the double agent and his unknown descendant:

| ??? | R. von Pöllmacher—DOUBLE AGENT | Anthony |

"By the way," Sean said just before he hung up, "a green-finch is a bird often found on the French coast at Normandy. Its French name is *verdier*. My contact found a written notation that read, 'V for Verdier, V for Victory!' I thought that was a neat side note."

I recalled Grandpa saying the Morse code "V" on the pen's cap had meant more than just "victory," and now I knew it meant *verdier*, the French word for "greenfinch." A neat side note, indeed.

Smiling, I sent Sean a text that started with "HOLY WOW!" and continued on with my profuse thanks and assurances that I would check in regularly. Then I put my rental car back in gear and drove back to the Hotel Sutton, anxiousness beginning to jump in my stomach. I needed to decode those last names and get this information to Detective Dupart. Even though Sean hadn't said there was a "J. Sutton" on the list, meaning Pippa's name wouldn't be one of the last three names, there was still something odd going on. I felt the urge more than ever to make sure she was all right.

FORTY

Mrs. P. was on the front porch of the hotel, looking to be in a slightly heated discussion with one of the groundskeeping staff about when to put down a fresh layer of crushed granite before the party.

"I'd like it done now, before the light rain that's expected," she was saying, her mouth turned down in a scowl. "That will help it to settle better for all the ladies who will be walking in heels."

The groundskeeper replied that, should the rains become rougher, it would wash away the new layer and they'd just have to do it again.

Mrs. P. went to respond, then stopped when she saw me trotting up the steps. "Lucy, you're back already. How was your grandfather?"

"Sleeping, but good," I replied. "I'm sure he'll enjoy the caramels as soon as he wakes up, though."

"Oh, I do hope so," she said. "You look to be in a hurry, dear. Is everything all right?"

"Huh?" I said, already distracted. I was wanting to grab my

copies of *The Thirty-Nine Steps* and get to Pippa's cottage. It was way past time I got those last three names decoded. Pulling open the front door, I said, "Oh, everything's fine. Pippa's going to help me with a little project, and I just want to get to her cottage before the rains start."

"Is there something I can help you with?" she asked.

"Thanks a bunch, Mrs. P., but I'm good." I flashed her what I hoped was an unconcerned grin and went inside. As the front door closed slowly, I heard the groundskeeper say, "Maybe we should ask Mrs. Sutton or Miss Pippa about the crushed granite," only to have Mrs. P. snap, "Mrs. Sutton is running errands and Miss Pippa is busy. Now do as I've asked so we can have this place at one hundred percent by the time the rains start."

Fifteen minutes later, I made it up the steps of Pippa's cottage, out of breath again from race-walking while lugging my tote and a carrier bag full of books. I felt relieved when Pippa opened the door, her curly hair in a high ponytail and a smile on her face. No possibly unbalanced prep cooks had tried anything on her, then.

"So what's this project you need help with?" she said, gesturing me inside.

I only hesitated a moment. "Pippa," I said. "I've been trying, and failing, to think of how to start explaining. Let's just say I've got a problem and I need to halve it big time."

"All right, then," she said, taking the bag of books from me. "I've got some coffee brewing. Let's drink and talk. But first, an update on Lacey Costin."

"Great. Lay it on me," I said, ready to hear all about Lacey being an unhinged stalker or something.

"Turns out, she wasn't working the day that weirdness with my Chinese food happened. In fact, she was visiting her parents in California."

I didn't know whether to say "Good" or "Rats!"

"I also went ahead and checked the security footage for that day, to see if anyone else messed with my food. Mrs. P. came and picked it up to bring to me, just like I already knew, but that's it. No one even touched it."

"A good theory, shattered," I said, taking off my coat and laying it over the back of Pippa's sofa, but leaving on the light-weight down vest I'd layered over my sweater.

"And we can shatter another one," Pippa said. "Detective Dupart called just before you came over. Lacey was cleared of Chef Rocky's murder, too. It seems when she disappeared from the security footage that afternoon, it was because Ysenia, the sous chef, asked her to make a run to the farmers' market. There's footage of her at the market during the time of the murder, which Dupart said was between eleven a.m. and three p.m."

"Well, at least we know she's not responsible for anything," I said finally. "That's something. Did Dupart give you any other information?"

Pippa shook her head. "Not really, except that they know the murderer came in through the backyard. They found evidence that a patch of Chef Rocky's herb garden had been stepped on, but Dupart declined to say anything else until they know more."

She made cafés au lait again, and we sat on the chairs in her office. "Okay, I've shared my news, now hit me with your half," she said.

And I did. I just let it all tumble out, explaining everything from Hugo's dying words and the Montblanc all the way to Sean's message where he confirmed the names on the list were indeed the descendants of the Operation Greenfinch spies. I then showed her the copy of Hugo's list where I'd written down the spies' names next to their descendants. The whole time, Pippa gasped at regular intervals, sometimes in shock, sometimes in excitement, but didn't interrupt.

"So, to sum up, there's three lines of code we have to decipher, and I need your help, if you're willing," I finished.

"Lucy," she said, "I can't believe you've had this on your shoulders the whole time, but I understand why you kept quiet." She held up one hand solemnly. "As the great-granddaughter of SOE agent James Sutton, if you had a copy of the Official Secrets Act, I would sign it. I'm not going to give any of this information away, I promise."

She couldn't have said anything that made me trust her more.

"Let's get to work, then," I said and handed her a copy of Hugo's list, with the three names at the bottom still coded as book ciphers. We moved to sit on the rug so we could spread out.

"Ugh, the weather has turned seriously icky," Pippa said, looking out the window of her home office as a light rain was beginning to fall. The wind was picking up as well, making it look more like a minor squall than just cold, misty rain.

"I'm not unhappy to be in here with lots of hot coffee and a warm dog snuggling up to me," I said, giving Boomer's belly a rub. He sighed contentedly, making Pippa grin.

"I'll take the first cipher, and you take the second," she said.

"Deal." I stacked the nine copies of *The Thirty-Nine Steps* into two piles, and we each took a stack.

I'd explained that Grandpa and I didn't yet know if the third number in each set of codes referred to the first letter of the designated word, but on this we got lucky quickly. On Pippa's first try, she not only found the copy that worked to decipher Hugo's full name—something I wasn't surprised to see—but it also confirmed Grandpa's theory of how the codes were encrypted.

We now concentrated on the last two ciphers. Though it was

likely one of them was my name, the question of why Grandpa hadn't been targeted earlier made me want to be sure.

I opened my copy and went to the page indicated by the first set of numbers. It turned out to be the end of a chapter with only a few sentences on the page. So, while the page number existed, the paragraph number and word number did not.

"This one's out for my cipher," I said and set it near Pippa for her to try.

Soon, Pippa found hers wouldn't work, either. "Unless some-one's first name happens to be 'Blorg.'"

My next book seemed like it was working—I got P-H-O-E and thought it would spell "Phoebe" or maybe even "Phoenix," if the person's parents had a hippie bent to them—until the next two letters were "A" and "I." I didn't think "Phoeai" was a name, either.

I quickly exhausted my last two books when they came back with "Sbbf" and, my personal favorite, "Gorf."

"Nada for you, too, huh?" Pippa said, and shoved her pile of books my way. She'd thought she was getting the name Charles or Charleen until it went off the rails and ended up "Charlpk."

Pippa poured us more coffee and we each took another book.

"What if none of these pan out?" she asked, writing down a "Q" as her first letter.

I sipped on my coffee and stretched my neck out. "Then I keep searching for other copies of the book," I said.

Pippa tossed her book aside quickly. "I'm going to bet there aren't any names starting with 'Q-S-B.'" She picked up the book that had given me "Gorf" and started working.

I'd found my first letter—P—and flipped until I was at the next designated page. I counted to the right paragraph, then to the right word and wrote down an "H." Then I got an "I" and an "L." Two more ciphers later, and I looked down at my list.

P

H

I

L

I

P

Philip! I thought in triumph. It was a man named Philip Something. I found the next three letters quickly.

P

A

S

Pasquale? I thought. *Pasternak? Passer?* I practically dove
into the book for the next letters.

U

T

Pasut? No, there were still three more letters. Passuter? Hmm,
was that even a surname? Quickly, I found the last three.

T

O

N

Slowly, my eyes ran over the letters again, then I raised my
head to look at my client—my friend—sitting right in front of
me, her head bent over her copy of *The Thirty-Nine Steps*, flipping pages at a fast rate.

The cipher spelled out Philippa Sutton. Pippa was short for Philippa.

For a long moment, I felt a wave of terror come over me. I'd just told her everything, feeling safer doing so because I thought she wasn't on the list. But she was. Pippa was being targeted.

Ridiculous thoughts like chaining Pippa to my side to keep her safe flew through my mind. I looked over her head at the framed photographs that hung between the two windows in her office, once more taking in the photo of her great-grandparents from 1945. I stared at it, calming myself by going over the facts I knew about James and Nell Sutton, listing their statistics like bullet points in my mind.

James Bracewell Sutton. Born December 5, 1920, London, England. Helen "Nell" Sutton. Born July 29, 1921, Corpus Christi, Texas. Maiden name . . .

Pippa was counting paragraphs on a page, then words. I saw her write what looked to be an "R" very slowly, as if in a trance, and then her eyes raised up to meet mine.

We could read the dread in each other's faces as we both turned our legal pads around to show each other.

PHILIPPA SUTTON

LUCINDA LANCASTER

However, instead of being frightened, I smiled. "I know," I said. "I know who she was."

"Who?" Pippa said, looking perplexed.

"The female spy in Operation Greenfinch, the one who exposed the double agent. She was your great-grandmother, Helen Sutton, maiden name Davis." Grabbing Hugo's list, I showed her that her own name, Philippa Sutton, matched up as the descendant of the spy I'd written as *H. Davis, American.*

"The 'H' stands for Helen, with Nell being her nickname," I told Pippa.

She blinked those big, dark green eyes. "But Lucy, it was my great-*grandfather* who was in the SOE. Great-Granny Nell was one of Eisenhower's secretaries, not a spy."

I grinned. "And what better cover could there be for a female spy who needed to be able to move around frequently than being one of the top brass's secretaries?"

I turned and pointed to the V-E Day photograph on her wall. "Your great-grandmother, she was in the OSS, I'm sure of it. Pippa, you're descended from not one, but two Allied spies."

Despite the situation, Pippa bit her lip and then broke into a wide grin. "If you're right, then, wow. I have to admit, that's *really* cool."

"Isn't it, though?" I said excitedly. I held up my hand and she gave me an enthusiastic high-five. Boomer lifted his head and thumped his tail as if in agreement.

Pippa shook her legal pad at me. "But look at this, Lucy. You're on the list, too."

I had assumed I was, so it wasn't a shock. Then I took her legal pad and really read it. "Wait a minute," I said. "This isn't my name. I'm not Lucinda Lancaster."

Pippa frowned. "You're not?"

I shook my head. "No, I'm Lucia Lancaster."

"Really?"

My lips couldn't help but curve up. "I was named after the character of Lucy Honeychurch in E. M. Forster's *A Room with a View*, which is my mom's favorite book. Mom always loved how Lucy's cousin calls her Lucia, especially when they're in Italy. I don't have a drop of Italian blood in me, but Mom liked it, so that's what I was named."

Pippa grinned. "I like it, too, and I'll have to call you Lucia now." Then she pointed back at the name. "But then who is Lucinda Lancaster?"

I started to shrug that I had no idea, then stopped and put my fingers to my lips. "I think I might know," I whispered.

There was a knock on Pippa's front door. Boomer was up on his feet with a woof.

"Pippa, dear, are you in there?" Mrs. P. called.

"For the love of Pete, this is the third time she's come to my door today," Pippa said. "I don't know what her problem is—she usually either calls or just makes a decision on her own." She huffed out a sigh. "I'll go see what she wants." Boomer's hackles had stood up and Pippa gave the top of his head a brief rub. "It's just Mrs. P., silly. Stop being such a goof."

"Pippa, dear!" said Mrs. P., sounding a bit agitated. Glancing out the window, I couldn't blame her. It looked like the temperature had dropped another ten degrees and it was still lightly raining.

"Coming, Mrs. P.!" Pippa called back.

"Close the door," I said. "Just in case." Boomer followed her out and the barn door closed smoothly on its rollers. I heard her opening the front door and the sounds of genial conversation.

I'd pulled my laptop toward me and found the database that logged obituaries. I typed in "George Lancaster," "Texas," and a date range that was in the last ten years.

The obit was long and full of lovely words for the man who had the same name as my grandfather, mentioning his youth in Houston and his time in the European Theater in World War II. I scrolled to the end, where it listed George's family members. I was picking up my phone and calling Detective Dupart before I could think twice.

His voice mail picked up. Frustrated, I realized he'd never take me seriously if I babbled, so I strove for a clear and believable message.

"Detective Dupart, this is Lucy Lancaster," I began, speaking slowly but with confidence. "I know this will sound weird, but it's important, so please listen carefully. My contact at the National Archives has found the information we need. I have the list of spies from Operation Greenfinch who match up to the descendants on Hugo Markman's list. I've also decoded the last three names on the list. One is Hugo himself. The second is Pippa Sutton—but she's here with me, and safe. The third, however, is a woman named Lucinda Lancaster."

I took a breath and continued. "Detective, I am *not* Lucinda Lancaster—my first name is Lucia. However, this woman named Lucinda is the daughter of a World War Two veteran named George Lancaster—which is coincidentally also my grandfather's name."

I paused, knowing I was about to give up Grandpa's secret, but it had to be done.

"This is important," I said, holding my phone tightly to my ear. "There were two George Lancasters from Houston in the war. One was a regular soldier, the other was an OSS spy. The George Lancaster the killer has listed is *not* the spy. I know this because the real OSS operative is my grandfather. This means the killer made a mistake in his research. Detective, the killer may be going after a woman who has no connection to Operation Greenfinch whatsoever, and I need you to make sure she's safe."

I finished the message by imploring Dupart to check on Lucinda Lancaster, telling him that, as of a few years ago, she lived in Flower Mound, Texas.

I hung up, hoping Dupart would get the message quickly. For my part, questions were popping up left and right.

If the killer had made a mistake in his research and had never been targeting Grandpa and me, then was it possible that

Grandpa's accident was just that—an accident? And what about my brakes? Could Frank have been wrong?

I found the video Frank had sent me and watched it in dismay. No, Frank had not been wrong.

I went to forward the video to Dupart, then stopped. I'd just left him a long message with a lot of information to process. I didn't want this video to overshadow the potential safety of an innocent woman. No, I'd forward it to him later. I picked up Hugo's list again, with all the names now decoded.

The killer made a mistake in his research. My own words to Dupart came back to me when I scanned the last three names.

I thought about Grandpa, being nearly run down. I looked down at my phone, at the video that confirmed my brakes had been tampered with. We both could have been killed, and that was no mistake.

"The killer figured it out," I whispered. "He knows he found the wrong George Lancaster."

"Would you like to know how I did it?" I easily visualized Grandpa's grin the other day as he told the story of how he got into the army at sixteen and three-quarters years old. *"They didn't cotton on to me because there was another George Lancaster and I passed myself off as him—at least initially."*

He'd been in his accident the very next day, hadn't he?

I stilled. I remembered the reaction Grandpa's story had received. How a pair of crystalline blue eyes had gone round. How she'd said, "Wouldn't it be funny if he had a granddaughter named Lucy, too?"

I swallowed, hard. *No,* my mind kept repeating. *No.* It couldn't be! Not sweet, helpful Mrs. P. "Don't even think such things, Lucy!" I admonished myself.

Yet similarly to when I looked at Pippa's great-grandparents and their stats came up in my mind, I couldn't help it now. With Mrs. P.'s pink-cheeked face and ginger pageboy swimming before my eyes, the ugly facts, like actual bullets, shot out at me.

Terrence had mentioned Chef Rocky was killed in a way that would have required black ops training or medical training. Mrs. P. had been a nurse for ten years before switching careers.

Uncle Dave had told me how Mrs. P. and her admirer, "Mr. H.," used to sit at the corner table at the Sutton Grand, eating gelato, and talking about World War II and their grandfathers. Uncle Dave had more or less told me Mr. H. was Hugo, but I'd taken that knowledge and put it in terms of Roselyn and her gambling secret. I hadn't for a second suspected Mrs. P. in Hugo's death.

And poor, poor Hugo. Did Mrs. P. poison him with radium chloride? She would have known the effects of various kinds of poisons. But how would she have done it?

I smacked my forehead with my palm. She collected old pocket watches. Radium chloride was used to make the faces and dials of clocks glow. I didn't know how long it took the chemical to kill someone. Days? Weeks? However long, there was enough time in between so that Mrs. P.'s hand in Hugo's death wasn't noticeable, that maybe it just seemed like his underlying health issues were merely getting worse. Until it was too late, that was.

I thought about how Pippa's Chinese-food leftovers had killed the gardener's chickens a couple of weeks earlier. Mrs. P. must have poisoned the leftovers, hoping to kill Pippa, but it hadn't worked. Did she use radium chloride there, too? Regardless, she hadn't tried again quickly. No, Mrs. P. was smarter than that. If she had, someone would have put two and two together sooner.

Other moments flooded back. The look on Mrs. P.'s face when I jokingly asked if her last name could have originally been Pohlmann, and her perfect East End accent as she told me about her mother, a hotel housekeeper, and her father, who was "good with cars."

"Me mum and me dad were about as far from being toffs as you could get. Hardly two shillings to rub between them their whole lives—though me dad always claimed he was the son of a peer. Mum never believed him, though."

I heard her words as if she'd just said them. I wondered if she'd used that accent when she'd spoken to Naomi Van Dorn, claiming to be Naomi's long-lost aunt.

Always stick as close to the truth as possible. That was what Grandpa had advised—and that was exactly what Mrs. P. had done, wasn't it?

Wait, I thought. She *had* screwed up. She'd screwed up this morning in asking me if the trouble with my car had been my brake lines, telling me Pippa had confessed the real reason we'd crashed into the juniper trees. Yet when I'd spoken to Pippa later this morning, she'd said she'd just woken up. There was no way Pippa could have told Mrs. P. about my brakes at all.

I stood up so fast, the blood rushed to my head.

"Pippa," I whispered in horror, staring at the closed barn door in front of me, which kept me from seeing into the rest of the cottage or to the front door, where she had answered a knock some minutes earlier.

Pippa had opened the door to a killer.

FORTY-ONE

I moved to the sliding barn door, but didn't open it. Maybe she was just in the kitchen. "Pippa?"

Silence. How long had it been since she'd gone to answer the front door? Five minutes? Ten?

"Hey, Pippa!" I called out again, trying to sound unconcerned. Nothing.

I didn't want to open the office door. I decided to go even louder, but keep it casual, like I wasn't rapidly becoming scared out of my wits.

"Hey, Pippa, I have something funny to show you. Come in here."

The silence was covering my eardrums like a thick duvet. There was no response.

Could Mrs. P. have killed Pippa and now be waiting in the house for me?

Oh God. I spun around. I needed a weapon.

I lunged for my tote bag. While it held a veritable slew of items from my knit cap to my folders, faux-snakeskin clutch with my essentials, and my little makeup bag, the only thing I could possibly turn into a weapon was my keys. I put them in my vest pocket.

Catching sight of a peppermint, I swore. Another bullet point was added to the list: the chocolate mint plant. Mrs. P. tracked it into the hotel, yes, but it wasn't from the knot garden, was it? No, I was betting it was from Chef Rocky's backyard. That's why she jumped so fast to take it from me when Boomer kept trying to get at it.

Boomer, I thought, my heart clutching. Had Mrs. P. hurt him, too?

Hurrying now, I moved around Pippa's desk, picking up a blue plastic letter opener sitting by some envelopes. It wasn't the knifelike kind, but instead a safety style that was flat, about the size of an egg, and was probably not good for cutting much. It did have a sharply pointed part for inserting into envelopes, however. I tested it on my palm and decided if I had to stab someone with it, it would probably break, but it would hurt enough before it did. I was about to put it in the back pocket of my jeans, then changed my mind and slid it underneath the left cuff of my sweater, against the inside of my wrist.

I looked into Pippa's trash can. Nothing except for papers. The pens we'd been using to decipher the last of Hugo's codes were basic ballpoints with a dull rounded tip, so from her decorative containers I grabbed a sharpened pencil instead, sticking it in the shaft of my right bootie. Lastly, I grabbed the two paperweights. The smaller, with the picture of Boomer, I slipped into my other pocket. The other, sporting a large red heart on a pink background, I grasped in my right hand.

None of it was much, but it was better than nothing. I moved back to the barn door, listening for sounds in the house. I was pretty sure I would have heard if Pippa had brought Mrs. P. into the house, whether at her invitation or against her will. Still, I steeled myself, then yanked open the barn door, ready to fast pitch the larger paperweight at Mrs. P.'s head.

The cottage was silent. No voices, no Pippa. I glanced around, craning my head to see into the kitchen. No Boomer, either.

I sprinted to the window, flattening myself against the smooth wall beside it, desperate to see if Pippa was out there and hurt—or worse. The shutter louvers were open. Carefully, and for only a split second at a time, I took darting glances out onto the porch and the immediate grounds.

It had all but stopped raining, though fat drops of water dripped in consistent rhythm off the porch roof. Across the vast lawn, I could see the hotel in all its graceful glory, but now I truly appreciated how much distance was between it and Pippa's cottage. Even if I stood outside and waved my arms, someone at the hotel would have to be on the second floor and using binoculars to clearly see me.

Mrs. P. had also gotten what she'd told the groundskeeper she wanted: all the outdoor prep for the gala had been completed before the rains. Not a single soul could be seen anywhere, including Pippa, Boomer, and Mrs. P. herself. Then I shifted to look left and saw a patch of buttery yellow fur lying still on the grass.

"Boomer!" I said, anguish filling my voice. I opened the front door and was instantly hit by a blast of cold wind. The temperature had dropped ten degrees. With the wind chill, the temp was no doubt close to freezing, and my lightweight down vest wasn't doing much to keep me warm. I grabbed my coat from the sofa and scanned all around once more for signs of Mrs. P. Seeing none, I raced out the door and over to Boomer.

He was breathing. He looked to be just asleep. Looking around, I saw a scattering of little dark nuggets that I recognized as Boomer's liver-flavored dog treats.

"He goes crazy for these things, for reasons only he knows. He'll do anything you want once he gets a whiff of them."

I put my hand on Boomer's side. His fur was soaked, and I worried he would get hypothermia. I didn't think twice, but took off my coat and placed it over the dog, hoping it would keep him warm enough until a vet could come.

I stood up, shivering and looking around for the larger paperweight, then realized I'd put it down when I put on my coat.

I was about to run back inside and get it, and maybe go to the kitchen for a better weapon, when a blast of icy wind hit me and made another one of Boomer's treats tumble over in the grass, looking like a large caramel.

I stifled a cry. The caramels! Would Mrs. P. have poisoned them, too? I remembered how I'd teased about sneaking one and she'd encouraged me to.

"You deserve one," she'd said.

Why, that conniving, evil . . . My fingers shaking, I found the contact I'd put in my phone labeled simply "Tom," and typed a text.

Caramels poisoned!

I hit send. Would he know what that meant? I started panicking. *Grandpa . . .*

To keep myself from going crazy waiting on Tom's reply, I looked around for which way Mrs. P. and Pippa could have gone. Due to the rain, there weren't any discernable footprints or a clear indication of which way they went. Could Mrs. P. have taken her down to Lady Bird Lake Trail?

My phone dinged and my heart skipped a beat.

Confiscated. None eaten.

My hand to my forehead, I made a slow spin, weak with relief. I was about to text him back when a couple of broken reedlike grasses caught my eye, and just beyond, I saw it: the path Pippa told me ran behind her cottage and into the woods to the temple-like folly.

I recalled her saying it was a place she had gone to since she was a child to escape when things got overwhelming, and that there was such dense thicket surrounding the folly that she hadn't been heard when she'd broken her ankle and was calling for help.

Yet I did hear it—a faint scream of pain in the distance.

"Pippa!" I cried, and nearly jumped out of my skin when my phone rang, Detective Dupart's name on the screen. I was holding my phone to my ear and saying, "Detective, bring help!" even as I took off down the path.

"Ms. Lancaster! What's wrong?"

I was running, following the path as it curved out of sight, snaked around a couple of trees, and straightened out again, the cold wind biting at my cheeks and whipping my ponytail around to lash me in the face.

"It's Mrs. Pollingham," I said. "The Hotel Sutton's front desk manager. She's the killer, and she has Pippa!"

"Ms. Lancaster," he shouted. "What happened? Where are you?"

I dropped my voice to a whisper. "She's got her in the woods by the hotel. Probably in the folly."

I heard a sound behind me and I whirled around, my arm and face smacking into the low branches of a young tree. Stumbling backward, I held on to my phone, but somehow my thumb slipped over the red button on the screen, hanging up on Detective Dupart.

I looked around. No one was behind me, so I pulled my keys out, threading them through my fingers, and plunged back down the wooded path. There was enough cover from the taller trees overhead that little of the ground had gotten soaked, but it was damp enough that my footsteps were muffled.

It muffled another's footsteps as well. I skidded to a stop, nearly losing my balance on the wet leaves, as Mrs. P. emerged from behind a large oak, holding a pistol with a silencer.

FORTY-TWO

❧

D rop the phone," she said, and gone were the warm tones in her voice. "And the keys."

"Mrs. P.," I breathed, letting my keys fall to the ground. I still had the smaller paperweight in my pocket. "Why are you doing this? Did you shoot Pippa?"

"Drop the phone. Now." She took a step toward me. If she hadn't had a gun, I would have tried out some of my self-defense moves. But the pistol in her hand and the coldness in her tone made me do what she said.

My fingers opened to let my phone drop just as Dupart called back. I tried to hit the red button again that would ignore the call so she couldn't see his name, but this time I missed.

The angry flush that crept up Mrs. P.'s neck and onto her cheeks made me take a step backward.

Ffft. I leapt out of the way with a yelp as my phone's screen shattered. I stumbled awkwardly onto a rock and fell, landing hard on the ground with an "*oof*," my right wrist taking the brunt of the fall. I sat up quickly, holding it gingerly.

"Oh, get up," Mrs. P. said, disdain flooding her voice, gesturing at me with her pistol. "If you'd broken it, it'd be obvious."

I stood up, attempting to wiggle my fingers and succeeding. My wrist was already beginning to swell, but she was right, it wasn't broken. Then I saw her looking down at something on the path. The paperweight had fallen from my pocket and tumbled toward her, landing so that it looked like Boomer's face was staring up at her.

"That dog's an idiot," she all but spat. "Stupid enough to take the liver treats, and then tried to bite me as he was falling asleep."

Good boy, Boomer, I thought.

Using her toe, she kicked the paperweight and it flew off into the brush. Then her lip curled. "And you're an idiot for thinking you could stop me." She used the gun to gesture me to walk in front of her. "Move, now, or you'll get a dose of what your phone just went through."

I made my legs work, though I almost couldn't feel them.

"Where are we going?" I asked. My teeth weren't just chattering from the cold.

"Oh, I'm putting you with little Miss Pippa. I'm going to have to take off after this and put the plan for the rest of my life into action, so I don't have time to deal with you two separately. So, you know, two annoying little birds with one stone—or two shots, as it were."

I looked over my shoulder at her. Over her black cargo pants and gray sweater, she wore a barn jacket in that heavy twill material. It, too, was black, but also nice looking, with large pockets, two of which were bulging.

I understood. She was dressed to make a trek through the woods and come out onto some part of Lady Bird Lake Trail looking like a stylishly dressed tourist who would blend in if spotted by anyone out walking in this weather. She was also dressed to blend into the night. And the huge pockets on her jacket said she could hide a pistol until she could dispose of it.

She made a noise of frustration. "Och, I'm so angry I had to do this today. I had a plan for you and Pippa on New Year's Eve. A couple of shots during the fireworks display . . . a shove into Lady Bird Lake . . . but you made everything go sideways."

I glanced over my shoulder, utterly speechless except for croaking out, "H-how?"

"I've been watching you, Lucy dear," she said. "When you came back from picking up your rental car this morning, I could tell you'd had news. Your face was all anxious, but lit up at the same time, like a little chipmunk who's discovered a stash of nuts. Then I saw you racing over to Pippa's house with your copies of *The Thirty-Nine Steps*. That's when I knew you were close to exposing me."

"But why, Mrs. P.?" I asked, trying to do the dumb act. "Why do you want to kill Pippa and me?"

My attempt earned me a harsh laugh. "Och, really, Miss Know-It-All Genealogist? I'm not buying that you haven't figured it out. Ask me things that are more meaningful to you, why don't you."

The first question I could think of was a silly one, considering, but it came out anyway.

"Where will you go?"

"My ancestral homeland," she replied, a note of happiness in her voice.

"England?"

"No, dear, Germany. About five years ago, I made contact with a cousin outside of Dresden. I've visited her on vacation and we've become close. She, too, believes Germany should have won the war, and she's working to keep the ideals of the Nazi Party alive in the fatherland. She's offered me a place to stay and live, and she's helped me create a new identity for myself."

I glanced back, in complete shock to hear her calmly admitting to the same twisted ideologies her double-agent grandfather had believed.

"What will your name be?" I asked. "Or will you be a von Pöllmacher once more?"

"Oh, look at you, pronouncing my family name correctly," she said in a singsongy voice, but didn't answer my question.

"All right, then," I said, and changed tack. "What about Hugo? Why did you poison him with something as heinous as radium chloride? In fact, why did you poison him at all?"

She made a dismissive noise. "Because it was apropos. He was as interested in the war as I was, and was always warning me to be careful when I cleaned my war-era timepieces that had glow-in-the-dark faces. It irritated me that he felt I wasn't capable enough to handle them properly, so I thought he might like to know what real radium chloride poisoning felt like." A note of gratification came into her voice. "It was easy. I was at the Sutton Grand all the time, no one thought twice. And I already had a reputation for sending him a whiskey as a nightcap. No one even noticed when I stirred in the scrapings from my watch faces."

She let her voice go to a stage whisper. "To be honest, I didn't even know if it would work, but he wasn't the healthiest man and I figured it would make the issues he already had *much* worse at the very least. Overall, I was so pleased with the effects."

I gave her a horrified, sickened look, which only made her chuckle.

"And Chef Rocky?" I said, my voice shaking. "Why an ice pick in the ear?"

I heard more mirth in her voice. "Well, I couldn't use radium chloride again, could I? So the ice pick was a convenient way to dispatch him. Years ago, I dated a very attractive ex-military man who taught me that move, and how to pick a lock and enter a house quietly, too."

"You've used an ice pick on someone before?" I squeaked.

"Only on a mannequin," she said with a little too much blitheness. "Of course, it was harder than I thought in real life."

"I'm glad you have some remorse," I replied bitterly.

She laughed. "No, dear. I meant that if I'd done it right, I would have been able to get the ice pick out, leaving no trace of it being there." She made a tutting noise. "Alas, it was not to be."

Bile rose up in my throat, but I swallowed it back.

"Pippa once told me you were stunned by Chef Rocky when you met him," I said. "Was that because you recognized him as one of your targets?"

I felt her tap me between my shoulders with the barrel of her gun. "Och, right again! My, you are good at this."

Her taunting voice made me want to swing around and kick her, but she was still talking, so I didn't.

"I'd been wanting to avenge my grandfather's death ever since I found out how he was betrayed, of course, but I never knew where to start."

"When did you find out?" I asked.

"Oh, about ten years ago," she said. "I learned that, after the war, my grandmother was branded the wife of a traitor and went from being a member of the landed gentry to losing her place in society. Still, even though she raised my dad in a small flat above a shop, she had contacts. Some were in the SOE, and she managed to find out both what had happened and the mission's code name. I never researched it until one day, about two years ago, after I met a genealogist much like yourself at the

Sutton Grand. She told me the mission may have been declassified and, if so, I could find out the names of those involved."

While I had no doubt my unknown fellow genealogist wouldn't have said anything if they'd known, it still hurt knowing Mrs. P. had been set on her path by someone like me.

Mrs. P. said, "Eventually, I started looking into it, and lo and behold, I found the spies of Operation Greenfinch."

"But how did you find out their first names so you could trace their descendants?" I asked. "I only got their first initials, last names, and code names."

"Worried I'm better at this than you?" she asked with a bark of laughter. "Aww, now don't you worry, Lucy dear. Their names are out there, all right. I just had more time to find them than you did."

"Right," I mumbled.

Mrs. P. was still musing on her accomplishment, the merry note back in her voice.

"Then I had to become a nosy genealogist myself and work to make sure I found *the right* descendants. After that, I got to pick and choose the descendant I felt was best worth killing. It was kind of fun doing the research and tracking down all my targets." I got another little nudge between the shoulder blades. "But I'll admit, you could've knocked me down with a feather when I realized I was already working for one of them. For the very great-granddaughter descending from Agent Helen 'Nell' Davis, no less."

I'll bet, I thought.

"But I knew I couldn't act fast. I had to wait, be an exemplary employee, and pretend to care about Pippa and her self-absorbed mother. If I did anything too quickly, I wouldn't have my life in Germany that's now waiting for me." Her tone became full of wonder. "Then, all of the sudden, just like it was fate, Pippa hired Chef Rocky. I'd just put him on my list not days before I met him, can you believe it?"

I bit the inside of my cheek to rein in a snarky response.

"And then! Och, Lucy, it was like the fates were smiling down on me, telling me it was time to put my plan into action, because Hugo *literally* walked into my life and fell in love with me. I'll admit, I'd been having trouble tracing the descendants of Agent Weissman, so at first I didn't know Hugo was anything but a weak old sap with a love of history."

"When did you realize who he was?" I asked.

"We began talking about the war over dinners and gelato," she said, sounding almost wistful. "He felt he could trust me, don't you know, and one night he opened up about his grandfather being involved in a mission that ensured D-Day would happen. How his poor granddaddy got shot by an evil double agent." Her chuckle became a cackle. "I could hardly believe it. I was being romanced by a descendant of one of the spies who unjustly killed my grandfather. This man was in my life, he thought he was my boyfriend, and he trusted me with his life and secrets." Her voice went cheerful again. "And I couldn't resist betraying him like his grandfather betrayed mine."

I felt utterly nauseated.

"Anything else, dear?" she said, sounding like her old self. "We're almost there."

We were indeed rounding another bend into a pretty little clearing. Just like in Pippa's photo, the folly's limestone facade seemed to gleam like a warm, peaceful beacon. I couldn't yet see Pippa inside.

"And what about me? I take it that you didn't know about my grandfather being one of two George Lancasters until he told you, but didn't you wonder when you heard my name was Lucy Lancaster?"

"I'll admit I did," she said, "but I'd done my research and knew what Lucinda Lancaster looked like, so I wasn't worried." She sighed. "But that was my mistake."

"I'm confused, though," I said. "You could have poisoned me or killed me so many times. Hell, you could have poisoned me the night Hugo died when you made tea for me. So why didn't you?"

"You know," she said, her voice again tinged with wonder, "I'm not exactly sure. I think I was just enjoying the wait. With you, the time needed to be right, and the same goes for Pippa. And while it turned out a bit more rushed than I wanted, I'm still getting to take you both out at the same time, so I'm happy."

She wasn't happy, she was stark-raving nuts.

"So you made the list, using a book cipher—to, what, keep your intentions secret in case anyone happened to come across the list?"

"Right again!" she crowed. "Plus, it was fun. I thought my grandfather might be proud. I understand he liked *The Thirty-Nine Steps* too."

I decided not to touch that last statement and asked, "I'm curious, how did Hugo find out about it?"

I heard her snort. "That damn man was as nosy and curious as you are. One day I left the code out at home, forgetting Hugo and I had a date. He'd already seen that I had several copies of *The Thirty-Nine Steps*." I could practically see her offhand shrug as we walked over the soft earth. "I guess he took a photo of it when I wasn't looking, became suspicious, and began deciphering my codes."

"Wait. You didn't know he'd found your ciphers?" I asked, surprised.

"Not at first," she said. "Nor did I know he'd sought you out. But it didn't matter. By the time he found you, he was a walking dead man. Though when you mentioned he'd dropped a Montblanc pen, I was a tad worried. He'd shown it to me once, so I knew about it. But I stood in the back parlor watching you after you saved it from Boomer, and you clearly didn't know what you'd found. That was when I realized Hugo had inadvertently given me more time."

Before I could reply—though I didn't know if there were even words to do so—Mrs. P. was shoving me over the threshold of the folly, taking me out of the cold wind into what felt like a round, nearly wind-free freezer that was about twelve feet in diameter.

Two cathedral-style windows with leaded panes let in much-needed light, but the only other details in the place were wooden benches hugging the perimeter, each made up of two wooden slats fitting into holes within decoratively carved limestone blocks and another block supporting the slats in the middle.

Occupying the center of the bench on my right was Pippa. Her hands were tied behind her back and looped around one of the wooden slats with what looked like twisted cording. It was shimmering in the slight glow of the folly, and I recognized it as the satin cording Pippa had bought for the New Year's Eve gala favors. I remembered seeing Mrs. P. cutting lengths of the stuff this very morning. She must have put the cording in one of her cargo pockets for just this moment, I thought wryly.

Pippa was shivering horribly, her head lolling like she was attempting to come back into consciousness.

I whirled on Mrs. P. "What did you do to her?"

Mrs. P. shrugged. "She was whining, so I had to give her a little bonk on the head to shut her up."

I took an angry step toward her, but Mrs. P. responded by grabbing my injured right wrist. I cried out, and tried to aim a kick at her. As I twisted, I felt something hard and plastic poking me under my left sleeve. I still had the plastic letter opener.

My twisting caused Mrs. P. to release me. Then, like a demonic cat, she lunged forward, shoving me in the back toward Pippa.

"Get over there and sit down."

As I stumbled forward, I brought my arms in close, like I was protecting my injured wrist, and slid the opener into my left palm. I cried out again on purpose as I landed in a heap next to Pippa. As I did, I forced my left arm around her back, feeling for her hands, pushing the little letter opener into her fingers.

"Lucy?" she said thickly. But her dark green eyes were focusing. I felt her fingers clamp down on mine.

"Boomer's okay," I said. "Just drugged."

Tears came into Pippa's eyes and she yelled at Mrs. P., "You're horrible! You told me he was dead!"

"Shut up," Mrs. P. snarled. "Both of you."

At that point, she seemed to decide that having me next to Pippa wasn't a good idea after all. Before I could fully swing around and sit down, Mrs. P. had grabbed the back of my down vest and hauled me to my feet again, shoving me across the folly floor to the bench on the other side. I managed to stay on my feet, but fell heavily onto the wooden slats. Looking up, I found Mrs. P. pointing her gun in my face.

FORTY-THREE

Turn sideways and put your wrists together behind your back," Mrs. P. demanded, gesturing with the gun.

Wincing, I did as she said, and before I could think of anything to stop it, I felt the satiny cording wrapping twice around my wrists. Then she wrapped it twice more around the backmost wooden slat of the bench, tying it off as expertly as she might a tourniquet.

I tried to move my hands, my injured wrist singing with pain, but it was no use. I only had one weapon left—the pencil in my boot—but there was no way for me to grab it.

Across the folly, Pippa was crying, her head bent low as sobs racked her body. I'd been hoping she would try to cut through the cording with the letter opener. Hell, its blade was so small, I didn't know if it could even cut through one strand, and by the utterly defeated look on her face as she cried, I guessed she'd attempted it, and failed.

We were both still tied up, and by the way Mrs. P. was pacing around, looking at us with a wild sort of feverish glee, we had little time on our side.

Then I remembered Dupart. Would he and his team be on their way? Would they even know where to look? I hadn't heard any approaching sirens at all as Mrs. P. was marching me toward the folly. But then again, would I? Pippa had said the woods offered a unique silence in the middle of bustling Austin.

There wasn't much I could do except keep Mrs. P. talking.

Remembering the motivation of the last killer I'd come across, I asked, "Mrs. P., is all this really because your grandfather was killed"—I just stopped myself from adding, "for being a traitor"—"or is this because, due to his death, you grew up with very little while Pippa and I had more advantages in life?"

She glared at me, then looked with disdain at her young employer. Then she shrugged.

"Honestly, I can't complain about my childhood. My parents gave me a decent life in Florida and I rarely wanted for much. At the Sutton property where my mum worked, they always let me come and swim in the pool, and I got to have my sweet sixteen party there. Yeah, it was real nice, for the most part."

"Then why?" I asked. "The least you can do is tell us." I jutted my chin toward Pippa, who was still crying, albeit more quietly now.

Mrs. P. walked over to me in a slow, confident manner. "Why, Lucy? Well, it's because I'd come home from school and find my father sitting and looking at his hands, which were always covered in dirt and grease, and calloused beyond belief. He'd just sit there, looking at them. And when I asked him one day why he did that, do you want to know what he said?"

She was waiting for my answer. "Yes," I said, my mouth dry.

Once again, she affected her working-class English accent. "'Love,' he said, 'It's because these hands were meant to be soft and clean. They were meant to butter my toast with a silver knife in the morning, grasp the stock of a fine grouse gun during the day, to cup a crystal port glass in the evening, and button silk pajamas at night.'"

Her clear blue eyes were far off, in the past, then they lasered in on me, almost making me want to flinch. She dropped the accent.

"He said the same thing every time I asked after that, which wasn't often. I was still young at the time and selfishly thought Dad just felt like he should have done better for himself and Mum and me. Still, as we both aged, me into my twenties, my dad into middle age, I watched him becoming more and more ashamed of the grease on his hands and only just being able to make ends meet."

She swung to face me. "It only got worse after my mum died, too. And soon, he was sick and dying himself, and that's when he finally told me the truth. Of what my grandmother found out, of who my grandfather was and what he did in the war." Her eyes had a fanatical gleam to them and her voice was righteous. "How he tried to turn the tide of D-Day, to turn England to the right side, to the side of *der Großdeutsches Reich*."

I saw Pippa go still at the outburst, raise her head, then blink in confusion. Like most Americans, she'd always heard "the Third Reich," not the German-language *der Großdeutsches Reich*, for "the Greater German Reich."

Mrs. P. hadn't noticed, though. Without warning, she'd rushed me again. She wanted me off guard, and it worked. I jerked back, banging the back of my head against the limestone wall. Her face was inches from mine, her arms on either side of me, caging me in. I saw the wild look in her eyes and her widening grin at how she'd startled me. I started to turn my face away when her smile gave way to that ever-present chuckle. It sounded sinister now, as puffs of her hot breath landed lightly on my cheek.

I made myself look at her. If she was going to kill me, she was going to have to look right at me to do it.

"But your grandfather," Mrs. P. drawled in acid tones. "He and his filthy cohorts stopped him. My grandfather was their leader before that. He was a sophisticated aristocrat, and a learned man, and those upstarts thought they knew what was better. They were the true traitors!"

She screamed it so loud, my head jerked back again and I felt my insides clench, waiting to hear the breathlike *ffft*. Instead, she pushed off my bench with surprising agility and wheeled round to Pippa, raising the pistol in her right hand.

As she did, however, she'd pushed off hard, making the slat to which my arms were tied bounce in its stone pocket and slide out a bit. My weight was on the foremost slat, so the change went unnoticed by Mrs. P. as she continued to rage. Inch by inch, I began sliding over, using my uninjured fingers to move the cording that attached me to the bench.

"And *your* great-grandmother, Miss Pippa?" The derision with which she said Pippa's name was almost sickening. "She seduced him! That hussy from the backwaters of Corpus Christi, Texas, seduced my high-born grandfather."

I felt the first loop of my binds come free as Mrs. P. pointed to herself with her free hand, as if she herself had been hoodwinked by Pippa's great-grandmother.

I was struggling to free the second half of my bindings from the slat and, for a brief, nauseating second, I saw Mrs. P. beginning to turn back toward me, when Pippa cried out, "My great-grandmother did what was right! She was brave!"

Mrs. P. turned back to her, her voice one of purest loathing. "That filthy woman made him think that she believed in his cause. Nell Davis was the traitor who ratted him out. *She* was at the heart of this treachery. And since I can't make her pay, you'll suffer for what she did." And as she raised her gun, the last bit of my binding escaped the wooden slat.

Hands still tied behind my back, I pitched forward off my bench like a drunken sprinter out of the starting blocks, aiming for Mrs. P.'s back and shouting, "Pippa, duck!" just as a screaming blond fury darted in through the folly's entrance.

Roselyn Sutton and I hit at almost the same time. I'd braced myself to head-butt Mrs. P. between her shoulder blades. Instead, Roselyn hit Mrs. P. like a battering ram from the side, and I smashed into Roselyn.

Mrs. P. was knocked off her feet and Roselyn and I both went down hard on the limestone floor. I managed to twist and felt the back shoulder of my vest tear as I skidded a few inches on the rough stone, my trussed wrists still behind my back. Stars popped into my eyes and pain shot through both arms. Roselyn, too, went flying off Mrs. P. and onto her hip at Pippa's feet. I watched the gun go flying out of Mrs. P.'s hand. I heard a breathy *ffft* and my heart about stopped, then I heard the sound of a chunk of limestone shattering.

Mrs. P. was stretching out for her gun, kicking her feet out like an angry mule, but Roselyn, who was now clearly in pain, still had a hold on Mrs. P.'s pant leg and was clawing at her.

Mrs. P. was much stronger than she looked and was gaining inches, though. I struggled to get up, but my left wrist wouldn't hold me and my right shoulder was shooting shards of pain to my nerve receptors. With a howl of agony, I rolled to my back and used my stomach muscles to pull myself up, my eyes squeezed shut with pain. I had to keep Mrs. P. from that gun!

"Don't. Move. Another. Inch."

I sucked in a sharp, terrified breath and opened my eyes, ready for the worst.

In a vision I felt would have made her brave great-grandmother proud, Pippa was standing, tall and strong, all tears gone. The gun was securely in her hands and pointing steadily at her front desk manager. One piece of the satin cording that had bound her wrists was hanging down, gently unraveling as it swayed like a feathery, silvery palm frond.

Mrs. P. looked up at Pippa with one last rage-filled expression, but her hand went slack just as Detective Dupart and his team rushed into the folly.

FORTY-FOUR

❧

"Here we are, the Lancaster Suite," Nurse Angelique sang out as she rolled me in a hospital wheelchair into my grandfather's room.

Grandpa was sitting up, his bruises making him look terrible, yet his expression was as bright as a summer's day. "Lucy, my darlin'!" He held out his hand to grasp mine.

And that wasn't just the painkillers talking in either of us, either, since both of us had refused anything stronger than acetaminophen. Of course, compared to Grandpa's, my injuries were just minor and mostly superficial, the worst being my wrist, which was badly sprained, and my shoulder, which was badly bruised.

"We have matching bruises now, Grandpa." I grinned, pointing to the one on the side of my forehead that I'd obtained during my collision with Roselyn, having smacked into one of the buttons on the lapel of her trench coat when we both flew at Mrs. P.

Before becoming a blond battering ram, Roselyn, it seemed, had been off running errands for the gala—all at the request of Mrs. P.—but had come home earlier than expected and was looking for her daughter.

"Actually," she'd told me as she, Pippa, and I rode together to the hospital, "I was hoping to discuss Mrs. P. with Pippa. I'd been feeling lately like she'd been overstepping her boundaries, and acting a little strangely." Meeting my eyes, she said, "When I got home, I parked at my cottage and was heading over to Pippa's just in time to hear you calling her name and see you go racing off into the woods."

Roselyn's face, unmarked except for dirt and one superficial scrape on her cheek, was set in a protective fury.

"I followed you, Lucy, and I was just about to call to you when I heard the silenced gunshot. I hid, but saw Mrs. P. taking you hostage. Then I followed y'all to the folly." She looked at Pippa. "I saw you crying, and heard all those *awful* things Mrs. P. was saying, and I just didn't think. I ran at her."

"You both did," Pippa said, smiling at us. "You both saved me."

"Yeah, but you got the gun away from her," I reminded Pippa. "Looking like quite the super spy, I might add. I think we all saved each other."

"We did," Pippa said, and Roselyn proceeded to fuss over her daughter for the rest of the ride, only letting up briefly when Pippa received a call from the vet where Boomer had been taken for observation. He would be fine, and we all breathed a sigh of relief.

Thankfully, my grandfather knew I didn't want to be fussed over, just like he didn't. We'd get enough of it from my parents, who were flying back early from Turks and Caicos to take care of Grandpa, and would no doubt add me to their nursing list once they saw me. Instead, Grandpa and I joked and laughed—but only after I gave him the minute-by-minute lowdown on everything that had happened since his accident.

"You know," Grandpa said, shaking his head, "I should have trusted my gut. The way Mrs. P. responded to me about there being another George Lancaster. It was overacted, a bit fishy, I have to tell you. But I was too determined to get that pen in case the microdot happened to be already on the viewer." He sighed. "I should have mentioned it to you, my love. It was the mistake of one who's been away from the game too long."

"What amazed me was how she used your rule of staying as close to the truth as possible. There was almost nothing Mrs. P. lied about, Grandpa," I said. "The truth became her weapon, keeping her under everyone's radar for so long. She only began to slip up when she started to rush."

Grandpa arched one white eyebrow. "Do you know how her grandfather, Reinhard von Pöllmacher, slipped up to Judith—Nell Davis, I mean—which led Nell to have to seduce him to get into his confidence?"

I'd given Grandpa the list showing all the real names of the spies he'd served with on Operation Greenfinch. It had moved him to see their names, and he'd run a finger down the list of code names, nodding at each one like he was seeing a list of old friends. Now I sat forward, all ears. I couldn't wait to hear more of the story. "How?"

Grandpa smiled. He'd already told me how much he'd admired Nell Davis Sutton, calling her "outstandingly smart and capable, with the courage of five men. I was proud to call her my friend, even if I didn't know her real name until today."

I could see the warm memories of her shining through the bruises on his face. I already had plans to videotape Grandpa discussing his wartime memories of Nell and her heroics so they could be added to the Sutton family video. With Pippa's permission, I would also submit the video to the Library of Congress's Veteran's Oral History Project, to be saved and viewed for generations to come.

That was, I'd videotape him once he recovered from his injuries and no longer had various shades of black, blue, and greenish yellow on his face. Until then, he had a date with Pippa on the second of January to meet at his favorite diner in Wimberley and tell her about her ancestor.

"Nell had just met her boyfriend," Grandpa was saying. "Pippa's great-grandfather, that is."

"James Sutton," I said.

"That's right. They met in the Dorchester Hotel, and they'd fallen in love. Soon after, she was paired with von Pöllmacher on a mission into France, where they had to play lovers. She told me she thought of James every time she looked at von Pöllmacher, and it worked a little too well. He misread her signals and confessed that he'd been in love with her—and her Aryan looks—since their first meeting."

"No," I breathed.

"It's true," Grandpa said. "She'd been a little suspicious of his allegiances for a time already, and one night of feigned passion on her part and a few hints about how brilliant she thought Hitler was, and Operation Greenfinch came into being."

"Wooooow," I said. "Wow, wow, wow."

"That was pretty much my reaction, too," Grandpa said. I noticed he was starting to blink more and I could see his energy was beginning to wane. I still had a couple more questions that couldn't wait, though.

"Any chance you've figured out who your good Samaritan was, the man who helped you the night of your accident?" I asked. "Which we now know wasn't an accident at all, but Mrs. P., wearing a wig and driving a rental car. She confessed, and they found the rental-car reservation on her computer when it was searched."

Mrs. P.'s anger and loss of control were such that when she was led away in handcuffs, she screamed about the Greater German Reich, how she had killed to avenge her grandfather and his love for the fatherland, and even sold out her cousin as being the driver of the car that had run over Alastair Newell when Mrs. P. had last been in Germany.

Dupart later told me that, once in custody at the APD, Mrs. P. had boasted of how easy it had been to kill Penelope Ohlinger once she convinced Penelope to come to Austin. They'd met for a walk when Penelope couldn't sleep and Mrs. P. had brought her tea laced with sugar and heart meds.

Later, Mrs. P. even ranted about her plans for killing Naomi Van Dorn and Fiona Kenland. Acting on my tip, Dupart had already contacted Naomi, who'd canceled her trip into Austin, but was recording her phone conversations with a British-accent-sporting Mrs. P.

As for Fiona, she'd twice canceled plans to fly to Austin to meet with Mrs. P. From what Dupart told me, one of Mrs. P.'s last admissions before her lawyer showed up was to say she'd nearly given up on Fiona and was thinking of just "hiring a hit man and being done with it."

Grandpa shook his head. "Such a waste to have so much hatred like that. It ate her up over the years. Did they find the Omega Weems aviator watch at her place as well?"

"Actually, they found it in the pocket of her jacket. She already had a buyer lined up and had planned to meet with him and make the exchange after she'd killed Pippa and me. How did you know about her having the watch?"

He shrugged. "Stands to reason, doesn't it? Plus, she had a

thing for watches. The Weems is extremely valuable. I'd bet she was hoping to cash it in before she left for Germany."

"Wow, right again," I said. "You're good at this, Grandpa." I told him that Uncle Dave was so happy to finally be exonerated that he'd sat down on one of the green sofas and literally started crying.

I snapped my fingers. "Speaking of Mrs. P., I found out why she was always called 'Mrs.' when she was never married. Pippa said she didn't like being called 'Ms.' or 'Miss,' and she didn't like her first name, either—which is Gertie, believe it or not—so Mrs. P. it was."

Grandpa just blinked bemusedly and shook his head.

"So, I guess you haven't met your good Samaritan?" I asked, bringing the subject back on track. "I was hoping to thank him for what he did to help you."

"Help me?" Grandpa repeated. "No, he *saved* me. Kept me talking, and wrote down what I asked and made sure it got to you. He's also the one who put a guard on me. He's a good sort, a truly good man." His eyes twinkled. "But I expect you'll get the chance to thank him soon enough."

He gave me one of his infuriatingly enigmatic smiles. I wanted to ask what he meant, and I also had a million other questions, but I could see he was rapidly becoming tired. I asked him one more question before I called Nurse Angelique back in to check him out and wheel me to where I could wait for Serena and Josephine to come pick me up.

"I've been meaning to ask you about the Montblanc Hugo left us. Do you still have the one that was issued to you? I don't recall ever seeing it in your collection."

"No, my darlin'. Mine was lost in service to a brave young Frenchwoman," Grandpa said with a grin and a yawn. "I caught a Nazi manhandling her just a couple of days before the Germans officially surrendered. I walked right up, pulled the cap off, and stabbed him in the thigh with the nib. Howled like a baby, he did. And when he yanked it out, he was so angry he threw it into the flames of his motorcycle, which the young Frenchwoman had set on fire in defiance. I helped her escape, and the Nazi was soon being marched out of town, limping badly, I might add. All in all, I feel like my Montblanc met a heroic fate."

I bent over and kissed his cheek. "*You* were the hero, as you've always been to us, and especially to me."

Once I was released, Josephine and Serena took me straight to Big Flaco's Tacos, where Flaco stopped in his tracks as soon as he saw me.

"*Ay, Lucia,*" he said, taking one look at my bandaged wrist and generally bruised appearance and immediately going into Scary Mexican Second Father Mode. "*¿Qué pasó?*" Rapid-fire Spanish followed that, which Josephine translated for Serena.

"To put it sans swear words, darling, he's threatening to find whoever did this to his beautiful Lucia and make them pay in ways that will have them screaming for their mummy and wishing they'd never been born."

Serena feigned an exasperated look. "I'd prefer to hear it *with* the swear words, please."

In minutes, I was seated at my favorite barstool and plied with all my favorite tacos, plus guacamole, queso, and churros with Mexican-chocolate dipping sauce for dessert. Flaco hovered around me, giving anyone who accidentally passed too near me such a stare-down that they veered away, giving the three of us a wide berth.

He also threatened to assign me a bodyguard, saying something about calling his son, and only backed off when Serena and Josephine promised they wouldn't leave me alone in the coming days, and because I swore to come for breakfast every day until he was satisfied I was healing properly.

Afterward, against my friends' protests, I went to the office. "I have some work I need to do, including editing the video with the two interviews I did this week with Pippa's cousins. And, to be honest, I could use a little bit of peace and quiet."

They relented, but only after seeing me safely into the office, where Serena laid out my next dose of acetaminophen and Josephine made me a big pot of Darjeeling tea.

Once they left, I let the events of the day fade into the background, letting my work soothe me back into equilibrium. The first thing I did was get ahold of Sean, as it was nearing the end of his workday in DC. When he answered, I spent the first twenty minutes updating him on what had happened and explaining how he'd helped me uncover a murderer.

"I can't thank you enough, Sean," I said with fervor.

"Anytime, my friend," he said.

"If that's truly the case," I said, "is there a chance I could ask one more favor?"

"Name it," he said with a laugh, and I explained about some extra research I'd done weeks ago that I was pretty sure I was correct about, but I needed verification.

"I'd love to do the verifying myself, but it will take longer. Any possibility you might have a researcher or two running around who could speed it up?"

Sean's voice was warm as he said, "You know, I think I just might." He finished by saying he'd get back to me as soon as he could.

FORTY-FIVE

❧

I t's a good thing you were already planning to wear this strapless dress," Serena said, pulling the zip up gently so as to not jostle my scraped and bruised right shoulder.

Predictably, it had stiffened and darkened overnight, though the spa day the three of us enjoyed had helped, with the facialist carefully avoiding my scrapes and the massage therapist putting warm, moist heat on my shoulder while she gently worked out the rest of my knots.

Except for Detective Dupart calling me to verify a few more details and the walk I took with Pippa where I filled in some gaps in the story and she fretted a little more about Roselyn, who'd disappeared yet again, it was a thoroughly relaxing day. While I didn't let the cat out of the bag regarding Roselyn and her work with the FBI, I did say to Pippa, "Your mom loves you and will come clean. Just give her a little more time."

The best part was a long visit with Grandpa. I brought him some tacos and we'd discussed all sorts of things, including my hopes that Sean could come through for me again. I'd marveled at how much better Grandpa looked and felt, too.

He would be able to go home tomorrow, and neither he nor I could wait. We spent the last hour deciding on gifts for Dr. Brozo, Nurse Angelique, and his still silent, still watchful guard, Tom, who'd leapt into action the moment he got my text and pulled a poisoned caramel from Nurse Angelique's fingers just as she was about to take a bite.

Now Serena turned me around to straighten my dress and nodded to my right wrist. "And you can hardly see the bandage with that silver cuff Pippa gave you as a thank-you. It complements this dress perfectly."

I touched the wide Tiffany cuff, thinking of the inscription Pippa had engraved underneath—three dots and a dash. She'd bought one for herself as well and would be wearing it tonight, too.

"You don't think I look too much like a disco ball, do you?" I said, slowly spinning under the lights of my room's bathroom to where the multitude of silvery paillettes on my mini-dress cast nickel-sized orbs of light against the walls.

Josephine held up my new heels. "Only if disco balls are beautiful, bad-ass genealogists who saved the lives of two women yesterday."

Serena put her hand on her hip. "Not to mention the lives of the other people that psycho Mrs. P. had plans to kill."

I smiled. Earlier, they'd already let me have a good cry about the fact that I hadn't been able to save Hugo Markman, Chef Rocky, or Penelope Ohlinger. It was a hard thing to come to grips with, but they helped me to see that if I'd had true knowledge of what was going on earlier, I would have done my damnedest to save any or all of them, and that made me feel a little better.

"Thanks, girls," I said.

"Now, how do you want to do your hair?" Josephine asked, pulling out a curling iron, a curling wand, and a straightener.

"Y'all choose," I said, shaking my hair back. "Do with me what you will."

"Hot damn. It's like Christmas and Hanukkah all over again," Serena told Jo, who gave a little excited squeal and began plugging everything in.

An hour later, Serena transformed my long, straight, dark brown hair into voluminous soft curls that tumbled over my shoulders and mostly hid the bruises on my right shoulder blade. Josephine had given me a perfectly done smoky eye and a neutral, blush-pink lip.

When Walter and Ahmad came up to my room and saw us three looking glammed up, they looked stunned in the best way and said all sorts of appreciative things to us. I was left as the fifth wheel, just as I'd known I would be, when we finally walked downstairs to the music coming up from the ballroom, but Walter offered me his other arm, and I took it, ready to thoroughly enjoy myself.

At least, I would enjoy myself until we all shouted "Happy New Year!" Then I already had my escape route back to my room mapped out. It was my mission to be out of my disco-ball dress and into my pajamas by ten minutes into the new year.

"Is it snowing yet?" I asked as we descended. I craned my head to look through the front door as another group of guests walked in, dressed to the nines.

Josephine laughed. "You can't tell by the fact that everybody is walking in without snow on them?"

I grinned. "You haven't been in Central Texas long enough to understand, Jo. It almost never snows here—and when it does, it's usually just a light flurry. You could walk through it and be completely dry in the time it takes you to cross the porch."

Serena, who was looking out the window like me, added,

"But it's still snow, and we reserve the right to lose our minds over it."

"Then I'll lose my mind over it with y'all," Josephine said in solidarity, almost sounding like a true Texan. Serena and I looked at each other, then said, "Too bloody right!"

As we reached the last step, Pippa came out of the bar in a metallic green slip dress. Her blond waves were straightened and pulled back into a sleek ponytail with a deep side part. She was laughing with Roselyn, and I confess I stared.

I'd known Roselyn for almost two months now, and I'd never seen her laugh. Not a real, happy laugh, at least. It absolutely transformed her. She looked gorgeous in a shift dress of gold silk with her hair piled up in curls on top of her head. She was visibly limping, her hip having been as badly bruised as my shoulder, but she was looking radiantly happy.

I turned to my friends. "Would y'all give me a few minutes? I'd like to talk to Pippa and Roselyn."

They wandered off toward the ballroom. Pippa hugged me gently, but with feeling, and Roselyn said, "It's over, Lucy. The man I told you about was arrested earlier today." She looked at her daughter and found Pippa's hand. "I've told Pippa everything, and she's going to help me stay on track."

"I'm really, really glad," I said, smiling widely.

Now Roselyn held her hand out to me. Surprised, I took it as she said, "I'm free, and Pippa's alive and safe because of you. I don't know how to thank you."

"You just did," I said.

Roselyn smiled, warmly and genuinely. "And now I think we all deserve some champagne and a damn good time," she said, and ushered us into the beautifully decked out ballroom teeming with smiling revelers.

I found my friends and finally, after a long week, let my hair down.

The five of us were in the bar as midnight approached. Pippa had joined us, holding the hand of a handsome guy she introduced as Alan. They'd known each other for many years, it seemed, and he'd come to the gala with his sister, who would be holding her wedding at the Hotel Sutton in the spring.

The group of us had long since commandeered the little area of high-top tables and black-leather barstools situated just inside the bar, talking and laughing and enjoying ourselves for the last hour. Serena and Walter had just brought us all fresh flutes of champagne when Josephine's boyfriend, Ahmad, said, "We're one minute out. Get ready!"

Serena caught my eye.

"*Stay*," she mouthed from across the table, but I shook my head.

Ahmad and Walter had their respective arms around my two best friends. Alan did the same to Pippa. I was happy for all of them, but I was finding myself looking over my left shoulder to eye the staircase that would take me back up to my room. I knew all three couples would be getting their romance on as soon as the clock struck midnight, and I didn't want to witness it for even a nanosecond longer than I had to.

"Here we go," Walter said, raising his champagne flute. "Ten, nine, eight—"

I started chanting with everyone else, and we could hear the ballroom erupting with the same words.

"Seven, six, five—" I saw Serena and Josephine's smiles change from happy to excited.

"Four, three—" I saw Walter reach out and clap someone on

the shoulder as I felt a warm hand slide down my left arm and take my hand.

"Two, one—" I looked down at my hand, then up into a pair of blue eyes with a little bit of green around the pupils.

"Happy New Year!"

The shouts were in my ears, but all I heard was Ben's voice saying quietly, "Happy New Year, Lucy. I'm so sorry."

I chose to believe him.

"Kiss me," I said, a smile rising up inside me and onto my face. He took my face in his hands and did as he was told.

FORTY-SIX

B ut I thought you didn't go undercover," I said. Then I arched an eyebrow. "Or is that some tosh you told me two months ago to get my goat?"

We'd moved to the back parlor, which mercifully had been devoid of both other people and ghosts. I'd shut the door, Ben had locked it, and we hadn't spoken for several minutes as our lips were otherwise engaged.

Finally, when my neck ached from tilting my head back, he seemed to remember I was short and led me to one of the leather sofas. He sat—my goodness, did he look handsome in a tux—and pulled me down gently onto his lap, careful not to jar my right side. There we didn't speak for several more minutes.

Finally coming up for air, he began explaining how he'd ended up ghosting me.

"I had to go to DC right after what happened with Senator Applewhite, but you already know that. I was only supposed to be there for a couple of days, but this other situation came up. I can't discuss it, but I understand you know the gist of it from Roselyn Sutton?" Now *his* eyebrow arched. "And, ah, maybe from being an amateur sleuth again and nearly blowing Roselyn's and my cover?"

"I plead the Fifth," I said. "And this is not about me, but about your explanation. Please continue, Special Agent Turner."

"I'm never going to stop you from poking your nose in, am I?" he said.

"Probably not," I replied. "At least, not if my genealogy skills can help save someone. It's not within me to back away if someone is in danger."

He nodded. "I figured as much." Then he grinned and kissed me again.

"Hey," I said, pulling away a bit breathlessly. "What gives? More explaining and less lip-locking, sir. How did you, specifically, get roped into going undercover?"

"This guy we just put away today, he fancied himself a sophisticated gangster of sorts. He liked to be around highly educated people who could talk history and art. Made him feel better for his men to 'look like gentlemen and speak like gentlemen,' as he put it." Ben shrugged. "I fit the bill."

I leaned back and looked him up and down, still digging his longer hair and dressed-up Han Solo vibe. "Heck, yeah, you do. Can you wear this outfit more often?"

He assumed his Fed Face. "We'll see, Ms. Lancaster."

For some reason, that sounded all kinds of hot now. We spent another few minutes not talking. After a while, he started chuckling.

I swatted his arm. "Hey, that's not a nice thing to do when a woman's kissing you!"

"No," he said, giving me his oh-so-charming grin. "That part is awesome. I was remembering the funny thing about my cover name."

I eyed him. "Do tell."

"It was Brent Embry, but that wasn't what it was in the beginning."

I remembered Pippa telling me Roselyn had a Brent Embry in her contacts and several calls from him. Things were making more and more sense . . .

"Do you want to know what it was supposed to be?" He put his lips close to my ear, sending delicious shivers down my spine, and whispered, "Brent Ebrington."

When my jaw dropped and I stared at him, he nodded his confirmation.

"I couldn't believe it, either. I'd gotten your email telling me about my ancestor named Ebrington Chaucer FitzHugh—which, you're right, it's a great name—but it's hardly a common one. So, I asked the guy who prepared my cover identity how he chose it. He said there's a pub in England with that name and he liked it, simple as that."

Ben's smile widened and linked his fingers through mine. "I had to tell him I knew a smart and seriously beautiful woman who was also a little more curious than is sometimes good for her." He gently stroked my bruised right arm, giving me more good chills that dulled the pain better than acetaminophen ever could. "I told him this smart and beautiful woman would recognize the name Ebrington and might be compelled to ask questions if she heard it. So, he changed it to Embry."

He was darn right I would have recognized it and asked questions, but I didn't get to say so because he kept talking. Really, this was the most I'd ever heard Special Agent Ben Turner say anything. I was quite enjoying it.

He swallowed, then looked up at me, giving me a clear view of his pretty eyes. "You know, I don't normally believe in signs, but I have to admit, I took the fact that they chose my ancestor's name—the ancestor you found for me—as a sign that you might forgive me for going radio silent on you without any warning or explanation."

I took his face in my hands. I'd been seeing some signposts, too.

"First of all," I said, "as the granddaughter of a tried-and-true spy who did what he had to do for our country's safety, I get your job requirements now more than ever. Next, as a history buff, I could name more examples than you can count of people like you who have set aside their own personal safety and reputation for the greater good, including, if you remember, your own ancestors."

He grinned, but I put a finger to his lips.

"Third, I couldn't call myself a professional genealogist if I didn't understand that people don't get a free ride in life, and making hard decisions from time to time is what got our ancestors to a place where you and I could be born and live and sometimes make hard decisions of our own."

I grinned, then felt my voice catch. He hadn't mentioned it, hadn't taken credit, but I now knew who Grandpa's good Samaritan was.

I stroked his cheek with my thumb. "But right now, the best and most important reason why there is no doubt I forgive you is that you saved my grandfather's life, Ben. After Mrs. P. tried to kill him with her car, you called nine-one-one, stayed with him, talked to him, and made him feel safer by letting him know I would be contacted. You must have told him who you were, because he told you the code name Greenfinch."

My voice went to an emotional whisper. "Then you got a guard placed on him, ensuring both his and my peace of mind. And now I know that *was* you I saw at the hospital, which means you went to visit him—all because you're a good man, and not to earn points with me. That, Ben Turner, descendant of Ebrington Chaucer FitzHugh, is why I'm eternally grateful to you."

I put my arms around his neck, letting my fingers run through his hair, and I kissed him with more passion than I'd ever kissed any man, and he responded in a way that left me without any more words. For a minute, at least. I still had to know a thing or two.

"Why were you in Wimberley in the first place, though?" I asked. "Did you know you were driving behind my grandfather?"

Ben replied, "To the first question, it was the base for my undercover assignment. The guy we put away liked living in a small town. To your second question, I didn't know it was your grandfather at the time, but I recognized him as soon as I saw him. Plus, he was able to tell me his name. I was just in the right place at the right time."

"But how did you know it was my grandfather before he told you his name?" I asked, still baffled. "Do you have some sort of dossier on me?"

Ben tilted his head back, a deep, sexy laugh erupting in his throat. "No. I've been in your condo, remember? You have at least five photos with your granddad in them, including that cool one from World War Two."

"So you were snooping?" I teased, arching one eyebrow.

"Observing my surroundings," he corrected, then changed the subject. "You saw me at the hospital?"

"Getting out of the elevator, yeah." I gave him another once-over. "I *really* liked that look with the scruff and motorcycle jacket." I gave him two thumbs up for extra emphasis.

"More than the tux?" he asked, pulling at his bow tie, which had gone decidedly crooked.

"I like both looks equally," I replied, straightening it again. "I'm a complicated woman with many facets, Agent Turner. Like it or lump it."

"Ms. Lancaster, I'm just fine with you being complicated and many-faceted." His smile faltered a bit. "However, speaking of complications, it turns out I'm not too bad at the undercover work. It seems I'll be doing more of it."

I thought about how I felt about that. As an independent person, I didn't need someone at my side every minute of the day. I just wanted someone who wanted to be with me as much as I wanted to be with them, however much time we got to spend together. I said as much to Ben, but added, "I do reserve the right to worry about you, though."

"I'm okay with that," he said. "And on that note, I do have one other thing to give you."

"Here?" I said, and he laughed.

"That, I hope, will come later, but it's actually something else. Something you were working on, that your granddad told me about and I was able to help with it. Would you go get Pippa and Roselyn?"

I was about to ask why, but his face smoothed into that infuriating look that said I wouldn't get any more out of him, so I slid off his lap and went in search of my client and her mother.

"I'll bring her right back," I told Alan with a wink. He looked like he'd been shot with cupid's arrow for sure.

The three of us walked into the back parlor, where Ben was unfolding a piece of paper that looked to be an email. I caught the address and saw it was Sean Nelson's.

"How do you know Sean?" I asked.

Ben grinned. "I'm a part-time history professor and I generally handle fraud cases, remember? I've worked with Sean many times on many subjects. He's a great guy."

He turned to Roselyn and Pippa as I stood, staring at him with all sorts of feelings rushing through me, including curiosity.

"Roselyn, I'm going to come right to the point," he said. "You explained to Lucy that you didn't want your genealogy traced because your German American grandfather was shot for being a traitor. That he was selling secrets to the Nazis, and they still shot him."

"What?" Pippa said, looking at her mother in shock. For her part, Roselyn's eyes snapped with embarrassed anger, and she had them trained on me.

Ben's voice was calming. "Before you decide to be upset with Lucy, let me continue. Now, Lucy here had already done some preliminary research on your family."

I blushed, and Ben gave me a hand motion that encouraged me to explain.

"I did, yes," I said, directing my words to Roselyn, "but I stopped looking at your paternal grandparents, Wilhelm and Anna Fischer, when I realized you weren't interested in me tracing your line."

I looked back and forth between mother and daughter, looking so much alike, and with so many traits of their ancestors.

"I'd requested your grandfather Wilhelm's service records at the same time I'd requested those of James Sutton's," I said to Roselyn. "James's still haven't come in, of course, but your grandfather's did. They were flagged with a request for posthumous commendation."

Roselyn's lips parted. "You must have the wrong man, then. Mine was a traitor. There's no way he would have been given a medal."

I shook my head. "I do have the right man. I went back and traced everything again, just to be sure. Then I asked my friend Sean at the National Archives to expedite the reason behind the posthumous commendation, but I haven't heard back."

Ben smiled. "That's where I come in. I wanted to do something special for Lucy. And when her grandfather mentioned that she'd contacted Sean about this information, I called Sean and asked that he send the report to me instead."

Now there were three women gaping at Ben. He cleared his throat a bit nervously, which almost made me laugh, and handed Roselyn the email. "This is what Sean found out."

Roselyn read it with Pippa looking over her shoulder. Their faces went from disbelief to shock to hope.

"Is this true?" Pippa asked. "Wilhelm volunteered to pretend to be a Nazi sympathizer to gain intelligence for the Allies?"

Ben nodded. "It was an eleventh-hour sort of Hail-Mary-pass kind of thing, or so it seems. They didn't have time to get a trained OSS or SOE agent in place, and Wilhelm, or Wil, as everyone called him, volunteered. He was a German immigrant and spoke the language fluently. As you read, he almost succeeded. By coincidence, one of the Nazis he had to engage recognized him as a childhood friend and knew Wil and his parents had moved to America."

Ben's expression was sober. "Roselyn, your grandfather was tortured, then killed. In order to retain the cover of the rest of the mission, they had to play him off as a traitor. But he wasn't. Just like Pippa's grandparents, your grandfather was a hero."

Roselyn stood, shocked, then her face crumpled. Later, she would tell me she wasn't upset for herself, but for her grandmother, father, and aunt, who, much like Mrs. P.'s grandmother and father, had been tainted by association with a traitor.

After a minute, Ben cleared his throat, his voice becoming very much the formal government official.

"Roselyn, both for your efforts to help us put away a very dangerous criminal, and also for what you and your family have been through, we would like to put forth a recommendation that your grandfather be finally, posthumously, awarded for his selfless bravery during the war. With your agreement, we'll start things rolling as soon as possible."

Ben would claim later he was attacked by two blondes. The smile on his face told everyone how much he loved it.

"Look," Pippa said, pointing out the window to Sarah Bess's lit-up knot garden. "It's snowing!"

It wasn't just some flurry, either. Fat flakes of white snow were coming down. The boxwood hedges were already covered in a thin layer of white, as was the grass.

"Want to go outside?" Ben whispered in my ear, hearing my excited squeal. He was already taking off his tux coat and putting it over my shoulders before I'd even said, "Heck, yeah!"

Roselyn said to her daughter, "Let's go get our coats and go outside, too."

The grandfather clock chimed one gong—it was an hour into the new year. Ben took my hand and led me out the French doors into the winter wonderland, the white fairy lights making the falling snow glitter like diamonds.

Ben kissed me again as the snow fell gently all around us. "Happy New Year, Lucy Lancaster."

"Happy New Year, Special Agent Ben Turner," I replied, making him laugh and kiss me again.

"Lucy!" Pippa called out. I turned to see Pippa and Roselyn on the porch. Her arm was around her mother's waist and they both looked happier than I'd ever seen them.

"Thank you," she said, "for everything."

I blew her a kiss, then extended my arm with the silver cuff, holding out my first two fingers. Pippa grinned and did the same to me in return.

"Peace?" Ben asked.

I smiled. "V for Victory."

ACKNOWLEDGMENTS

I'm incredibly grateful to my fabulous agents, Christina Hogrebe and Jess Errera of Jane Rotrosen Agency, and to everyone at Minotaur Books for all their enthusiastic support of me and my books. Thanks especially to my incredible team: Hannah (both of you) and Nettie in editorial, Kayla in publicity, Steve and Mac in marketing, and my copyeditors and proofreaders. David Rotstein also deserves a special thanks for designing another utterly gorgeous cover.

Many thanks go to Alice Braud-Jones for letting me interview her about genealogical procedures, for taking the time to read over my book for accuracy, and for giving me extra fascinating facts to add to Lucy's world. Thank you so much as well to Mary Anthony Startz for discussing genealogical research tips with me, and for introducing me to Alice.

I'm also indebted to my wonderful uncle, Doug Perkins, for talking genealogy with me over the years and for being a great writer, editor, and inspiration who has always cheered me on.

Another round of thanks goes to my friend Sergeant Doug Thomas of the Harris County Sheriff's Office, for once more being my go-to person for answering all manner of police-related questions.

And huge thanks to my writer friend Catherine B. Custalow, MD, PhD, who graciously answered all my questions about how a certain character could have died, with the amused understanding that I might have taken some liberties with the knowledge to suit my purposes.

Last, but not least, thank you so much to the International Spy Museum and the unnamed yet very helpful advisory board member for so kindly answering my questions about microdots, and to the lovely specialist at the National Archives for giving me such great information about World War II research.

If there are any errors in the genealogy/research world, medical world, spy world, or the law-enforcement world, they're definitely mine.

To all my friends and to all the readers and book clubs who have embraced my taco-loving genealogist Lucy, thank you. Y'all are amazing, truly.

Of course, I'm forever grateful to my parents for their love, encouragement, and absolutely everything else. I'm so incredibly lucky in my lineage, that's for sure.

Read on for an excerpt from FATAL
FAMILY TIES—

the next installment in the Ancestry
Detective mysteries,

available soon in hardcover from
Minotaur Books!

ONE

❧

"Lucy, you have to help me!"

I just about jumped a mile off my barstool and the taco I was angling toward my mouth with the speed of the ravenous hit my cheek instead. Juicy pork carnitas dribbled down the left side of my face and several thinly sliced radishes spilled onto my plate.

A paper napkin appeared, and then another. I snatched them and tried to mop myself up before anything dripped onto my white silk blouse.

"You have cilantro on your chin." Another napkin fluttered in my face.

Removing the offending herb, I turned with narrowed eyes and then felt them pop open again in surprise. There, sitting next to me at the counter at Big Flaco's Tacos, was Camilla Braithwaite, one of my three least-favorite former coworkers.

"Camilla?" I spluttered. "What are you doing here? How did you even find me?"

In answer, she pulled a magazine from her purse and dropped it down on the counter. It landed on the edge of my bowl of queso, sending precarious ripples through the warm, spicy cheese dip. Hastily, I moved the dish away as she jabbed her index finger on the magazine. The cover and several pages had been turned back so it was open to an article near the middle. Camilla's striking, light brown eyes were intense, almost as much as the scent of her perfume.

"I took a chance and went to your office, even though it's Saturday. Josephine—she's British, right? She was speaking Italian on the phone when she let me in, but when we talked she sounded like the Duchess of Cambridge. Anyway, she said you were here. I've come to see you, about this."

With one more jab of her finger for emphasis, I looked down.

The Battle of Just Plain Bull: The inflated life and continued lies of America's last Civil War soldier.

Despite my irritation, I picked up the magazine. "Hey, I saw this headline a few days ago." I flipped to the cover to be sure. Yep, it was *Chronology*, a national publication put out by one of the biggest and best museums in the country, and known for making articles about history so interesting they inspired many a social media discussion, and even a few movies. "I get the digital version now, but it's on my list of articles to read." Glancing at some of the photos, the history-loving side of me was thrilled. Despite myself, I smiled. Dang my naturally sunny disposition! It came out at the worst times.

Camilla didn't return my smile. "So you haven't read it yet."

"Nope," I said, handing her back the magazine with my left hand while picking up my fork with my right to spear some of the fallen carnitas and radishes. Adding a squirt of lime onto my forkful, I savored it, wishing Camilla and her flowery perfume would go away so I could enjoy my lunch in peace. I was finishing up a client's genealogy project today and if I didn't lollygag at Flaco's like I normally did, I could complete it by early afternoon, leaving my Saturday evening open for much better things. Glancing out the taqueria's glass doors, where March had brought sunshine and springtime weather, I felt my spirits lifting at the thought of the romantic plans I had in store for tonight with—

"Read it now," Camilla said, interrupting my daydream and turning the article back around. My eyebrow arched. "Please," she added.

With a stiff toss of her head, her thick russet-colored hair obediently swished from her collarbone to behind her shoulders. It'd been nearly four years since I'd last seen Camilla. Yet, during the sixteen months I'd worked at the Howland University Library in Houston, where I'd been a staff genealogist and she one of three research librarians, I'd come to recognize she only did that particular move with her hair when she was stressed. When she was relaxed, she brushed it back with her hand.

In truth, Camilla Braithwaite was normally fairly even keeled. In fact, of the three, I'd liked Camilla the most. She'd been easy going and had a good sense of humor . . . when she and I'd been alone, that was. When the other two research librarians—namely, Roxie Iverson and Patrice Alvarez—were around and push came to shove in the library's social pecking order, however, Camilla had been a lemming. She'd followed the mean-spirited direction of the other two, treating me as if my niceness and generally happy personality were traits they found irritating rather than worthy of appreciation. In appeasing the small-mindedness of our coworkers, Camilla had helped me feel like a permanent outsider. So, she'd become my third least-favorite.

"Why is it so important I read this?" I asked, holding up the magazine with one hand. With the other, I scooped up a hefty bite of my fallen carnitas, just succeeding in delivering them to my mouth without incident as she replied.

"Because I need you to prove it's not true."

TWO

❧

My curiosity grappled with my perhaps saner instinct to get up and walk out the door. The last time Camilla had asked me to do something for her, it was a project she couldn't be bothered to do herself. Then when I'd completed it and our mutual boss had complimented the final product, Camilla had taken credit for my work.

"Why me?" I asked her now. "You're a researcher, and a very good one. Why can't you do it?"

"Because it involves the type of research genealogists normally do, and that's not my forte. Nor Roxie's or Patrice's, you know that."

Darn right I did.

"Then why haven't you asked Ginger?" I said. "She's an incredible genealogist, and right there, in-house, working with you."

When I'd worked at Howland University, Ginger Liening had been my direct manager, a senior genealogist, and taught the Genealogy Studies courses. I'd adored working alongside her—when I got the chance to, at least. As an entry-level staff genealogist, I'd often been tasked with helping research librarians as much as Ginger. Roxie had claimed they needed my help, but what they really wanted was someone to do their grunt work. Since I'd needed the job, both for experience and money, I hadn't been in a position to do anything but say yes to every project.

"Ginger retired and moved to Arizona with her husband six months ago," Camilla said.

"Dang it, that's right. I sent her flowers and everything. I don't know where my mind was." Scooping up another bite of carnitas, I said, "Though surely y'all have hired a replacement since then. Why not ask her or him?"

"Him, actually," she said. "Trent—that's his name. He does a decent job, yes, but I want someone who does what you do."

Camilla's cheeks turned a bit pink, which I'd never seen happen to her before.

"Which is?" I asked, though I suspected I knew what she meant.

She cleared her throat. "Look . . . back when we worked together, you . . . *cared*."

"You say that like it's a bad thing," I grumbled, but Camilla went on regardless.

"I saw it when people came in, wanting help with their ancestry," she said. "You understood how the past could affect a person or their family. That's what I need, someone who cares when things are sensitive."

I blinked. That wasn't what I expected.

"Not because I . . . you know . . . helped solve a couple of mysteries late last year?"

"A couple?" she said, the furrows in her brow deepening. "I only heard about the one with the senator."

I wanted to kick myself. At my request, the FBI and the Austin Police Department had worked to withhold from the press my name and assistance in uncovering a murderous hotel front-desk manager's attempts to take out the descendants of eight World War II spies, one of which included me. Instead, all of the kudos had gone to Detective Maurice Dupart and his team at the APD, and I'd been relieved to remain out of the spotlight.

"Never mind," I said hastily. Taking the magazine from her, I flipped through the article's pages. "You'd better order something," I said. "This puppy is six pages long and I don't speed read."

Ana, Flaco's best waitress, seemed to have heard me and offered Camilla a menu before placing a small bowl of freshly made guacamole in front of me with a grin.

"*Flaco me dijo que necesitas esto*," she said.

I grinned back at her. Yeah, Flaco was likely right. I probably did look like I needed some guacamole.

As usual, I could see Flaco multitasking at his grill, wielding tongs in one hand and a ladle in another, all while glancing over his beefy shoulders from time to time, keeping an eye on his customers, and especially on me. Julio "Big Flaco" Medrano already treated me like his fourth child, but after my genealogical projects and general nosiness had gotten me into some hot water last year, he'd become extra protective, watching over me like a huge guard dog with a handlebar mustache.

Camilla ordered a Dr. Pepper and eyed my guacamole. I used a tortilla chip to scoop up the gently mashed avocado spiked with fresh lime juice then mixed with chopped red onions, cilantro, jalapeños, and tomatoes. She asked for an order with tortilla chips for herself as I began reading.

His name was Charles Edward Braithwaite, and he was a coward, a deserter, and a charlatan.

I blinked up at Camilla. She had a smattering of freckles across her nose and full lips, which were pressed together in dismay. I turned back to the article.

After that explosive first sentence, the article about the life of Corporal Charles Braithwaite of Houston, Texas, who had the distinction of being the longest-lived soldier from the Civil War, was interesting enough that I was able to block out the crunching noises Camilla was making as she plowed through her guacamole.

I read that Charles Braithwaite was born in Houston in 1842 to a family so poor he and his siblings rarely had shoes. As a youth, he often stole food to feed his brothers and sisters, but was known for being able to slip away before anyone noticed, and thus never got caught. He intermittently worked for farmers in the area, picking raspberries, pears, and cotton, but never held steady employment.

However, in August of 1861, at age nineteen, Charles was finally caught trying to make off with several heads of cabbage, but escaped incarceration by enlisting with the Fifth Texas Infantry Regiment as they prepared to fight in the War Between the States. The Fifth Texas became part of Hood's Army Brigade and fought in many well-known campaigns under General Robert E. Lee in Northern Virginia, including Seven Pines all the way to the Battle at Appomattox Courthouse, where Lee eventually surrendered to General Ulysses S. Grant, beginning the end of the Civil War.

Charles Braithwaite, however, lasted for only a couple of those battles. According to the article, he deserted his regiment on September 1, 1862, after the bloody campaign at Manassas, Virginia, which came to be known as the Second Battle of Bull Run.

I read on. The article claimed to have evidence that, instead of going home to Houston after deserting his regiment, Charles made his way south to a small town in Louisiana, where he hid until the war's end. After finally returning to Houston in 1865, he soon found no one had heard of his desertion, mainly because his regiment had been all but decimated at Antietam and other subsequent battles. It turned out that Charles Braithwaite had few cohorts, if anyone, to check his past.

For years thereafter, Braithwaite lived quietly. He married, had three children, and worked at a lumber company, rising up to the title of foreman. He eventually retired, having been known for being a fair boss and for hiring and promoting Black men at his lumber company. He'd also provided his children with enough food on the table that they never had to steal themselves.

There were two short paragraphs that read favorably toward Charles. The reporter wrote Charles "dabbled as an artist," occasionally submitting illustrations to local Houston newspapers of the time. He even returned home from his hideout in Louisiana in time to be in the crowd at the famous Emancipation Day announcement on June 19, 1865, when Major-General Gordon Granger of the Union Army stood on the balcony of Ashton Villa in Galveston, Texas, and announced the freeing of all enslaved people under General Orders Number 3. A photo in the middle of the article showed the drawing of what Charles saw that day. He'd beautifully captured the jubilation of the Black residents at hearing the news of their freedom at what would later become known as the first Juneteenth celebration. While the *Chronology* reporter called most of his other drawings "generally simplistic," it was admitted that Charles had a talent for drawing people.

The next paragraph then briefly laid out Charles's well-documented support of the Black population in Houston and Texas, including working with the Freedmen's Bureau, stumping for political candidates who supported the rights of Black people, and, later, vocally opposing racial segregation laws.

His children Nathaniel, Edward, and Henrietta, and later their children, often accompanied him as well, and followed in his footsteps. It was also mentioned that Charles gave to the poor, supported women's suffrage, and was adamant that education and medical services be a high priority.

Yet that was as close as the reporter went in a positive direction. In 1920, the article stated, when Charles was seventy-eight years old—having already outlived most people born in the mid-1800s—he recognized his golden opportunity. He began to embellish himself and his time in the war for his own profit, giving his rank as corporal instead of what it actually was: private.

Braithwaite, still spry and healthy, began taking speaking engagements, first in Houston, then in other parts of Texas, and eventually travelling throughout parts of the South. As his fame for being a surviving Civil War soldier grew, parades were given in his honor and he was feted at nearly every turn. In his hometown of Houston, Braithwaite Park was named for him, as was Braithwaite Elementary. Later, as the Second World War drew nearer, two scholarships were set up in his name for underprivileged students looking to go into the armed forces.

The reporter disparaged Charles, who had become known as an advocate for the growing Black community, for suddenly being willing to make money off his time as a Confederate soldier. Yet, it was still conceded that Charles refused to glorify the war and the aims of the Confederacy in his popular talks, often rebuking anyone who attempted to encourage him to do so. Instead, he spoke of his fellow soldiers' hardships, the suffering, watching his friends die, and often exalted the bravery of all soldiers—Confederate and Union alike—in battle. And the audiences ate it up.

I paused in my reading. The article was indeed an exposé, but it had been well-written thus far, walking the line between giving the hard facts and being downright accusatory, and tempering it all with a bit of praise here and there. I flipped through the last two pages, which contained several photos and a couple of fairly inflammatory pull-out quotes, including one that read *"Braithwaite went so far as to invent a fellow soldier named Powers in his journal, writing about him as if this young private had been his friend, though no such soldier existed."* I could see why Camilla was upset, sure, but I was beginning to feel like she was being overly dramatic about insisting the article's allegations should be debunked.

After taking in a photo of Corporal Braithwaite as a handsome young man and noting he'd passed down his high forehead and cleft chin down the ages to his descendant sitting next to me, I glanced back at the first page to check the reporter's name.

"Camilla," I said, "It sounds like this Savannah Lundstrom did her research. I sympathize with you on what she says about your ancestor, I really do, but I have to say, I'm not seeing anything in here that warrants being proven untrue."

I ran my fingers over the photo of Corporal Braithwaite in his full-dress uniform, then met Camilla's eyes. "It's a shame he deserted his regiment, yes, but we don't know why he did. It could have been post-traumatic stress disorder, for instance. PTSD is hardly a recent occurrence, you know. They had different names for the symptoms back then, calling it everything from a feeble will to mania. In fact, the heart palpitations of panic attacks were often called 'soldier's heart' and were chalked up to practically everything other than true psychological conditions. War is hell for everyone involved, and Charles could have been suffering such mental anguish that he just ran." I softened my voice. "It's possible he wanted to go back, but feared being shot on sight for desertion. I think judging him solely on that one act when we can never know all the facts is a little harsh, especially when we know he went on to be an upstanding man in most every other respect."

Pointing to a paragraph on page two, I said, "Case in point, Ms. Lundstrom even acknowledges your ancestor spoke out on behalf of Black people and their welfare long before he became famous, and was known for being one of the few to hire and promote Black men at his job with the lumber mill. She even admits that, while he made his fortune off of recounting tales of being in the Civil War, he spoke about what it was like being a soldier, not glorifying the Confederacy."

To this, Camilla nodded, saying with pride, "Yes, my ancestor's anti-racist views are well documented, and my family upholds those views to this day." Then she fell back into a strained silence, and I picked up the baton again.

"All right, then. Despite his one questionable act of leaving his regiment, I say you should be proud of him, the person he was, and what he accomplished on the whole."

I went to close the magazine. "Camilla, I'm sorry, but I don't think I can help you with this and I really need to get back to my office. I've a project to finish up and I really don't want to work late tonight. I have a—"

"Keep going until the end," she cut in, before I could finish with the words *a date tonight with my boyfriend.* What I wouldn't have added, but really wanted to shout from the mountaintops, was that my boyfriend was a handsome FBI agent who'd just come home after a long undercover assignment and would have a whole week off to spend time with me.

I gave Camilla a look of undiluted exasperation and felt a little proud of myself for that small act. Four years ago, in any dealings with Camilla, Roxie, or Patrice, I'd reined in any feelings or action that wasn't friendly or helpful. I had to for the sake of keeping both my job and maintaining a peaceful work environment.

Now, though? I was my own boss and I owed Camilla nothing. Or next to nothing. I had no desire to be rude or disrespectful to her, especially for reasons as silly as office-hierarchy pettiness. To me, the better way to do things was to live well and happily, without giving consequence to the unworthy people in one's past.

That is not to say it's always easy when one of those people is staring you in the face and practically demanding your help.

"Please," Camilla said again, and with a pleading note in her voice. "Keep reading until the end."

I felt myself relenting. Darn it if I weren't a nice person who was willing to keep giving people chances! I scowled and went back to the article, though it didn't take much longer for my grumpy face to change to one of astonishment at what I read.

Before they knew it, Charles Braithwaite and his family were earning money hand over fist, and his children and grandchildren were suddenly being welcomed at the best houses and social events in Texas and beyond. The formerly poor Braithwaites had moved on up to houses in the finest area in Houston, and they didn't let anyone forget it.

At the time of Private Braithwaite's death in 1945, it is estimated he and his family had earned around $75,000—the equivalent of over a million dollars in today's money—for his appearances as a Civil War veteran. Braithwaite made no bones about his appearance fees, either, and he didn't care from whom he took money. In 1925, Zacharias Gaynor spent a month's wages to have Braithwaite come to his house for dinner, a regular custom throughout history that often served to increase the host's social standing. It did nothing for the Gaynor family, however, and Zacharias, after spending all his family's money, was later was sentenced to eight weeks in debtor's prison, losing his job in the process. We can only guess at the hell his family endured during that time and afterward. But did Braithwaite care, or return the man's money? Of course not, and he only continued to milk his fame even when he became feeble, deaf, and nearly blind from cataracts.

Such was the delight at having a real-life Civil War "hero" in their midst that some local companies even spent a bundle just to have Braithwaite, who was semi-bedridden by this time, sit in the backseat of a car and listlessly wave a hand in one parade or another, mutely shilling for some company he no doubt couldn't even name.

Oh, but his children and descendants were smart with the money Braithwaite gained. The three clans stemming from Charles and his wife Violet spread out over Texas and the United States, no longer the descendants of a man who stole as a youth and deserted his regiment as a soldier. No, the families even today continue to live off the image their ancestor so carefully cultivated from his lies. They still speak of Charles Braithwaite's valor, hard work, open-mindedness, and honesty whenever they can, holding him up as a paragon for the greatest kind of American, not caring that the money their livelihoods were founded upon was hardly that of a great man, but instead of the most selfish of cowards.

It seems that, even today, escaping the truth is still a Braithwaite pastime.